THE BETA'S BARGAIN
TEA RAVINE

Copyright © 2024 by Tea Ravine

All rights reserved.

No part of this publication may be reproduced, distributed, or transmitted in any form or by any means, including photocopying, recording, or other electronic or mechanical methods, without the prior written permission of the publisher, except as permitted by U.S. copyright law. For permission requests, contact Tea Ravine.

The story, all names, characters, and incidents portrayed in this production are fictitious. No identification with actual persons (living or deceased), places, buildings, and products is intended or should be inferred.

Book Cover by Blue Shadow Designs

CONTENTS

A note	1
Dedication	2
1. Onyx	3
2. Falcon	13
3. Onyx	15
4. Silas	23
5. Onyx	29
6. Onyx	38
7. Grayson	48
8. Onyx	56
9. Onyx	63
10. Falcon	72
11. Onyx	80
12. Onyx	87
13. Dylan	95
14. Onyx	102
15. Silas	106
16. Onyx	113
17. Onyx	120
18. Grayson	127

19.	Onyx	134
20.	Onyx	142
21.	Falcon	150
22.	Onyx	157
23.	Onyx	166
24.	Onyx	175
25.	Dylan	183
26.	Onyx	190
27.	Onyx	199
28.	Onyx	210
29.	Silas	217
30.	Onyx	222
31.	Onyx	228
32.	Onyx	236
33.	Grayson	240
34.	Onyx	244
35.	Falcon	254
36.	Silas	258
37.	Onyx	263
38.	Onyx	267
39.	Onyx	277
40.	Epilogue- Onyx	281
Acknowledgements		285
Also By Tea Ravine		286
About the Author		287

A NOTE

This book is a work of fiction. Any resemblance to persons dead or alive is pure coincidence.
It is also a work of art and does not accurately portray real life or real world places.
In other words, this book came out of my head.
I dreamed it up.
It's all pure fantasy.
Have fun. xxx

DEDICATION

Throw off the chains.
Be who you were born to be.
Don't be afraid.
Fly.

This book is for Ron. Who loved gardens
Birds, broken and otherwise
and me.
You were loved.
And will be missed.

One

ONYX

I push the helplessness and the thick fingers that encircle my wrist away. My icy smile is the only weapon I have. I throw it at the rich alpha who has me cornered. He's already thinking he's won, I can see it. His salacious leer makes my skin crawl, but I can't call out for help, even though it is just feet away. The venue is glittering. Rich men in tuxes scan the room, rocking back on their heels, trying to find something to entertain themselves. Women in beautiful dresses move gracefully through the crowds, pecking other women on the cheeks and flashing their teeth in warning grins. And betas like me slide through them all, invisible. This isn't a celebration, it's a hunting ground. And I'm caught.

The trick is to be boring and unobtrusive. Serve the drinks and don't get noticed. Offer the expensive canapes with your eyes fixed over their shoulders. Don't see them as people, see past them. That's how you survive the night.

After four years, I should be used to it. I should excel at it. So, I'm not sure how I got in this position tonight. I'm close to the wall, behind the crowds. This area exists in all the venues and every party I've ever worked. I call it no-man's-land. It's where the predators hunt. I know better than to be tricked into being cornered so easily. A mistake of this magnitude could cost me more than just my wages. He just asked for help to find his wife. I was just trying to help. So simple, so stupid.

I grit my teeth and back away, keeping my wary gaze on the alpha in front of me. There's a code of conduct amongst the designations. Alphas using their bark to compel people is considered bad form. I've seen too many abuses of its power to even pretend to entertain the thought that I'm safe.

A male omega passes, and my eyes flit to his black tux. It's worth a fortune. He's beautiful in a dark and masculine way that I'm sure leaves women seething with jealousy. A huge smile spreads warmth amongst the crowd and in his wake leaves a trail of oranges in the air. The smell tickles my nose, and I discreetly rub my finger against it to hold back a sneeze. His presence is the perfect distraction and the answer to my prayers. The alpha turns, unable to resist the lure, and I use that moment to duck under his arm, past the potent scent of cigarettes, and into the nearest hallway.

He won't give up. I know alphas like him, the pursuit is half the fun, so I keep moving, running without running. I let the wash of irritation mask the fear that was rising. If I get busted not working, they'll dock my wages, and I need that money. I can't remember when I ate last. I know it's been a day or two but my head swims, leaving me feeling strangely disconnected from my body.

"Hey, beta, beta, where are you?"

The drunk's stupid voice sings out over and over, ruthlessly herding me away from the party. I walk quicker, slamming open a door and then stopping short. I'm both trembling with the need to run and held in place, star stuck.

The woman in front of me is stunning. She's wearing crimson but even if she were in a potato sack, she has the kind of beauty that just screams class and elegance. Her green eyes scan my face, and I find myself dropping my gaze in deference.

Alpha.

I'm frozen, wondering if I need to run past her or go back into the party. I hear the fumbling calls of the alpha. Both of us flinch and look towards the hallway where the doors are.

"Run," she whispers in a husky voice. "I didn't see anything, but if anyone says anything, say you know me. My name's Scarlet Waring."

I run my eyes over her again, unable to believe this miracle. "Onyx Davies," I say in a hushed voice. I force myself to smile and then run past her. If I can just make it to the kitchen, then perhaps I can disappear into the crowd of servers.

My relief upon stumbling into the kitchen gets a couple of the wait staff's attention. A woman named Moira, who has a wide smile and just seems too nice to be working here, leans close to me.

"All right?"

"Yeah, now I am," I say out the side of my mouth. A tray is pushed onto the stainless steel bench, and I pick it up. I pause at the kitchen door, composing myself, then I turn, backing into the door so it opens, and I go back out into the fray.

THE BETA'S BARGAIN

The night drags on. The Scarlet woman is the talk of the party. Her pack, the Knights, came in on white horses and rode off with her. It's so romantic, and my pathetic little heart adores it. The party takes on that strange, mythical stage where the party guests are so drunk they are behaving like idiots instead of people, and my feet and body are aching so much that I could cry. The minutes are hours. Hunger and pain make it hard to smile.

A stranger passes me in the hallway and holds the doors. I look up and suck in my breath. This man is handsome and young, maybe a year or two older than me at twenty-three, but I know him. I've seen him around in many unexpected places.

"Are you working tonight?" I ask him.

He shakes his head, refusing to answer. He always refuses to answer me. I don't take it to heart.

"I can't meet you in the park tonight. I have to go home."

He cocks his head to the side and then steps towards me. I suck in my breath, wishing that I didn't smell like alcohol and quiche. I peer up at him as he gently presses something into my hand. His eyes are dark, his face in shadow, always in shadow. He leaves as quietly as he appeared. I watch until I'm sure he's gone. When I glance down, there's a roll with potatoes and meat inside.

I close my eyes so I don't cry. This man might be the one bright spark in my miserable life.

For hours, I work, I don't see either my saviour or the alpha again. I keep jumping at shadows, but they never appear. As the last guests leave and the cleaners come in to take over our jobs, I follow my colleagues to the staff section of the giant hotel.

The women chat in soft, tired murmurs, while the guys veer off, heading to their lockers. Making friends is something that should be easy. I guess it is when you don't have so much to lose. A sharp stab pricks me deep in the chest, but I push it aside and focus on what's important.

Our boss for the evening walks towards us, not even flinching on those four-inch heels. She looks like she might live in them. I envy her ability to dissociate from her pain. Yvette Daniels smiles with her crimson lips and hands out envelopes with our wages in them.

"As this was short notice, everyone gets paid in cash. You did a wonderful job this evening, people. Treyfield Pack was impressed and pressed upon me their desire that I report their thanks to you."

She smiles, looking each one of us in the eye. I wonder if it's part of her training or if it comes naturally to her. She makes us all feel important and like we're part of the huge cog that is Treyfield and Hastings corporation. The huge empires dominate the industries of department stores and hotels.

You want luxury, go to Hasting hotels run by pack Treyfield. You want to wear the best clothes money can buy? Shop at Treyfield department stores. The Treyfield Pack are household names.

Getting in with this company has been one of my short-term goals. They look after their employees. Their wages are above average. They allow sick days and leave. To work for them would be a dream come true.

I've been filling in at parties as a temp for four years. Taking calls and jobs even after I've worked a twelve hour day just on the chance I might get the tap on the shoulder.

Yvette waits until most people leave and approaches me as I'm putting on my worn and crappy boots.

"Miss Onyx Davies?"

"Yes, ma'am."

"Uh, your name has come up a lot recently. We've taken notice of your hard work and dedication and would like to present an invitation for a long work placement with the option to retain a full-time position when the term comes to fruition."

"Yes!" I blurt out.

She laughs, but I can see she's a bit startled by my eagerness. "I admire your enthusiasm, but hear me out. The job is working at the company's country hotel. Silver Rocks Resort."

My mind boggles. The resort won awards for its amazing gardens recently, and there are rumours that another garden will be revealed soon.

"You'll be attending a seven-week event, helping to chaperone the guests. The first week or two will be training."

"When do I start?" I blurt out without thinking.

"You need to go to do an intake assessment. If you agree and all goes well, you'll get on a bus and leave right away."

I hesitate, my excitement fading. Disappointment crushes me. I can't take this job. "I have a dependent. I can't take the job, I'm sorry." My disappointment must show on my face because she reaches out and rubs my shoulder sympathetically.

"It was made clear to me to let any potential employees know that dependents and partners can come and stay in the employee' cabins on site. The information pack will have everything you need to know. Should you do well, you'll be offered a position at a hotel with a training package and a future with Treyfield Pack in hotels or department stores."

I wheeze. My ears are ringing. I don't think I'd be this happy if I won the lottery. "Yes. Yes. Yes."

She smiles tightly, and I can't help but think she's not overly happy with my capitulation. "Excellent. Well, just be at this address by eleven am. Oh, and Onyx, the wages are three times per hour what you earned tonight."

She turns and walks away like she didn't just drop a bomb on me. I cling to my locker, trying hard to keep myself upright while my head rings with her words.

I have to get home, pack up. We need to get ready to go. I'm going to ace that assessment.

I grab my stuff and race out of the hotel and onto the street. It's going to take me a long time to get home from this side of town. I try to take the straightest course, but the buses have stopped running, and my feet ache.

I don't end up getting home until nearly dawn, and by then I collapse in exhaustion on the couch. My stomach rumbles, but I ignore it. We don't have food in the house, we rarely ever do.

I must space out because the next thing I'm conscious of is waking up to a face that's almost identical to mine. Silver shakes me roughly, and I'm pulled out of the abyss. Her face is soft and round. Where Silver's eyes are a clear crystal blue, like the sky, like our fathers, mine are not. Her lips are plump and inclined to curve up even when she's unhappy. My face is more angular, my eyes are blue but like slate, and my lips are thin and curve down.

Mama always said I was the child with the entire world on my shoulders. Silver was the twin, with her heart in her eyes. We're as different as night and day, even if we look remarkably alike. She is the omega, wanted, watched, and loved. I'm the beta with freedom to go unnoticed through the world. We are chalk and cheese under the skin.

"Did you get them?" Silver barks.

I put my hand in my pocket and pull out the baggie of pills and the roll that my hero saved for me. I hand it over, ignoring the pang in my belly. Those suppressants cost me three times what I paid last month, but Silver needs them. If she goes into heat, any choice that she might have will vanish. I promised our father on his deathbed that I would protect her.

"There's only thirty," Silvie says when she inspects the bag.

"Prices went up."

Silver gets up and stomps away from me. "That's crap. Fuck!" she shrieks and whirls back to me. "What are you going to do about it?"

"I'll get some more. I know I said that last time, but I found them, didn't I? Have I ever let you down? It was take these or nothing. I'll find more."

Silver sits on the couch arm and puts her head in her hands. "I won't end up in one of these packs, Nyx. You know what I want. What I deserve. I want a pack that can afford to look after me, that can afford to take care of me. Who will treat me like the omega I am and cherish me."

"I know," I say in exhaustion. Her request isn't that much to ask, except for the fact that her standards are impossibly high. She won't accept any of the packs that might court her here. Only the best for Silver Davies.

"I refuse." Silver paces the space with growing agitation. I sit up and put my head in my hands. I'm too tired for this. If she gets too worked up, a tantrum will follow. I can't deal with her shrieks this early.

"I understand that. I'm trying, Silvie." My jaw cracks when I yawn, unable to hold it in anymore.

"Try harder." Silver snaps.

I fall silent, the pain and weight of being responsible for everything crushing my soul. "I got a job. There's a cabin for you to stay in. It's at the Silver Rocks Resort."

Silver whips towards me. Her whole face lights up. "A resort? The Silver Rock, that's Treyfield Pack's resort. When are we going?"

I check the time on the brick I call my phone. "We have a couple of hours. Let's pack up, get ready to leave, and go get something to eat."

THE BETA'S BARGAIN

The rain pours down, instantly soaking my pants. The only thing I'm grateful for is that my pants are black, so maybe no one will know. Silver races ahead with the umbrella, laughing with a tinkling joy that is attracting too much attention. I can't find it in me to stop her. She stands under the awning of the convenience store and raises her eyebrow before glancing at the door.

"We had breakfast."

"I'm hungry, Onyx. Come on, I need to eat. I can't be on a bus that long and be hungry."

Her whine grates on my ears, and I push away that voice of reason in deference to keeping the peace. The street is filled with steam as the rain hits the hot concrete. I pause and spot my favourite person leaning against the alley wall. My heart jolts, and I smile despite the situation. I glance back, but Silver isn't watching me. I take another long look at him.

He's got a very compelling face with an angular bone structure that makes him look almost pretty. But right now, he's frowning, his full lips turned down. I sneak into the convenience store and get two drinks and two rolls with chicken, cheese, and mayo. Silver will kill me, but it will be worth it.

Instead of coming out the front door, I go out the back and sneak into the alley. My stomach flutters as I approach him. I reach up and brush my wet hair out of my face. I should have tried to dry off. Fuck it. Why do I get so nervous around this guy?

"Hey," I say and feel my cheeks burn. "So, I, uh, wanted to say thank you."

He turns slowly in my direction like he can't believe his ears. His eyes widen. "You're here."

I tip my head to the side and smile widely. "I am."

He swallows hard and stands up off the wall. Beads of rainwater run down the side of his face, dripping from his wet hair. I'm suddenly stricken at the thought of never seeing him again. It just seems so unfathomable. I wish I could see what colour his eyes are. The dull grey of the day has turned everything a menacing hue, leaching the colour from around us, stealing this one last wish from me.

"I know we never exchanged names. It's a thing, but I'm leaving town."

"You're leaving?"

Am I imagining the panic in his voice?

"Yes, I'm going to interview for a job to go work at Silver Rocks Resort for Treyfield pack. Lucked out with that one."

His face twitches, and I inhale a strong, almost bitter scent of lemons.

"Treyfield Pack?" He murmurs. "Of course, they know." He lets out a deep sound that could be a growl.

"Um, so, anyway, I don't have time. I just...well, you've been the only friendly face, and you keep saving me."

"You saved me first." He says bluntly.

I blink, my words vanishing. "No, I-"

"You fed me and told me where I could find a place to stay. You saved me first."

"It was just a sandwich and some advice." My cheeks burn.

"It saved my life." He insists.

I peer up at him and shrug uncomfortably. "Here!" I shove a sandwich and drink into his hands.

"What? No!"

"Take it. Please. Just...don't forget, we aren't all bad."

He tries to shove the sandwich into my hands, but I step back.

"Make a bargain with me instead." I suggest.

His eyes widen, then narrow in suspicion. "What kind of bargain?"

I hold out my free hand. "If I ever see you need help, I will be on your side. I'll help you wherever you are because we're friends."

"You-" he cuts himself short and stares at my hand. He takes it in his larger one. Tingles curl deviously up my spine, and I wish I was braver. "I will be on your side, too."

"No matter where we are in life, I'm your friend." I say with a small smile. "And you're mine. This is just the start of our story."

He shudders and almost closes his eyes. His fingers tighten on mine for a moment before he abruptly loosens his grip and lets me go.

"Don't go," he pleads suddenly.

I bite my lip and look away. "I have to. I need to feed my family. It's a good job."

He frowns down at my gift, and when he looks up, his eyes are even darker, full of something I don't recognise. "Okay, fine. But if this is just the start of our story, we write the rest of it together. My name is-"

"Uh!" I cut him off, feeling a strange lump in my throat. "No names. Just...be safe, okay. I'm really glad we met. And don't forget our bargain. You and me, Mystery Man, our story starts now."

I take a step backwards and then another. He follows, but I force myself to turn away and jog towards Silver. He doesn't come after me, and though a huge part of me wishes he would, I'm relieved because I know that reality is cruel, and Silver would chase him away.

"Where were you?" Silver snarls and takes the sandwich and drink.

I snatch the drink back and open the container, drinking three mouthfuls of juice. It will have to do me.

"Needed the toilet."

"Ugh, don't be so vulgar."

I shrug. "You asked, Silvie. Come on, let's get out of here. I'm going to be late."

I brush my pants and walk into the office, trying hard not to stare. I'm damp, and it's obvious that I am. There's nothing I can do about it. Embarrassment is a second skin when you're poor and desperate, I've discovered. We're up, I don't know how many levels, and I feel like I'm an eagle perched in the sky. The windows are enormous. How do people even work here? I'd spend hours just staring at that view.

Yvette waits for my eyes to return to her, then she smiles.

"This is a contract for employment. Take a seat, and I'll go through the code of conduct, get your signature, and then we can take a quick photo and get you on the bus."

The process takes little to no time. But my hands shake even after I've signed everything. This job could get Silvie and I the first home we've had since Mama and Dad died. It could buy her what she needs to attract a pack. I could be free.

My father's last words to me go through my head. *A beta is good for everything else. An alpha is good to lead, to protect, to provide, but an omega is a gift to everyone. You owe your sister, you owe her for this mess you made for us. You owe her for her dead parents.*

My father was as mean as a snake. But he is right about one thing. Mama died, and it was my fault, and the only thing I can do to make amends is find my twin her happily ever after. Silver is vulnerable. I'm not. As a beta, I have all the freedom. But with Silver, I've got even less than she has. Her designation has trapped us both, and the only genuine answer I can find is to make us respectable again and get her a pack. Her freedom will set me free.

This job can get us on the road to that goal.

I smile politely for the photograph and take the lanyard with the passkey. The key will get me into the resort, but I will need to go to orientation right away to get a second key that will allow me access to the hotel.

"How are you feeling?" She asks. Her tight bob is like cut glass. I wonder how she keeps it like that or how she walks in those shoes. They look excruciating and very pretty.

"Good. Overwhelmed. Looking forward to getting to work."

"The first few days are going to be training. So be prepared. Simon Shultz will be in charge of overseeing all the guests. He's a lovely man but loves people who have an eye for detail." Yvette smiles. "Just do your best, Onyx."

"I will, ma'am."

"Good. I knew you were the right choice."

I smile at her as she walks me to the elevator.

"Welcome to Treyfield employment, Miss Davies."

The words make me shiver. I can't stop smiling. Dreams really do come true.

Two

FALCON

I glance sharply towards the door and remove my glasses. The energy that goes through my penthouse makes the hairs on my body rise. I huff out a sound and clear my throat. Silas tenses on the couch and shifts so he's sitting up. His lips twist as he steadies his jiggling knee. Grayson jumps off the treadmill before it stops and, in long strides, reaches the door.

This is the moment. All our plans, months of work. It starts now.

He yanks it open. I put my hands flat on the desk and stare at my favourite employee. Yvette Daniels walks in looking like a million dollars. She's polished and ruthless and far too many men underestimate her to their peril. If she scents blood in the water, she will attack. But I hold her leash. Outside of my pack, she is one of two people I would say I trust.

"Come in." I growl.

She waited for me to say the words. Just how I trained her. I want to shake her and have her behave differently today. I want her to give me the words I need to hear. She purses her lips and gives Grayson and Silas a polite nod.

"She's taken the bait, sirs. She's signed up to work for the resort, and she's on the bus." Her voice is calm and holding just a touch of reticence.

The relief of those words takes a moment to go through me.

I close my eyes to savour the victory. Yvette lets out a shriek, and I jerk forward in surprise to see Grayson spinning her round and round.

"You are the best, Yvette. I knew we could count on you." He crows loudly and smacks a kiss on her cheek.

"Keep your lips to yourself, Gray. My girlfriend will take your head." Yvette warns, but I can hear the pleasure in her voice.

Right, I need to get things moving. We're moving our base of operations to the resort. I reach for my tablet and freeze. There is so much I need to organise. I bite the inside of my cheek, relishing the pain that lets me know this is real.

Silas is still silent, but his guilt is keeping him from happiness. That's fine. When we fix everything, he will be himself again. We will all be ourselves again. I stand up and then pause, frowning as my gaze lands on my assistant.

"You're still here."

Yvette frowns.

"Rude much?" Gray snorts a laugh and slaps Yvette on the back. "You need a raise?"

"No, Alpha Waters, he's paying me too much, anyway."

"Good, but never turn down a good raise. I'll have Simon organise you a bonus."

Yvette grabs his arm. "I want vacation days."

Gray laughs. He smirks at me and answers her without looking. "Done."

"What is it?" I ask impatiently. "Why are you still here?"

"There are two, sir."

"Two?" My mind tries to conjure what she could be talking about, but I come up blank.

"Two girls. I was informed that they are twins. They are both going to the resort." Yvette clarifies. "Twins, Alpha Treyfield."

I lean back in my chair and smile. Now, it all makes sense. I love it when my hunches pay off.

Yvette stares at me and then drops her chin and turns on the stiletto heel and leaves.

"Now, they are ours." I say in triumph. Silas and Gray move in closer as I begin to talk. The plan we've set up is about to be put into play. We all have our parts. This will be our all or nothing. I fire off a message to my private investigator and lean back in my chair.

We will get our omega.

Three

ONYX

"Right, I've investigated the whole place, and it's not going to be that bad!" I say to Silvie with false cheer. My fake smile makes my cheeks ache, and I drop it almost at once.

I'm dead on my feet. I've been studying at night and working under Simon and his crew of robotic managers for the last four days. Lack of sleep is killing me. Silvie has wanted me to explore the resort and take her out during the evening hours. I can't do everything, but she's bored. So she wants to talk and have me report all the details to her and ask me a million questions, and she just doesn't let me sleep. My eyelids feel heavy, and my eyes are burning. I didn't get to eat today, either.

"I hate it. I want to go home." Silver barks out.

"We can't, Silvie. I signed a contract." My voice is tired and lacks the politeness I normally have.

"I hate it here, Onyx." She stomps away from me and walks into the bedroom. "I want to go out."

"You can't, Silvie." I sit on the wooden chair and put my head in my hands. "Please."

"I have to get out of here. This place is a nightmare. Please. It's like a prison."

"The event starts in a few days," I try to explain, "there are people everywhere. You could get caught."

"Pur-lease!" she snaps sarcastically and rolls her eyes. "You can't keep me here!"

I groan and rub my fingertips into my forehead. She's working herself up into a lather. If this keeps going, she'll be screaming at me within the hour. The idea of it makes my throat close up.

"One little walk." I spit out quickly when she pauses. "One walk, I'll show you the pool, and then you come back, and you let me sleep."

She beams at me, and the expression almost makes it worth it. The problem is that one little walk, or candy, or anything is never enough. She always wants more, so the relief is short-lived, and I know it, but I can't stop myself from being happy that she's happy. I push myself up into a stand and head towards the door. She puts her arm through mine and almost drags me into the door frame.

"So, I painted my nails today. Do you like? Rose gold."

"Pretty." Where did she get the nail polish? I'm not stupid enough to ask.

I let her waffle on as I lead her through the rows of cabins and down along the path until we get to a gate that says Staff Only.

"All right, we're entering the resort proper now, Silvie. No messing around, and be ready to run." The forest has given way to cultured gardens and paths that are immaculate. Everything seems to be made out of white stone here.

"I will. Of course, I will." I don't believe her.

My nerves don't dance. They are jumping up and down, flexing with each heartbeat and stray thought. What if someone sees us? What if I lose the job?

The pool is massive, a great, big, deep in-ground pool surrounded by gardens and walls with vines. It's got a fountain at one end and a spa off in the corner. Around the pool, on the white stone ground, are two dozen lounges with tables and towels. It really is beautiful. I should relax, but my anxiety only gets worse. Silvie runs ahead of me and stops at the edge of the pool. Her eyes are enormous when she looks back and smiles.

She's so beautiful. When she smiles like that, I wish we were kids again, before we found out our designations and my father's words twisted us into warped versions of who we used to be.

"I'm wearing my swimsuit."

I frown, repeating the words in my mind, panic growing. My eyes widen, and I reach for her arm. She shakes me off. "No, Silvie, you can't. I'd lose my job, we'd have to leave. We'll starve." I sound like a broken record, and she's tuned me out.

She pouts and then removes her dress, anyway. "Stop being such a buzzkill. One little swim. It will be fine."

"Silver, get your ass away from that pool right now." I snap.

"Not a chance," Silver says and looks back at me. "You need to live a little."

She dives into the pool and disappears beneath the water.

My heart is beating triple time. I can see all my hopes and dreams going up in ash, and she's...she's flipping around like a damn otter and giggling like a little kid. Every time I start to say anything, she dives under the water again.

I crouch by the side of the pool, slapping the water to get her attention, but she spits water in my direction and disappears under again.

"Silver, please," I beg.

I catch movement and turn in that direction. I'm frozen in terror. My fears of losing my job pale compared to this shitshow. A group of guests, all male, are coming this way. I know they're guests because we've been forced to memorise the dossier of all of them. All sixty-eight of them.

This group is a pack of alphas that don't have an omega. Julien, Derek, Mitch, and Toby are young and rich. In my opinion, spoiled rotten, but I'm not asked for my opinion. I just have to serve. There have been whispers among the other betas that they are bad alphas.

And they've seen us, and they're coming our way. I catch the lead one leering at me, right until a breeze lifts his hair. He freezes, and then his attention focuses on my sister. I inhale and catch the cotton candy scent over the chlorine.

Fucking damnit!

I glance from them back to the pool and crouch at the edge. "Please, Silver, please." I whisper, waiting for her to surface. It takes several dives, and they're almost on top of us when she pops up just near me and spots the pack. Her eyes go wide, and she sinks down to her nose in the water.

Why is her scent so strong? Cotton candy floods the air, muted by the pool water, but it's there, and it shouldn't be. Isn't she taking the suppressants? I try to think of something, anything I can do, but there's almost nothing except throw myself in front of my sister and make a loud enough noise that they back off.

And pray.

"Hey, beautiful." Julien croons and crouches beside the pool. "You want to come out and say hello?"

Silver shakes her head and drifts towards the middle of the pool.

I look up to find the alphas already staring at my sister. Mitch strips out of his t-shirt and kicks his shoes off. He's got more muscle than brain.

No! I step between them and scowl.

"Move along." I say, putting my deepest, most pissed off voice on.

"No, we just want to talk to the pretty omega," Toby says and brushes his hair back, giving Silver a flirty wink.

Oh, crap. Silver smiles back, and I can smell the candy scent get sweeter, stronger. I almost gag on it, but I'm so busy panicking that I'm not sure if it's fear or the scent.

"Of course, you do, but you can't." I step between them and the pool, but they're all craning their heads around, flexing muscles, and ignoring me. Mitch's jeans drop, and now he's standing there in boxers, licking his lips and flexing bronzed skin.

"Stop! Right now!" I order. "Stop. You stay away!" I shove at Julien, but he just laughs at me and bats me away.

Toby crouches by the side of the pool. His nostrils flare, and he smiles. That smile sends all kinds of alarms screaming through me.

"Silver, get back." I warn her. "Go to the other side of the pool, get out, and run."

She doesn't move.

"Stop. No one move." I try again. "Silver! Now!"

One of the alphas grabs my wrist and squeezes it as he moves me. I go stumbling, landing hard on my knees. The pain brings tears to my eyes instantly. I wheeze at the throb of fire in my skin.

The alpha is pushed away from me and ends up tripping over a chair. I look up and find a man in a leather jacket standing between me and the alphas. A familiar scent of lemon surrounds me.

No way.

"We can't touch him." One of the alphas whispers. "That's Dylan."

"Excuse me!" Simon appears between the alphas and glares up at them. "I'll take care of this situation, alphas. Thank you for your help."

The four giant men move away, with reluctant glances over their shoulders. I make a mental note to spit in their drinks as I get to my feet and brush the dirt and dust off my knees.

The guy with the leather jacket turns to me, and I go still. His skin is olive, and his black hair is cut close to his scalp. He's got huge honey-coloured eyes and this thick muscular body. I know him. Of course, I know him.

"Stalker." I whisper in awe.

THE BETA'S BARGAIN

His lips curl upwards, and I bite the inside of my cheek and try really hard not to throw myself into his arms. It's such a welcome relief to see a familiar face.

"Mr Dylan, can I offer you an escort to your room?" Simon says.

My boss looks between us with a polite frown. His slicked back hair is perfect, and the white shirt with the logo looks as pristine as it did twelve hours ago. Simon is my goals.

The man in question shakes his head, with his eyes still locked on me. He doesn't even remove his gaze from mine when Silver rises from the pool.

The lemon scent wraps around me, and I hear Silver growl. I turn towards her and see the way she's staring at him. My eyes go wide. No way. How did I miss that?

Holy hell, he's an omega.

The budding, ridiculous hope that I've had over the last few months shatters like brittle glass. He's so far out of my reach, he may as well be on the moon.

"All right, fine, but you're explaining to them what's going on," Simon says and transfers his gaze to mine. "And you broke the rules. Come with me and bring your sister as well." He reaches out to one of the chairs scattered around the pool and grabs a towel. He throws it at me.

I wrap it around Silver and quickly usher her after Simon. My sister is quiet. I think she's finally realised she's done something wrong.

My stomach bottoms out, though. I should beg and plead, but I don't even know what to say. I did the wrong thing. This is all my fault. I'm supposed to protect her, and instead I've doomed us both.

What are we going to do? A crack of a stick behind me has me turning, and I'm startled to find the omega, Dylan, following us. My heart jolts, and that sick mix of giddiness and anxiety causes me to almost trip. I catch myself easily but feel my whole body heat.

"Dylan?" I ask stiffly as we follow Simon.

"Yes, I'm Dylan Wyrven."

"Onyx Davies. And my sister Silver." I admit softly.

He reaches out and clutches my fingers, giving them a squeeze before he lets me go. We don't say another word, which is good because I don't even know what to say.

He's an omega, so he obviously doesn't work here. Or at the parties I've seen him at. But why is he homeless and starving?

Simon leads us into his office. "Take a seat." He lifts his phone and presses a button. "Sir, I have a situation here. Of course, we'll wait for you."

We wait in silence for ten minutes when the office door opens, and a huge alpha enters the room. The power that radiates off the man makes my knees tremble. He eases behind Simon's desk and sits down, staring at us.

He barely looks at me, but spends a long time studying my sister and Dylan. This alpha is really attractive, with a Mediterranean look about him with a thick head of hair and exotic eyes. He's not as pretty as the omega beside me, but he's compelling in his own sense.

"You can't stay here like this, omega."

I think he's talking to the male, but then I realise he's addressing Silvie. My twin reaches for my hand and clings to it. But then she straightens up, drops my hand, and sniffs. I catch the moment she catches his scent. Her body language dips into a supple, relaxed state, and her eyelids drop. Her candy scent fills the air, stronger than before.

"I've got nowhere else to go." She barely whispers.

"What do you want in life?" He asks and leans back in the chair, his eyes flick to the male omega but completely pass over me.

"I want a pack, a family, a home." Silver lists off. I'm not even really listening to her. I'm too busy observing the alpha. What does he want here? Why does her answer make him smile in such a fake way? He's subtle in testing the air, but he is doing it. Does he like her scent? I hate the idea of him wanting Silver, but I can't pinpoint why. It just feels wrong.

"I can give you those things." He says in a seductive croon.

He drops that bomb and leaves it hanging. The guy beside me goes as stiff and still as I do.

Silver's eyes bulge, and she lets out a tinkling laugh that makes me want to kill her. It's flirtatious and coy.

"How?" I bark out, interrupting their private meeting. "How are you going to provide those things?"

"By letting you join our party as a guest. A very special guest." He almost purrs at her, completely ignoring me again. My anger grows, sharpening as I stare at this arrogant man. I bet no one has ever told him no before.

The male omega reaches out and grips my other hand, somehow knowing just when I was about to grab the world's best boss' coffee cup and hurl it at his head.

"We'll provide you with food, clothes, anything you need. Makeup. A stylist. You can meet and indulge in your flirtations and make connections. All I ask is that you sign an NDA and not report anything that happened."

"I would never do that." Silver coos. "This place is a dream. I'd love the opportunity to visit."

"I know you wouldn't, but my lawyers will kill me if I don't get your signature." The alpha leans back in his chair, smug and pleased with himself.

The smell of lemon sharpens, turns bitter, and somehow soothes the rage that's rattling around inside me.

I hate it. I hate him. But it's what she needs. This is Silver's chance. It's a no-brainer, and I hate it.

"I don't think-" Silvie glances at me, for once hesitant. Vulnerable. "Onyx?"

"You should take it," I say with a firmness in my voice that I don't feel. "It's very generous, thank you, Alpha."

The asshole still doesn't look at me.

"Just a question, Alpha, but am I fired?" I ask in a rough voice.

He finally looks at me. Finally sees me, but only for a moment before he dismisses me again. "No. You can continue working for us. Just stay out of sight and keep your head down."

Got it, Alpha. Do your job and don't be seen. How many times have I been told that in my life?

He gets to his feet, and we do the same. As he rounds the desk, he moves close to Silver and lifts her hand to his lips and murmurs something. She goes pink and nods her head.

"You can leave." He says to me without even looking at me. "Dylan, sit down."

I stare at Silver, but she doesn't turn around. She just looks like she's won the lottery, so I start walking towards the door.

I'm shoved suddenly, and I hit the wall hard. I turn and find myself with an omega pressed against me, my front to his back. He's growling, and the alpha is staring, his mouth and eyes wide.

"Her? Is it her?"

If I wasn't so afraid, I'd be offended about the way he's speaking about me, but this alpha wants to hurt me. I can feel it in the air around us. I've done something terrible, but I have no idea what.

I move for the door, but the omega, Dylan, I correct myself, grips my wrist. He moves with me, opening the door for us. His touch is warm, comforting. I'm finding I like the way his hand bracelets my wrist.

The alpha is suddenly between us, pulling him back, but Dylan does something I've never seen an omega do before. He lets go of me, takes the shirt of the alpha, slams him against the wall, and growls.

"The beta?" The alpha asks in shock. "No, we thought-"

Dylan slams him into the wall again. This time, with so much aggression that even the alpha falls silent.

The Alpha finally shifts his gaze from the furious omega's to mine, staring at me like he can't believe his eyes. I think he finally, really sees me.

I stiffen, standing up straight, and glare back. Alphas are a dime a dozen. I'm not ashamed of what I am, despite how appalled he looks.

Dylan lets out another furious, threatening sound, then he lets go, walks back to me, grabs my wrist, and drags me out of the room.

The door closes, and I glance back, unsettled by how much the look that alpha gave me hurt.

Four

SILAS

I arrive in the penthouse with no memory of how I got here. I've stopped just beyond the lift doors, barely able to see or think. Tight shudders run up and down my spine, and it takes everything I have to contain the rage. My tie feels like it's choking me, and my shirt feels too tight. I can still feel the female omega's fingers on my hand, her scent in my nose. Bile races up my throat, and I close my eyes and fight to keep it down. How did this happen?

Grayson pauses near the couch and studies me. He rakes his fingers through his blond hair, and his grin, with all those dimples that I love, slowly fades. He reaches out and pulls on a singlet, covering up all those chiseled muscles, like by doing so he's putting on armor. I hate that his hopeful expression withers and dies, but I have nothing good to share with them. Nothing.

Falcon comes out of his office rolling up his shirt sleeves and sits on the couch. His calm expression lingers on me, pulling out my secrets without my say so. Falcon is beautiful in a cold way, in an untouchable way. But when I look in his eyes, I see safety. I see unconditional love. I can't face it right now. His white shirt is unbuttoned two extra holes, which is unusual, and I focus on it so I don't have to meet Falcon's intense gaze and admit I failed. "So?"

"He hates us more than ever." I run my fingers through my hair and scowl at the carpet. "I just, I don't know what we can do anymore. Is this a punishment? Is this rebellion? Can't he see that we're sorry?" My voice comes out in a roar of pain.

Falcon leans forward, his eyes, the colour of the shallows of an exotic island, narrow as he focuses on me. They can be ice cold like glaciers or change to the aquamarine that is sparkling at me now. He clears his throat and I snap my attention back to what we're talking about. "What happened?"

"It worked. Our plan." I walk around and throw myself on the couch. "The twins came out. One is a beta who works for us, and the other is the omega. Just like we guessed." I smile ruefully as Grayson perches opposite me. "That beta has been hiding her twin this whole time. Masking her scent with scent deodorisers. Giving her suppressants. Keeping her in that hovel. I had them. I had them right there in my pocket. All I needed to do was find out her price."

I stand up, pacing back and forth. I wind back and slam my fist into the wall. "We were wrong!" I howl.

Falcon stands up. "Silas, what happened?"

His question contains a bite, a demand, but I fight it, shaking my head in denial as the events replay in my mind.

"It's the beta." I rasp out.

"What's the beta?" Grayson asks.

I swallow hard and rip my tie off. "He wasn't interested in the omega. Oh, she's pretty, but her scent isn't appealing at all. Not to me, not to him. But the beta…I couldn't get close." I turn to Falcon, moving into his space, leaning over him, gripping his shoulders. "He wouldn't let me. He stopped me. I dismissed her. I tried to get rid of her. He's even more furious with us. Whoever that investigator is, fire him. He said that he smelled the person Dylan was following, and it was the omega. It wasn't! It's *'very much'* the omega." I blurt sarcastically, shaking my head, unable to grasp how badly I ruined our plan.

"He wants the beta?" Grayson mulls it over. "That makes things easier and harder. Our omega is slippery. Always with the surprises. He is a worthy catch."

"He isn't ours," Falcon says tersely.

"Yet," Grayson says and gets up with a bounce. "He isn't ours yet. But he damn well is, and we all know it. But the question is why a beta? What has she done for him that we haven't been able to? Is this revenge? Is she a shield?"

I follow Grayson towards the vast windows. "She's nothing special. Not beautiful. Nor is she clever, talented, or intelligent. This beta is average across the board. She blends in with all the workers we've had over the years, and you'd never look at her twice. She is nothing exceptional."

"So, our options are to separate them," Grayson says and leans against the window. The sight makes me nauseous. "We could, theoretically. She does work for us. We could send her to the other side of the world to work."

"And risk driving him further away? Risk more months of desperate searching?" Falcon growls. "No. We need to start playing his game now. It was our mistake, us that fucked up. We hurt him, and if we want to earn his forgiveness, we need to work with, not against."

"What are you saying?" I ask stiffly.

Falcon goes to the bar and pours three glasses. I join him and take mine.

"Let's court him." Falcon says.

I stare at him for a long moment. "Are you insane?"

"No, I'm not. I'm saying let's court him properly. Let's woo him and win him away from her. She can't have what we have. We're his scent matches. He needs us."

"So ridiculous," I mutter and shake my head. "Wooing an omega twice."

"Got a better idea?" Falcon asks coldly.

I stay silent because I don't. But I'm surprised Grayson stays quiet, too.

The glass of whiskey keeps me company while I try to get through some of the emails I have to answer, but in the end, I can't resist. I open up her personnel file and scan the contents before starting again at the top.

Onyx Laural Davies. Twenty-three years old. High school dropout. No college. Her address is an area that should be condemned. I make a note to speak to someone when we get back to town. She has glowing referrals from every single person she's worked for. Words like hard working, respectful, takes initiative, polite, no trouble, good with customers, willing to learn. All the words a businessman like me loves to hear.

And yet, she's protecting her hidden omega sister like a vicious dog.

I exit out of the office software and do a general internet search. No socials. That's odd but not unheard of. Ah, here we go. I click on the link and pause at the photo of a fireman supporting one of the twins as they walk away from a massive house fire.

Her mother died in the fire when the twins were sixteen. Their father spent months in hospital before he succumbed to his wounds. But by then, he'd wracked up significant debt. The insurance wasn't paid out due to there being some question about whether it was deliberately set. In the end, it was ruled an accident, though. But that may not be the truth. I get chills just thinking about this evil bitch with my omega.

I only find a bit more information after that. The pack that was courting the omega disappeared when the funds dried up, and after that, both sisters disappeared. The beta resurfaces a year later and starts working. Often taking multiple jobs in a single day. The omega never resurfaces.

"I know all about Silver. She had an extensive social media page when she was younger, and she never deactivated it. I know she loves shiny things. She dreams of having a pack. She is the exact kind of omega pack's dream about. Flirty, gorgeous, feminine." I mutter.

Nothing like my Dylan.

But we never looked into the beta. I don't know what food she likes or what colour her eyes are. I know nothing about her other than this information in her file, and it's not enough.

What I know is that he found her at one of our events. I don't know when, but it's the only time they could have crossed paths. There's a pattern. On the events she works as a temp, he stays the whole night. If she left, he left. He followed her while we spent months searching for him.

For a few short weeks, seven months ago, Dylan was ours. And life was better than I ever dreamed it could be.

Then we blew it. I slump in my chair.

But this. It has to work. The entire event has been planned meticulously with the only goal: to get him here. Every day tailored to bring him back to us. He returned the thirty invites we sent him. So, I set about finding out why. And I find her, them.

I grind my teeth so hard my jaw aches. Just the idea of her touching him. Ugh, I can't stand it.

Sure, I pulled strings. I bought her, plain and simple. She's got more than enough money as her salary to keep even her greedy eyes pinned. I'll reveal to Dylan what she's like. I'll show him she only cares about money. She isn't worthy of him.

I load up the security camera and flick through them until I find them. Of course, they're together. I seethe as she sways towards him. Seducing my omega. I should just kill her.

No.

I stalk towards them before I register leaving the penthouse. They're sitting in a dark corner of the restaurant. It's luxurious and empty. The low lighting really sets the romantic mood. She's leaning across the table, her plain black hair, dull and lifeless, her smile is just-ugh! Dylan, on the other hand, is fixed on her. He tracks the movement of her hand and wrist as she talks. He smiles, and it brings me to life and destroys me. His dark hair is shorter than I've seen on him, and he looks thinner. He's obviously not eating enough. But he's Dylan, and he's beautiful. There's only one issue. He's looking at her and not me.

I want to destroy her.

My feet stop without my say so when I see them. She is talking a lot, and he's just staring at her. But it's the look he gives her that causes my heart to clench. It's soft, it's fond, it's deep caring and understanding. It's the look he reserved for us. For his alphas. For me. It's hard to breathe. My hands are shaking, and I step out of sight just as he looks up and scans the room.

"Listen, Dylan, you don't mind if I call you Dylan, do you?" My Dylan shakes his head. "I appreciate your help, but I'm used to dealing with alphas. I'm not worried about that one."

I clench my hands tight. She should be.

"You haven't said a word."

Dylan smiles. "I prefer to listen to you."

His voice. Oh, I've missed his voice. I still hear it in my dreams. I've yearned to hear him say my name.

She blushes. I can see the change in her cheeks from here. I clench my fingers so hard my knuckles hurt.

"I don't like to talk much."

"Oh, that's fair." She brushes her black hair behind her ear, and I want to cut it off.

"You're one of the guests here." She nods to herself and glances around. "I shouldn't be sitting here with you."

My eyes widen as the dawning realisation that she doesn't even know he likes her rises in my brain like a sunrise of hope. She is at a disadvantage. We have the home field. We have some time.

"I better get home and pack up Silvies' stuff for her. I mean, if she wants it."

She stands, and Dylan does, too. He moves close to her, but she dances back away from him. Nervous.

"You can call me Nyx." She holds out her hand.

It's nothing, it's professional courtesy.

He tilts his head to the side, smiles that precious smile, and reaches out, enclosing her hand in his. He may as well rip out my heart and kill me.

I wait until she's gone before I step out from behind the wall. He doesn't acknowledge me at all. That hurts. It really hurts. I reach out for the hand that he touched hers with, but he snatches it back.

I close my eyes and struggle to breathe evenly.

"Why her?" I ask in a whisper.

He glares at me, his gaze turning frigid.

"Why? I'm just trying to understand why?"

"You wouldn't understand. Fuck off, Silas. I'm here like any other guest." His eyes lift to look past me, and I hear the high giggle. I stiffen and reach out, resting my hand on his arm.

"You belong with us," I say, and I'm not sure if it's a command or a plea.

He snorts in derision and stands taller, slamming his hand, into one pocket of his jeans. Where I can't reach it.

"The only thing I do know is that with you is the last place I want to be." He glances at the woman who moves closer to us. "Enjoy your evening, Alpha Hastings."

I pull out a chair and sit at a table, staring at the spot he just left, reeling from the venom in his voice. He stalks out of the restaurant, uncaring of my pain, unmoved by my torment, leaving me broken at the table. Haunted by my own failures, again.

Five

ONYX

It's hard not to fidget. I'm shoulder to shoulder with a man who smells like garlic and a woman who's sniffing is driving me up the friggin wall. My mask of polite interest is getting hard to hold. Silvie didn't come back last night. Not for her things, not to sleep. I should be happy for her, and a huge part of me is, but I can't help but feel she's just abandoned me.

She kinda has.

But I can survive in this world. She can't.

Simon walks past, discussing last-minute reminders and barking out orders. I absorb the information with half an ear. There are easily over a hundred staff lined up in this room. All of us wearing identical white shirts with black slacks and shoes. The quality of the clothing is excellent, the best I've ever worn. I almost raise my hand to check my hair and make sure my ponytail is tight, but at the last minute, I keep my arm still. We are the perfect face of the Treyfield Resort.

My feet are aching from the new shoes, and my eyes are burning. My jaw aches from fighting the yawns, courtesy of spending the night up waiting and listening for any sign of Silver. I feel gross like I just need a month in bed.

Upon our arrival, uniforms were given out, but this morning, they gave us our name tags, shoes, and a bracelet that identifies us and our location in real time. It can't be taken off except with the master key. The silver metal is pretty, with roses engraved into the cuff and a number. 266.

I am now reduced to a number. It leaves a bitter taste in my mouth.

The woman beside me sniffs again, and I bite hard enough on my tongue to taste blood. I side-eye the line of staff to my right. They are all standing at attention, blank expressions on their faces. I get a horrible thought that perhaps I'm standing next to robots. The urge to giggle grabs hold of my stomach, and I bite my lower lip to suppress it.

Simon's gaze pauses on me for a moment before he continues on. The impulse to laugh dies away as the torture resumes.

The double doors are thrown open, surprising us all into spontaneous flinches. It's so unexpected that Simon falls silent and approaches with a wary smile. A man who I suspect is Simon's assistant scurries to hold the door open and almost doubles over in a deferential bow.

A man walks in with such an air of command that I want to duck away and hide. He's got classic good looks, a strong face, with a wide jaw, eyes with thick black lashes, and a slim body with broad shoulders. Lips that look like they could smile prettily or cut you to the core. Not a hair is out of place, not a wrinkle can be seen on his immaculate charcoal suit. But his eyes are piercing, and as they land on me, I fancy he knows who I am, that he sees me, and then I remember that I'm a beta, and men like that never look at me.

The second man who enters has thick blond hair. He smiles at the room, and I feel a flutter in my stomach. He moves like a jungle cat. He looks like he should be modeling underwear.

The last is the man from yesterday, but today, it's like I'm seeing him for the first time. His hair is slicked back, and I notice that his brown eyes are dark and deep and they look soulful. He looks like someone I would want to be friends with.

The three of them together send crackles of electricity into the air. They have an aura that cows us lesser mortals. I'm holding my breath, staring with wide eyes.

Three tall, broad, and handsome alphas walking in like they own the place...Oh, no. No way. These are they, the Treyfield Pack. The Alpha's who own the company. No, I checked. They're not supposed to be here. Simon said they were in the city and wouldn't be coming here.

Oh, my god. Treyfield Pack gave Silver a room and...what do they want from her? I feel sick and put my hand against my stomach without thinking. The movement draws their eyes. I freeze like a baby deer in the headlights of ravenous wolves.

What are their names? Why can't I recall the information?

The longer they stare at me, the more my cheeks heat, and the harder it is to keep still. My skin twitches, and I want nothing more than to step back and let the line of workers absorb me into their ranks.

THE BETA'S BARGAIN

There is something personal and predatory in the way they are watching me. Like I've already done something wrong. Which I guess I have. I stifle the urge to laugh again and fix my gaze on the wall behind them.

I've served glasses of wine in the most daunting of settings. These alphas are just men. They bleed like the rest of us. *Breath in and out, Nyxie.*

They arrange themselves around the room, two of them moving and watching us like we're cattle. Simon and Elaine take up spots on an equal distance apart in the middle of the empty space in front of us. Perfect little management robots. A throat clears, and my gaze darts back to them, the alphas, who are now stopped in front of us like they're about to give us a speech. The alpha with the blond hair is leaning against the wall, absolutely content with his lot in life. Not participating at all.

A frisson of anger ripples down my spine, and I suppress it quickly.

"Welcome to the Treyfield Empire's first annual Omega Meet."

My eyes widen, and I stare at the arrogant man in front of me as he speaks. Omega Meet?

"My name is Falcon Treyfield. You'll recognise my name as my fathers created many of the department stores you now shop in. The Treyfield name has a hundred years of history behind it, and today, we're adding one more."

The olive-skinned alpha walks with polite aggression, gesturing with his hands. "My name is Silas Hastings. My family has been in hotels even longer than Treyfield's been in shops. When we came up with the idea to have a retreat that caters to matchmaking omegas and packs, we got excited. People will be able to see what we really care about. What we are..." he waves his hand in a circle, "passionate about. We hope you will enjoy the energy and do us proud."

"And I'm Grayson Waters."

Murmurs explode. I hold my tongue, staring at the man against the wall.

"My family is in technology and now owns the largest research laboratory on the planet. We believe in giving back to the community. We believe in giving happy endings."

I snort.

The three alphas snap their heads towards me like I've shot a flare into the room. Panic turns my blood fizzy. I hold my breath until they look away.

"There can be no mistakes." Falcon says. "No errors. The next few weeks must be perfect. You must be perfect." He saunters up and down the line. I see men and women alike suck in their stomachs and straighten up. He comes back this way and stops right in front of me. "I will allow no distractions." He turns his head really slowly and meets my eyes.

There's this magnetic pull towards him that tries to grab hold of me, but I push it aside and embrace the anger. This man encompasses everything I've learned about alphas working for them. Rude. Arrogant. Entitled.

I'm just a beta. I'm not a distraction. I'm nothing to this man. So I smile faintly, letting him see that I'm not cowed.

His eyes flash, and for a moment, I get this idea that I've just woken a sleeping titan.

"Every alpha wants an omega to join their pack. And every omega wants an alpha pack to call their own. So, this weekend has been opened to packs and omegas specifically selected by a team and invited to participate."

He doesn't mention betas at all, and I hear him loud and clear. Serve our drinks, bring our food, don't talk, don't touch, don't look. Be there, and don't be seen or heard.

I swipe my expression clear and stare at the door with an acute expression of boredom.

"This is a charity event."

I bark out a laugh before I can stop myself.

The atmosphere turns dangerous before I even smother the sound. Grayson Waters pushes off the wall and stalks towards me. He looks like a shark. I can even see his gleaming white teeth.

"Something funny?" He raises a brow in challenge, and I'm just too tired to resist.

"No one in this building needs this kind of charity. So you may as well call it what it is."

Simon hisses, but I don't take my eyes from Grayson.

He smiles and holds up his hand, stopping my boss in his tracks. He leans in close so only I can hear him. "There are two people in this building who need charity."

I stiffen. "If you feel a need to threaten someone, please, look me in the eye when you deliver it. I promise I'll respect you more." And then I panic because I need this job. Why did I say that? "Alpha Waters." I lower my eyes and dip my chin, but the movement is sarcastic and the tone bitchy.

I'm dead. Actual stone cold dead. I can't believe I just said that.

Grayson throws his head back and laughs, leaving me confused and tense. His index finger drags lightly across my hand. I flinch, and he smirks and walks back to his spot on the wall. The spot he touched tingles, and I twist my wrist and rub the skin against my pants.

Mama always told me to think before I spoke. She would be slapping me across the head for this. Dad might have beaten me to death for ruining Silvie's chances. Just thinking about them opens the ache inside me. The pressure to get Silvie a good life weighs heavily on my exhausted shoulders.

"You'll be paired up and assigned an omega or alpha pack to shadow. You'll carry out such tasks as fetching, carrying, delivering food, drinks, messages, requests. There is no such thing as no to our guests, they will have the ultimate experience. If you don't think you should do something, you go to Simon or Elaine and let them handle it. You will be on call 24 hours a day."

My eyes widen. What?

Hopefully, they pair me with Silvie. But that hope dies almost as quickly as I think it.

"Onyx Davies?" Simon calls out. He's holding a black leather-bound folder in his hands. My stomach drops. I take it gingerly and flip it open. It's the pack from the pool. Pack Drest.

"Mr Simon, sir, this isn't going to work-" I try to explain, but Simon and Elaine hiss, and I shut my mouth. I can't help but notice that Elaine looks like a younger, less powerful version of Yvette.

I know what happens when you get between a pack and what they want. Alphas, especially rich ones, can be really vindictive. Fine. I close the folder and keep my head high while they hand out more.

The door smashes open, startling almost everyone in the room for a second time. It bangs on the wall, the handle puncturing a hole. A man stands backlit by the lights beyond him, there's something familiar about him, but I'm too struck by the rage pouring off him. Lemon wafts into the room, bitter and sharp. My eyes widen as I realise it's him, it's the omega. I risk glancing up and down the line of people. I want to go to him, protect him from everyone in here. Why, though? He's not my responsibility, and yet, he feels like he is. Perhaps it's because of us being semi-friends. I stay exactly where I am, my body tense and ready to spring across the distance.

Simon moves to meet him. "What do you think you're doing?"

I tense, shifting my foot forward.

"Simon, back away." Falcon barks out, much to my relief

Dylan lets out a hiss and stalks further into the room, finding a spot perfectly in between all three alphas and Simon.

A moment later, a harried Yvette jogs in behind the man. She goes straight to Falcon and whispers in his ear while shooting a glare at Dylan. That glare has me frowning at her. I want to step between them and stop her from looking at him.

I tune them all out. Dylan is struggling. With each passing moment, his agitation grows, and I can't stand it. His chest rises and falls, and as he turns in my direction, his expression becomes clear, and he is livid.

He ignores the alphas and searches the line until he finds me. As he passes Silas, the alpha makes a move to touch him. He dodges it, knocks Falcon's hand away, and gives Grayson a warning look.

Is this some kind of joke? Is someone setting us up for a prank?

My skin feels hot and cold, and I shiver as he walks straight over to me. He stops less than a foot away and stares down at me. My heart throbs painfully in my chest. I'm aware of all the curious stares and the fury of the alphas. The room feels dangerous.

"Dylan, what are you doing?" I whisper. I glance around and find all eyes on us. A cold sweat breaks out, and I shift my weight from leg to leg.

Falcon looks at me sharply. I can see all the questions he wants to ask on the tip of his tongue, but wisely, he holds them back.

Dylan takes the folder from my hands and flips it open, his lips curling, and his eyes growing dark. He reaches for my hand and holds tight as he turns around. He hurls the folder at Falcon. Pages of information rain into the air, and the big alpha just stands in the middle of the storm, impassive, staring at the omega holding me captive.

There's a tension in the room that feels different from anything I've felt before.

He tugs me against him, and his scent gets strong, wrapping around me and turning sweet. I can't help but feel I'm being used as a shield, but I can't work out why or how.

"I'm working," I say softly to break the silence.

"Release her!" Silas says furiously in a low voice, but he doesn't bark.

"She's mine." Dylan growls. I don't think anyone but the alphas, Simon, and I heard, but still, my face burns.

Mine? Mine! My brain is melting. I'm melting. Wow, no wonder omegas swoon when their alphas say it. It suddenly makes total sense to me. *Yes. I will step into fire for you, incredibly hot male specimen of an omega. I will be yours.*

34

No! Bad, Onyx. Control yourself.

The tension rises and rises until, finally, Falcon lowers his gaze to me and says clearly, "Simon, reassign Onyx to Dylan."

"But, sir-"

"Do it!" Grayson barks.

Simon nods. "Consider it done, sirs."

Dylan turns us towards the doors, but Grayson is there, cutting us off. "Don't you dare just leave like that."

I flinch, thinking he's talking to me, but he's talking to Dylan. He pulls me out of the omega's arms easily and shoves me away. Dylan and I both attack at the same time. I grab his wrist, breaking his hold on my hand just as Dylan shoves the alpha back. We bounce back together again, and I clutch at his hand this time.

"I can't get fired," I whisper.

"You won't," Dylan says loudly. He lifts his chin and stares at Grayson.

Silas steps between Grayson and Falcon and looks at me. "Please, Miss Davies, if you could, I'd appreciate it if you could be Dylan's employee. He's the most important guest in this hotel. Anything he wants, give it to him. Treat him as you would us."

I snort a laugh and cover my mouth when all three alphas look at me. "Sorry, it was a little bit funny." I lean into Dylan and pat his arm. "Don't worry, I'll be much nicer to you."

I jerk in fear when three savage growls erupt into the room. They control themselves quickly, but the sound lingers in my mind. My heart pounds, and I find myself standing behind Dylan, who guides me backwards out of the room.

"Go away, Dylan. We have work to do," Falcon says and dismisses us.

Dylan retreats slowly, pulling me with him.

"You know them?" I ask hesitantly.

He hesitates. "Sort of."

I snap my jaw shut as he leads me into the silver lift. There are six lifts in the foyer, but the two on the end are gold and silver. I haven't been on either of them before. The inside is polished silver with delicate art déco type designs laid into the frames of everything.

It's beautiful.

The door opens, revealing a suite that is far bigger than the other rooms I've seen. The furniture looks new and extremely modern and expensive. There is no sign of personality anywhere in this room. It's expensive and boring.

I let out a whistle and then whirl back to my new friend.

Who is this man? And why is he looking at me like that?

I walk to the window and admire the view before I turn back again. He's moved closer. Silently.

"I'm getting the sense that things are complicated here. Those alphas know you, and they're very angry at me."

Dylan snarls.

I freeze and tilt my head to the side. "So, they are. I'm guessing they don't like that we're friends." My head nods with a jerk. "I can understand that. Just makes them small-minded idiots."

His expression turns blank, and he shakes his head. That's a damn lie.

The elevator opens, and Grayson walks into the room and leans on the glass beside me. He doesn't notice the thick tension Dylan and I have as we watch him. I remember my mother talking once to her friend while I wasn't meant to be listening. Her friend said that the alpha they were watching was sex on a stick. Now, I had no idea what that meant, but right now, watching this alpha leaning on this wall...I think I completely understand. He is brain-melting level hotness, and that half lidded, sleepy look is straight out of all my frustrated R-rated fantasies.

He studies the omega and then turns to me. Focuses all that hot, sexy alphaness on me. My knees get weak, and I stumble back a step. Sweet lemon blooms in the air around us, and for some reason, that makes it even harder to think. Knowing the omega is as affected by this alpha as I am is the sweetest torture.

"I believe we got off on the wrong foot." His voice is seduction itself. His clothes are tailored to show off every asset he has, and even the tiny scar on his chin just emphasises his perfection. Blue-green eyes narrow, and soot covered lashes lower to hide his amused gaze.

He is an assault on my senses. I feel drunk.

"Did we?" I say when I remember what he said.

"My name is Grayson Waters. Alpha in Pack Treyfield."

"Okay?" I glance at Dylan for instruction, but he appears frozen, his eyes all but drinking in the alpha in front of me. Okay, um, wow. I should probably leave.

"We've heard good things about you, Miss Davies."

I sniff and stalk across the room to the kitchen, but when I get there and turn, Grayson is on my heels, and Dylan is on his. I step back and find the giant kitchen is far too small with such enormous men in here.

"I'm here to fill you..." Grayson murmurs and glances over his shoulder, pausing, with a wicked smirk, "In on your duties."

Is it hot in here? My mouth is parched. My brain scrambles as I finally duck past them both and into the lounge again.

"Stop," Grayson says in a low voice.

There's just a hint of bark, but I stop dead, shuddering as his fingers come up to enclose my shoulders. He squeezes them in a way that leaves me wanting to weep with the urge to beg for more then slides them down to my waist.

"You need to listen to me now, beta." His voice is like a caress.

I hold perfectly still as he removes his fingers. His fingers return to my waist and drag over my hips. I catch my breath and shudder as he moves away. I'm on fire. Actual fire.

"There. You're all set." Grayson moves away, and I bolt, putting the couch between us and staring warily. Paper rustles, and I glance down to find a folded up piece of paper in my pocket. I pull it out and open it, reading through my duties quickly.

"For the sake of appearances, try to at least pretend she's here to work, my love," Grayson purrs.

My gaze shoots to Dylan, who has turned white. His fists are clenched, and he's breathing hard. But the air is still full of the sweetest lemon scent I've ever smelled.

"Out!" Dylan growls.

"I'm going. I'm going." Grayson gets on the lift and turns around to face us, giving one last cocky wink before the silver doors close and take him away.

With his departure, he steals the energy in the room. I move to the couch and sit down, putting my head in my hands.

I have to keep focus on the end game. Silvie. But when I look up and find Dylan staring at me, I'm not sure what game I'm even playing anymore.

Six

ONYX

Moira sidles up to me as we prep the dining room for the packs and omegas to come down to get their breakfast. It's a job I've done so often I don't even need to think about it. The huge dining room looks different today. Perhaps it's all the white table clothes or the windows that have been opened to allow sunlight to pour inside.

I sometimes forget how luxurious these places are because I work in them so often, but this morning, I can feel the divide.

"You are all everyone is talking about, girl." Moira's dark eyes appear liquid but are full of laughter and life. Her lips are wide and almost always smiling, and her hair is as curling and springy as her personality. Over the last week, her constant attempts to befriend me have worn me down, and now, I actually look forward to seeing her when I go to our joint duties.

I jerk my head up and narrow my eyes. "Yes, well." I honestly have no excuse or logical reason to give these people. My circumstances are better than a best seller right now.

"That omega, wow. And the tension. It could have cut glass." She rolls her eyes back in her skull and fans herself. "So fucking hot."

The white top she's wearing is really tight across her breasts and really emphasises her thin waist. I never feel jealous, but looking at her, I get intimate with the feeling. Would Grayson react to her the way he did to us last night?

"That omega?" I ask and slide the cutlery trolley closer so we can load the tables.

"Dylan Wyrven. Mystery omega. No one seems to know anything about him except that he belongs to the pack."

My head jerks up. He belongs to a pack? That's news to me. "What pack?"

"Dylan belongs to Treyfield. You knew that, right?"

Oh. Wow. Those words crush me. My mouth works, but no words come out. I replay every moment I've had with Dylan and feel the weight of my stupidity incinerate me.

I try, but I really struggle to see Dylan in that world. My Dylan is a shadow, following me around glitzy parties. He's a man in a holey jacket in alley ways. Dylan is my rescuer at parties. He doesn't belong to them; he belongs to me.

I avert my eyes so she doesn't see the sheer insanity that has stolen over me. An omega, mine? What a joke.

"Oh, my god, you, like, totally know nothing, don't you? Girl, you need to stay informed." She shakes her head, sending brown corkscrews bouncing around her shoulders. "Right, so seven months ago, it's rumoured that the Treyfield Pack was about to enter a bonding ceremony with the omega in question. But just before they were to go ahead and do it, he ran and disappeared."

"Why?"

"No one knows. But he didn't go home. He just vanished. People thought he was dead. Or they locked him up. Or any number of things. The newspapers kept showing sightings, but I have to admit, I didn't believe it until I saw him yesterday. It reminds me of that missing Donahue heir. He took off. No one knows where. Richer than the Treyfield pack combined. If I had that kind of money, you wouldn't see me running away. But your omega, he was pissed."

"That's...tragic." I say sadly. I know where he was. Starving in the street. Following me in the dark. How did he end up so far from home?

"How so?"

"They found each other, they had happiness, and it was snatched away. It's sad."

Moira gives me an odd look and wheels the trolley to the next table. I pick up the cloth and wipe the forks as I place them.

"It wasn't tragic, it was a scandal. Treyfield Pack are *the* pack. If you could become a part of their world, you'd never want for anything ever again. You don't run from them."

"They might be abusive, misogynistic assholes." I say dryly. "They could be controlling narcissistic whores."

"Do you think so? Really?" The voice snaps with ice-cold fury.

I whirl so fast I have to catch myself on the table. Silas is standing there with a hurt look that doesn't even pretend to look sincere on his face. If anything, I think the alpha might be amused by my statement. His black shirt is pristine and reveals a tapered waist and broad shoulders. He sweeps his hair back, and I notice he hasn't shaved. The dark stubble just makes him look even more appealing.

"No, sir. I'm just using examples of why we should not judge a pack by their newspaper headlines. I certainly don't know you well enough to state if that statement is factual or fiction."

Silas stares at me with those dark eyes, and I get a horrible feeling that I shouldn't have said that.

"I don't know whether to fire you or just walk away," he murmurs. A laugh outside the dining room draws his gaze, and for a moment, he looks hunted. I peer at the door, but when no one comes in, he relaxes.

"She didn't mean it, honest, sir. We were just talking about..." Moira trails off, her cheeks turning a ruddy red, and she drops her eyes.

"You were just gossiping about us in company hours." Silas nods in understanding. "Well, let me fill in the blanks, Miss Davies. My name is Silas Leonidas Hastings. I was trained to take over this empire from the age of fourteen. I have zero workplace reports, infractions, or warnings against my name. Not a single complaint. I know how to deliver your fantasies in a one weekend long stay at my hotel. You want to watch mermaids while you dine? I can make it happen. A marathon of the hottest men in the world in your bed, I can have them here by lunch. You want a chocolate fountain and a ball gown that will turn you into a fairy tale? Let me be your fairy godfather. Whatever your price is...Miss Davies, I can afford it."

He moves in closer and closer until we're parted by just a tiny amount of space. We're not talking about gossip anymore. He's really trying to find out my price. A frisson of fear chases away the cobweb-like spell he's placed on me.

Dylan.

Silver.

The intimate way he spoke leaves no doubt to his intention. No doubt that I'm supposed to crumble and agree to anything.

Silver needs this chance. I will not jeopardize her dreams for this alpha's revenge or whatever it is he wants.

I peer up at him and smile tightly. "Not my fantasies, Mr Hastings. I am, after all, just a beta. If you will excuse me, I need to get back to work."

I can feel his eyes on me the whole time I load the tables, but when I finish and turn around, he's gone.

I'm confused by the mixture of disappointment and relief that I feel but shrug it off and chase after Moira as the waiters bring out the food.

An hour later, and I really hate this job, but I grit my teeth and hold in my irritation by pasting a bored expression on my face and counting the window panes.

We, the hired help, need to stand to the side against the wall. We need to be ready to jump to our charges' aid, cutting their potatoes or testing their food for poison. I force my eyes closed so none of that bitter thought leaks out. It's humiliating, and I've never had to do anything like this before.

I'm really not a good fit for this job.

It's for Silvie, I remind myself over and over.

Her voice has me snapping to attention. I turn my head and spot her walking into the room. She's laughing, happier than I've seen her in years. She's surrounded by handsome men. The dress she's wearing is floaty and violet. Her hair gleams. She looks incredible, like some kind of fairy princess.

I smile wide and blink back tears. She walks past me. I know she sees me because her face darkens, and she hesitates. It's a micro-expression so small that most people would miss it, but not me. I've known her too well for too long.

I lift my arms up to waist height, the beginning of an invitation. Silver just bites her lip and then takes the arm of the alpha beside her and walks straight past me. There's a strange combination of triumph and disappointment as I watch my sister step into the role she was born for.

"Holy cow bells, you're a twin." Moira says beside me.

I wince and snort a laugh. "Cow bells?" I shake my head, amused despite the pain in my chest. "Apparently, not today."

I refocus on Silver; I can't stop the sting, the burn of humiliation. She's right to distance herself from me. Of course, she is. Despite that, I have to blink hard a couple of times.

Those alphas didn't even see me. We're close enough in looks that we can pass for each other, and they looked right at me but didn't see me.

I hear my father's words in my head. Just a beta.

"Um, hey, your omega is heading this way, and he looks mad as hell." Moira hisses in my ear.

I glance around and spot him marching towards me. He saw me from across the room? And like magnets, the alphas appear, too, their gazes finding him and following his path straight to me.

"Shit. What do I do?" I wipe my hands on my thighs and glance sideways, wincing at the growing attention.

Moira giggles. "Honey, go with that man. He's determined, hot as fuck, and his eyes don't look anywhere but at you. Lock him down."

"He's an omega," I hiss back.

"Yeah, but he looks like he's made his choice." Moira throws in. "Good morning, Omega Wryven."

He stops in front of me, searching my face for something.

"Hi, Dylan, can I help you with something?" I lean in close and smile. "Would you like me to cut up your bacon?"

"Yes."

I'm frozen as my humour vanishes and panic replaces it.

His lip twitches, but he grabs my wrist and pulls me with him.

"Um, I know you don't like to talk, but can we…slow down or stop for a second?" He ignores me, and it's all I can do to keep from bashing into people as they adjust their chairs and take their spots at tables. And why is he dragging me straight towards those alphas?

I trip, but he turns suddenly, catching me, and sets me on my feet. Our gazes lock, and the room fades away. All the sound and all the colour. All I can see is gold eyes and black pupils and lashes. Black and gold becomes my world.

He takes my wrist more carefully this time and moves us through the room. I feel dizzy and off kilter. Suddenly, I don't want to talk. I want to replay that moment over and over. I want to think about how I feel and what happened. What is happening to me?

We stop at a table, and he pulls a chair out. I shake my head and pull away. I need to get back to the wall.

"Dylan, what are you doing? I can get fired for this. You're making a scene." My weak whisper of a protest is barely audible.

He growls, sits in the chair, and pulls me down onto his lap.

I go still, and all the words just leak out of my brain. I have nothing. I rest my fingers on the arm holding me and sit perfectly still, not looking anywhere but at the plate in front of me. His thighs are hard, and his arms surrounding me are bands of warmth. My whole body is alive, focused on every part of us that is touching. I force myself to ignore the growing heat simmering between my thighs.

"Well, this is going to be entertaining this morning." Gray purrs and leans across the table to grab a plate of butter. His arm brushes along mine, a spark of something both pleasant and painful charges my skin, and I gasp. I jerk my eyes to his arm, I could have sworn he had long sleeves on. I scowl when I see he's rolled up his sleeves and is flexing those muscled forearms. I stare, lost in the hypnotizing movements.

"Gray!" The commanding voice forces me to suck in air and breathe again. Silas is seated on our right, sitting with perfect posture and looking supremely unconcerned. Falcon is opposite me, his brows down, and that aura is almost menacing. It was from him the command came.

Wonderful. I'm so getting fired.

"Get her a chair," Falcon says in an air of complete command. Someone explodes into action, and a few moments later, a new chair and place setting are added. I calmly but firmly remove Dylan's arms and sit beside him. He reaches out and pulls the chair closer to him and glowers around the table.

Breakfast with wolves. A nice way to kick-start digestion.

"Did you memorise your duties?" Silas asks as he cuts into a crepe.

It takes me a moment to realise he's talking to me. "I did, Alpha."

"Excellent. Tell me." He cuts another piece and takes a bite calmly before pinning me with a glare.

I open my mouth, glance down at my food, and set my utensils down. "General tidying, making sure he arrives at the assignments, delivering messages and requests-"

"And the rules?"

"Be there but not seen or heard. We are not their friends." My voice slows and stops as I stare at Silas, silently pleading for the humiliation to end. "We are forbidden from forming attachments or engaging in a sexual relationship. We may not threaten them with violence or blackmail, manipulation or-"

"That will do." Falcon says sharply. "She understands her place."

I flinch at the sharp command.

Silas sets his knife and fork down, having finished his crepes. "Very well. We have a meeting now, anyway. Come along, Miss Davies."

I look down at my plate, still full of food, and sigh as I push to my feet. Dylan grips my wrist and stands slowly beside me.

"Really?" Silas growls. "She is an employee. My employee. Not yours. And she has a meeting."

A silent battle rages between the four men, but it's like I don't understand the language. But the room feels dangerous.

"Oh, Silas, you are such a tyrant. Go terrorize someone else." The feminine voice is full of amusement and teasing and familiarity.

I expect him to lash out, but he just closes his eyes and shakes his head.

"Hazel, what are you doing here?" Gray snaps.

"Oh, there was no way I was missing this shitshow. Hey, Dylan. How's it going? Do I need to beat them up again? I did after you left. I made sure they suffered."

I turn as she approaches, and my mind shorts. She is the most delicately beautiful person I've ever seen. Her features are elfin, her brown hair is shot with blonde highlights, and even with my dulled senses, her jasmine is a powerful hit. She's smiling at us, and it's kind and warm, and I don't even know why. Who is she?

"Haze...we talked about your stalking." Grayson says evenly. "It's not cute anymore."

"I know, but I'm bored, and I have to come and see what my big brother is fucking up."

"We're not fucking anything up," Grayson growls and moves to her side. He puts an arm over her shoulder, and my stomach tightens uncomfortably. I look away from them and find Silas plucking at the cuffs of his dress shirt, completely unconcerned. Falcon has his eyes closed as if he's praying.

"You could be watching a pack of your own," Falcon says.

I watch the female omega reel back; her face going white. "Cold, Fal. Really cold." Her tone is glacial. "You know perfectly well that I don't get a happy ending, unlike some who squander their chances."

He sighs, and his face contorts with regret. "I know. I apologise."

She draws herself up and sniffs. "Go away. I want to talk to Nyxie and Dylan."

"Now, Hazel," Gray begins, but she turns on him and smiles slightly.

"I will cause a scene and recite every single one of your embarrassing moments out loud. Or you can just go away."

THE BETA'S BARGAIN

Clarity is like a cloud breaking through. She's a sister. A younger sister.

The alphas get up and leave.

"You need to teach me that," I say to her.

She winks at me and flops into Falcons seat. "You're really pretty."

I frown. "Um, thank you."

She looks at Dylan. "I can see it. You do you, boo." She says and blows him a kiss. Then she just stands up and walks away.

I stare around, bewildered, until Dylan leans in close to my ear. "Eat."

"Did she do that so I could eat?"

Dylan smiles slightly. "Eat. That was Hazel Waters, Gray's younger sister."

My mind is officially blown. I start eating my cold bacon and eggs while Dylan sits close enough to stop anyone interfering. It's like we're in our own little world. I just don't know how the world is going to end. But breakfast never tasted so good.

The day passes as more and more people check in. I find myself either with Dylan or running errands and helping out the other staff. Before I know it, night has landed. I'm supposed to move into Dylan's suite. It's not expected of all guests, but some of the high enders have requested it. Simon found me an hour ago and let me know that I would be moving in with Dylan, no questions asked.

I hoist my backpack over my shoulder and close the door on the empty cabin. I take the long way back, slipping through the trees and avoiding the other staff. Preparing for an event like this is a massive undertaking, and tempers are frayed.

The resort is enormous, and I find myself near the gardens. None of us have been allowed inside them yet. They're doing a big reveal in the final week, which looks like it will be incredible. Huge hedges keep nosy guests from seeing inside, and guards posted on the entrance keep them out.

I round the corner and stop.

Dylan is backed up against the hedges. He shakes his head. His jaw is tight and his eyes wide. The three alphas move in closer.

I don't know what he's so afraid of, but he's afraid. I'm their employee. I could walk away and say I saw nothing. But I like him, and they gave him into my care. I'm moving before I can think things through.

I'm sorry, Silver, but it's the right thing to do.

I slip between the spaces easily enough and stare up at them. They are terrifying. They look like monsters. Huge, towering alphas, men with all the power and no compassion in their expressions. It's a repetitive nightmare, a situation I find myself in often in my line or work. One I've been lucky to escape. Powerful men taking and taking, and people like me, like him, we have no chance. I won't let them destroy Dylan. I push my back against the omega and push at them. When they don't move and someone growls, I react instinctively.

My palm crashes against someone's face. My hearts pounding, and I'm suddenly covered in a cold sweat, but my act seems to freeze all four of us.

"You can't do that to a guest!" I stutter shout at them.

Silas cradles his cheek with one hand, staring at me like I'm an alien.

"You can't intimidate people into doing what you want. He's scared, even I can smell his fear." I snarl, and when Falcon moves, I step into his path and ball my fists. They can take me down easily, they can crush me. But I'm going to do everything I can to protect Dylan. "Don't you touch him," I snarl. "Don't you dare."

"You're misunderstanding the situation, Miss Davies." Falcon says coldly.

"Am I? Have you got an omega up against a wall, intimidating him despite his obvious fear, trying to force him to what?" I throw a look at Grayson, and then Silas. "Force him to bond with you?"

"No! Never force him to do that!" Grayson growls. "Just listen."

"And how is that any better? You're taking his choice, his autonomy, away from him." I snap back.

"We just wanted to be able to talk, to explain." Silas says softly and glances away. "But you're right. We're doing this all wrong."

Falcon holds his ground, refusing to move for a long moment. "You don't know the situation, Miss Davies. But, no matter. You're correct. We'll be more patient next time."

"I've seen how alphas behave. I've seen how no can mean yes to them, and I've seen them leave ruins and wrecks behind like they're nothing. Just because you're stronger doesn't mean you get to just take all the time. You have power and wealth and the designation, but be better!" I scream. I'm breathing so hard I'm almost sobbing.

Dylan's hands are on my hips, holding me to him.

Falcon opens his mouth, but he can't seem to get anything out.

Our eyes meet and hold, and I'm aware of the way my hair is sitting in a messy bun. My faded grey hoodie with the holes in the sleeves. I'm aware I haven't slept properly in days, and I'm aware of the huge valley of differences between us.

He can have anything he wants in the world, anything. I don't have that luxury. I don't even have a home to go back to.

He steps closer, but this time, his focus is on me, and it's not anger in his eyes but curiosity. Falcon inhales and murmurs three words before he turns on his loafers and stalks away.

What on Earth did he mean when he said he loves coconut?

Seven

GRAYSON

Falcon calmly crosses his legs and sips at his coffee. That disaster that happened down in the grounds is still flashing through my mind. I'm not a monster. I can't even with that beta. That she could think that we would…I shake my head, trying to dispel the thoughts. Falcon said we needed to come back up here and regroup, rethink the situation, so that's what we've been doing most of the day. I think I need to go and hurl my stomach contents up. I would never, ever hurt my omega. Here we are, curled up with our tails between our legs, licking our wounds at home instead of celebrating with him. *FUCK!* I just can't get over their reactions!

"She doesn't understand the situation."

Our penthouse is lit with dim orange lights, and it bounces off the cream low couches and the thick white carpet. It's intimate and perhaps romantic on any other night. Today, it's just the only way we can face each other.

"I think it's pretty damning." I say to him and flick Silas a hard glare, too, just because. "We not only cornered him, but we orchestrated this entire event to force him to come back. Hell, we even tracked her down and brought her here under false pretenses."

Falcon snarls and uncrosses his legs. "It's different. We love him."

"But we hurt him." I point out. "We destroyed his trust."

"Not we!" Silas spits and turns towards me, away from the window he's been broodingly staring out of for the last few hours. "Not we. We didn't do it."

"I know," I say weakly. "But he thinks we did, so we need to prove ourselves. Grand gestures and all that and win him back."

"He might not love us anymore." Falcon says calmly. "Has that occurred to you? He might choose another pack."

The words send ice down my veins. "Don't say that. We're scent matches. We'll never find another omega who will be as perfect for us as him. We can fix this."

"Silas, any ideas?" Falcon asks tiredly.

Silas barks out a bitter laugh. "Ask the beta." He snaps sarcastically.

The words fall between us and ring in my head. I frown and consider it. I sit up and throw myself across the space to kneel beside Falcon. "That might work." I breathe, my stomach clenches, and I can't get the silly grin off my face. "Holy shit, that might fucking work!"

"Excuse me?" Silas growls. He stalks towards us and stops. I can see the unsure frown, that insecurity poking through. Silas might be rough and cold, but he feels it more. His parents tried to turn him into a robot, but he's got too much feeling inside him. It can't be contained. He's good and sensitive, and he just feels the world more. We just need to get him to come out of his shell.

The way he did with Dylan.

I stand up and pace the room. The white marble shines as I race into the kitchen and grab my tablet, bringing up the security feed of Dylan's room. It is the only thing I know how to do on the stupid machine. She's handing him a mug of something. When he doesn't pick it up, she wraps his hands around it. It's exactly what I'm talking about. I rewind the footage.

"Look!" I crow. I turn it around and show them. "She cares, and he trusts." I say, and when they both stare at me, I rewind it and show them again. "She cares about him," I enunciate slowly, "and he trusts her."

Silas moves closer and stares at the screen. "How is this possible? When did they even meet? What has she done to win him over?"

"Who cares?" I shrug my shoulders happily. "This beta is our way in."

"And? You think we can use her? Order her to help us?" Falcon frowns. "Seems unlikely."

"She's protected her omega sister all these years, and now she's protecting him. I say that we ask her. Explain what happened and ask her to help us."

"Ask?" Falcon's brows drop into a forbidding frown. "She'd never go for it."

"Why on Earth would she want that?" Silas snaps.

I look at my pack mates and seriously want to strangle them. How can they not understand this woman?

"Because she cares. She wants them to be happy." I mumble. "Like I want Hazel to be happy. She'll help us."

"I don't think she feels sisterly towards our omega, Gray." Falcon snarls.

"No, but she does feel something towards him." I retort. "She cares, and we can use that. Use her to get to him. To get him to listen to us."

Falcon nods slowly. "Fine, we'll speak to her tomorrow. Right now, I'm going to bed. I see no reason to be awake."

Silas waits a few minutes and disappears, too. I putter around but end up grabbing my tablet and finding my way to the office. I set up my desktop with the security feeds and actually do some work for a while before I find myself watching the beta's twin. She's up late in the piano lounge with a pack, and she is flirting heavily. The entire pack is captivated. She's going to do well for herself.

Without intention, I flick the camera to his private suite. They're both sitting on the couch, side by side. He'd got his feet on the coffee table...but he's not watching the movie, he's watching her.

Why? What is it about her?

She stood up to three alphas to protect him. That takes guts. More than guts, it borders on suicidal.

She's funny and smart. Caring and nurturing. Diligent and hard working.

I jerk myself out of my thoughts. What am I thinking, listing her merits? I squint at the screen. She's beautiful, too, in her own way, though too skinny and exhausted. Slate coloured intelligent eyes with black hair and lashes. Her lips are thin, but she's expressive. She can't hide her feelings, though she tries. She's not obviously curvy, but she's all feminine.

What does he see in her?

She jumps and buries her face in his arm. Her fingers curl on his wrist. It hurts to see her touching what only my pack should be touching. But now I'm also a little intrigued.

I shouldn't be.

We agreed as a pack. For our own sanity. Just the four of us.

But he's looking at her like that.

And it's hot. And intriguing. My cock is half hard, and I fight to ignore it. But his eyes are burning, and she hasn't even noticed. She flinches and bites her lip, Dylan and I both stare at the spot her teeth hold skin. My heart beat sounds deafening in my ears. What does she taste like?

"What the fuck am I doing?" I shut the computer screen off and lean back in my chair.

THE BETA'S BARGAIN

Images flood my mind, but I replay the way he stormed into our employee meeting. The blaze in his eyes. I imagine slamming him up against the wall, our lips clashing together. Lemon sorbet. I reach into my pants and stroke myself. It's not long before I'm hard. I rub my thumb over the tip of my cock, spreading the pre-cum around, imagining it's Dylan's hand. He'd open his mouth, dragging his lower lip up my cock and flick his tongue around the head. I fist my cock, moving into a steady rhythm. I'd grip his hair and thrust into his open mouth, listening to his greedy slurps. I feel a tingle in the base of my spine. My groan is loud in my office as my muscles tighten. Right before I come; I see her on her knees, her mouth open as I slip between those perfect lips.

I come hard, moaning, and reach for a tissue, cleaning myself up.

Shit. I throw an arm over my eyes and lean back in the office chair.

For days now, I've been trying to ignore this mild obsession. I've been fighting it off. But night after night, she appears in my fantasies.

Over and over.

I'm sick. I know I am.

I need my omega.

I wake up, courtesy of my own scream, thrashing around violently in the bed as I fight off memories. My door bursts open, and Silas flings himself onto the bed and wraps himself around me. His naked skin against mine is a blanket of warmth and safety dragging me out of hell. I shudder in his hold as reality slowly comes back to me. First the feel of Silas, then the scent, then the rest of the room.

I'm not in that basement, and I'm not missing. I'm safe with my pack. The words repeat until I almost believe them.

"It's okay. You're safe now." Silas murmurs into my ear. He kisses a path down to the bite he put on my skin and sucks hard on the spot.

It's not to arouse, it's just to remind me of where we are. I ignore my throbbing dick and hold him close until he pulls back and rolls so I'm laying with my head on his shoulder.

My heart beat slams against my chest, but I'm safe in Silas' arms. I turn and throw an arm and leg over his body, needing to be closer.

"Same dream?"

"Yes." I say hoarsely. "The basement. I was trying to protect Haze, but I couldn't."

"You haven't had one of those for a while," Silas points out and wraps his arms tighter around me.

"I haven't been feeling this crappy about life for a while," I say in exhaustion.

I miss the affection and intimacy of sex, but since Dylan left us, we have, by silent agreement, stopped being intimate with each other. It's unspoken, but the truth is that nothing feels right without him.

But tonight, I need Silas.

I roll us so that I'm leaning over him; I reach above him, curling my fingers in the pillow and flex my body against his, then I press my lips to his, forcing my tongue into his mouth. He groans and reaches up to clutch me closer to him.

"Gray, what?"

"He's back, but I want you, Silas. Tonight, I just want to be with someone I love."

Silas groans again and pushes me up, kissing me harder. His hands move over my back, dragging at my shoulders, fingers digging in almost painfully. It's desperate, like we've been away from each other for too long.

I love it, the feel of my alpha, the taste of his skin, the way he holds me. My hips grind, thrusting against him, feeling his hard cock against mine. I reach down between us, encircling both shafts with my hand. I grip tight and moan as I thrust against him. Silas tears his mouth from mine, tilting his head back on the pillow and letting out a hiss that makes me stroke us harder.

This is going to be short. It's been too long. I'm already on the edge.

Silas pants, dragging his hand down to my ass and thrusting up, fucking my fist and driving me insane. I love this man, this alpha. He's beautiful and mine.

"Silas!" I moan, plead.

He growls in my ear and yanks my hair. "Come on me."

His words are enough to send me over the edge. I grunt, thrusting harder and as I splurt all over Silas' stomach. My toes curl, and I fuse our lips together. All I can taste is his figs and sea salt scent.

"Silas!" I pant. "Please."

Silas tenses, arching up into my fist and gasping. His hot seed coats my fingers.

We both lay there, unable to move. I stare down at him and slowly remove my fingers, letting us go.

"You all right now?" Silas asks. The words are intimate and full of concern.

I get up onto my knees and crawl off the bed. I return a minute later with a washcloth and clean hands to gently clean Silas.

"I'm all right now." I say and lay down beside him. He holds his arm out, allowing me to lay my head on his shoulder.

"He's going to forgive us, right, Silas?"

"Yes. We'll make him." Silas soothes. "We're going to show him we'll be the perfect family for him."

A couple of hours later, I sit up and pull on some clothes. "I'm going to the gym."

"Mmm, I'm going to sleep then." Silas murmurs.

"Hey, Si?"

"Yeah?"

"Thanks."

"Love you," Silas murmurs before I hear a snore. I'm captivated by the way his hair falls across my grey pillow cases. I'm almost tempted to skip the gym and just get back into bed with him.

No, he needs to sleep, and I need to run away from whatever the fuck happened inside my head last night.

I catch the lift to the gym. The room's empty, but it's still dark outside, so I'm not surprised. I am, however, relieved. I put my playlist on the speakers and run. Running from my pain, from my demons, running because the only other thing I want to do is self-destruct, and that won't help anyone.

Half an hour later, I almost face plant on the belt.

My omega, my Dylan, walks in. It takes him a moment to spot me, but when he does, he stiffens and stands there, unsure. I make a quick decision and ignore him to focus on running. But I watch him like a hawk.

He crosses over to a machine, another treadmill, on the other side of the room and starts working out. I keep running until I'm panting and my legs are burning. I need to stop, but that leaves me with another problem.

I can't walk away from him.

He ignores me while I war with myself. *Just walk away, Gray. Leave the omega who hates you alone*. But I can't. He's ours. He's mine. I've missed him.

I can't stand this. I can take his hate, his rage, his despair, I can take it all, but I can't handle his apathy.

I'm feeling dangerous. Needy. I want him to look at me. See me.

I stare at him as I walk towards him, daring him to make eye contact in the mirror. He refuses, and it just enrages me a bit more.

"I love you." I whisper. "I love you." I say it louder. "I fucking love you." I shout.

He doesn't even flinch.

"I miss you. You are the only one. You're my only one."

He doesn't respond. It hurts, but I don't blame him. We're losing him.

I reach out to touch his shoulder, but he jerks away from me. He explodes off the machine and charges me. Gold eyes glint with fury and spark with hurt. It rips me apart. I hit the wall hard and stare at him as he cages me in.

"I love you," I whisper. The desperate sound is the most honest thing I've ever said.

He trembles, and the fury builds until I think he might hit me, but he doesn't. Instead, he closes the distance and presses his lips to mine, hard. Our teeth clash. I taste blood. I don't care. It's a kiss from my omega. Lemon fills the air, and I would happily drown in it. I grip his ass, dragging him closer to me. The hard bulge in his shorts rubs against mine.

I moan. It's ecstasy. It's heaven. It's home.

He's there and gone. Tearing himself away, putting space, too much space between us. He picks up his stuff. I watch as I try to get my brain online and then panic when I realise he's leaving. I grab his arm before he can disappear.

"You still love me," I smile at him, triumphant.

He closes his eyes, and a look of disgust crosses his face. It's like a knife in my chest. He yanks his arm free.

"I just wanted to shut you up." His deep voice growls. "You smell like Silas." He snaps defensively.

I laugh and beam at him. He shoots me a dark look full of warning, and I hold my hands up and zip my mouth.

I have to bite my lip as he stalks away, leaving the gym with that bloody aura of 'you can't touch me' that's had me hard since I first laid eyes on him.

He still loves us. I lick my lips and taste him on my skin. I knew he still did. The last few months of him freezing us out, it's finally thawing.

My omega kissed me.

What a beautiful morning. What a wonderful day!

I bounce into the penthouse and unfurl the bond a little bit. Silas sits up, his head turning in my direction from the breakfast table, while Falcon stalks out of the bathroom.

I grab my tablet and bring up the security footage from the gym and show my pack. Twin blasts of yearning and despair mingled with the sweet notes of hope fill the air.

"He hasn't moved on," I whisper. "We still have a chance."

Falcon sits down and watches it over and over.

I sit down opposite him, Silas at the head of the table between us. "Now, about the beta-"

Eight
ONYX

The opening speech of the great Omega Meet is flowery, pretty, and so boring I wish I was in my bed sleeping. I wonder if watching paint dry would be more interesting. I spend half the time listening to Falcon and Silas speak wondering who wrote it for them because I find it hard to imagine that they wrote it. It's too facetious. It doesn't sound like them at all.

But, finally, they wrap it up and declare this event started. There is a polite sound of startled applause before the alphas return to the table that I'm once again shackled to. Only then is the food brought out.

My cheeks burn, and there's no way I'm meeting anyone's eyes. I shouldn't be here. Yet, Dylan has his hand firmly wrapped around mine and won't let go. Once again, I'm the piece of a puzzle that doesn't belong.

"Will you be joining the archery event this morning, Dylan?" Falcon asks as he cuts up his eggs with a knife and fork. He is meticulous, each bite is almost evenly, perfectly sized. I feel grubby just thinking about eating in front of him.

Dylan, as expected, ignores the alpha's question. I catch a flash of frustration in Silas' eyes before he slumps.

I sit back, eating almost mechanically as I watch the way they interact with him. Grayson almost reaches out to refill his drink but, at the last moment, changes his mind. Silas' eyes flash when someone almost bumps into him. Falcon gets him more bacon before he can speak.

Oh. OH. They really do care about him.

I switch my attention to the omega beside me. Every now and again, he trembles. I thought it was because he was scared. That's not fear. The scent of lemons is strong around him whenever they're around. He likes them, too.

That is devastating. But reality, a horrible voice inside my head, whispers snidely.

I chew on a mouthful of toast and catch sight of Silvie. She's happier than I've ever seen her. Having the time of her life in a world she's never gotten to experience. Dylan has a chance at a happy ending here.

Maybe he has a good reason for hating them? Maybe...

"How do you know if the omegas find scent matches?" I ask curiously.

The alphas all pause, their intimidating stares locking on me. Silas is the first to clear his throat.

"When you meet your scent match," his eyes drift to Dylan, "it's like the world is suddenly filled with colour and sound, and a language you didn't know the words to suddenly makes sense in your brain. You can't imagine being without them or making them hurt." He trails off and forces himself to look at me.

Beside me, Dylan is stiff.

I exhale and nod. "If you would excuse me, I need to use the ladies' room."

Loitering outside the gold lift makes me feel creepy, but sure enough, Falcon walks into the foyer and stops.

"Something you need, Miss Davies?"

"Uh, yes. I'd like a meeting with you, please. Now." My words come out in starts and almost stutters. But, to be fair, I think anyone would be struggling to communicate in English with this giant alpha and his icy stare pinning them.

He walks closer and presses the lift's button. The doors open, and I...can only stare. How rich do you have to be to have a lift decorated this elegantly? Flowers and vines are carved into the handrails and engraved on the gold mirrored surface. It's truly its own work of art.

The penthouse is...very, um. I mean, you can tell it's expensive, but it's so white like a showroom. I can't imagine someone living here. But the views out the windows are incredible.

"Come and sit down." Falcon offers and takes a seat on the lounge.

I choose one opposite him and sit down. My pulse jumps and races when the lift doors open, and Silas and Grayson walk inside. Both of them spot me and freeze.

"I thought we were doing this later?" Grayson said.

"She asked for a meeting," Falcon replies with a disdainful glance at me.

"Yes. I, uh, did." I swallow hard. "You hurt my friend."

The three of them stiffen before Silas and Grayson walk to sit down beside Falcon. It's interesting, the differences in the way they sit. Grayson slouches, his legs spread wide, looking relaxed and completely terrifying. Silas wraps his arms around his chest and crosses his legs, closing himself off. But Falcon sits upright and relaxed, but his body is pointed at me, and his attention on my face doesn't waver.

How is it possible that sitting can be intimidating? Should I be practicing this? Do they get lessons?

"What are you here for, Miss Davies?"

"You hurt him." I say before I can think. "I want to know what you did."

"That has no bearing on you whatsoever," Falcon says evenly.

"It does. It matters a great deal."

"Why?" Silas asks. "Why does it matter?"

I glance at them again and think about Scarlet and Barren. The infamous Raptore pack with their new omega Missy. Happiness. I want that for Dylan.

"Because the answer will determine whether I actively go against you or whether I help you."

"You're aware you work for me." Falcon says with amusement.

"I'm aware of that, sir, but you gave me to Dylan and told me to treat him well. Protecting him and helping him find happiness is part of my job."

"Is it now?" Falcon almost purrs.

"Why? Why would you help us?" Silas asks. There's so much distrust in this alpha.

"I'm not helping you. I'm helping Dylan. It's been a long time since I had a friend. He chose me. It's the least I can do." There is a regret inside me that is so heavy it weighs me down.

"Some might call this above and beyond," Grayson murmurs. "Others call it being meddlesome."

My temper snaps. "Do you want my help or not? Because you three suck at wooing him back."

"And what do you get out of it?"

"Nothing. I want nothing. If anything, I want the board wiped clean for what you've done for Silver."

"Silas, get the footage." Falcon snaps.

THE BETA'S BARGAIN

Silas grumbles but pulls out his phone. A moment later, a TV descends from the ceiling. The screen turns on. Silas walks out of the bathroom in a towel and stops.

You can see him arguing with a woman. He points down the hallway and shakes his head.

A moment later, Falcon and Grayson appear. A door opens, and the female throws herself at Silas, kissing him hard. Dylan appears on the bottom screen, watches long enough to completely shatter him, then turns and runs.

A moment later, Silas throws her off, and security appears.

"Huh."

"What?" Silas growls defensively.

"Curious question." I warn with a finger up. I'm hesitant to ask this, to offend them.

"Yes." Falcon says in a dangerously low voice.

"Why doesn't he trust you enough to listen to you, to hear you out?"

Silas drops his head in his hands. "My mother. She kept making comments about Dylan being male. About heirs. About a female omega she picked for us."

I blink twice and sit back. "Huh."

"What now?" Falcon asks with a tinge of annoyance.

"Nothing, it's just...nothing." I sit forward. "What makes you think he wants you back?"

Silas presses his screen a few more times and another video loads. I can see a gym and Grayson and Dylan. The Dylan on the screen jumps off the treadmill and charges Grayson. The kiss is hot, explosive; it shakes my entire world, and it's on a screen.

I clear my throat and avert my eyes. But I feel cold. Hurt, even. I have no claim to him.

"That was this morning." Falcon says.

"I see." Is my voice too high?

"Nyx, may I call you Nyx?"

I give Falcon a tight nod.

"You have to understand that should this plan of yours succeed, you will lose him."

I stare because he's crushed me, with words, he's just crushed me. And he knows it, and he doesn't care.

"Why?" I ask.

"Because we are the most prominent pack in Silver Falls. Our lives and the expectations are lined out for us. You don't belong here."

I laugh. "So, I can't be friends, then?"

"Of course not. That would be unseemly." Falcon states coldly. "So, now you know our terms."

It's not a hard decision. Staying with me means alleyways and clothes with holes. It means hunger. Being with them would give him the world. Not just wealth but love. "I'll help you fix things with him."

"Thank you," Grayson says, and I think he means it wholeheartedly. Silas flicks the screen off, and it retracts into the roof.

"If you'll excuse me, I have to go-"

"How are you doing this?" Silas asks, mirroring me and standing.

The lift door opens, and Dylan springs into the penthouse. He spots me and stalks to my side immediately.

"Sit down, Dylan. We're not harming her." Falcon says in exasperation.

"Or firing her." Grayson adds with a wink.

His scowl is so fierce. Am I wrong? Are these alphas bad people? They don't feel bad, just spoiled. Their workers adore them. The wages are incredibly generous. I've never heard any rumours of any wrongdoing on their behalf.

"We've offered Nyx a position on our research team. It's permanent. She will travel to all our hotels and see how customer satisfaction can be improved, but she'll start with this event." Silas explains.

It's an incredible offer for someone like me. Why don't I want anything to do with it?

"She gladly accepted and signed the papers." Grayson says. He still hasn't unfurled from his lazily reclined position.

Dylan looks at me, searches my eyes for the truth, and I think he sees my secret, but then he just ignores it.

"What did you do to her? What did you offer her?" Dylan's deep voice trembles with fury.

Falcon stands up and throws his hands in the air. "You're going to believe the worst of us no matter what, aren't you? So, go ahead, believe it. We made her cry. We threatened her job. Her sister. Her home. We made her sob and hate herself. She's so traumatised she wants to run back to the hovel she calls home, with its flickering street light and broken windows, and hide under her lilac woolen blanket, with its rat-gnawed holes, until she thinks we've gone away."

My attention snags and hooks on the alpha. My heart is pounding now. There's a creepy feeling of violation turning my blood to ice.

His gaze tears from Dylan and lands on me, and for the first time since I've known him, Falcon Treyfield looks like he can't believe what he just said. He appears lost for words and shocked at himself.

I cross to stand shoulder to shoulder with him. "Did you go into my house?" I hiss.

He shuts his jaw with a snap. My ire raises as I stare at the guilty tic in his jaw.

"Do you do that with all your employees?" I ask, only a fraction louder.

A shiver runs up my spine, and I stiffly walk away from him. I stare out the window, looking at the rolling forests and the blue, blue sky. So perfect from this pane of glass.

"It would be easier for them to report their findings and help us with the event if they stayed in the guest suite. It would also help with contest winners getting the platinum rooms as a reward." Grayson drawls out.

I want to stab him with a pencil. In the eye.

The last thing I want to do is get a front row view to this shit show. I consider my options. I could tell Dylan the truth and watch him run and be miserable again. Or I could try and find a way around Grayson and his fat mouth, but one look at him torpedoes that idea. I have no choice. I'm moving in with Treyfield Pack. Grayson is sneaky and underhanded, and I don't approve of his methods. At all. But I turn with a smile and beam.

"That sounds wonderful."

"No!" Dylan growls.

I glance at him and shrug. "You don't have to. You're not employed as The Customer Satisfaction Officer."

Dylan's unhappy rumble echoes around the room. I turn away so I can look out the window again.

I feel him approach, not hear, I don't see it, my body feels his. The hairs rise, my skin feels the air displacement. Everything in me is attuned to this man.

"Do you really want this?"

I reach out, and his fingers slide between mine. "It's a really good offer for a beta like me," I whisper.

"You can do better," Dylan whispers.

"It's nice that you believe that. But the reality is that I can't. I rented a crappy one-bedroom apartment that didn't have a kitchen, heat, or electricity. I can barely make ends meet, and I work two or three jobs a day and barely sleep. This job is security and stability and a warm, safe place to sleep. I'd be an idiot to turn this down."

I hesitate.

"If you want me to tell them to go to hell, I will. I'm on your side here, Dylan. Your opinion is the only one that matters to me. So, tell me, are we doing this, or are we taking our chances out there?"

He stares at me for a long moment and then startles me by tugging me into his hard chest and wrapping his arms around me. I hesitantly lift my arms and encircle his waist. Wow, he smells good and feels incredible. But what's worse is how my eyes prickle, and I want to just stay in this moment forever.

"I'm doing this for you," He whispers. "Everything I do is for you."

His lips land on my forehead, and something inside me tilts, and when I feel steady again, I realise my entire world has changed.

Nine

ONYX

The sunshine is like a warm blanket that keeps trying to lull me to sleep. I could almost pretend that the last couple of days hadn't happened. Could almost forget the rollercoaster of highs and lows that's been my existence. I tilt my head back to get some more of the sun and catch motion out of the corner of my eye. Dylan shifts his weight again, leaning towards me, removing my ability to pretend with one sexy wriggle of his shoulders.

Damn him. Why am I so affected by this omega?

"You don't have to stay with me. You can go and get involved." I gesture to the lawns where groups of people are laughing and talking.

He snorts and folds his arms over his chest. Somehow, I know his answer, and I can't help but be grateful. I follow his gaze and want to groan. The omegas and alphas are all on the wrong side of tipsy and are getting creative with the croquet mallets. One young alpha has his mallet between his legs and is thrusting his hips as he chases a giggling omega around.

"Does anyone even like croquet?" I ask absently. "I don't even know the rules. What's the point of it even? If I had a mallet like that, I wouldn't want to softly tap a ball. I'd want to whack it and break things."

Dylan snorts and gives me a sidelong glance. "We can come back tonight and smash things."

"Promise?" I ask and frown as an omega falls sideways, giggling when she hits the ground. It takes five people to haul her up.

I search until I spot Silvie hanging off a different alpha from the ones she's spent the last four days with. He leans in and kisses her neck. She laughs loudly. The impulse to rush in and protect her is strong. She doesn't know him. Why is she letting him kiss her so intimately? But I restrain myself even while I keep an eye on her. Would I care if she was making out with strangers if she were a beta? No, but an alpha has the power to lock her into a life of their choosing forever.

It doesn't matter. I don't think she's going to hear anything I have to say. She hasn't even spoken to me since the office. I've tried, but she's pretending I don't exist. I've worked at dozens of venues with heaps of different kinds of people, serving them, knowing I was going home to a ruin with no food, but not a single person has made me feel the way she's made me feel. Like I'm two inches tall. Like I'm embarrassing.

It's humiliating, but I can understand why she's doing it. Oh, boy, does that make it all worse. Understanding sucks.

There have only been a few times in my life I've been disgusted by my sister's behaviour. This is one of them. Maybe she was like this at the Omega Academy? I didn't attend the school with her; I went to the normal school with the rest of the betas. Even then, before the fire, I kept my head down.

Silvie is the extrovert.

Dylan's knuckles brush the back of my hand. "Don't go into your head, Nyx."

I frown up at him. "How do you always know?"

"Because we're friends."

"Friends?" I ask with a teasing grin.

"The best of friends," Dylan whispers. "And friends know when friends need help. So, this is me throwing you a lifeline."

I turn my hand, gripping his, trying to ignore the flutters. I stare into his eyes until I have to tear my gaze away. My cheeks are on fire, and my stomach is flipping wildly, but there's a happiness that's making my chest light.

"This is me taking the lifeline." As friends. Purely platonic friends.

"Well, the afternoon's games seem to be going well."

I jolt violently and pull my hand free of Dylan's. I let out a curse and turn to smile up at Silas.

"You scared me. They are going to start destroying things soon." I jerk my head to the lawn. "I hope you have people available to carry them all inside."

Silas shrugs. "I'm not surprised. And we are always prepared at Hastings Hotels."

That takes the wind out of my sails, and I slump. "Your guests are happy. They love the drinks, the service, the choice of activities, they love the resort." I hesitate. "But they are bored and destructive and-"

"Any signs of matches?"

"Not yet." I say through my teeth. "So, you don't care about this?" I wave my hand towards the group.

"Fantastic work." Silas says and rocks back on his heels.

My glare should have burned a hole into the side of his head, but alas, the hard-headed alpha simply ignores me. I can feel Dylan's tension building and frantically think of a subject.

"Your mother is very famous. I imagine it must have been hard to live with her." I ask the question without much thought, instantly wishing I'd bitten my tongue.

Silas blinks and turns to me. "That's not really any of your business."

I bare my teeth with a smile. Fuck it, that's the most reaction I've gotten from him in four days of this new job. "Sure, it is."

He spits a word in a language I'm not familiar with. It's unbearably hot. "My mother is awful. She is critical and always held me to a standard I couldn't reach. Everyone thought she was wonderful, though. No one knows what she's really like. She is the ultimate actress."

I stare at him. "My father was similar. I was born for one job and one job only, and I could never do it well enough. My mother and I both failed to be what he decided we should be. His expectations could never be met."

Silas is silent. I can feel his eyes boring into me. "Did you stop trying?"

I bark out a laugh. "Not as yet."

"How sad it is that our parents have been so disappointing in our lives."

I smile tightly but don't look at him. Dylan is quiet beside me. For a few minutes, the three of us just watch the groups of men and women interact.

"Can I bring you both a drink?" Silas asks. The question is soft, without his normal snarl.

You could knock me over with a feather. I know Dylan isn't going to accept it. So, I do it for him. "Yes, please. We'd love one. But no alcohol. I'm working."

Silas' dark gaze looks me up and down, and then he turns and walks away.

"Well, he's friendlier than he used to be. Perhaps I misjudged him," I say with a chuckle.

"Interesting game you're playing, Nyx." Dylan says slowly, and I can't help but note the disapproval in his voice. "Interesting and obvious."

It's not the first time he's said my name, but I find myself shivering in response. It makes me daring and want to take a risk. Anything that gets his attention. What road is this madness taking me down?

"I'm not playing a game, Dylan."

He bumps my arm with his. "Liar."

"Not lying." I protest. Definitely lying.

Silas returns with our drinks. I take mine gingerly.

"You two should go get some rest before the dinner event begins." Silas says. "Dressing will take some time."

I consider that. "I'm good, I'll just wear my uniform."

"Uh, no. That's not going to do." Silas murmurs. Peering first at me and then at Dylan.

The omega straightens, and I can feel him getting ready to fight on my behalf. I have to do better at this. Causing fights isn't going to find any happy endings.

"I don't own a dress." I say quickly and feel my cheeks burn. Sharing my truths after so long of being so secretive is hard.

"Oh." Silas says. "Well, I can-"

"I'll do it." Dylan growls low and aggressively.

I glance between the two of them and take Dylan's hand. "Sure, that sounds…well, having a tooth pulled actually sounds more appealing, but okay, you can dress me."

Silas snorts a laugh and then smiles.

Oh, dear alpha, beta, and omega, the man is the most stunning sight I've seen in my life when he just smiles. Why the hell doesn't he lead with that? It takes me a moment to recover my wits enough to turn away from him. My knees are weak, and my chest feels heavy. I have the strangest urge to giggle.

I clear my throat twice and then take Dylan's arm. "Right, let's go."

The omega chuckles darkly, sending another unpleasant surge of awareness. I press my lips together and determine to ignore it.

The dinner goes off without a hitch. Incredible acts of musical talent and dancing skill stole my breath. The simple black gown hugged my body, even though I kept tugging the hemline down. It made me feel beautiful for two minutes until I saw Silver glittering in a pale blue gown. After that, I just took a mental step to the left, pretended that I was wearing my uniform, and effectively ignored it.

But now...there's no ignoring the uncomfortable situation I'm in. I'm on the gold lift with the alphas and their omega. I don't belong here, and our reflections show that loud and clear.

The door opens, and they wait until I get off before walking past me. I loiter close to the lift doors, suddenly very, very unhappy with my decision to move into the penthouse with the Treyfield Pack. What was I thinking? Every night since has been harder than the night before.

"I'll walk you to your room." Falcon says, breaking through my panic.

I abruptly turn and stalk after him. He leads me down a long corridor. I reach out and twist the handle before he can, almost slamming the door in his face.

All the bedrooms are on this side of the penthouse. Grayson has the room next to mine, but the other three bedrooms are further down the hallway.

The room is nice, dark with clean lines. The king-size bed feels too big for me, but I could worship the bathroom. I've been here four days, but there's almost no sign that I'm here. I'm not sure how I feel about that.

I pace as long as I can, trying to wait the pack out. They'll go to sleep soon. There's only so many times I can pace the confines of the room before thirst gets the better of me, though, and I end up creeping out when everything's been silent for a half an hour.

I creep out and find the penthouse in semi-darkness. I don't have to worry about the dress rising up my thighs like I did at dinner, and without those evil contraptions called shoes, I feel more like myself.

A quick search of the cupboards reveals glasses, and I drink some water before I return to my room. My pulse is jumping, and I startle in the dark. I feel like a thief at night, sneaking around where I don't belong. I search for the lights, but I can't find them, so I just approach my bed and lay down on it.

Instantly, I know something is wrong.

"Well, hello there, little beta."

I let out a shriek and scramble off the bed, smashing into a wall that should not be there.

Grayson, because that's the only alpha it could be, lets out a laugh and grabs my wrist, tugging me back onto the bed. He murmurs something and pale light erupts from a half sphere on the wall.

"Sit down, let me look at that."

I stop struggling because I really need to calm my heart rate down and, to be honest, my elbow is throbbing. I sit on the bed as he extends my arm towards him and checks.

"No blood, but you're going to have a nasty bruise."

"Thank you." I mutter and put some space between us.

He leans back with his hands behind his head and stares at the ceiling. There's something not quite right about him, and not for the first time, I wish I have the ability to scent feelings and emotions in people's smells. I get one leg off the bed and then pause. I can't leave him like this.

"What's wrong, Grayson?"

"Call me Gray." He says shortly.

"Okay, Gray." I say hesitantly.

His eyes flick to me. "Lay down. I promise I won't touch you, but I have to turn off this light. My head's killing me."

I hesitate. Everything urges me to leave but one tiny little morsel of compassion. I lay back on the pillow on the other side of the immense bed and stare at the ceiling, too. With another soft murmur, the light goes off.

"Why are we staring at the ceiling in the dark?" I ask.

"I don't sleep well." Gray shifts, and I can't help but imagine his huge, toned body on the bed beside me.

"Oh. I can understand that." Is my voice high? Damn it!

"You don't sleep?" Grayson asks in a gruff voice.

"Well, I enjoy sleeping. It's just that I'm normally either working or in pain, so I just can't." I wrap my arms over my stomach, but that feels weird, so I put them back at my side.

"My sister and I were kidnapped when we were little," Grayson says with a sigh. "So, when I close my eyes, I have a tendency to relive it."

I turn towards him, staring at the dark spot where I know he's lying. "That must have been awful."

"They kept us for two weeks. I was twelve, and she was six."

"I'm so sorry that happened to you, Gray. You must have been terrified." And I mean it.

"I don't like to sleep because when I sleep, I remember it all again when I wake up. Plus, I have terrible nightmares, and it's embarrassing."

My heart goes out to him. It shouldn't. But I'm a sucker for a sad story, and the voice of the man beside me is not that of the confident alpha I normally see.

"I can stay for a while, if you'd like?" The instant it comes out, I want to bite back my words. I want to scream at myself for my impulsive mouth. I want him to say yes.

There's a long pause where I prepare to leave the room in a flood of shame.

"Stay." Gray murmurs.

It's one word. But it feels like a door just opened.

I curl my hands up under my chin and lay there in silence, staring into the black. My thoughts race, but I force myself to think of all the jobs I need to get done tomorrow. Eventually, sleep wins.

***

I wake up because I'm hot. Unbearably, uncomfortably hot. I struggle, but there's a weight over my waist holding me down.

I blink at the object several times before it suddenly makes sense. Fingers curled over my ribcage, stroking in a way that has butterflies exploding to life in my stomach. Am I dreaming?

There's an arm holding me down. I sit upright, struggling up and away, frantically looking beside me.

The events of last night come back. Gray is laying on his side facing away from me. It takes me a moment to realise that it's not his arm that's pinning me. I whip my head to the other side and find Dylan staring at me.

I freeze.

"Morning," he says and smiles.

"Morning." I reply, stunned.

"Mmm, morning." Grayson says, rolling towards us. He seizes my waist and drags me onto him. He cuddles me close, nuzzling into my neck, and yawns into my chest. My nipples tighten painfully, my skin flushes hot.

Oh, boy, I bite my lower lip hard as I try to work out what to do.

I have never had a man this close. I'm both terrified and frozen at all the strange feelings that are happening faster that I can process.

I try to get off him by sliding my leg over his hip, but that brings up another problem. A big problem that drags a groan out of him and causes tingles in my core. It's so startlingly new, so unexpected, that I just freeze there. With the bulge pressed right up against the thin undies I'm wearing. I can feel everything. Oh. Boy.

"Now, this is a whole new layer of fun that Silas and Falcon will not appreciate." Gray grabs my hips and rolls his.

I gasp as the tingles turn to fire. Slick arousal seeps between my legs, and I'm instantly terrified he'll feel it. My eyes dart from him to Dylan and back again. Grayson has never, ever looked this sexy, and when he lets out a groan, I think my brain gives out.

I whip my head towards Dylan, but the omega just watches me.

The door opens, and Silas walks in. "Have you seen-" He stops mid-sentence and opens his eyes wide, I know because I've turned to watch him.

"Let me go," I whisper, desperate, unable to take my eyes off Silas as he slowly takes in my damning position.

Gray lets out a rumbling sound that rips my eyes back to his face. His smile is slow and sexy. "This is a wonderful way to wake up."

"I could do without it." I snap back, but my voice is husky and lacks the oomph that I try to put in.

He shifts his hips again, and that bulge rubs against me in a way that makes my core clench, and my limbs want to collapse on him. To plead for him to...what?

I let out a growl and try to throw my leg over.

His grip tightens, and all I end up doing is rocking against him, causing us both to let out guttural groans. Causing another wave of crippling pleasure that has me gasping.

"Let me go!" I call out, almost beside myself.

His hands leave me, and I struggle, finding my legs weak but manage to throw myself off him and get pressed up against the wall.

I'm breathing hard, and my body is feeling things I've never felt before. All eyes are on me.

"I have to go." I say quickly and rush around the bed and out of the room.

Silas doesn't say a word, nor does he try to stop me.

I find the smiley face on the door right next to mine and groan as I enter it and pull it shut behind me.

I drop my head in my hands and groan. What is wrong with me?

I remember Grayson's story last night, and I remember enough to know that he fell asleep. I wake easily, so he must've had a nightmare free night.

Maybe I did some good after all, right before I fucked it all up.

Ten

FALCON

I lean back in my office chair and swivel so I can stare out the window at the views of Innis Falls Forest. It's a glorious view that I knew as soon as I saw it I had to make mine, but today, I have nothing. No thoughts. Nothing but a vividly painted image in my mind that should not be affecting me the way it is.

Silas had informed me an hour before of what happened this morning and of Gray's behaviour. One hour of thinking about it. One hour of fantasising about it.

I could shout at him. I could sit and talk to him until I'm blue in the face, but Gray will be Gray. What was interesting is that Dylan ended up in there, too. Where the beta goes, our omega will follow, apparently.

But how do I make that stop? How do I make him stop looking at her and start looking at us?

And why can't I stop imagining the beta riding Gray while our omega watches from the other side of the bed?

The view doesn't give me the answers I need. I stand up and stalk through the penthouse.

Simon meets me on the ground floor. He's dressed in the white and black uniform and carries it well. I check for creases but, with satisfaction, I note there are none. Simon's hair is dark and carefully combed back. His blue eyes convey only the slightest interest. His face is a polite mask. Exactly as it ought to be. He's much slimmer than I and much smaller than his older brother Adrian, but the Doctor and I don't get along at all, our personalities are too similar. Simon suits me perfectly.

"How's it going?" I bark out. Yvette joins us, walking silently with a tablet in her arms.

"The event is going well. I've had three reports from the staff of inappropriate overtures from the guests. Several objects have been vandalised. But other than those normal teething problems, the event is going off as a success. The planned events and activities are all booked out. I'm seeing the formation of several mergers and alliances."

"Fantastic. How are the staff?"

"We have a few standouts. A woman named Moira has formed a close friendship with an omega named Jade and has gone above and beyond to teach the girl confidence. Louis is getting along really well with Pack Michaels. Our chef fired two of her kitchen aids but says she doesn't need them. The gardeners worked late last night to get the last beds weeded."

"Good. Yvette?"

"Security is good. No problems with the press. We've had zero attempts to access the property, and it appears we've managed to keep the event under wraps."

Yvette and Simon exchange a deep look with each other that only serves to irritate me.

"Sir, about the girl..." Yvette begins.

Simon swallows hard and glances away from me. I can see they are both scared, and they should be.

"What about her?" I growl.

"It's just, I don't know whether to replace her position with the omega—" Simon explains. "She's not qualified to work for such an esteemed guest. I'm concerned. We're concerned that it will look bad."

"Not to mention how it's coming across, a staff member sitting at your table, eating with you, sitting on your omegas lap," Yvette adds hastily.

"No." I bark. I won't tolerate this line of conversation. "Am I not Treyfield?"

"Yes, sir." They both say at once.

"Whatever I choose to allow, the storm will weather because we are Treyfield pack, and no one would dare question us."

"No?" Simon queries. His face goes pale. "I mean, yes, of course, sir. You're absolutely right."

"Just leave the two of them to me." I say grimly.

"Yes, sir," Yvette says and looks down at her tablet.

"Yes, sir." Simon breathes.

"How is the twin?" I ask instead.

"She is..." Simon's normally impassive face twitches, "she's." He stops, and I stop with him, turning so we're face to face. "She's not making any friends with the omegas, and the attention that she is garnering isn't the kind you'd want to encourage, sir. I've been wondering if we should intervene."

"I'll consider it."

I walk around the resort with them, listening to the individual reports and adjusting my instructions. Silas normally handles the day to day running of the hotels, but I need something to do this morning. Something to keep me occupied. Keep my mind busy.

"All right, thank you, Simon. Keep me apprised of any issues."

"Of course, sir."

"Yvette, I want you to keep working with security and our public relations team. I'm going to be distracted for the next few weeks. If there are any issues, bring them to me, but otherwise, I'm entrusting this event to you."

Yvette blinks a few times. "Does that mean?"

I nod sharply. "We're going to attempt to win back our omega. So, we'll be stepping back, Silas, too. It's a tremendous opportunity for the both of you to show me what you're capable of. I'm looking at creating two new positions if this pans out so that we can step back a little. I want you both helping to run the Treyfield empire."

Their eyes widen. Yvette looks almost like she might cry.

"Thank you, sir," Yvette says in a breathy tone.

Simon swallows hard and nods sharply. "Oh, good luck, sir."

"Thank you. Can you handle the resort, Simon?"

"Of course, sir, it will be my pleasure."

Yvette grins. "Everything will be fine. Good luck."

"Good. Have at it then." I snort as she walks away with a bounce in her step.

The world falls away, and I find myself pausing inside the doorway to the Sunflower room. The yellow colour goes perfectly for tea and nibbles. Or so I'm told. Personally, I've been trying to destroy this room since I first saw it. It's garish and offensive and worse yet, Sila's mother, Vienne, adores it. All the more reason.

An omega with red hair spots me and blushes hotly. She looks like she's going to approach, so I give her my best glare. I can see her courage wilt and fail her, and in moments, she turns and flees. Good, now I can focus. I'm about to leave when I catch the low voices from inside the room.

"But you know them, right?"

I vaguely recognise that voice.

"I have met them." Onyx says evasively.

"Then you can introduce me."

"No, Silvie. I can't. I am an employee."

"Fine," Silvie laughs, "then you have to do what I say, and I say I want to meet them."

"Not going to happen." Onyx says firmly.

There's a silence.

"Do you think that I'm not good enough?"

"No! Come on, Silvie, that's not what I meant. I'm saying it's not appropriate for me to introduce you."

I want to applaud her sense of self-preservation.

"Fine. Don't introduce me. Tell me about them."

Onyx sighs. "There is nothing to tell. They are my bosses."

"How can you be so selfish? You should be helping me."

"I am helping you. I know you can't see it. But I am."

"Then give me what I need," Silvie hisses. "I deserve this. All those years, I stayed hidden at home, and I lost my potential pack. I was alone and heartbroken, and you weren't there."

I bristle and hold back the growl. Why am I getting so defensive over the beta?

"I was working, Silvie. We've had this discussion many times. I didn't abandon you. You had food, clothes, suppressants, your treats. I kept a roof over our heads."

"And here we are, and I have a chance to become *the omega* of the pack world, and you are denying me and refusing to help me."

"It's my job. If I get caught, I get fired. I don't get paid, and you get shown the door. You'd sacrifice it all for that?" Onyx growls.

"For love, I would sacrifice anything."

"You're not in love."

"I could be."

"Silvie," Onyx stretches her name out, sounding firm and cold. "I will not introduce you to the Treyfield pack."

Suddenly, the realisation of exactly what Silver is asking dawns on me, and I feel that darker side of my personality rise up. There are many ways I can destroy the young omega. Her chance, her one freebie that Silas bestowed on her, will be ruthlessly ripped away, and I will dump her and her sister right back where I found them.

No one from Treyfield, Hastings, or Waters will hire them. No one will touch them. They will be blacklisted all over Silver Falls, and if I make that decision, the society will follow.

I step back when I hear a chair scrape, ducking into an alcove. Silvie storms out of the room a few minutes later. Onyx comes to the door and watches her. She wears the same expression of exhaustion that I so often find on my face.

"It was wise of you to turn her request down."

She turns her head and finds me in the shadows.

"Of course, I turned it down. I'm your employee, not your friend."

I study her. "Your work ethic is unusually strong." I pause, letting the compliment sink in. "And yet, mornings like this morning happened. Would you care to explain how that came about?"

"Can I say no?"

"Not if you want to continue living here easily." I say the words with a slight rise of my shoulders. I step out and gesture for her to walk beside me.

"You have no lights."

"Pardon?"

"I couldn't find the light switch. I needed some water, and when I went back, your lights were impossible to turn on."

"I see. I'll get right on that." And make sure it never causes an issue again.

She narrows her eyes. "So, I went to lie in what I thought was my bed, and lo-and-behold, there's a man there. We talked about the fact neither of us sleep well. I fell asleep, and so did he. It was a simple accident."

"Falling asleep in someone's bed is not an accident."

Her eyes flash. "Have you not been so tired you've fallen asleep on the couch? Have you never, ever seen someone-" she cuts herself off and blows out a breath.

Realisation crashes through me, and I don't know whether to be appalled at her suicidal tendencies or amazed that she appears to be completely genuine. Did she stay with Gray to look after him?

"I'm aware of how Gray feels about sleep." I concede.

"I just...wanted to help."

"Why? What are you getting out of it?" I can't help the skeptical tone.

THE BETA'S BARGAIN

"Well, a conversation with a person who isn't ordering me to get them something. Learning that there's a really happy, smiling man who hides a whole lot of pain. A man who reminds me a lot of me."

"I'll be requiring you to sign NDA's."

"Of course. I'll sign as soon as you bring them."

I hesitate. I hadn't expected her to agree quite so quickly. She looks at me, and I find myself staring at those blue-grey eyes and wondering when she got so pretty.

She smells so faintly of coconut, it's just the perfect amount. I love coconut, but the scent of her is growing on me. What is it about this strange beta that arrests me? There is both an old world air about her and a naïvety that makes me want to corrupt her. The contradiction is compelling. A beta saving omegas. A beta taking on alphas, standing between alphas. I can't say I've seen it before, but I've never seen anyone stand up to us the way she is.

But there's one thing I've learned in life, and that's if it looks too good, it's a lie.

I give her another once over. "Excuse me, then."

She smiles faintly and walks away from me. I watch her leave. I, Falcon Treyfield, watch a beta leave. As soon as I realise what I'm doing, I turn away from her with a curse.

Dylan is standing not far away, watching me. I dream of his expression morphing into a welcoming smile the way he used to, but today, he just scowls harder.

I walk towards him, daring him with my eyes to run, daring him to hide. He holds his ground, but his shoulders tense. I wonder if he thinks I'm going to hurt him.

"Dylan."

He lifts his chin and meets my eyes. Lust sizzles in my blood, and I shift my body even closer so that only a hand span separates us.

"Leave her alone."

The words take a moment to sink in, and the lust vanishes, leaving me cold and empty.

"I will not hurt her. I'm not a monster, Dylan."

He flinches like I've struck him. He looks away, and I realise that he looks lost. I hate seeing that expression on him.

"Have a drink with me."

He hesitates, and I can almost feel the longing.

"One drink with me, please, omega?"

I've said the wrong thing. I know it the second the word omega leaves my lips. His expression stiffens, and he takes a step back, shaking his head before he jogs off in the direction the beta disappeared.

"Fuck!" I say and stalk towards the lifts.

I just need a few moments alone. A few minutes without the pressure. The phenomenal pressure.

All I care about is him. The impulse to watch three empires burn to the ground just so I can have him has been riding me since the day we met.

I remember it so clearly. Our eyes met at the bar. He was four people down. I didn't even catch his scent, I just looked at him and knew. His scent filled the room, and I watched the moment he caught mine. It was instant. It was fate. It was destiny.

The omega who shook my entire world.

We had him, and we lost him.

I scowl as I turn around and follow the path they took and find them sitting in the garden. She looks up and sees me and gestures for me to join them. Dylan turns, and his face closes off, but I saw the look.

That look was soft and full of emotion. That look was reserved for me, Silas, and Gray once.

I cross towards them and startle when Onyx steps up and wraps her arms around my waist.

"Thank you for the present."

I frown, unsure what she's talking about, and then I spot the key to the library. I'd asked Simon to give it to her earlier this morning.

"Can you take us there?" She asks hesitantly, but I catch the subtle manipulation in her eye. She could find it easily. "I'm afraid I don't know where it is, and it would be nice to have an expert give us a tour."

"Sure." I find myself foolishly agreeing to her request, still struggling to wrap my mind around her. Is she manipulative or naïve? Is she a siren or an innocent? Maybe she's all of it.

Nyx walks ahead of us, filling in the silence with chatter that I realise is her not giving us time to think. When we get to the library, she vanishes, laughing and calling out her discoveries.

Dylan stands stiffly beside me. The last time we were in here was the first time I knotted him. The memories press on me.

"We aren't giving up on you. We didn't do what you think we did, and we're not going to just quit. You belong with us. You deserve to be happy, too, Dylan."

His hands clench, and I take my chance, moving quickly and pressing my lips against his. He stands stiffly, his hands on my shoulders, not pushing, not pulling, and then his lips suddenly move, soften. I kiss him the way I've been dreaming. All-consuming and like I want to crawl inside him and make him mine.

He kisses me back.

It's the first time since he left that I've really allowed myself to feel hope.

And then he breaks away, pressing his palm against my chest and closing his eyes while his chest heaves.

"Falcon," he whispers.

My name, he says my name. Like he wants me to rescue him. *I promise, baby, I will.*

I press against his palm. "Not giving up. Not now. Never. You're the only one we want."

He sucks in a shuddering breath, and his eyes get cold. He doesn't believe me. That's fine. And because I can see he's close to breaking, I turn and leave. It kills me, but I force myself to do it.

The beta's incessant chatter becomes the anthem of my determination. With each step, I hear her voice in my head, and I formulate a new plan.

Eleven
ONYX

I've got hundreds of notes on the tablet. The email that they've provided has asked a few specific questions, which means someone is reading what I'm doing. I'm still not sure if this is a real job or not, but I'm hoping it is. So, I'm doing my best. I make a few more notes about the quieter omegas, the ones who aren't as pretty nor as confident. There are some packs as well hanging back, who aren't as committed to finding an omega, they appear to be here just because. I've interviewed them, and they've all been forthcoming with me, and I've forwarded that information to Silas.

"Come."

I glance at Dylan and shake my head. "We can get some good information at dinner."

"Nyx. Come."

I roll my eyes and stand up, stretching out my aching muscles. "All right, where are we going?"

He leads me up to the penthouse and then opens my door. I don't know where the alphas are. Their absence should make me feel less anxious, but it feels oppressive and dangerous without them around. I don't like the way my brain's thinking regarding those men. I seem to be forgetting that cats have claws.

"For you," Dylan says.

I peer on the bed and stop when I see the beautiful gown. It's a smokey grey with thin straps.

"I can't wear that."

Dylan rolls his eyes. "Put it on."

I shake my head. "No."

"Nyx." He growls.

I whirl and find him too close. I freeze, staring up at him. His expression changes, and his pupils widen. He moves slowly, leaning towards me. His lips brush against mine. I suck in air. I haven't blinked, and he hasn't looked away. He pulls back and studies me for a moment before leaning in again. This time, his arms go around my back and pull me up against his chest.

The tantalizing scent of sweet lemon fills the room. That scent is his. I might not be able to smell it like an alpha, but it's burned into my memory now. But with his lips pressed firmly against mine, I can taste it. It's a drug.

I whimper into his mouth and move my lips under his. Kissing him back. Oh, no, I'm kissing him back. I have to stop. It feels incredible. His fingers spread wide around my back, sliding up to my shoulders. I feel so safe in his arms.

I tear myself away, and he lets me go.

He stares at me. I stare back.

"We shouldn't have done that." I blurt.

He straightens, nods, turns, and walks out of the room.

I stare at the door. He just left. He didn't ask. He just accepted it. I should be relieved, and yet...I shrug it off and look at the dress.

Fine. I'll wear it.

Dylan spots me when I walk out in the silver gown. He gets the same look on his face that he had just before he kissed me. My stomach flutters, and I look down at the dress, smoothing it over my thighs. I'm unable to look at him a moment longer, if I do, he's going to know that I think that black shirt is sinfully right on him and makes me want to spread my fingers across the expanse of his body and pop each little button open.

"Okay, ready." I say with false bravado.

He turns with me and falls into step exactly beside me. My arm brushes the black shirt he's wearing, and I have to bite hard on my lower lip to stop from making a sound.

We arrive in the dining room, and I almost trip. Silver is sitting at our table. She's leaning against Gray, fluttering her lashes up at him.

Dylan tenses beside me.

"Do you want to go somewhere else? I'm not really hungry." I peer up at him, trying to read his expression.

He hesitates and then shakes his head. "Scared?"

I scowl. For an omega that is prone to broody silences, he sure knows how to get his point across with just a word or two.

"I'm not scared. But it's not going to be fun."

We arrive at the table and take our seats. Silver hasn't noticed that she's lost the attention of the alphas. I watch her, waiting for the exact moment. It happens thirty seconds later. Her back stiffens, and her eyes spark.

She looks up and hits Dylan with a glare that makes me stiffen. My small movement draws her attention, and she focuses on me. The venom in her eyes is shocking.

"Silver." I say with a hint of frost in my voice.

She blinks twice, and a happy, generous smile appears on her lips. But I can't shake that icy chill that's surrounded me.

"Hello, sister. You look almost nice. It's a shame that isn't your colour. You remind me of Prudence."

My cheeks flame, and I look down at the gold cutlery. Prudence was a poor girl in our neighbourhood that Silver used to tease mercilessly about her weight and acne. She's got a family and a husband who loves her, though, unlike us. I liked Prue. She was sweet and kind.

"She looks beautiful." Gray says loudly.

Silver laughs. "You're being kinder than you have to be. I'll help you with your dress next time, Nanna, I promise."

The nickname makes blood rush from my head. I clench my hands into fists in my lap and bite the inside of my cheek.

"Nanna?" Gray asks with an edge in his voice that Silver misses.

"Oh, it's the nickname my father used to call her before he died."

Falcon shifts his weight. I feel the heat of his thigh beside mine. It's reassuring, and I get the impression that Falcon just did that deliberately. "Fascinating."

"Is it?" Silver says with another tinkling laugh. "Enough about us. Tell me about you. I want to know everything. What makes Falcon Treyfield tick?"

"Coffee and the blood of people who piss me off." Falcon says in a deep rumble. His hand slides over my thigh, down to my knee.

Liquid heat simmers inside me. I suddenly feel naked at the table.

A waiter puts a plate of food in front of me. I look up at him and smile. "Thanks, George."

"Your welcome, Nyx."

The food looks more like art than food, and I sigh heavily looking at it. I miss stews, lasagna in big whopping sheets, plates of fries with a crumbed chicken breast and gravy, a plate full of good, wholesome food. Food I haven't had since my mum died. Why does my food have gold glitter on it? I'm going to count how many mouthfuls this is, but it looks like maybe a generous four.

Wings. That's what I want. Sticky, sweet, messy wings.

"Oh, this is lovely, simply gorgeous." Silver purrs and leans on Gray's arm. Gray, to his credit, does not look happy, and sends Falcon and Silas dark looks at every turn.

Dylan stiffens, and I reach out and place a hand on his thigh. I take a bite of my food and almost choke when I turn my head and find Falcon glaring at me. With more caution than I wish, I remove my hand.

I don't listen to the conversation. Just eat what's presented, try to stay calm, and shrink further and further into myself with each of Silver's jabs.

I know why she's doing this. I'd hoped years of poverty would help her attain some level of common sense. But apparently the air of entitlement hasn't gone.

"Our father was an alpha," Silver says.

I pull myself out of my daze and focus on what she's saying.

"He didn't love our mother, though. She was just a beta." Her words, I've heard them so many times, but never like this. "Just like Nanna. Beta through and through."

Dylan reaches out, and this time, the heat of his hand blankets my thigh, stopping the ice spreading in my veins and the tears that are trying to fall.

My dessert doesn't appeal to me, so I wipe my mouth with a napkin and push my chair back.

"If you will excuse me." I say and notice that no one at the table acknowledges me. I'm already invisible. But the second I stand up, Dylan does, too.

He steps in front of me, grabs my wrist, and drags me through the dining room like he's on a mission. I don't know where he's going, but I'll go with him. The shame and embarrassment is a thick fog in my head, and I'll take any help I can get.

We get to the pool, and I pause.

"What are we doing here?"

He reaches out and grabs a handful of my dress near the waist, pulls it up to mid-thigh, and knots it. He's so close, and the scent of lemon turns sweet. I love the line of his jaw, the dark stubble, and the scar on his right eyebrow where the tiny hairs have turned white.

He's gorgeous, and he kissed me.

"Why did you kiss me?" The words are out before I can think. My cheeks burn, but I don't take them back.

He pauses and then finishes the knot before he stands up. I inhale swiftly. He's right there in front of me. Our mouths are so close. Is he going to kiss me again? Do I want him to?

He steps back and pulls off his shirt. I watch as he kicks off his shoes and then points at mine. I have an impression we're going to sit and kick our feet in the pool, and I kinda like this idea. With a side glance at him, I kick off the heels and step to the edge.

Dylan grabs my hand and pulls us both into the pool. I let out a startled shriek before the cold of the water floods over my head. I kick to the surface and flick my hair back before I start to laugh.

Dylan is nowhere to be seen. I tread water, turning slowly, and then I'm suddenly pulled under. With a happy laugh, under the water, I dive and kick free, but when I turn, he's there, his body melding around mine. I wrap my legs around his waist as he brings us up to the surface.

I choke and laugh again, clearing my wet hair from my eyes.

I throw myself backwards, but he holds onto my ass so I just float in the water with him above me. He strokes a hand down the center of my chest. It's so sudden and erotic. My laughter dies.

Suddenly, I'm aware of the throb between my legs. I'm aware of the silence around us. The lapping of water. The way my skin has pebbled and is so sensitive where his fingers have touched me. My lips tingle. Everything in me wants him to close the distance between us, erase it like it's not there. I sit up, resting my hands on his shoulders.

"Dylan," I whisper, and he lets go.

I swim away from him and press my back to the side of the pool wall. But he follows, pressing into me. I can almost touch the bottom of the pool, but he can stand, and he uses that to pin me to the side.

"I need to kiss you," his voice is silky smooth, and it sends a thrill through me. His lips find mine, his tongue entering my mouth, filling me with the taste of lemon lollies.

He pulls back, resting his forehead against mine. "I want you."

Three words. Three guttural, heartfelt words that echo inside me.

"We can't." I protest with the last shreds of my sanity.

He growls and presses against me, then he lifts me, and his lips trail down to the place on my neck where my shoulder meets. "I want you. I want you for me. I need...I just need...you. Just you."

His words melt my brain. They seer themselves into my heart and soul. I will never ever forget this moment. It means too much. No one has wanted me since my mother died. And here is this beautiful, incredible man, and he wants me. Worse, I want him.

I wrap my arm around his neck and lift myself even further up out of the water until we are face to face. The water laps at us, and I realise we've moved further into the shallows.

"I'm not going to hurt you, Dylan. I'm trying to save you. You need to trust me." It hurts to say the words, probably because I mean them so much.

I press my lips to his gently and kiss him the way he kissed me. But guilt and reality pull me back, and I laugh and search for a distraction.

"I'm going to tell you three true things about me. And I want three back. You don't have to tell me now."

"Why?"

"Because if you know these things, you might trust me." I clear my throat and look into his beautiful eyes. The pool is steaming now, and I've never had a moment like this. "My dad called me Nanna to hurt me because he blamed me and my mother for the fire."

Dylan shakes his head and presses close, kissing the corner of my lips.

"It wasn't your fault. I heard about it. It was an accident."

I close my eyes, trying to shake off the guilt that always comes. "It doesn't even matter. He died believing it was my fault. Nanna is someone who should have taken care of things. It was sarcastic and bitter and a taunt, and Silvie knew that. That's why I was so quiet at dinner."

Dylan doesn't say anything, but then he doesn't really need to, his expression is so easy to read. He's outraged for me. I have to look away to hide my shock at the flutter in my chest.

"I hate this job, but I've never had a dream of being anything else. I think my sister's dreams became mine." I say and fiddle with his shirt button.

"What are they?"

"A pack." I say with a laugh. "Silly, isn't it? A beta with a dream of a pack? But I was told to make her dreams come true, and I spent so long dreaming her dream that I think it became mine. I imagine a house full of love. Lots of children. Cuddling someone by the fire, cooking with someone else, finding safety with another. I just imagine big love, more love than can be..." I trial off.

Dylan closes his eyes, but when he moves, he spins us into the middle of the pool.

"Tell me the last one."

I don't have to think about it. I know exactly what I'm going to tell him. "When you kissed me earlier today...that was my first kiss."

His eyes turn liquid. The scent of lemons overpowers the chlorine, and when he moves towards me, I'm powerless. I just stand there, helpless, as he gathers me up.

Twelve

ONYX

I pull back before he can kiss me. "Your turn."

He stares at me, and his lips turn down. "The Treyfield pack are my scent matches. I met Falcon at a bar, and I just knew. When he brought Silas and Gray to me, it was like heaven existed. I've never been so happy. Scent matches are rare, but when you find them, it's it for you. Well, I thought it was, until I found you."

I suck in a breath and stare at him with wide eyes. There's no choice. I have to ignore the last part of that confession. I'd assumed they were all scent matches, but I hadn't known for certain. "No wonder they're acting insane."

He snorts.

"Okay, okay, second one."

"I love pecans. My mother used to bake pecan pies. They always remind me of home. I ran away from my family, so, uh, well, I haven't seen them since I ran from the pack." He sighs. "I miss my mother."

I frown. "Dylan, that's awful. You must be so lonely. Why don't you call her?"

"And say what? I'm miserable, and I messed everything up? My pack are overbearing morons, and I don't even know who I am anymore? No, I needed to find out who I was and who I am."

I wrinkle my nose at him and then become aware of the way my hands are sitting on his shoulders. We're so close, but it doesn't feel weird. It feels natural.

"Do you know who you are?" I whisper.

"I've been stalking you." Dylan confesses, ignoring my question.

I stare at him, and my heart skips a beat. It should be terrifying, but with those words came a clench in the vicinity of my heart that sends an empathic line of pleasure straight to my core. My breath seizes in my lungs, and my thoughts scatter.

"You...stalked me?" I ask for clarity.

"Since you fed me that first day in the alley. I was almost dead. We haven't been meeting by accident. I've been following you." He says in a rush. "God, that sounds creepy."

He stares at me. There's no sign of a smile. He's not yelling out, he's not joking. I can't help but find it...endearing.

"You stalk me." I say with a tiny smile I can't hide. "Specifically me?"

"Yes, specifically, exclusively you."

He relaxes against me, leaning in with a soft growl.

I push away from him as the wash of feelings rips reality cold and raw over me. I'm supposed to help him get back with his alphas. What the hell kind of false fairy tale have I fallen into?

I look over and notice the strangest thing. A statue of a fat little dog with its tongue lolling out sits in the shrubs, a cat perched with watchful eyes beside it. You can't see it from any angle around the pool, only when you're in it looking out.

"Look at this."

Dylan comes closer and has a look. "That's Grayson's influence. He leaves a signature wherever he works."

"A cat and a dog?"

"I know. It's weird, but that's Gray for you." Dylan studies it intently.

"We better get back." I say instead.

Dylan sighs and lets me go, and I swim away from him and towards the pool ladder. I climb out and shiver in the cold air. It feels like the pool was a dream, an alternate reality. Dylan glances around and then hoists himself out of the pool. I watch, mesmerised, as his shirt, now a second skin, allows me to see his arm and back muscles flex. Water sluices off him, and he unfolds, standing to his full height.

He truly is a beautiful man.

I turn away and pick up a towel, trying to wring as much water from my dress as I can. I pick up my shoes and stare towards the hotel, refusing to look at the omega beside me.

There's a tension that I know is entirely of my own creation between us now. Every step of the walk back digs it deeper. Silas comes out of the staff rooms and stops, his eyes traveling up and down Dylan and then me.

"Evening."

I incline my head stiffly. "Good evening, Alpha Hastings."

Silas presses the button, and when the lift door opens, he gestures to allow us to enter first.

I'm so hyper aware of the fact my nipples are tight, the dress is clinging to me closer than a second skin. Also, I'm dripping water over their perfect lift. I chew on the inside of my cheek, wondering if I should say anything or just leave it be.

In the end, I choose silence as the best defense. The doors slide open, and I'm confronted by so much skin and muscles that I stumble back against the lift wall and press against it like it might be able to absorb me.

Grayson flexes and then looks up all innocent like. "Oh, hey. Didn't expect you back so early."

I know he's talking to Dylan, but the way his eyes linger on my chest makes me burn. The doors aren't shutting. I have no choice but to brave it. Now, do I run or walk with my head high?

I edge out, watching as the alphas turn to follow Dylan. The way to my room is clear. I take a chance and move quickly, only to hit a solid wall and stumble to a stop as I practically bounce off Silas' chest.

He puts his hands on my shoulders to steady me. An electric current goes down my body from where he's touching. I lose my ability to move, staring up at him. He doesn't look down at me, just moves around me and let's go.

I'm invisible in this room. I could be naked, and no one would see me.

The thought stings, even though I know it shouldn't. Even though it's completely wrong of me. I'm ashamed of myself as I walk down to my room.

A quick shower and a change into sleep shorts and a tank top later, and I find myself in the hallway, sneaking back towards the lifts. I just need some air.

The lounge is dark, but suddenly, a screen lights up and illuminates Silas' face. He peers up at me. I hesitate only a moment and then walk past him. I'm allowed to get water.

I think.

"Dylan is annoyed with you and mad at us."

"Me? What did I do?" I ask, outraged.

"You left him here with us. I believe."

I ponder that for a moment and then scoff. Then I stop, and I actually wonder if he does feel like I abandoned him. Perhaps I shouldn't have done that.

"He's mad at us because that was an obvious ambush."

I blink. "It was?"

"Of course. Grayson has a gym up here and access to the gym downstairs. He doesn't need to be lifting weights right near the door."

"Oh."

I finish pouring myself a glass of water and sip it slowly at the island.

"My mother organised all that." Silas says.

"All what?"

He laughs softly and shakes his head. "I tried to warn them when they wanted to form a pack with me. My mother is a controlling force of nature. She is incredibly manipulative. I underestimated her. We all did."

I set my glass down and move closer, still with a huge lounge between us.

"She organised it. My mother," the words are a curse, "kept pushing and pushing. She made comments that ripped him apart. She made sure to point out that he was less. The way your sister did with you all night. We tried to use our manners to combat her. Never said a sharp word or put a stop to it, we didn't want to cause a scene. We let words lay in the air between us. Words that infected our pack. My mother is pure poison, Onyx."

"Is he?" I ask. Silas frowns. "Is he less?" I clarify. "Is he what your mother says?" I'm almost afraid of his answer.

Silas laughs, but it fades away, and a deep softness takes over his face. "No, he's everything."

I can feel the honesty in his words. The relief and regret that runs through me is excruciating.

This sad alpha shuts off his laptop and stands up. He pauses in the frame of the hallway light.

"Goodnight, beta."

And just like that, the peaceful moment is shattered. The spot where he was standing is still pulsing with the contained aggression. He used words to pierce me with this time.

I feel naked and like I need another shower.

With a mental snarl at myself for letting their harsh words get into my head, I pad back to my bedroom. I've just got my hand on the door handle when I hear a muffled sob from the room beside me.

I hesitate, staring at it, but in the end, I slip inside and creep towards the bed.

"Grayson?"

He whimpers again.

"Gray?"

I reach out and place a hand on his arm. He moves so quickly that I can't even anticipate it. I'm suddenly on the bed, with him sitting on my hips, his mouth bared in a vicious snarl.

Even though my body trembles, I reach up with a shaking hand and cup his cheek. I try to ignore how hard I'm trembling.

He blinks several times, and the enraged expression changes to one of confusion.

"Onyx? What are you doing in here?"

"You were whimpering."

"So, you got into my bed?" Grayson smirks and rolls to the side but keeps me pinned with a single, huge thigh over my hips.

"I did not get into your bed. I touched your arm, and you just...magicked me here."

"Magicked?" Grayson laughs. "I have skills even I'm unaware of. Holy hell, I'm a next level alpha."

"Shut up." I hiss at him. "You just did this pull and flip, and the next thing I knew, I was pinned."

Gray is silent, his smile fading. "Did I scare you?"

I study the intensity in his eyes and shake my head. "Not at all."

His face transforms, and a huge grin appears. "Oh, then you liked it?"

My mouth works, but no sound comes out. "No!" I finally almost shout.

"I think you did," he says in a low voice that makes my stomach flutter.

This alpha is deadly.

The door rips open suddenly, and I twist my head to see a man outlined in the light. He comes into the room and pushes the door closed. My heart thumps almost painfully in my chest, but then Dylan peers down at me. He slides into the empty space on the bed and shoves Gray's leg off me.

I sit up, but two arms pin me down again. I grumble and adjust my body until I'm comfortable, but then they move closer. It's strange to have two huge bodies plastered on either side of me. Kinda nice but intimidating. I vividly remember Dylan's kiss and feel my lips tingle.

No, this is wrong!

But then I notice that Gray's fingers are on Dylan's arm.

My eyes widen as my brain joins the dots. I'm the invisible buffer helping them to grow back towards each other.

There's a small amount of comfort in that. But it's also distressing in a way that I refuse to analyse. I lay there for a long time. Dylan searches his alpha out in his sleep. One arm curling over me to press against the skin of Gray's chest.

It's sweet. It's excruciating.

The alpha moves in his sleep, burying his face in my shoulder. Shivers run over my skin, and I find it hard to breathe.

Dylan makes a sound that's similar to a growl, and when I turn my head, I find his eyes wide open.

"You can't growl if you came in here and contributed to this…fiasco!" I snap in a whisper.

He moves closer to me and drags his teeth down my shoulder. I shudder. My nipples go hard, and I feel a warmth and ache between my legs that makes me press my thighs together. It's an effort to keep my breathing regulated.

I hear his soft laugh as he does it again. I squirm and then freeze, my breath puffing out of me when Gray makes a sound that is deeper than Dylan's growl. He shifts his weight, and I feel something long and hard pressing against my thigh. Where are their clothes? My internal brain squeals. Why aren't they wearing underwear? The baffling mysteries of this moment are there and then gone in a poof of a breath from Gray.

I might not have experienced a lot, but all the years of living where I've lived and attending the parties, I've seen things that have opened my eyes to a universe of sex. I'm not shy. My eyeballs have bled with how much I've seen.

But experience, not so much.

And a prevalent thought keeps circling. This alpha is not mine.

He grinds himself against me and then growls again. I feel Dylan's reaction to the sound. The way he stiffens and lets out an almost inaudible moan in my ear.

Do I help them or stop them? I feel like I'm walking a tightrope, and I've got no idea where it's going. Only, what will happen if I fall?

I reach for the omegas hand and guide it down to Gray.

I stare at the roof, refusing to allow myself to even move as Dylan wraps his hand around Gray's dick. The sounds are impossible to ignore, and the movements are more erotic than I could have dreamed. Sinuous bodies moving against me. I think of sheep and anything and everything else, but the ache between my legs grows. I get wet, and the urge to moan gets harder and harder to suppress.

My breathing saws in and out of my lungs, and each touch from the two men is burning with painful pleasure, driving me higher and closer to losing my reason.

It feels like it takes forever, but then Gray stiffens. He lets out a grunt, and I feel a hot, wet splash on my ass cheek.

Dylan leans up and grips my chin, opening my mouth and invading with his tongue and all that lemon. I can't do anything as I realise Gray is still teasing Dylan. The hard fist against my belly, Dylan is still thrusting into me. His hand reaches back and grips my ass, dragging us closer together.

I whimper into his mouth.

Dylan kisses me the whole time, keeping my attention on him. And then, with a cry into my mouth, he stiffens and grinds himself into me. The wetness is much more this time, and I find myself so close to the edge of my own orgasm that it's almost painful.

I lay back panting and then try to struggle free.

"No. Stay." Dylan growls and locks an arm around me.

"I have to get cleaned up." I protest.

He makes an unhappy sound. "Stay."

"He likes you smelling of us. We marked you." Gray says with a smile that makes me nervous.

I peer at them, and then with a grumble, I reach down and pull off my shorts. Leaving just my lace panties.

I roll back onto my side and lay there, ignoring them. But then someone's hand rolls down over my ass, dipping dangerously close to the inside of my thighs. For a moment, I wonder what it'd feel like. Would it stop this ache inside me? But then I remember who I am. I remember my job, and I decide in that moment that it's not worth the price I'd pay tomorrow.

"Stop!" I hiss out desperately. If my body had a voice, it would be howling at me, but I'm blurring lines here that shouldn't be crossed. I'm aching for the omega and the alpha. This is so wrong.

I'm not sure if they will or not, but the moment I say it, all movement stops, and the hands disappear.

It takes me a long time to get to sleep.

Thirteen

DYLAN

She's avoiding me. I'm not surprised after what happened last night. I'm not even sure how it happened. Just her and him and the dark. It was so easy to fall prey to the feelings for them I've been resisting.

Still, this morning, she is staying one step ahead of me, merging with the groups of people I no longer feel comfortable with. I wonder what she'd think if she knew I grew up with people just like these, in a world just like this. Would she be surprised? Would she look at me differently?

Would it surprise her to learn how much I hate it? How those months of having nothing, of living alone, were some of the most raw and powerful of my life. The cut throat mentality of stepping on each other to get more is everywhere. It isn't exclusive to the haves, but an act of kindness when you have nothing means so much more.

Despite that, my alphas seem different. Or at least I'd thought when I'd fallen for them I'd believed they were different. And that's the crux of the matter. I was jaded and cynical before I met them, and still, I fell. My hormones and instincts decided before rational thought could. I trusted them, and I was wrong.

But with Onyx, it's all different. She saved me, a stranger. She is everything good and kind in this world. I look up as she smiles at Moira. She doesn't realise how much she lights up a room. The staff admire her and listen to her; the omegas respect her, and the alphas find her intriguing. She commands attention and doesn't even realise it.

I didn't lie when I said that I stalked her. I did it just like I'm doing now. As she flits around smiling and being the invisible help, I'm a dozen feet away, following in the shadows. That's how I first saw her. I'd been about to crumble, to admit defeat and go home. I was sneaking into a hotel where I knew I might find someone who could take me home, and there she was. Her back was straight as she marched straight up to the alpha, shoving a glass into his hand. She'd being smiling and distracting an alpha while a young waitress with a tear-streaked face made a desperate escape.

I didn't think anything of it. Not until three weeks later when my money had well and truly run out. Not until I finally learnt what being hungry really feels like. When I sat weakly in the back alley outside the convenience store, I watched her count her money, go inside, and come out with two sandwiches and two drinks. Another person bounced around her, talking incessantly, and then walked into the park. But she picked up some rubbish, a wrapper of some food, and put it in the bin. At that moment, she turned her head and spotted me staring at her.

Destiny? Fate? I don't know, but it felt that way to me.

It took her two seconds to decide. Two seconds to give up her food. She gave me food. She saved me. Perhaps my life. Her kindness saved my soul. She brought back hope.

So, I followed her. That night and every one since.

And while she might have saved my soul all those months ago, she repaired my shattered heart along the way. She is mine. I won't give her up.

But she's running. Did we push her too far? No, there was no fear in the sweet coconut scent of her.

I'm watching her so closely that when she looks up, those strange eyes of hers catch the light, turning silver in parts and blue in others. She locks eyes with me, and her cheeks pinken, but she smiles.

She's radiant.

I watch her talk with Hazel and another omega with red hair, I think the omegas name is Laurel. A pack lingers closer than I'd like, but they aren't looking at my beta.

"She is really good at talking with people, isn't she?" Falcon says from beside me. "A bit like a chameleon."

I curl my lip at his words, refusing to look where I really want to, at the alpha beside me. He doesn't deserve it. "She's not like that...she's wearing a mask."

Falcon focuses on her. "Are you going to forgive us, or is this a futile exercise?"

I grind my teeth and focus on the beta. She looks over and sees Falcon. He gestures to her, and she excuses herself, moving lithely through the crowd.

With every step that she gets closer, her true expressions bleed through, and I see the real her. Cautious, intrigued, wary.

"What is it about her?" Falcon murmurs.

"She's my magic." I say and step away from him, closing the distance between us. She peers up at me, and I reach up to finger comb her hair behind her ear.

"Dylan?"

"You look beautiful this morning." I say with all the truth that I have.

Her eyes glitter and crinkle at the edges. How can eyes smile? Hers can.

"You look beautiful all the time," she says back with an easy grin.

Falcon approaches and stops too close to me. The unspoken claiming makes me want to slap my arm into his chest and bounce him back a few steps.

Whether she knows what he's doing consciously or not, her instincts do, and her smile vanishes as she steps back, carefully removing herself from his little aura cloud.

She turns away and spots her sister heading in our direction. I don't say a word as Silver approaches and sidles in-between Falcon and I, and though part of me wants to tear her apart, the other part of me spots the open opportunity to gather all of my betas attention.

"So, Mr Treyfield, I'm really enjoying the party, but I was wondering if you had a garden?"

"We do."

I snort and take a step towards Nyx. She cuts me an amused glance that tells me she knows exactly what I'm doing. The noise in the room is loud, but it fades away with her smile.

"Would you care to show me?" Silver flutters her eyelashes at Falcon, and I turn back, snarling.

Falcon cocks his head to the side, watching me.

Don't do it. I mentally shout at him. *Don't you dare do it!*

"I'd be delighted to show you." Falcon says in a deep voice.

Wrong answer, asshole. I turn on my heel, sweep Nyx into my wake, and stalk out of the ridiculous yellow-coloured room. Fuck that alpha and his games.

"Hey, slow down!"

I hesitate when I hear her shout at me and stop. We've taken several turns, and even I'm not even sure exactly where we are. I let go of her wrist and pace back and forth in the narrow hall. All I want is the open, empty parklands I've been sleeping in. I hate these narrow halls and all the lights. It's just too bright, too close.

Onyx grips my shirt, and I come to a halt, breathing hard.

"What's wrong?" She asks me.

I exhale and cut a glance to the left. The corridor remains empty. "Nothing."

"Okay, that's not nothing. You can tell me, Dylan. I thought we were friends?"

I swallow hard, frustrated and pissed off. I can't explain it. It's too humiliating. I don't even fully understand it myself.

"Hey, everything all right?"

I whip around, ready to throw myself at the intruder and rip his throat out, only to find Silas standing there. For a moment, fury chokes my words in my throat, and then, all at once, my anger drains away. Silas has that effect on me. It's all in the eyes. He melts me. All my reasons, my logic, my senses.

"Falcon is showing Silver the gardens?" Nyx asks cautiously.

Silas jerks his eyes to me, alarmed. "He wouldn't do what you're thinking."

"I'm not thinking anything." I grit out. My hands clench with the effort to contain my emotions. "I don't care."

Silas and Onyx exchange meaningful looks before he moves closer. His fig and sea salt scent washes over me, relaxing my senses. I inhale deeply, drawing more of it in before I can stop myself.

Silas, my alpha, moves into my space but slowly in measured, careful movements. He lifts his hand and strokes the side of my face, trailing down until his thumb brushes the base of my neck.

"He wouldn't do that. We meant the vows we gave you, Dylan."

I reach out and snag Onyx's wrist, and everything comes a bit closer to being in focus. I pull her close so she's pressed against both of us.

Silas glances at her and then focuses on me. The scent of her combines with ours, mixing and blending with a subtleness that makes my mouth water. Silas' brown eyes, with the myriad of shades, try to convey all the promises and invitations, but I don't want to hear them. Instead, I focus on slate blue.

Silas shifts his arm, but she reaches up, freezing when he growls. She resumes the movement, and her hand lands gently on his forearm. His white shirt is too white and too pristine. Nyx grips his arm, and, stiffly, she moves his wrist from my waist, guiding it up to rest over my heart.

"Tell him again." She hisses.

"We won't betray your trust again," Silas whispers.

I stagger towards him, baring my teeth. He wraps his free arm around my neck and holds me close. There's an urge to fight, to throw punches, to make him hurt, but I won't risk hurting her. I can't, so I allow the soft stroke of his hand down my back. I ignore the way he breathes in my scent and lets out a breathy little sigh.

He leans in closer still, and his lips graze my cheek. For a moment, all the longing and yearning is just too much. I want him.

But then I remember that day. Those feelings, and I remember how much it hurt. Never again. I pull back, bringing her with me.

She cranes her head to look behind me, and I turn, finding Grayson leaning against the wall. He's wearing a jacket and no shirt like he was halfway dressed and got a call. I guess, in a way, he had. But I hadn't expected him to come.

"Need a hand, Dylan?" His mocking, teasing tone doesn't match the gentle concern in his eyes.

I bare my teeth at him and pull Onyx close to me, both to keep her safe and to keep me sane.

"I do not." I bite out.

"Well, Silas would love to-"

"Do not finish that, Gray." Silas barks out. He's always been able to read the room better than Gray.

"You're too serious, Silas. Look at him, he wants to have a little fun. Don't cha, baby boy?"

I snarl, loud enough to get both of their attention. "I'm not your baby boy, not now, not ever."

Grayson tilts his head to the side and moves closer, shifting around me, his fingers brushing my ass, making it tingle. I bite back the urge to growl. He moves like a shark, unerring in his direction. Certain. His mouth on my shoulder, his fingers in my hair. So quick, before I can slap at him. Dividing my attention from the more subdued but no less powerful threat of Silas.

Onyx tries to escape, but I pull her up against my side. The alphas, for their part, ignore her. It enrages me. Which is confusing because I don't want them touching or looking at her. But pretending she doesn't exist is worse.

A door opens at the other end of the hall. I turn to look over my shoulder and spot Falcon. He approaches slowly, adjusting his tie as he walks. He is the most intimidating of the three of them. When he gets close, he simply reaches out and tries to take her from me.

He tries to take her from me.

My barely leashed temper explodes. I lash out at him, shoving hard at his chest, and pull Onyx into my arms, snarling viciously at the three alphas who aren't mine but are currently threats.

"Onyx," Falcon says in warning.

"We had a conversation about ambushing and manners, didn't we?" Onyx snaps back. "You're the idiot who was set on goading your omega into a response. How stupid can you get?"

Her cheeks immediately redden, and she looks up guiltily.

Falcon's face gets that stiff, tense mask that hides the rage he's feeling. I don't take my eyes off him.

"That's not what's going on," Gray says helpfully.

We all ignore him.

Onyx turns in my arms and wraps her arms around my waist. "They just want to talk. Surely, a conversation wouldn't hurt."

I peer down at her and narrow my eyes. "No!"

"One little conversation." She pleads.

I glance up at Silas and his carefully composed mask. "One conversation."

"I need to show you something. I need you to watch it to the end, and I need you to have an open mind. This isn't an attack, Dylan, it's evidence."

Silas pulls out his phone and hands it to me. I look at the security footage and hiss. How dare he? How fucking dare he?

But Onyx grips my hand before I can throw the phone.

"Can we watch it, please?"

She doesn't know the pain she's causing me. I reluctantly nod. She presses the button and holds her hand over mine. At first, I'm barely paying attention, but then I do a double take and rewind it. I watch it over and over.

Maybe seven or eight times.

The horror of the revelation is staggeringly huge. It's epically life changing and completely devastating.

I fucked up. I made a mistake. They didn't do anything with the other omega. Oh, god.

THE BETA'S BARGAIN

No. It changes nothing. I can't trust them. The other omegas will never give up. I don't deserve this pack. The Treyfield pack. They should never be mine.

I stare at the screen, but I don't feel right, and now...I don't even want her near me. My vision goes white and black, and I hear a ringing in my ears. My face is clammy with a cold sweat that makes me shiver. I step back out of their grips and move away from everyone. One step at a time until I'm running.

I run as fast as I can, but I can't escape the words, I can't escape the whispers. She's there with a thousand faces. The omega they deserve, the one who can carry on their line. The she's that aren't me.

Broken me. Poor, ruined me. Unworthy. Undeserving.

How could I ever think that I could deserve her?

How could I ever think that I could have them?

Fourteen

ONYX

All right, so Dylan has just taken off like the hounds of hell are after him, and I have no idea why. All I know is I'm now in a hallway with three very large, furious alphas.

"What just happened?" Falcon barks.

"I don't know," I say through numb lips.

He reaches out and grabs my throat. I feel like a rag doll in his grip as he pushes me roughly up against the wall. There's no way to avoid his gaze, so I meet it head on. I'm scared right now, terrified. Dylan's not here to save me, and I've never been around an alpha this mad.

"What do you think just happened?"

I hesitate because I really don't know if Dylan wants them or not. I'm guessing based on his reactions. "Falcon," I plead, "I don't know, but I can find out."

Falcon leans closer and then pauses, his nostrils flaring as he inhales deeply. I tremble, my thoughts scattering to last night. His expression turns puzzled. He just studies me, and then abruptly, he lets go and steps back.

"Grayson, I think we need to have a conversation."

"But Dylan-"

"Onyx can deal with him. You, Silas, and I need to have a conversation."

I don't miss the threat in those words. I peek up at Grayson and find him smirking. He winks in my direction and then shoos me away.

"Run, little beta."

I don't wait for a second invitation.

As I leave, I don't quite run, but I do move quickly and keep moving until I'm at least three entire rooms away from them. Only then do I settle down enough to think logically.

THE BETA'S BARGAIN

There are several places I can search for him, but it will take me all day. I hum as I walk towards the foyer. I spot the security desk and get an idea.

Simon warily watches me as I approach.

"Hello, sir. Um, so Falcon, well, Alpha Treyfield has instructed me to find Dylan, but he took off. It's imperative that I find him quickly."

Simon studies me in silence and then reaches for the phone. He presses a single button and then lifts the handle to his ear.

"Alpha Treyfield, yes. I have the beta here- Okay, sir. Yes, sir. I will, sir."

Simon puts the handle down and studies me intently. "I'm to give you whatever help you want."

I take a breath, trying to steady my nerves. I don't think Simon is ever going to like me, but then again, I haven't seen him like anyone. He doesn't appear to have friends. With his slicked back black hair and his intense eyes, he comes across as cold and intimidating. "Can I please see the security feeds?"

"Come around this side of the desk then, Beta Davies."

I wince at the verbal slap he's just given me and creep around the desk while he instructs a man named Gavin to pull up the footage.

"There!" I point to a screen.

Gavin follows screen after screen until I know the direction and what area of the resort Dylan is hiding in.

"Thank you." I say and rush out of the main building. The day is overcast and dark like a storm is coming. I don't know why, but I don't want him alone in this. I run through beautifully manicured lawns and the forest that surrounds the resort.

It takes me an hour, and just as I spot him, the heavens open, and thunder cracks across the sky. He huddles deeper, his arms tucked tightly around himself as he stares blindly at the ground in front of him.

I approach carefully. I can't miss the scent of pain, even with my dulled senses.

"Hey," I mumble. I don't want to spook him.

He turns his head in my direction and then looks back at the dirt.

"You've got everyone freaking out."

"I was wrong."

I shrug. "Even the perfect can have an off day."

"I'm not perfect!" He snarls.

"You seem to be to me." I say in a whisper back to him.

He shoots me an incredulous look. "I'm a mess. I ran from my alphas-"

"You stood up for yourself and your rights. How many other omegas could have walked away? Would have walked away?"

"I don't deserve-"

With a frustrated snarl, I close the distance and straddle his lap, putting us chest to chest, nose to nose. I shiver with cold as rain drips down my clothes, soaking me. It drips off both our faces. "Tell me what you don't deserve again, omega."

"I don't deserve-"

I slam my mouth down on his. I tease his lips and taste the salt from his tears mixed with the rain.

"You deserve everything." I say to him, "You are kind and righteous and stronger than anyone I've known. You stand out among the crowds."

"You didn't see me."

"I'm not allowed to look at the stars, Dylan." I say quietly.

His arms close around me, pulling me even tighter to him. "I'm broken. I don't shine so bright. You can look at me now."

"I'm looking. I shouldn't be, but I am."

"What do you see?" He asks bluntly.

"I see an omega who needs his alphas. And I see alphas who are trying to make amends. They love you. It's plain to see. Will you give them a chance?"

The struggle is transparent. I reach out and brush his hair back from his face.

"I can't..." He says at last in a pained gasp.

"You could try. Courting again? Could you do that? A clean slate."

"Why are you doing this?" He growls, refocusing on me. "Why are you sending me to them?"

I blink at him. "Because they are your scent matches. Because you seek them out in your sleep." He blinks in surprise. "And because I want more than anything for you to be happy."

"What if being happy isn't with them? What if it's with someone else?"

My stomach gets all fluttery hearing his words, but I push the side of me that has dreamed of hearing those words away.

"Do you really believe that?" I ask. "You can have the fairy tale. Three princes who adore you more than life itself. Who are trying, Dylan. Everyone can see they are."

"I don't want the fairy tale. I want more." He whispers, and then he kisses me.

My heart is thumping in my chest, and all I can taste is him. I pull back, aware once more that I'm breaking the alpha's trust and sabotaging their scent match. There is something seriously wrong with me.

"We should go inside. You need to talk to them."

He's silent for a long moment. "Yeah, I guess I should. I need to apologise."

I try to let go of his hand, but he clings to it and leads me back to the resort.

There's something deeper between us now. The air is thrumming and pulsing with a tension that wasn't there before. I'm afraid to speak in case even the smallest sound knocks down this house of cards.

He doesn't lead me to the penthouse like I think he will but into the employees only section and to a room that is off limits to all but the owners. I hesitate, but he drags me unerringly inside.

"There's a shower, and we can get a change of clothes." He says quietly and nudges me towards the bathroom. I go inside but turn to look at him as he pulls the door shut. It's intimate and feels strangely like we're in our own little world. Like the falling rain took us to a faraway place. I can't hide my smile as I go into one of the stalls and get under the hot water, acutely, painfully aware that he's in the stall beside me.

Fifteen

SILAS

The path back to the penthouse is blurry and forgotten while the images replay in my mind over and over. I blink and find myself sitting on the couch. Grayson is stretched out opposite me, and it's only the tug in the bonds that keeps me from exploding into a vicious fit and tearing the room apart.

Falcon perches beside me, his menthol scent surrounding me. Familiar and cool.

"This plan isn't going to work," I say the words softly, but I know that they'll hear me. I rub my eyes with my palms and let out a groan that rises into a roar of helplessness.

"What happened?" Falcon says as soon as the sound dies away.

I let my hands fall to my sides. Are they numb, or is it my whole body that's numb?

"He loves her."

Falcon stiffens, it's the slow tightening of muscles of an apex predator. His attention, already so focused, zeros in on me and pins me to the spot.

"Say that again."

"The plan isn't going to work because he loves her." My voice is bleak. The betrayal and the shock of knowing that he found someone else while we hunted for him is strong and painful.

"How do you know?" Grayson asks and leans forward, his elbows on his knees. His movement flops some of his blond hair down one side of his face. He absently brushes it aside and scans the room as if he's expecting one of them to appear.

"They were talking, and he said...he said he wants more." The words sound strange coming out of my mouth, absent the shock that I'm feeling inside. They sound hollow, hurt.

Falcon stands up and paces, reaching up to tug his top shirt button open. He rolls up the sleeves of his black shirt as if he's preparing for a battle. Grayson shifts his attention between the two of us, a small frown drawing a line between his brows.

THE BETA'S BARGAIN

"I can see where he's coming from," Grayson says with a shrug. "He's spent his whole life living in a cage and meets us, and we try to give him the world while everyone else said he wasn't enough. He ran for good reason, and he found her. I mean...if she's the more-"

"Are you willing to give him up to her?" I snarl. "You should have seen them. He is ready to give her bonds today, and she's more than halfway in love with him herself."

"So, what do we do-" Gray shouts at me. He surges up, but with a hand motion from Falcon, he falls back, his words cut short.

Falcon clears his throat. His stiff posture has relaxed, and he smiles. It's so disconcerting that I'm stunned silent. "It's simple, really. He's left us with no choice. I know that knowing he's out there, I would never want another. So it's him or nothing."

"Agreed." Gray says firmly and folds his arms over his chest so that his muscles bulge. He doesn't look at me, and it scrapes at my temper.

I nod finally, but my neck feels stiff and strange. I agree, but I'm not sure where they're going with this.

"So, we court the beta, too." Falcon's words are said in the same way he delivers everything; absolute confidence. For a moment, they don't even sink in. Horror spreads through my veins like poison.

"Have you lost your mind?" I shout into the space. "She's a beta. Our parents would have a field day. The media would have a field day. She isn't even from a reputable family." All the possible future problems slam into my brain faster than I can acknowledge them.

"I don't care about the rest of the world, Silas," Falcon says coldly. He raises one brow and unfolds his sleeves, almost daring me to keep arguing. "I only care about what makes him happy and this pack, and if she is the happy, then he will have her. I will gift wrap her and use her as bait to lure him back into my arms, and I won't feel a shred of guilt for doing so."

I lick my dry lips. This is insanity. We can't do that to her. To us. "She'd be trapped. It's her life, too." Am I pleading?

"She'd be rich out of it. She'd be living a dream." Falcon insists, and I can see him falling into this idea, there's no way to change his mind now. His eyes darken, and he bites his lower lip and paces while staring into space.

"We'd be throwing her to the wolves." Gray shakes his head. At least he's a little hesitant.

"She'd have her own pack to defend her." Falcon snaps and whirls on us, he puts his hands on his hips and scowls. "Now, this would have been better if it had never happened. If Vienne had kept her damn nose out of our pack, but she needed to control her son. Silas, we hurt him. We have a brief window of time to win him back. I've already had to turn several of our family away from the resort, but they know we're here doing something. We are running out of time."

Fear renders me silent. My hands tremble as I remember the last vicious conversation with my mother. The omega of her choice standing in the background trembling as security moves to drag her from my hotel.

I remember the desperate search that grew my panic like a bleeding wound. He wasn't in the room, then the floor, then the building, and then he wasn't anywhere. I barely remember the weeks after.

"How are you going to convince her?" I ask, and the numbness has spread to my lips.

"We are going to court her. Woo her. And through her, him." Falcon says firmly. Decisively. His eyes lighten with his white smile, there's a dimple in his cheek, but it's the devil's dimple, I'm sure of it.

I run my hands through my hair and stand up, no longer able to contain the racing energy inside me. I stride to the kitchen, rip open the fridge, and pull out a beer before turning back.

"This is insane!"

Grayson shrugs. "It's not so crazy. She feels right."

I stiffen and stare at him. "Did you help this to happen?"

"I wouldn't say help exactly. She was trying to help us, I think." Gray shrugs his shoulders.

"You don't know what you've done!" I thunder.

Falcon and Grayson turn towards me and stare.

"She is now the female who will bear our children." I grit out. "Think about how that is going to go down with my mother."

Grayson winces. "Ah, yeah."

"She will be the woman raising our children." I look between them both and see the clarity dawn on their faces. "She will go through hell being with us. Hell."

"So, you're willing to lose him?" Falcon asks.

"I'm saying that it's worth more than a second of thought. It's worth a conversation!" I roar. The bottle shatters in my hand. I ignore it.

"This is the conversation." Falcon says.

"No!" I round the island and get up in front of him. He's taller than me, but my shoulders are wider. I shove him back a bit, just to get his damn attention. "This is you telling us what is happening. As usual."

Falcon inhales, and I watch that glacial mask come across his face, shielding all expression. "Do you have any other suggestions?"

"No!" I snarl. "But I damn well don't want to be dictated to, Falcon."

"Um, should we come back later?"

I swivel my head and find the beta staring at us, with Dylan right behind. He grips her wrist and takes a backward step towards the lift that has all of us tensing. Her eyes drift over us. I wonder what she's seeing, and then she locks onto my hand.

"You're bleeding."

I, what? I peer around in confusion before I realise she's staring at my hand.

"Let go," she says calmly, and then she crosses the room and takes hold of my wrist. I stare down at her, perplexed. I could kill her and solve all our problems right now. But that coconut is mellow, and the anger is draining away. She tugs me towards the kitchen and gets me to hold my hand under the cold water while she pulls the first aid kit out.

She's quick and gentle, focusing only on the wound as she dries it and then cleans and finally bandages it.

I start picking up glass with one hand, but she shoo's me away and tidies up while I stand there as helpless as the rest of the pack.

Falcon raises an eyebrow.

There is no other answer, and we know it, I know it. But I surely wish there was one. I incline my head and damn the beta into hell with us.

"So, Dylan and I were thinking about skipping the dinner tonight."

I look at her sharply and notice her wet hair and the employee clothing of a white shirt and black slacks, the uniform doesn't sit right on her. "We can go over the reports here if you wish?"

She flicks me a smile, and I notice, possibly for the first time, that it's sweet and, though crooked, quite beautiful.

Have I ever looked at her as anything other than a threat?

I replay every single interaction we've had and close my eyes as I realise that the poor thing is probably going to hate us forever.

"Alpha Hastings?" Onyx calls from the couch she's perched on.

I jerk my head up, looking at her. "Call me Silas, please."

She nods and indicates the spot on the couch beside her. I move quickly, taking the seat, and throw myself into my world as I try to ignore that mellow scent.

She cares about Dylan. She cares about my business and her work. Everything I assumed about her was wrong. I really have no idea who this woman is at all.

But maybe we have a chance to learn.

"Silas?"

I make a humming sound and look at her. Her cheeks turn pink, and I wonder what that's for, but then she smiles slightly and points at the tablet.

"Now that we're a few days in, some of these omegas and these packs have segregated from the main group. They appear to be after more refined activities."

"Refined?"

"Reading groups, theoretical lectures. Political debates. Art showings, and the more...cultured activities."

I peer down at her report. "Interesting. You said Hazel is one of these people?"

"Yes."

"Hazel would know. Gray, can you get your sister up here?"

Grayson sits up. "You want Haze's help? Do you know what can of worms you'll be opening?"

"Is she still moping?" I ask.

Gray's face falls into a dark shadow. Ever since her pack chose another omega, Grayson and Hazel haven't been the same. She pretends and smiles, but he's so protective of her. We all are.

"It will give her something to do." I insist. "We can call it a trial."

"I'll see if she's available." Grayson says evenly, stands up, and disappears into the lift.

"Gray and Hazel...I still struggle with it." Nyx whispers.

"You and me both. But they both have a stubborn streak a mile wide, and they'd do anything for the person they love, just like...." I trail off, aware that I've stopped talking about Gray and Hazel, and my mind has drifted to Dylan without my permission. I'm not sure how to continue speaking. He is in everything. He is my world, and being without him is agony. He invades me whenever my guard is down.

She licks her bottom lip, and I follow the movement. "That is a truly amazing thing. To care so much that you'd do that for someone because you love them." Her eyes, that deep blue, almost grey, stare at me with so much understanding.

"Like you with your sister." I say with false lightness.

Her face leeches of colour, and her shoulders roll in. "Not the same. I can only try my best, but I don't often succeed in doing right by her."

"She's here. I didn't get a chance to tell you how much I admired your composure when we first met. It must have been strange and frightening, and you just gave your sister this chance to better her circumstances. That is...incredibly selfless."

She searches my face as if seeking the lie. "Not selfless."

"No?"

"If my sister gets a pack, then I won't have to work so hard to keep us fed and housed. It's selfish, too."

It's hard for me to wrap my mind around the concept of not having food to eat. Or not having a place to sleep. I can literally walk into a number of hotels and sleep in any bed I want. My family own multiple homes. Falcon's own homes are numerous, and Gray has, at last count, four, but he's welcome at a whole host of other packs' homes.

Food and lodgings. Clothes and safety have always been easy to come by.

"Is it hard living like that?"

She freezes and then closes the tablet. I think she might move away, but instead, she leans back into the couch; her gaze distant.

"It's dangerous. It's so easy to get sick. Your belongings are difficult to replace, and people will take them. You can't afford to 'own' things or get attached. Men are...it's dangerous. Drug use is rife, as is crime. Learn to sleep light, react faster, keep secrets."

"And you work so hard..."

"To get us out, Silas. It's all to get us out of that life. While Silver is with me, she puts both of us in more danger. Suppressants are expensive. I have to bag my clothes before I come home because I can't afford to have her scent on me. Alpha's with money don't like to hear the word no."

A fury that I've never known rises, and I move slowly, leaning over her. "Has that happened here?"

She blinks, frozen like a deer in the headlights. "Not here."

"If it happens here, you will give me their names." I order.

She inhales, shuddering, but I don't move away.

"Are children important to you?" She asks.

I cock my head to the side, wondering how much she heard. "Yes, and no. I want a vast family with lots of children. But they don't have to be mine. I just want to raise a family."

Across the room, I catch Dylan listening intently to the conversation.

"So you'd be happy to adopt or foster?"

"Yes." I say easily.

"Wow, that's really...cool."

"You don't want children?" I ask her.

"I mean, I'd love a big family, but my life is hardly a safe place to raise a child." She admits. "But it's good to know you want a family, and it doesn't matter where it comes from."

And now I feel like she's not talking to me.

Dylan's tension eases, and he turns away from the conversation. Falcon's words slam into my brain.

Okay, Falcon. Courting the beta. Out of the corner of my eye, I watch Dylan pace near the huge window. Court Onyx to win Dylan. All right, Omega, you've left me no choice. I'll take the beta, too, if it means I win you.

"What got you interested in working customer service?" I ask and turn my body towards her, listening intently and cataloging every gesture and micro-expression she makes.

All's fair in love and war.

Sixteen
ONYX

Silas sat with me for hours last night, asking me questions and chatting. He's intelligent and sensitive, attentive and empathic, all of which surprised me. I know more than I ever thought I needed about him. I know he enjoys helping at rescues. He doesn't get along with his family. He feels the weight of expectation and resents it.

I found myself deeply interested in his conversation, and every time I went to leave or search for Dylan, I'd be drawn back into a conversation that made me forget time was passing.

It was fun. It was nice. New. Just thinking about it leaves a smile on my face. Just thinking about him leaves me with a strange fluttering feeling in my chest.

But this morning is this morning, and I do not know what today will bring. Maybe that's why I haven't been able to open the door and make myself leave.

I inhale and then force myself to step out into the danger zone. I can hear people talking and follow the sound. My gaze is drawn straight to Falcon. Who is...he is...holy shit, I think he's actually a god.

He turns his head and spots me, his frown crinkling in confusion. I can't look away from all the golden muscles, though, and the way those sweat pants sit on his hips. Where are the rest of his clothes? Where is the suit? The stiff shirts? Those shiny shoes?

Falcon crooks a finger at me. I couldn't resist if I wanted to. I stumble over to him and stop, dropping my eyes to stare at his toes so I don't start drooling over his washboard abs.

"You're with me this morning, little one."

I jerk my gaze to his. "What?"

"Dylan and Silas need to go out and handle some pack business, so it's you and me."

"Oh, I can go and help-"

He lifts a hand and presses a finger to my lips. "I need you."

Oh, man, that is so unfair. My resistance is swept aside. My hands are clammy, and there is a voice inside my head screaming for help not to embarrass myself.

"Okay. So, paperwork or research?" I ask helpfully.

He studies me with a perplexed little frown. "Interesting."

"What is?"

"The fact that you don't seem to see yourself as a woman. Just a worker."

I almost trip over my feet.

He sits on the couch and hooks his arms over the back of it. "What if I said I haven't been able to stop watching you? What if I confessed that I touch myself while thinking of you?"

My cheeks burn, and I can't look at him. "I'd say that it's not fair to tease me, Alpha Treyfield."

He sits forward. "I'm not teasing."

I force myself to look at his face and freeze, captivated by the animation and interest I see staring back at me, and then he blinks, and it's all gone.

"Come. I do have some work to attend to, and your eyes would be appreciated."

I follow him into his office and wander around, taking it in. It's huge, with one glass wall that is black. The window is from floor to ceiling, and the other two have bookcases and shelves.

The desk in the middle of the room is a huge black monstrosity with a laptop in the middle, and that's all. It's stark and minimalist and everything I didn't think Falcon would have in a study. And what is the purpose of that black glass wall?

"Come and sit." Falcon points to a chair beside him and takes a seat in a huge computer chair.

"We've talked with Hazel, and she's got several ideas for rooms to talk. She also thinks some more recreational activities might aid things."

The way he says those words causes my brain to short-circuit.

"What kind of things?" I clear my throat and focus on the email.

"Private walks in the woods to look at different species of plants. Bird-watching. Stargazing."

I cough and nod. "That all sounds good and plausible. There's a woman named Moira who knows a fair bit about plants, and a young man named James who knows stars."

Falcon exits that email to fire off another one to Simon. I watch the long lengths of his fingers float across the keyboard.

I swallow hard and stand up, but his arm snaps out, and he snags my top and drags me back down.

"I was just going-"

"No." He says firmly.

"That's not really very fair."

"I'm a very cruel and unusual man. Ask anyone."

"I have. They speak of you with fondness."

His eyes widen, and his mouth parts.

"They say you are good and fair. A kind boss who drove a woman to the emergency and stayed until her burn was treated. You helped another worker get out of debt. Your workers respect you. They might act nervous, but it's because they are in awe."

"You can't know that."

I lean in close, smiling. "I'm one of your workers, boss."

He stands up suddenly, and I do, too. His hands move faster than I can anticipate, snagging my upper arms.

His kiss is punishing. It rips past all my defenses and steals my sanity. His kiss freezes in my mind, becoming one of those forever moments that I know I will never forget. I can't move my arms, but he walks me backwards until I hit the shelves. Stuff falls, but he doesn't even break away. Menthol tingles in the air, and I moan, opening my mouth, only to have his tongue press in, stealing even more of me. I am changed by his kiss.

He draws back. His lips are wet and slightly puffy. I want to kiss him again.

"You're full of surprises." He whispers, and then with a growl, he pushes himself away from me and the shelves and drags a hand through his hair. "Fuck, you taste like coconut."

"I do?"

He gives me a sharp look and grabs my wrist, dragging me back out to the main room where I find Gray lounging on the couch. He looks almost asleep. He's not wearing a top again and is just in his work out shorts. I bite the inside of my cheek and force myself to look away. I think there's a little drool, but I refuse to check.

"Stay with Gray."

Gray's eyes open, and he lifts an arm for me to come close. I sit beside him, but he drags me into his hold and curls around my back, throwing a thigh over my legs.

I squirm and let out a little whimper.

"Careful, Beta," Gray whispers in my ear. "You sound needy."

I freeze, and he chuckles darkly in my ear. I try to stay as still as possible, and it's not hard. Gray is like a sedative. The warmth and smell of his mango scent relaxes me so much I end up asleep.

When I next open my eyes, Dylan is sitting beside Silas on the couch. They are both smiling at each. Silas is talking, using his hands to describe a project he's interested in starting, and Dylan is listening intently, looking carefree and...dare I say it, happy?

Falcon makes a sound, and I twist and find him sitting beside me. He crooks his finger again, and without thinking, I crawl out of Gray's arms and into his lap.

It's like I'm in one big dream. None of this feels real.

Falcons arms come down around me, and I lean into his chest. I'm not sure what's going on, but I can't find it in me to resist. And then I feel the vibrations, the deep, soothing sound. My eyes close as I press closer to him. Has it been there the whole time?

I think so. But I've only just become aware of it.

What is it?

It's coming from Falcon. I think. That's crazy, isn't it? I press my hand to his chest and lift my head.

"What's this?"

"Purring." Gray whispers from behind me. "He's purring for you."

That is too intimate. That's for mates or someone special, not for me. I scurry off his lap, tripping and landing heavily on my knees.

"Onyx?" Dylan asks sharply, half rising from the couch.

"I'm okay, Dylan, jeez, I just need to pee." My quick joke covers the tension, but still, I close my eyes and curse my own foolishness. I shouldn't have got up. They have a chance here with him. It's working, and I ruined it.

I scurry off to the bathroom. I'm in there for a while, staring at myself in the mirror. Who even is this person? I don't even recognise myself anymore. My cheeks have colour, my eyes are sparkling, and my lips are still puffy.

The door opens, and Falcon slips inside.

"Does my purr scare you so much you need to run?"

"No." I say at once and then look away, catching the red lie on my cheeks in the mirror. "Yes."

"So, which is it?" Falcon murmurs and moves behind me. He sweeps my hair all over one shoulder and then runs his hands down my ribs to settle on my hips.

I suck in a breath as he moves me back against his chest. "I don't know why you're doing this."

"It should be obvious." Falcon murmurs and kisses my neck.

"And yet, it's not." I hiss back. I reach up and tug at his hair, stilling his movements. "You don't like me. You don't know me. You've just gone from wanting me to disappear off the face of the planet to this? I think not."

Falcon grins in the mirror. "You think so poorly of me. But you kiss me like you think the world of me."

"No, I-"

"You do. Perhaps, Miss Davies, it's because I know that you feed the poor with the last of your money. Or it could be that you are so fierce in your protection of my omega. Maybe it's the kindness you work with or how hard you strive to do each task. Perhaps it's that your silky dark hair and almost thunderstorm eyes have been haunting my dreams, and I'm sick of resisting."

His fingers spread wide, covering my stomach.

"Perhaps we're just all under your spell now."

"Perhaps you have a silver tongue." I throw back at him.

He laughs, and I can't stop my body from responding to that sound. Silas' smile, Grayson's aura, Dylan's heart, but Falcon's laugh. It melts my brain.

"Perhaps we'll show you." He murmurs and sucks hard on my neck. A bolt of pleasure lances through me, going straight to the junction of my legs.

"Falcon, stop. Think of Dylan."

He lets go abruptly, our eyes meet in the mirror, and I see the seriousness on his face.

"I am." He vows.

Which makes no sense at all.

I pant and put space between us. "Your omega needs to trust you. This isn't a trust building exercise."

Falcon shakes his head. "You get a reprieve for today," He says and stalks out of the bathroom.

I wait a few minutes and then return to the lounge room. I almost go straight to my bedroom, but the idea of being alone with any of them near a bed is too much temptation.

Falcon has disappeared, but Silas and Gray are still lying on the couches, and Dylan grabs me and pulls me close as soon as I return. The thick smell of candied lemons thickens, I turn my face into his neck, inhaling deeply. The tension that's in his body eases as I play with the hem of his shirt.

"Productive day?" I ask him.

"Meh."

I listen to them chatting about the business and then catch a mention of the gardens.

"I can't wait to see them. When is the first tour?" I ask.

Gray sits up slowly. "You want to see the gardens?"

I bounce and turn to him with a smile. "Of course. The sheer mastery behind their creation is a once in this lifetime. The creator is one of your employees, isn't it? I've seen some of the smaller ones in photographs. I've always wanted to see the Gardens of Treyfield for myself."

Dylan and Gray exchange a look before Gray gleefully pulls me into his arms and hugs me, laughing.

"Okay, you are my favourite person."

I glance at the others for clues, but they are tight-lipped. "Um, why?"

Falcon closes the fridge. I can't help it, but just looking at him causes a frisson of awareness through me. "Grayson designed and oversaw the creation of every garden."

"What?" I shriek. "I mean, I knew you worked on them, but you designed them? They're incredible."

He laughs.

I struggle and twist in his grip before gripping his cheeks. "You're the brilliant mind behind those perfect gardens?"

Gray laughs and then kisses me hard. I respond by throwing my arms around him and kissing him back before I freeze and tear myself away.

"Ha." Gray says smugly. "You forgot to hate me," he sings and winks teasingly.

"What are you all playing at?" I think my words are quiet, but it silences all four of them.

Falcon tilts his head to the side and watches me intently. "We're not playing at anything."

That statement doesn't instill me with anything but more questions. I lift my chin and stand up.

"There will be no more kissing." I say firmly.

Dylan clears his throat. I look at him, and there's a large part of me devastated with my proclamation.

Falcon puts the milk back in the fridge and stalks towards me. I back up, but I don't get far before Dylan' scent surrounds me.

"No more kissing, huh?" Falcon sounds positively delighted.

"No!" I try to say firmly.

He leans in close, his lips stopping but a hair's breadth from mine. "Fine, no kissing until you ask nicely."

I scoff. "Not going to happen."

He reaches out and runs one finger down the centre of my chest, stopping just above my naval. My whole body gets shivers, and my lungs lock down, refusing to let me breathe in or out.

"There are plenty of other ways to seduce you."

My jaw drops. He just laughs as he walks away.

Seventeen
ONYX

Though my bed remained free of uninvited guests, my mind did not. All night, I tossed and turned, playing everything over and over. The only conclusion I came to in those long hours before the sun rose is that I'm doing a disservice to that omega. I could throw myself into this situation and really experience, grow some memories for my life. The truth is that I want Dylan, but I want his alphas, too.

Instead of having breakfast in the penthouse, I make a break for it and disappear downstairs where I can get some space to think. I'm too busy peering over my shoulder to catch the movement in front of me. My arm's gripped in a painful hold, tearing a shocked squeak from me. Silver hauls me into the yellow sitting room and pushes me up against the wall.

"Where are the alphas you keep serving?" Silver snarls.

Serving? What am I, a tavern wench? I pull my arm free of her hold.

"Hi, Silver, nice to see you again. It's been a while. Yes, I'm doing fine. How are you?"

"Oh, you're always fine. I just want to know about them. Everything you can tell me." Silver brushes her hair behind her ears, and I'm momentarily distracted by the diamond earrings she's wearing.

"That would be a serious breach of my contract, and I would be fired immediately and never get a job with Treyfield again." I snap at her and take a seat. I grab a scone from the middle of the table and butter it. Then add a thick layer of apricot jam.

"So?"

I cut her a sharp glare and resume slathering my scone. "So, we need this job."

"Not if I land them as a pack. You'll never have to work again. We can organise, like, a lump sum payment." She takes a seat beside me and steals my scone.

I stare at her and reach for another scone, break it in half, and repeat the slathering. "I'm not doing that."

Silver's face morphs, and I see the side of her she tries so hard to hide. "You owe me."

"No, I don't."

"It's your fault we don't have parents. It's your fault we're broke. And it's your fault my pack left me. You owe me, little sister." Her rage is not new, but it isn't hitting the same way it normally does. I take a bite of the scone. It's delicious.

"Onyx, I swear to god, you will pay if you ruin this for me."

I shudder at the venom in her voice, but I'm not truly worried. She would never let anyone see her like this. She won't cause a scene here. I can hear people on the other side of the door.

"Get me an in with that pack."

"They have an omega." I snap back at her.

"Nothing is signed yet." Silver leans back with a smug smile, and for the first time, I focus on her. Her hair is perfect, with shine and volume. The new cut is styled to show off how round her face is. Her eyes have eyeliner that goes from black to smokey grey, and her lips glimmer coral. But it's the clothes that melt my brain. I've seen those clothes on recent celebrities in magazines. How did she afford them?

How long do I have to work to pay them back? There's a panicked whistle screeching in my brain.

"Silver, where did you get those clothes?" I manage to get out in a strangled whisper.

"My friends bought them for me. You can pay them back later. Especially since you're friends with the pack now."

I stare at her, feeling the blood drain from my face, leaving me dizzy and feeling so very old. "I will not do it."

Silver fluffs her hair and spins in the seat so she's facing the table. She reaches out with one perfectly manicured hand and plucks a muffin from the basket. "You will, though. Because you always do."

"Why not one of the other packs?" I plead. "Just pick someone else."

"Because I want that one."

Fire ignites inside me. "You're not having that one. Pick another." I snap at her.

She gives me a sharp look and then lifts a shoulder and lets it drop casually. "Fine. I mean, sure. But, you know, how would they feel about all the jobs you've done?"

I glare at her.

"Your threats aren't getting anywhere with me." I snap at her. "All my jobs were honestly done. I'm not ashamed of where I've worked."

Silver smiles, but it has no affection in it. She's dropped her mask completely. This is the sister I know.

"Do they know all the jobs you've worked? Do you?"

I turn in the chair so fast I almost fall off, but she stands up and walks away from the table without a backwards glance. Unsurprisingly, she's immediately surrounded by alphas vying for her attention.

My stomach churns painfully, and I put the scone down. I couldn't possibly eat now. I think I know what she means, but there's no way. She wouldn't, would she?

Grayson slides into a seat next to me and smiles. "Phew, I thought she might actually stay here."

I peer at him absent-mindedly. What the fuck did Silver mean when she said that? The only thing I can think of is the couple of times she disappeared. Has she been pretending to be me? The thought rips through my confusion, leaving nothing but horror behind.

I feel sick all of a sudden and suck in a breath to calm the roiling in my stomach.

"Hey, Onyx, breathe. It's going to be okay. I can leave if you want."

I grip his hand and cling tightly to it. The last thing I want right now is Silver getting her paws on him.

"Talk to me, what's going on?" Gray whispers, and it's almost as if he cares.

"I just..." I open my mouth, but nothing comes out. What can I say? My sister is a two-faced tyrant and only I know it?

"All right. So, I have a present for you. I was going to take you there later and romance you into a flurry of love. But let's go now, huh? No love-bombing. I swear."

He stands up, dragging me with him, and leads me out of the yellow room. In fact, in minutes, I find us outside in the misty morning.

"Where are we going?" I ask, trotting to keep up with him.

He grins and winks at me, then turns to the path with the garden. I stumble, but he catches me.

"Falling for me already, ah, if only I'd known the way to your heart was down the garden path."

He laughs and wraps an arm around my shoulders as we slip inside. The guards discreetly move back into place. And then all around us are ten foot high shrubs. The sounds of the world vanish, and it's just him and me.

"So, this garden is, well, for lack of being poetic, it's how I see my father's relationship with my mother. That's the inspiration. It's also how I feel about Dylan, but I try really hard not to tell anyone that."

My heart's thudding wildly, and I can't stop smiling. Grayson is so much more than he appears. He's creative, considerate, and vulnerable. All these parts of him I never would have guessed existed. He's a good man, I can see that now. He's worthy of Dylan, and I, well, I like him, too. He makes me want to explore, try new things, and relax. It would be easy to fall in love with this alpha.

"Why?" I have to clear my throat and repeat the question, but when he looks at me, my stomach flutters, and my cheeks warm.

"It's hard to put myself out there. I'm happy and carefree, tough, you know? But I'm an alpha, and I run an empire, and I'm supposed to know what's right. I'm not supposed to be creating love sonnets with flowers and shrubs."

"Why not? You're an artist. People need beautiful places to fill their hearts."

"That's the other half of my argument," Gray says wryly and leads me around a corner. I stop dead and just take it all in. "It's like Alice in Wonderland."

"Exactly. Love makes the world seem insane while being perfectly logical and reasonable. My mother and father are insane to everyone but them. They are cold and cruel and live in their own world, but it's because of how they feel towards each other. They are the essence of that story."

There's a massive, red-leaved maple tree in the middle, with a creek that runs in front. A checkerboard is made out of two different colour grasses, while statues appear to hang from the very sky. Vines form doorways, and beds of flowers line the paths of white rocks.

"It's beautiful, Gray."

"I think so. It's certainly my better work. You see, the concept has been haunting me since I was about sixteen. The problem was finding a balance of madness that encompasses the story and peace that a garden like this needs to give."

"I feel both of those things. I feel wonder, excitement, peace." I say and reach out to put a hand on his arm. "It's lovely."

Gray smiles at me, and this time, his expression is more vulnerable, more real.

He removes his arm and holds his hand out to me. Without hesitation, I reach out and slip my fingers into his grip. He walks me along, talking about the flowers and the design process. Even the selection of the maple and its transportation has a remarkable story. The tree would have had to have been cut down.

He rescued a tree.

By the time he finishes speaking, and we've walked through several more sections of the garden, I know I'm never going to be able to look at him the same. I also know that I really like this alpha. And I didn't really expect to. It's one thing to find them attractive, it's another to like them as people.

I like all three of them. Perhaps more than like.

I push that thought aside and focus as he leads me through a dark archway. The path breaks into pieces and then vanishes, leaving the people that follow the path in a sphere of green vines and white wild roses.

"This is a very similar place to where I met Dylan for the first time. Falcon had told me about him, but I didn't believe him."

"It is?" I peer around with more interest.

"I was exploring gardens at a party that was boring me to tears. They didn't design it to look like this. It was an accident. But I walked in, lost, swearing because I couldn't find the path back to find Falcon, and he was just there. He turned and gave me this look that warned me off," Gray laughs, "or at least it was supposed to, but I was entranced. It took a long time to convince him we were sincere. I stood and talked to him, but it wasn't until I told him about the roses and how they should be red that he listened." Grayson laughs again at the memory. "The irony is not lost on me. Perhaps I should start talking to him about roses again."

"You have another chance." I insist and put my hand on his chest. "I will help you."

"Why?" Gray asks suddenly. "Why will you help us? You don't know us."

"I know, but you're hurting. He's hurting. I can see it, and I can help you." Helplessly, I look away and shrug my shoulders. "I want to do a good job."

"We both know this is now more than a job between us all. We torched that intent days ago." Gray lifts my hand and kisses my knuckles. "Dylan's changed too much. He needs more." Gray says and spears his fingers through my hair. "And maybe...so have I."

His lips crash down on mine. I gasp, and his tongue pushes in. Mangoes fill my nose, and then he pulls back.

"Did you ever dream of having more?" Gray whispers.

Did I dream of more? Of course, I did. But I'm just a beta. The words don't feel right anymore, but I push all that aside.

"Of course, I dreamed of more," I whisper.

"How far did you dream?" Gray asks. "All the way to the top?"

I open my mouth and stare up at him.

"Dream of me from now on, Nyxie," Gray whispers, and then he pulls me back against his hard body. His hands move from my hair and slide down, cupping my ass and pulling me closer to him.

"I like these black work pants you wear. No one else can see just how perfect you are," Gray growls and kisses down my neck.

I search for and find a bit of control, of reason.

"We shouldn't be doing this. What about Dylan?"

Gray's head snaps up, and he growls. "He's watching."

My eyes open wide, and I twist, looking around until I spot the omega. I expect him to tell me off, shout at me, something, anything, but as soon as our eyes collide, it's like a spell has been lifted. He storms towards me and grips my hair at the base of my nape and yanks hard enough to pull my head back.

"Do you want my alphas?" Dylan asks.

There is no way to answer this without hurting him. I need to rip the bandaid off.

"I know I'm not supposed to, but I find them attractive," I admit in a hushed whisper.

Dylan smiles. "Good."

He reaches down with his free hand and flicks the button of my pants undone.

"Have you done anything like this?" Gray asks.

"No," I whisper. I'm still watching Dylan as he slowly unzips my pants.

"Maybe we should take this inside-" Gray murmurs, but Dylan's hand slides inside my pants, and I arch against him with a gasp.

The feel of someone else touching me is both terrifying and so erotic I don't want it to end. I don't want this to end. I grip his wrist as he strokes, and then I widen my legs. Gray curses and moves behind me, pulling me back so he's supporting my weight.

"Ask me to kiss you, Nyx, please," Gray begs.

I squeeze my eyes closed and moan. My hips arch against the omega's hand. "Kiss me, please, I need it."

Dylan pulls his fingers out, revealing how wet I am. I watch as he puts those digits in his mouth and closes his eyes as if he's savouring it. Gray growls and merges our lips together. My mouth fills with the taste of mango, and I throw an arm around his neck, holding on.

I shift my legs, suddenly aching and needy. My nipples are painfully tight, and I need, I want more. The thought that it's the middle of the day and people could be just on the other side of these hedges drives the excitement even higher. I'm so close, the pressure is almost painful. I need more.

Dylan drops to his knees, dragging my pants and underwear with him, exposing me to the garden air. He helps me out of them and then he lifts one of my legs and stares. My cheeks burn.

"Well, hell, looks like this is how we're playing this," Grayson growls. His hands shift, and suddenly they're under my shirt, climbing up my ribs to grip my breasts. I cry out as his thumbs brush across my sensitive nipples.

"Grayson! Security needs you!" Falcon shouts from close by.

I stumble away from both of them, my cheeks burning. I reach for my pants and pull them back on and then slip my shoes on. Shit, what did I almost do?

Grayson lets out a growl and gives Dylan a long look.

"So close," He murmurs.

I don't wait to see what Dylan says, I just run back to where I find Falcon standing, his hands on his hips. He looks at the three of us and frowns slightly.

"I didn't realise you were giving a tour." Falcon directs the words at Grayson, searching his face.

Gray snorts. "I was trying something new."

Falcon's eyes sharpen. "Any success?"

"We were so close," Gray growls.

I blush bright red.

"Sorry, Alpha," I murmur. "I'll get back to work now."

He reaches out, grabs my hand, and drags me back through the garden. "Not your fault. This is entirely on Gray. But I am sorry I didn't come a few minutes later."

I think I hear a 'me, too', but I don't look around. Nope. That way lies madness.

Eighteen

GRAYSON

I exchange a glance with my omega, and the pair of us trace the fleeing beta with a one-track mind. We were so close. The taste of her is in our noses, our mouths. I can feel her pressed against me.

Dylan catches up to her and grabs her hand. She peers up at him with pink-stained cheeks and this expression that is three parts hunger and seven parts affection.

She is falling in love with him. No, she is in love with him. It's written on her face every time she looks at him. Now, how do we get her to feel those feelings towards us? I'm not sure that I've ever pursued anyone for anything other than casual sex, with the very distinct exception of my omega.

But winning him was more a case of waging a war.

I follow them up to the penthouse and go into Falcon's office in order to deal with the problem of the beta's sister and her behaviour. The staff wants us to shut her down, but I want to leave it to buy more time. I'm there for an hour arguing with our security team, more frustrated than I can tell, when Falcon comes in and sits behind his desk.

"What happened in the garden?" His face relaxes, and he undoes his tie and throws it on the desk.

I hang up on the guy on the phone.

"Nothing. It almost happened, but then it didn't. You have the worst timing." I sigh and rub my forehead. "He was all for it. Bad, terrible timing, Falcon."

He grunts and leans back in the chair. I'm about to stand up and leave when his glass window turns opaque. As it is, I get halfway out of the chair and end up stumbling. I reach out so I don't fall, grabbing hold of Falcon's bookcase. Hell, I don't even care what I broke. I'm riveted.

In the other room, Silas paces around our beta. Her chest is heaving, and she's standing in just a thin, black, lace bra that does nothing to hide her, and stockings and a lace garter. Her panties are gone.

"Holy shit, Silas, you prick," I breathe and move closer to the glass wall.

Behind me, I hear Falcon get up and move to the front of his desk, leaning on the corner closest to the glass.

Dylan approaches from off to my right. He stops in front of her and puts his hands on her hips. I can't see her anymore, but I can see his shirtless back, all those muscles, the toned skin. He's got a fresh scar on his shoulder and more definition in his upper body, but he's still our incredibly sexy Dylan.

He suddenly kneels. My cock was already on the way to being hard, but seeing him kneeling before her has me instantly rock hard and weeping.

"Shit," I breathe.

Falcon makes a strangled sound, but I can't look away.

Silas approaches from behind and wraps his arms around her, settling them on her stomach. He's talking, but I can't hear anything. I really want to hear everything. Silas flicks our wall a taunting smirk, and suddenly, we have sound. Someone has the remote hidden.

"On the other side is Falcon's office. Now, we don't know if they are in there or not. But that's part of the game. You can't see in, but if they are lucky, if they are in there, they can see you."

"How do you know they'd even want to see me?" She asks, and I growl in response.

"Because I know my pack, and I know that they'd really want to see this," Silas says calmly. "Now, the rules. They're really simple. If you move, we stop. We start again when I say you can. Do you want to go ahead?" Silas' words are cold, but the tone is superheated and seductive.

He could sell you a vacuum cleaner without you knowing what you were buying.

I put a hand on the glass and flick the button on my jeans, opening my pants so I can fist my cock.

"Yes."

I exhale with a rough purr and tilt my head back, thanking whoever is up there looking out for us.

Dylan leans forward, kissing down her stomach and across her thighs. He doesn't go straight in, but he's showing more restraint than I would have. She gasps and makes little reactive sounds with every single touch.

Silas slides his hands up her body, cupping her breasts and squeezing. He fishes her out of the lace, dragging it down under her breasts. Her tits are perfect, small and with dusky nipples that Silas cups and almost presents to us. Damn him.

She gasps and moves her arm. I can see she's almost beyond thought. I want to touch her so badly, but I don't want this to stop. Just as I think the word, Silas says it.

"Stop." Silas says. He waits as her arm returns to her side. "Start."

He plucks her nipples, and I consider banging on the glass and shouting at him to take the bra off. I want to see her without a stitch of clothing on.

Dylan finally makes a move, lifting one of her legs onto his shoulder. She gasps, and her back arches. The sight makes me harder than ever. I fist myself slowly and then let go and spit in my hand. Fuck, I can just imagine sliding into her. Or him while she fucks his face.

I grip the base of my cock harder when she moans. Her head thrashes to the side and Silas laughs lightly.

Her hips move…

"Stop." Silas says in a mocking tone.

I growl, wanting to bury Silas somewhere. She pants and opens her eyes. It takes a moment before she realises.

"Start." Silas growls, and his hands disappear. A moment later, the bra falls off. She's beautiful, she's lovely. Her skin is creamy and unblemished, and it's just begging for my mouth and teeth. I'm going to mark all that skin up and leave a roadmap of everywhere I've been.

I thumb my slit and groan as she shudders. She's boneless in Silas's arms, and Dylan is moving really quickly now. It's going to be over soon.

Her hips jolt forward, and her back arches.

"Stop," Silas purrs.

She groans and jerks her body back into the position. "Please!"

But not too soon.

"Wrap your arms around my neck," Silas growls.

She reaches up, and he reaches around, gripping her breasts, squeezing them in his hands. He whispers in her ear, and she moans.

I can just imagine all the dirty things that Silas is saying to her.

Her arms tighten, and Silas smiles at the mirror as her head thrashes. "Stop."

"No!" she wails. "Silas, please."

She returns to position, but it's harder this time. Her skin is flushed, and her chest is heaving. Dylan has his face buried in her cunt, eating her like he's devouring her.

"Fuck, yes," I growl. "Make her come."

Falcon stumbles forward, slamming his hand on the button on the side of the wall.

Silas runs his hands over her stomach, up her breasts, before he grips her throat. Her eyes go wide, almost entirely blacked out. She looks towards the glass, and her eyes lock on Falcon and then me. Shock, arousal, need. It's all there on her face, and it only ramps up harder.

I'm going to come for her. Come on this glass so she knows I want her. I jerk myself harder, faster, thrusting into my fist. My balls tighten. I don't take my eyes off her.

"Come for me, baby," I whisper.

Silas says the words for me.

She shatters. Her whole body shudders and tightens, her hips thrusting towards Dylan. That cry, oh, god, that cry. The pure rapture on her face is mesmerising, and it sends me over the edge. I grind my teeth and let out a fierce growl as the base of my spine tingles, and the pleasure pours through me. Streams of cum shoot out and coat the glass, but I continue stroking my twitching flesh. My fingers claw, and I curl in over myself, but I never take my eyes from our goddess.

Silas draws back with an evil smile.

"Well, looks like we caught both the fishes."

Dylan glances over his shoulder, quickly taking in the scene. His eyes are molten, needy, an omega who needs his alphas. I want to fix him. I want to be the one to make him feel better.

Silas gently covers Onyx up with a black satin robe and tugs her towards the door. I wait until I hear their footsteps go past, and then I approach the room.

"Who do you want, sweetheart?" I ask softly.

He shudders. "Both. I want you both."

Falcon closes the door gently behind us. "You've got us."

THE BETA'S BARGAIN

She blushes when she sees us but lifts her chin and meets my eyes. Yeah, having her in the pack will not be a hardship at all.

I walk over to her and kiss her cheek. She jerks away, putting her hand to the spot.

"What was that for?"

"Um, for the incredibly hot peep show that I'm going to be jacking off to for the next decade."

Her face turns cherry red. "Gray!"

"You looked beautiful, and I wanted you. I wanted you before you did it. Now, I just want a taste. A touch. Anything. Everything."

She stares at me as if I'm speaking another language. As if I couldn't possibly mean what I'm saying.

I reach for her hand and creep it unerringly to my semi in my pants.

"I want you. Simple. But seeing that…you looked perfect. My hottest fantasy."

She shudders, and then her fingers relax, and she curls them around me. My eyes roll, and I flex my hips, thrusting my hardening dick into her palm.

"No more of that. Food first," Falcon says.

She wheezes and instantly lets go of me. "Sorry."

"Sorry? Sorry! Do it again. Anytime. Hell, you just want to hold on to something. My dick is willing and ready."

She gives me a side-eye, but I can see a gleam of amusement in her eyes.

"I have to tell you, I was surprised. I thought you were new to all this."

Her face turns that interesting colour again. I admire it and decide I'm going to make turning her this colour a thing.

"I am new. I mean. Yes. I haven't done…any of it. But I worked in a lot of clubs, restaurants, and lived in a lot of bad neighbourhoods. There isn't much I haven't seen."

I lean in closer, throwing an arm behind her. "Do you have a preference? We all like to experiment a bit."

She's looking anywhere but at us, but the entire room is waiting for her answer. "I don't know. But I liked what we did," She whispers.

"Exhibitionism for the win." I waggle my eyebrows at Silas.

She peers at me and then at the others.

I lean in closer, pressing my lips to her ear. "Falcon likes restraints. I like being outside and games."

"Games?" she asks.

"Well, maybe we're playing hide and seek. Or chase. Or maybe tag."

She thinks this through, and then her eyes go wide.

"Marco Polo," I whisper. "Think of me as a big kid." I suggestively waggle my eyebrows. She bats at me.

I laugh and glance at Dylan. I vividly remember what he likes. Being pinned down and fucked until he can't move. Knotted.

Falcon walks around the couch and hands out slices of cake. I put half of it in my mouth in one bite.

She watches me intently.

"So, sleeping with me tonight?" I ask right as she takes a bite. She chokes, as I expected, leaving me rubbing her back and dragging her into my lap.

"Onyx, you don't have to do anything you don't want to." Falcon says clearly.

I give him a hard 'what-the-fuck-are-you-saying' glare.

He ignores me and stares at her. "You do not owe a single person in this room anything. We hope that if you want to share our beds, you will do so because you find us attractive, but if you don't wish to, there is no obligation."

She gapes at him. "Everyone finds you attractive." She says at last. It's about the last thing I think she will say.

I burst into laughter and squeeze her tighter. "Oh, you are adorable."

"Dylan, they talk about you all the time. How sexy and hot you are. The alphas and omegas."

I don't like that at all. I go still watching him. My heart aches when I spend too much time studying him. Dylan cocks his head to the side and shrugs. But then, to my surprise, he leans back into Silas's arm.

I stare, my heart thudding hard in my chest. He's willingly embracing a member of our pack. He allowed us to give him some relief earlier. Is this actually working?

"Can we watch a movie or something?" Onyx asks.

"Sure." Falcon sets it up and then bring over drinks and snacks.

She glances back and sees him sitting alone. I can almost see her brain working. I wait, wondering if she'll be brave. Most people aren't with Falcon, he is terrifying.

She heaves a sigh, crawls over my lap, grips my hand, and then leans into him.

Falcon's surprised. It might not be visible for the rest of the mortals, but I can see the shock in his eyes. It fades after a while, and he gets comfortable, rubbing her head with his long fingers. I lift her hand and kiss the back of it.

It's the most peaceful night we've had...in ever.

And all because of this beta who refuses to give up and continues to surprise us. I find my eyes drawn back to her and Dylan over and over and note that I'm not the only one.

Nineteen

ONYX

I can't stop looking at them, even when I know I should look away. My cheeks have one setting at the moment, and that is scorching. And though that seems to give Gray joy, Silas' wicked and watchful eye is the one making me feel unsteady.

I glance at Falcon beside me in the lift and exhale again. He's in a white shirt with a dark blue jacket over the top. He looks untouchable. Yesterday, in the room when I'd looked through the glass, his eyes had roamed down my body and back up before stopping on my face. The bulge in his pants had been unmistakable. But he hadn't uncrossed his arms, he hadn't touched himself.

He reaches out and presses the emergency button. I let out a squeak when the lift shudders to a stop. Falcon keeps his chin down and his eyes averted from me, though I watch him out of the corner of mine. There is nothing threatening about his stance, but my tension rises as the seconds pass. *What is he doing? Should I say something? Should I just stand here, silent?*

"I can smell your fear."

I blink as those words fall between us. I have to answer it as honestly as I can. He'll smell the deceit. "I'm not afraid of you. I'm afraid of what everything means."

"Let's test that theory."

I only get a moment of warning and then I'm pressed against the corner of the lift. He lifts me, resting my ass on the rails. I grab at his shoulders, keeping myself steady as his mouth finds a spot on my throat that makes me melt. I gasp as he sucks hard and then runs his teeth over it.

"I could make you ours right now," Falcon whispers.

I've never experienced such polar longings as I do at this moment. A huge part of me wants to tilt my head to the side and beg him to do as he wills. But another, even larger, part of me can't believe them. Won't believe them. Being trapped by a bond would be terrible if it turned out I was right.

He waits through my hesitation and then licks up over my jaw and seizes my lips in a kiss that leaves me feeling weak.

"Falcon," I plead.

He growls and pulls at my thighs until I wrap them around him. "It's good you asked Gray to kiss you. It means I can kiss you whenever I want."

I'm confused until I vividly remember Falcon telling me to ask nicely and then me begging Gray in the gardens. Damn.

He slides his hand up the inside of my skirt. My skin shivers and heats in his wake. Until he reaches my underwear. He strokes lightly, pleasure coils, and then his fingers are inside the barrier. He curls them inside me, pumping, the feeling of being stretched makes me pant into his shoulder.

"So wet for me, Nyx. You want this? You want Dylan and Silas and Gray, but you want me, too, don't you? What will you do for me?" He whispers against my lips.

"What do you want?" I gasp out as he changes the angle, shoving those fingers deeper.

"I want the answer to a question," Falcon says after a moment.

My trepidation vanishes, and I smile against his lips.

"I would give you that for free," I gasp out and tilt my hips so I can thrust against the movement he's creating.

He seizes my mouth in a kiss that makes me forget where we are. I tear away from him, my body tightening, locking on his fingers as my release rips through me, fierce and unexpected. He thrusts a few more times before he rests his head on my shoulder.

"Answer me this, while my fingers are inside you, while I've allowed you to retain your freedom."

His words are harsh, but I get a sense that it's some kind of defensive measure, so instead of rising and biting, I let the comment roll past unchallenged.

I peer into his eyes, now on my level. The pale colour seems to change with his emotions, cold and mercurial as arctic ice or as warm as the shallows of the tropical seas.

"What?"

"What do you want from our pack?"

I hesitate. What I should say is a pack for Silver. A job. What I really want is something different. I go with my heart. "I want a memory of something different, something good."

Falcon's eyes widen slightly. His lips part, and I taste menthol on his breath a moment before he kisses me. As he does, he pulls his fingers out and then wraps his arms around me in a hug.

"You are a strange individual, Nyx."

"People say that a lot," I admit with a smile.

He helps me adjust my clothing and hair and then undoes the emergency stop button. We go down in silence, but his hand holds mine right up until the doors open.

"The plan was a success!" I announce as I stalk into the penthouse. I look around. There's no one to be seen.

"Gray?"

I wander around and then tap on some of the bedrooms. All of them are empty. Wandering down the hallway, my steps pause outside Falcon's office, thinking about that glass wall. I press a hand to my stomach to soothe the sudden butterflies the memory invokes. The office is empty, but I find myself drawn into the room. The glass is clear, and I look and see what they saw.

From here, there's a dark room with the bed lit up by lights overhead. The bedding is navy blue satin, and the carpet is thick and plush. There are no windows in this room. It's very intimate.

I suck in a breath, trying to ignore the way my body heats as I imagine what they saw. As I remember how I felt. I look at the spot where Gray emptied himself, but it's been cleaned up. I reach out and trace the spot with my finger and shudder.

What am I doing? *I'm letting myself have a moment*, I think with sudden determination. I run my hands over my breasts, squeezing hard, before I pull at my nipples. My breathing comes faster. No one's here...I could...

The window turns black. I see my reflection in it. A few seconds later, the office door clicks shut and locks, and then the light turns off. My skin crawls, and the hairs on my body lift. I shiver and strain to hear any sign of life.

Hands grip my waist and hold me still. "Stay," Silas whispers in my ear. He trails his lips to my lobe and bites hard enough to pull a moan from me. My eyelids flutter closed as my head falls back.

"What?" I moan incoherently.

"Shh," he whispers and starts peeling my clothes from me. "My pack hadn't touched each other when we lost Dylan. We couldn't. Before we met him, we used to touch each other all the time, but in our pain, we lived like strangers." Silas lifts my hair, and his nose runs over my neck. My back arches, and his hands pause in their frenzy, reaching to lie over my bare stomach, lingering for a moment. I think Silas has gone into a memory somewhere. He pulls himself out a moment later.

"But the hunger is back." Silas whispers in my ear. His fingers drift down, and I hold my breath, but they turn away, and he resumes tearing at my clothes.

In minutes, I'm naked in the dark. My fingers twitch, but I lift my hand to cover his. But so is he.

"Silas?" I murmur. "So, you're all involved with each other?"

He moves my hair and kisses my neck. "You're so lovely. Yes. I love them, and they love me. Is that a problem?"

I shake my head. "No. It's a relief."

He chuckles darkly.

His fingers reach down and stroke me. I gasp, trembling, as his fingertips dance over my clit. The pleasure spirals are rising in me. In the dark, where only my moans are audible, where the only thing I can smell is him, there is a freedom I've never experienced. It's addictive.

And then the glass turns clear. Just like that. The light surprises me into frantic blinking. I look up to the bed to see a sight that turns my blood to fire inside.

Grayson is lying on his back on the bed, and Dylan is thrusting hard into his mouth. Behind him, Falcon is thrusting against Dylan. The scene clarifies, making sense in my pleasure-drunk mind. Fucking him. Oh, my god.

My core clenches, and I feel moisture run down the inside of my thighs. Silas laughs softly and presses something much larger than a finger against me.

"Put your hands on the glass," Silas whispers.

I do as I'm told and watch as Dylan arches his back, his teeth gritted as he comes into his alpha's mouth. There's no sound, but somehow, that makes it hotter.

Silas kisses my shoulders and runs his hands over my body. I know what's about to happen. It occurs to me to stop it, but I want memories. That's what I said to Falcon, isn't it? I wouldn't stop this for job security for the rest of my life.

What's wrong with me?

Silas growls, and I don't care. All I want is him.

He pushes against me and then slips in suddenly. The feel of him is strange. There's a burning, stretching feeling, but it feels good, too. He pulls out and thrusts up again. It's like he flips a switch, suddenly, the feel of him is nice. More than nice. But the shock of having him inside me and the new sensations have chased me back from the edge.

He must think this feels good, too. He keeps murmuring about perfection in silky pockets of heaven. The words make me feel powerful. I curl my fingers on the cold glass and push back against him.

"Just a little more," Silas growls into my ear.

He isn't in yet? Oh, lord!

He thrusts again, and this time, goes deeper still. I gasp. He feels so deep inside me, so deep. So big.

"Does it hurt?" Silas asks in a harsh whisper.

"No, it feels good, just weird, too."

He grunts and pulls back, then he pushes in again. My eyes roll, and I let out a little cry. Protest, welcome, needing, wanting. All I can feel is him. All I can see is the omega getting railed by his alphas.

Falcon is not holding back, not like Silas is. I wonder if I could take it. If I could handle what he's doing.

"Can you...can you do what he's doing?" I ask hesitantly.

Silas pauses in his movements, his hands grip my hips to hold me still.

"You want me to fuck you, little beta?" Silas asks. "The way Falcon is fucking Dylan? Fuck you until you're mine. Fuck you until you've got my cock imprint inside you?" Silas growls, and his fingers squeeze, pulling me back against him.

"Yes. Like that. I want to know...what it feels like." I pant out, almost sobbing at the exquisite feeling inside of me.

Silas pulls out of me and grabs me by the waist, moving us until I'm bent over the desk. He plants a hand in the middle of my shoulder blades, keeping me still, and kicks my legs apart.

THE BETA'S BARGAIN

"You watch our omega. You watch him," Silas growls. "Watch them fuck him. How hard and mercilessly Falcon fucks him. Think about how he's going to fuck you."

Then he plunges into me in one stroke. The speed and strength of the move steals sound from me. I open my mouth in a silent cry, my whole body reacting to his invasion by screaming across my pleasure nerves.

He hammers into me again. And again. In and out. Thrusting and grinding. At times, he leans over me, pulling up as he thrusts deeper, whispering all the filthy things he's going to do to me.

Things I don't even understand, but, oh, I want to.

And I'm helpless. In a way I've never been before. I'm vulnerable, but I feel powerful. The way he clenches at my hips with his fingertips, the way he growls into my ear and seizes my throat, sucking painful marks onto my skin.

My body and mind are his. He reaches around, burrowing his hand between me and Falcon's desk, and strokes my clit.

"Falcon's going to come in a moment, and you, my love, are going to scream my name. You hear me? Answer me."

"Scream, yes." I pant.

I claw at the desk. The sound of his flesh hitting mine is so damn erotic. The combined smell of us in the air. I memorise every moment of this. The stretching ache.

Dylan looks towards us, his head whipping around. His eyes darken, and he grips the bed and roars. Falcon snaps his hips faster, his eyes on us, too.

Silas laughs darkly. "Now, Beta. You come now."

He pinches my clit hard, and I come. I scream his name, and I tighten around him, squeezing his cock, and then he snarls and bites my shoulder, thrusting up into me. I feel a hot spurt of his cum paint my insides. And then his thrusts ease, and his hold eases. He slumps, breathing hard, and nuzzles my shoulders.

I lie there panting. The wall is black again. Silas gently pulls himself from my body, and I gasp at the feel of emptiness and the fluids running out of me. I go to stand up, but he pins me back down. His fingers touch me, and he shoves them back inside me. Again and again.

It takes me a moment, but I realise he's pushing the fluids back inside.

The thought makes my head spin and my core clench. That needy, wanting feeling comes back. I bite my lip and let my forehead thump on the desk in embarrassment.

The door opens, and Falcon walks in. He stands there for a moment, only the light of the hallway from the open door illuminating us. I feel no judgement from him, nothing but curiosity and a growing heat.

"Silas," Falcon warns.

"She will carry my heir," Silas growls darkly. "My child."

"What?" I shout, and now I attempt to struggle out of his hold. "I did not agree to that. There need to be words. Lots of words."

"Fine. Next time," he growls. I expect him to back away, but I let out a gasp when I feel his hot breath on my ass.

Silas growls, and then his tongue swipes between my legs. I go still. Trembling. He licks again. This is so dirty, and it should be wrong, but I love it. I moan and clutch at the wood, spreading my legs wider.

Falcon comes to lean against the desk. "He needs to have you again, and then he will calm down. Don't worry about what he says right now. It's an alpha thing." He's naked, and his dick is starting to thicken again in front of me.

Can dicks be pretty? If they can be, Falcon's is as perfect as the rest of him. Thick, hard, and with veins that beg to be traced.

"Uh-huh," I moan as Silas' tongue probes inside me.

Dylan comes into the room. I can't see his face, and I wish I could. I wish I could tell what he's thinking. Does he hate this? I moan as Silas probes his tongue inside me.

"Silas, she's sore." He says in a tone I've never heard him use. It's deep and a purr that makes me want to climb into his lap.

It has the same effect on Silas.

The alpha growls and licks one more time before he stands up and walks over to Dylan. The two of them collide, ripping at Dylan's unbuttoned jeans and slamming against that window. Falcon sighs and lifts me into his arms, then carries me out of the room.

I smile dreamily and yawn. The low-key arousal is still there, but I am sore.

"Did you get what you wanted?" Falcon asks.

"It will be a perfect memory." I say into his shoulder.

He shakes his head and presses a kiss to my temple, then drops my naked self into Gray's lap. Grayson pulls me into his arms and gets us both comfortable under a blanket. He's got a satisfied gleam in his eye.

"Cuddle time, little beta."

"That sounds perfect, Gray."

Twenty

ONYX

Four days have passed since my deflowering event. They haven't touched me. They cuddle me, sit with me, talk with me, but no one has attempted anything more.

I almost wish it would go back to all the sex. Instead, I've been discovering things about them that make them real. Make them...special. These men are exceptional, and I think I'm falling into a danger zone. Running head first towards the edge of a cliff. I know it's there, but I can't stop.

Yesterday, Grayson and I sat and worked through the entertainment part of their hosting duties. The singers and artisans that are getting paid mightily to lend their voices. He's got a lot to say about the arts, and he's so passionate about all forms of it.

Gray watches me doodle. "I can't do that anymore. Not without thinking of my father," he says, leaning back in the chair. He flicks a quick look at the woman on stage banging her bongos and adjusts the crisp white shirt he's obviously got an urge to shred.

I wonder if he knew how hot he looked in that shirt if he'd still hate it.

"Why?" I ask, not really paying attention.

"I wanted to be an artist. I loved to draw. Whenever I was supposed to be studying, I was doodling. So, he would punish me."

I jerk my gaze to his. "He what?" Gray's dad has just made my enemy list. How dare he hurt baby Gray!

"He punished me. I'm meant to rule empires, not doodle. Don't worry, Hazel isn't allowed to create her finger paintings, either, but she's stronger than I am, and she does it, anyway." There's a flatness in his eyes when he says that, like he doesn't see himself as strong or artistic.

Which is crap! I push away the paper and pen and turn in my seat, reaching out and gripping one of his huge hands. His eyes stop bouncing around the room and focus on me.

"You create the gardens. Those magnificent, amazing works of art." I hold up my hand to stop his protests. "Your father is a moron. Art is the heart of society, and you are more talented

and envied and celebrated than you know. But don't worry, Gray, I'll make sure you see it the way I do."

"Yes, I do create them, but they're just gardens. They aren't like Hazel's paintings. My father and I had a full-blown fight, and he threatened to disown me when I came out as the designer. I laughed at the time. I said with all the bravado of Falcon and Silas that I'm part of the Treyfield pack now. My wealth is nothing compared to Silas'. But I still can't pick up a pen and just draw without hearing his words in my head."

"Your dad sounds like a dick," I grumble.

He laughs and agrees.

I left it, but the memory of it lingers. I know what it's like to have a dad who's a dick. Beneath the easy-going countenance, Gray is deep and sensitive. He is fierce and emotional. Perhaps even more so than Silas, but when he loves, he loves with all of him. I can see how much he loves Dylan, Silas, and Falcon. He can't hide it. It's transparent in everything he does.

Silas had paused in the kitchen two days earlier and wrinkled his nose at the fish.

"You don't like fish?"

"No. I hate the taste."

"Me, too."

He glances at me over his shoulder. Silas is beautiful when he isn't smiling, but when he smiles, he is gorgeous. He tempts me in a way the others don't. He tempts me to try all the new things. To push boundaries. To be a little daring. He's this suave, polished man in a suit with this darker side, and when he invites you to join, he does it with that smile.

How can a girl say no?

That conversation led to us spending the day in the kitchen cooking and tasting food. There's something undeniably sexy about a man barefoot in the kitchen in sweats and a tank top. But, more than that, he's attentive, charming, and funny. It was easy to open up about my life and tell him about the various skills I've learned over the years. He listens and makes me feel heard.

Falcon I have learned little about, his past is a vault, but I watch the way he makes drinks and prepares snacks. He handles the phone calls from irate family members. But Falcon takes care of his pack, his employees, and anyone under his protection, anticipating their needs and never looking for thanks. He's the one who organises security for us when we go downstairs. He urges us to bed and does a lap of the penthouse, turning off lights and making sure it's safe. Falcon is the one who, when he sees we're getting stressed., he gets on his knees and rubs his pack's feet or brings them their favourite food or holds them.

The powerful head of Treyfield has one duty in his heart, and that is taking care of his pack. It's endearing. It's more than that. It's a sight that stops me dead with twin blasts of awe and longing. Yearning.

Dylan has transformed. The longer he is around the pack, the more open he becomes. His laugh is infectious, his smile is heartbreaking. But the peace in him, the happiness...it's transformative. I wouldn't recognise him now. He's totally different, but it suits him.

And he's free with his affection, including me in it. He makes me feel special; he makes me feel like more. He is my best friend, and his happiness is my happiness.

Spending time with them is slowly drowning me in feelings I know will destroy me, but like an addict, I'm helpless to stop.

I see them now, how they fit together. Like pieces of a jigsaw. This pack is a perfect fit.

They line up in suits as I come out of my room. I'm dressed in a gown of deep purple. It clings like a second skin and looks like water. The only reason I walked out dressed like this was because of Silas' whispered complement earlier today when he chose the dress. I've got on black lace gloves that rise to just past my elbows, and Falcon had one of the staff come up and help with my hair and makeup.

I don't look like myself.

The night is incredible and like a fairy tale. They are attentive, and we laugh and live in this bubble. Dinner is divine, even if it is spoonfuls of food covered in glitter. I clap politely when the artist stands up and bows. She leans into the microphone again and croons another song. Dylan puts a hand on my thigh and leans in to press his lips against my ear.

"Do you want to see something?"

I nod.

He takes my hand and pulls me through the tables. I spot my sister sitting with a pack, but her glare momentarily arrests me. There is so much hate and venom in it.

Dylan pulls me down a hallway and into a door I've never passed through before, and I forget all about her. It's a giant cinema.

"What are we doing here?" I ask him.

"Are you feeling healed?" Dylan asks and drops his eyes to my abdomen.

My cheeks blaze. "Yes. I'm healed. Jeez!" I look away and bite my lip.

"Ah, good. So, Grayson is bored."

My attention sharpens in a single second. "Are we playing a game?"

Dylan grins. "Hide."

I hesitate and kick off my shoes before bolting in the opposite direction of Dylan. There's a thrill that is indescribable to knowing the alphas are going to be hunting us down. I hesitate and then choose a row in the middle of the back block. The trick to this is going to be to keep moving.

A minute passes, and then another, and finally, they come in. I don't even need to look. I can feel them in the air. The doors are shut and locked.

I press my hand against my lips to suppress a giggle.

"Ready or not, here I come." Gray's voice booms into the enormous room.

I shift closer to the end of a row and wait until I can see where they are. Falcon walks up slowly and gets to my row. He looks in my direction, but I'm positive I'm hidden, and then he takes a seat.

I lick my lips and watch him. He turns his head and looks to the front.

Silas and Gray are chasing Dylan around. He is flying over the chairs, leaping from space to space. It's effortless and amazing. He's managing to stay away from them, too, but eventually, he's pinned by Silas. Gray turns his attention and looks for me.

Holy hell. There is something about him that has come alive.

I'm going to make this hard for him. Really hard.

He prowls towards the back, searching each row. As he gets closer, I crawl as quickly as I can to the other side, and when I see him step up; I slip down a single step. He keeps going up, and I descend, moving to the bank of seats on the left. I look around. There has to be somewhere else I can hide. I spot the curtains down the front and ponder it. If I could get across the distance, I might get there. He's already checked them, too.

I check his location, and then Silas', and then I work my way down. At the floor level, I crawl almost under the seats to the wall and then, in really slow increments, I work my way to the curtain and slip behind it.

I hear them get close twice and then move away again. And then someone charges at me. I let out a shriek, slip free of the curtain, and bolt.

Gray's arms wrap around me at once. He throws us both to the ground and growls in my ear. I still, the instinctive nature of prey to freeze when caught by a much larger predator.

"I thought you'd left," He growls and bites at my neck, small teasing scrapes of his teeth. I can feel the length of his cock pressed against my ass. I'm not surprised by how hard he is.

"Gray," I whine.

He pulls me up on my knees and rips my dress down at the front, and then the material is gone. I'm not wearing a bra, just a small, black scrap of lace that the woman who brought my clothes called underwear. Gray plucks at them as if they offend him and then tears them off me.

My knees get weak, and I lean back against him to stay upright. Holy crap, he literally just ripped my clothes off. *Swoon*.

"Like that, did you?" Gray murmurs. "You'll like this better. Dylan. Get down here."

The omega is already naked. His cock sticks out hard in front of him. It's not the first time I've seen him naked, but it's the first time he's been naked with me. I want to taste him. I want to touch him, but he suddenly seems uncertain.

Gray frowns. "All right. Go entertain Silas. Falcon will help me."

"Help you what?" I ask with a bite to my voice. I can't help the sting that Dylan didn't want me.

Gray pinches my nipple in retaliation. At first, there's fiery pain, then the pleasure that seems to be in a direct line with my pussy. My core tightens on nothing. My hips arch, and Gray laughs.

"Oh, you're so responsive. Perfect."

I don't get to say anything else because a very naked Falcon stops right in front of me. His cock is huge. It's got a slight bend and veins that I want to trace. My mouth waters. What would he taste like?

"You don't have to do anything you don't want to," Falcon says.

I peer up at him, confused.

Gray makes an impatient sound. "On your knees, Alpha."

I hiss as Falcon drops to his knees in front of me.

"Take him in your hand. Put him in your mouth. Touch. Explore," Grayson whispers in my ear. "Just make him regret giving you an out."

A thrill burns through me, and I bite my lower lip as Gray's hands travel over my ass.

I reach out and take him by the root. He's softer than I imagined. Velvet over steel. I stroke towards the tip. Falcon exhales roughly. A bead of liquid appears in the slit. I study it and then drop to my hands and knees and put my lips over the tip of his cock.

He grips my hair and lets out a shuddering moan.

"Yes, that's it. Make this alpha your bitch. Show him how powerless he really is," Gray teases, and I get an urge to giggle. Gray presses close, his thighs pushing mine out, and then I feel him. He rubs his cock up and down before he presses inside me.

I gasp, and Falcon surges inside. It's disorientating at first, having them in me, unfamiliar sensations and tastes and feels. Gray bottoms out and then slaps my ass, causing me to gasp. Falcon pulls out with a growl and pushes back in.

Oh.

The taste of him is addictive. I lick the underside and suck before bobbing my head down as far as I can go. I gag slightly and drag myself off him.

"Oh, fuck yes, do that again," Gray murmurs and surges into me. "Suck his cock and teach him who's in charge."

I smile around Falcon's cock and then hollow out my cheeks. Falcon hisses, and I look up at him as best I can. He's watching me with this intent that I want to break. I want him moaning, helpless. I wrap my hand around him and squeeze lightly.

A hand on my head urges me back down, and I do as instructed. This time, I breathe through my nose. My eyes water, and the hand draws back.

"Gray!" Falcon snaps.

"She's good, she loves it." Gray thrusts into me, impaling me on Falcon. I choke and gag and draw back.

Holy shit, I love this.

"So good at this," Falcon murmurs. "Her mouth is perfect, tight and hot. You're perfect, Nyx."

This time, when he presses against my lips, I take him all the way to my throat. He groans, and his fingers clench in my hair, holding me still.

"I want to fuck your face," Falcon says almost incoherently.

"Do it," Gray hisses as he slaps my ass again. I hear him spit, and then a thumb strokes the tight muscle of my ass. There's a moment of fear, but I push it aside. This is about memories, and it feels so good.

Trust.

"Do it." I say to both of them.

Gray growls, and his thumb slips inside. I let out a whimper and open my mouth as Falcon pushes inside me.

I lose track of everything. There are just so many feelings and sensations. Tears run from my eyes as Falcon pumps inside me. His growls and groans have me dripping around Gray. But Gray, damn him, is effectively fucking me in two places, and I can barely think. I need more. I need it harder; I need...something.

"I'm going to cum," Falcon puffs out.

I reach out a hand, gripping his ass as he tries to pull away. He curses and thrusts back into my mouth, stiffening with a shout and pouring himself down my throat. He gasps and leans back, dragging himself from my mouth.

"You're amazing," He pants. "So amazing. Thank you."

"Yeah, she is," Gray growls and then he pulls out, leaving me empty and on the edge. He lays down and crooks a finger. I've seen this a lot at parties. I know what he wants, but I'm nervous. I edge closer to him and then straddle him.

"Just line us up and sink down. Easy, peasy." Gray teases and flicks my nipples with his index fingers.

I bite my lower lip and look around. Dylan is leaning forward on one of the chairs, his cock rock hard, watching intently.

I close my eyes and then reach between us, and I line him up. It takes me a moment, but then, when I sink down, my eyes widen. This position is different again. I let out a strangled sound.

Gray sits up and pulls me close. "Now, fuck me, princess."

The man melts my brain cells. My hips begin to rock as he mouths my breasts, dragging his teeth over my nipples. I slam myself down on him harder and faster, but I can't get what I need. I push at him until he lays back.

"Please?"

He growls and rolls us. His thrusts are wild and out of control. He pulls at my legs until they are up around my shoulders and pounds me until I'm screaming. I detonate around him. My body clenching painfully, gripping his cock, milking him. My toes curl, my fingers clutch at his shoulders, and I scream. He lets out a roar and pulls out, coating me in his release. I lie there, my pussy fluttering, and aftershocks making my limbs shake.

What was that?

Gray looks up at Silas and shakes his head. "You were right. She's life-changing."

I'm too dazed to try to decipher the words. I just lie there, breathing hard, wondering how I'm going to go the rest of my life never feeling that again.

Gray drops on me, snuggling and kissing my neck and cheek, and finally, my lips.

"Thank you, Beta. Nyx."

I look at the happy, satisfied smile on the alpha's face and nod once. "Thank you."

But a frisson of unease slips through me. Of discontent. I flick a glance at the omega and find him already dressed and walking away.

Twenty-One

FALCON

What my plan was, I can't even begin to remember. I watch her movements through the rooms. When she isn't in my sight, she's in my mind. Dylan has become as much a watcher as we are. Lingering with his potent fragrance, driving us wild while we watch her and him watching her.

It wasn't supposed to be this way. I lean back in my computer chair, watching the screen as she goes from person to person, talking for a few moments before moving on. My omega follows her closely.

It wasn't supposed to feel like this.

I turn away, looking away from the room and out at the landscape. Grey clouds are rolling in. The weather is taking a turn for the worse. Silas and Grayson are scrambling with the staff to move the events planned for the next few days inside, and the ones that can't be brought in, to be replaced.

And I'm up here...dealing with this shit.

I turn back to the screen and pick up the phone. "Simon, take them to the Fortress and wait for me there."

I swing my jacket over my shoulders and straighten my shirt. This unpleasantness is best to be done right now, before I lose my mind and do something I regret. I would not be suited for a life behind bars.

I let all thoughts of Dylan and Onyx slip into the back of mind, lest I tarnish them with the foul deeds I have to perform.

I don't pause to ready myself. I march into the room, instantly taking in the seven alphas lounging around the immense conference table. Three of them are so similar in colour of red hair, blue eyes, and too much weight in their mid-section that I can't even distinguish them from the other. The other four are just average alphas, nothing notable about them. I dismiss them from my mind and focus on the woman. She's got steel hair and a pinched nose with heavy blue eyeshadow on. Her dress suit is perfectly tailored for her and screams wealth, as does the thick rope of pearls around her neck and the jewel-encrusted brooch pinned on her chest.

"Ah, the Empress of Hastings." I give her a mock bow and smile through my teeth.

"We're staying, Treyfield, set us up with rooms." Her voice is low and deep and full of command.

I glance at her large entourage and spot the thin woman almost cowering against the wall.

"I believe I told you not to set foot in my sight ever again," I say with deadly warning.

The woman shrinks back. Her thick, dark brown hair is too shiny, her eyes too large. Her dress is as expensive as the suit. I know the omega can't afford it, which means Vienne Hastings organised this. Just like she organised the event that almost cost me my omega.

"Treyfield, I want to speak to my son."

"You'll remove yourself as soon as the weather lets up," I growl. "Simon will show you to your rooms."

Simon, who has been silent and invisible at my side, nods and steps forward. "If you will follow me."

Empress Vienne stands up slowly, her eyes promising that this isn't over. I don't move an inch as she circles the table and comes to stand directly in front of me. This woman barely resembles an omega, but somehow, she rules over her entire pack and the empire her father and grandfather created.

"That omega will never be good enough for my son," She spits.

"That omega is the love of his life and will be his omega. Further, he is too good for your son," I snap back. "Stay out of it, Vienne. I'm not going to warn you again."

"You can't hurt me, Treyfield."

"But I'm not just Treyfield anymore." I breathe. "We now have the weight of Silas's inheritance, the Treyfield empire, and the Waters empire."

Her eye twitches, just a little bit, and I know I have her scared. She won't give up because she's far too smart for that. But she's uncertain she's going to come out on top. I can see it in her eyes.

I smile and watch as those beady eyes narrow. I feel a rise in tension in the air, but I don't even look around. She might have seven alphas, but she's the one who runs things. Just as I run my pack. They will follow her lead.

"You will see your son when I allow and not a moment before. Try to go around me, Hastings, and you will find out just how fierce and instantaneous the wrath of Treyfield really is."

"Really, Treyfield, is there any need to be so vulgar?" She breezes past me. "Take me to my room," She snarls at Simon.

I turn and watch them file out, the younger omega being kept within the tight circle of the older alphas. For a moment, from the back, she looks like Onyx. The thought makes me irritable. The sight of them brings a deep darkness up. I want to grab them by their throats and strangle them all until they are dead. I want to pitch each one of them from the roof.

It's far too much of a coincidence that they are here again, just when things are starting to go well.

I close my eyes and wait until I hear the door click shut. The room stinks of her foul cinnamon scent. I pull out my phone and send a message to Simon to get someone in here to scrub the room clean.

Silas is going to freak out when I tell him his mother is staying in the resort. Grayson is going to level the penthouse, but it's Dylan's reaction that really concerns me. His reaction I fear.

Just trust us, trust me.

She walks into my office and gently shuts the door and leans against it. On any other woman, I might think she was coming in here to seduce me, but Onyx is wearing leggings and one of Dylan's jumpers. Her hair is in a messy bun on her head, and she looks tired but determined. I lean back in my chair and lace my fingers over my waist.

"And here I was thinking you might come to romance me." My teasing brings a hint of pink to her cheeks, but a moment later, she scoffs and walks towards the desk. She leans against the side where Silas fucked her recently. Just the memory of it makes my dick get hard. I lean forward and reach for my mug of coffee. The bitter liquid catches in my throat, causing me to splutter.

"There's something wrong with you." She says in a low voice. "You're not eating. You're hiding away in here."

I lean back in my computer chair, amused, and smile at her. "And how would you know?"

"You take care of this pack, Falcon, but today, you have been hiding." She edges closer. "It's strange."

The door opens again, and Dylan stalks in. He doesn't stop at the desk but continues, leaning over me and kissing me like he's a drowning man. Oh, the taste of him is something I'm never going to get enough of, but I hold myself still, refusing to allow my control to snap. Just a hint of caramel is enough to send me to the edge of a rut, but it's like he rolled in it.

Dylan pulls back, his eyes dark with challenge. I let go a bit and grip his chin, slamming my mouth back against his. I run my hand over the muscles of his back, and then grip his singlet and pull him closer.

"Don't start what you won't let me finish, Omega," I warn.

He stares at me, a dimple popping in his cheek, and then he tilts his head to the side, exposing his neck. Fierce, ravenous hunger erupts in me, but then I catch the hesitation and fear in his scent.

Not yet.

I close my eyes and put my hands back on the arms of my chair, gripping them so tight I think I might break a couple of fingers. "When you can offer me that without fear, I will give you everything I am."

Dylan's eyes widen, and he cautiously extracts himself from my hold. "I offered. If I wasn't sure-"

"Omega, you're afraid, still. It's okay, let us earn your trust. We have time," I soothe.

Dylan jerks back away from us. "Sure. Later."

Onyx looks between us, a small frown between her brows. She tugs at the sleeve of the jumper until her hand is swallowed. Dylan stalks past her, slamming the door shut and making her jump.

I stare at the door with regret.

"You did the right thing," Onyx says in a low voice.

"DId I? I'm not so sure." I rock back on the chair, swinging it so I'm facing her, and then I refocus on the reason she's here. "You're very observant."

"Only with people. I think it's a survival thing. I read moods and pick up habits and tells quickly."

I watch her. "And you're certain there's something wrong with me tonight?"

"Yes."

"And you're in here because..."

She flounders for a minute, her cheeks turning pink. She plucks at her sleeve again. "You helped me, and you care about Dylan. I misjudged you at first." Her blush deepens, and I smile, watching her.

She looks up and smiles back at me, and everything inside me goes still. There's nothing special about her right now, but it's like I'm seeing her for the first time. Wisps of hair float around her face. Her eyelashes sweep down and up, long and as dark as a raven's wing. The light coconut of her scent teases me.

The alpha inside me rises and inhales the scent.

Deep inside my head, I hear my voice growl two words.

She's mine.

I stand up, following my instincts. I grab her wrist and pull her towards me. She stumbles into my chest, peering up and then back down at my shirt.

"Always shirts," she says, and I'm momentarily confused.

"What else would I wear?" I ask in amusement as I brush back those wisps of hair.

Her eyes close, and she leans into my caress. "Something less stiff. Like a tee-shirt or a jumper."

"Ah, but if I did that, the sheer magnetism of my aura would have you on your knees."

She laughs lightly and then wraps her arms around my chest. "You're a much better alpha than I thought you were, Falcon Treyfield. I'm really glad I had time to get to know you."

She lets her arms drop, but I wrap mine around her, holding her, trapping her because I'm not ready to give her up yet.

"There's nothing wrong that I can't take care of," I mumble. "But thank you for checking."

"Okay. So, you're telling me to butt out, right?" She relaxes and curls her arms back around me.

"No, I'm telling you I'll take care of what is bothering me and that you don't need to worry. It's a small matter." I lean forward, pressing my face against her hair and inhaling that coconut scent that is driving me nuts. "Was your mother like you?"

She nods against my chest. "Silver and I look like her. But she was a beta like me. She was so kind, though, and happy. She was always singing, off-key and a beat too slow to the song, and she'd always make up the words, but she was happy, you know. Even though Dad wasn't. She made these little puffs out of pastry and hotdogs. They were so good."

"My mother is a cold and hard woman. But she will fight to the death for you once she decides you're worth it," I say to her and wonder why I'm telling her this.

"Where is she now?"

"On a beach somewhere getting some sun with my father's assistant."

"Your father's not with her?"

"My father died. He was one of the world's biggest assholes. My mother was in love with his assistant. The day he died, they took off on a holiday that hasn't ended. We all knew about it, even my father. He refused to divorce her out of spite because he hated her, but she came from money and standing. But she got the last laugh."

She hums and taps my chest. "How long ago was that?"

"Oh, I don't know, about twelve years ago. I didn't spend much time with them growing up, my father had rigorous ideals for how I should be. Mother could only save me so much."

She pulls back, and I grab the front of her jumper and pull her close.

"Where did you come from?" I ask her. "I don't tell anyone about my family. But somehow you're getting inside my head, little beta."

"I was always there, Alpha Treyfield, in the shadows, serving guests. But I'm glad I'm in your head since you're in mine."

I study her, seeing the tiny scar on her forehead, the crinkles at the side of her eyes. The way her lips are this shade of pink that I didn't even know existed, and those eyes of hers, they sparkle. Her eyes aren't just plain slate; they are gun mental and slate and indigo and cobalt and all the sparkles of life.

"Me, too," I whisper. I frown in consternation and then let her go.

"Come and have dessert with us. Snuggle with your omega. He needs you," She says and takes my wrist in her hand. I feel the contact with my whole body.

"Still trying to fix us up?" I murmur.

"Of course," she laughs softly. "I don't think you'll need me for much longer, though."

"I think you're going to be disappointed when you discover the answer to that, Miss Davies."

She looks at me over her shoulder. "I don't understand."

I shake my head and put a hand on the door before she can open it. I cuddle her from behind, pressing my body up against hers. She's so small and soft, such a contrast to Dylan. My body craves both of them.

"Falcon?"

"Yes?"

"Do you know why Dylan is avoiding me?"

"I have a feeling it's because of us," I explain.

"Oh." She stiffens. "I shouldn't have touched you. I...oh, I didn't think about that."

I laugh softly and breathe into her neck. "I don't think he's worried about you touching us." My hands trail over her hips, drawing lazy circles. "I think it's more a case of he doesn't like us touching you, but he doesn't know what to do about it."

She goes completely still. "I don't think-"

"He wants you so much his instincts are driving him to want to challenge his alphas for you. You have magic, Onyx Davies. In your skin, in your voice, in your soul. You have captivated and entranced us all. You have made our omega angry. That is a gift."

Her eyes are wide when she twists to look up at me. "That can't be right..."

I lean down and kiss her forehead. "Watch for a while then, little observer, you will see that I'm always right."

Twenty-Two

ONYX

No matter what way I look at my behaviour over the last couple of days, I can't see a way to make up to Dylan what I have done. I pace the foyer of the hotel and chew on my lip as I blindly go over and over it all. Where did I go wrong? Was Falcon right?

I turn on my heel and spot Silver coming out behind me, out of a lift that is just sliding its doors shut. There's nowhere for me to go, the huge windows and glass doors have my body in silhouette of sunlight. I could go outside the hotel, but she wouldn't hesitate to punish me for it. Resignation hits hard.

Silver's face is scrunched up, and she's almost shooting daggers at me. My face drains of blood, and I look away. I forgot about Silver. Wow. That's new. Another person I've let down. And I have nowhere to run.

She flips her hair and yanks on the thick checkered jacket as she stalks over to me. It's early. There's no one else here. She still looks around, just to make sure there's no one who will spot her. Only then does she reach out, her fingers biting into my upper arm and drags me to the side of the room.

"Why haven't you helped me meet them yet? I need time alone with them to win them over." Her whine is bordering on a hiss of rage.

"I'm not going to do it, Silver." I tug my arm free, wincing at the scrape of her nails.

"Then you doom us both," Silver snaps. "You selfish bitch. After all I've been through, all the suffering alone and holed up, protecting you, staying with you so you weren't alone. Dad suffering…"

She trails off, but I'm already back in that space, reliving those horrible days. Guilt crashes through me. The fire, the hunger, the debts, all those pages and pages of bills, and losing the house, our home, our belongings, and then learning to live in this terrifying reality. I relive it all in seconds.

"Let me help you find a different pack," I say earnestly and reach out for her hand.

"You really aren't going to do this for me, are you?" Silver's shocked. She backs away from me. "I can't believe this."

I stare at her. My lips are pressed into a thin line to stop any words from escaping. Her brows lower, and she snatches her hand back.

"Fine. I can't believe it, but fine. I'll set my sights on another pack."

I watch her cautiously. "Silver, I'm sorry-"

She holds her hand up and slashes it through the air between us. Her shirt swishes as she moves, the blue brings out her eyes and makes her look younger than she is. "I don't want to hear it. I see how it is. Your true colours come out when you get a bit of attention." The jab is cruel and untrue.

She's behaving like a kid. Has she always been like this? Have I always given in?

"No, that's not it! Silver!" I try to reach for her, but she throws her hands dramatically in the air.

My exasperation has me folding my arms and shaking my head.

I keep trying to call her, but she stalks away from me. At the door, her body language turns lighter and happier, and she laughs as she pushes the door open.

I glance at the desk and find a girl standing over it, staring with her mouth hanging open. She blinks a few times and shakes her head. "Fucking crazy omegas."

I turn away so I can pretend I didn't hear the betas whisper. She's not wrong. My sister seems fucking crazy. She's worse here.

I think.

With a sigh, I push open the doors and walk outside. I'm supposed to be meeting Dylan here, but I suddenly wish I wasn't. The weather has paused in its continuous drizzling, but it looks like it's about to open up again any minute now.

I lean against the wall and close my eyes. Last night with Falcon, I thought my heart was going to explode out of my chest. This game I'm playing with this pack is going to destroy me. Their touch is addictive, the sex and kisses are, too, but it's the hugs and the hand-holding. The sweet moments that are melting my defenses like an ice cube left in the sun.

They are inside me. A future unfurls like a vision before my eyes. I can see us now. A fantasy life that I can't have. And just imagining going back to my life without them is devastating. The sheer emptiness of my world without them in it...how can I go back to that now? I know what it's like to be with them. But I know what it's like to be without them.

How can I give it up?

Dylan appears on the path, walking towards me. His black jeans hug him like a second skin. The purple shirt and black vest are startling, but it looks right on him. I push off the wall as he gets close. He scrapes his hand through his short hair and looks away from me.

"Did you sleep well?" His growly voice vibrates through me, and I almost close my eyes in the pleasure of just hearing him speak.

"I did." I clear my throat, feeling a strange heat inside my limbs. "You?"

"Yeah, it was all right."

I meet his eyes and get the crashing image of falling deeply into stars. He leans in, but the doors to the resort bang open. The group of alphas and a red-haired omega stop and regard us. The omega laughs and walks the other way, whispering.

Dylan growls and grips my wrist and tugs me after him. I have to jog to keep up. My nerves are firing like lightning's being conducted along them, butterflies and smiles. Trembling fingers and short puffy breaths. Nerves and excitement.

Dylan stops at a building and pulls out a set of keys. It takes him a moment to unlock the door, but then he's ushering me inside and closing it behind us. The inside is clean, but the walls are painted with a rain forest mural. There's a door on the other side of the room that's blacked out and a desk that's unmanned.

"What's going on?" I ask warily.

I barely get the words out when he backs me up against the wall. His hands find my hips, gripping hard enough to bruise. I let out a moan, my head tilting back. Dylan leans forward and kisses me. He nips at my bottom lip until I open for him, tangling our tongues together.

He's my addiction. My weakness. I'd do anything for another kiss, another moment, another touch. I'd kill just to see another smile.

The world turns too fast, gravity flips, I see stars; he crawls inside my soul. All of my world changes as he breaks the kiss, leaving me panting, my knees weak, pressing against the wall to hold me up.

His smile is slow but satisfied. "Good morning."

I bite my lower lip and close my eyes. "That's the best morning." I say to myself but hear him chuckle. "So, you're not mad at me anymore?"

"I wasn't mad at you," Dylan growls and leans closer, sniffing at my neck. He lets out a sound that's like a chuff. Whatever it is, it makes my stomach clench. I tilt my head to the side, giving him room. "I was mad at Falcon."

"You're working it out with them, though, aren't you? They love you." I say the last three words in a hushed whisper.

"Love isn't trust," Dylan murmurs and licks the spot. I shudder and lift my hands to cling to his shoulders. If I don't, I know I'm going to embarrass myself and fall. He sucks at the spot, licking and teasing, dragging his teeth over it. "I trust you."

"But why?" I plead with a groan as his teeth drag over my shoulder.

"When have you given me a reason not to? You're honest." He kisses my shoulder. "Kind." He grabs the strap of my dress and peels it down. I don't know why Dylan insists on me wearing the dresses and nice clothes, but I don't feel at all like an employee, and losing the battle of the clothes was the least of my concerns. I know what I am, don't I? "Smart. Sexy."

I'm leaning heavily on the wall, my chest rising and falling. Trying not to melt as Dylan kisses his way across my chest. I reach up and cup the back of his neck.

"Dylan? Are you sure?"

"More sure than anything."

He pulls my dress down, and because I'm not wearing a bra, my breasts spill free.

"Damn, Nyx," Dylan whispers and reaches up, cradling me.

My flesh aches, my nipples harden, and an answering throb in my pussy makes me moan. I run my fingers through his hair as he ducks down, sucking at my breast, leaving marks on my skin, then seizing my nipples in his teeth and tugging.

I push myself up, thrusting my tit into his mouth, keening for more. Instead of finger combing my hair, I'm holding him locked to me as he suckles. With each tug, I'm lost in the wave of ecstasy.

"Dylan, please."

He switches to my other breast. I pant and hold on to his shoulders. He growls and peels my dress down even more, running his fingers over my skin, exploring every inch of me. His mouth follows his fingers, exploring with his tongue and the gentle scrape of teeth. My skin breaks out into goosebumps as he drops to his knees in front of me.

"You're so beautiful," Dylan whispers.

My eyes open, and I look down and disagree with him. "You are."

He smiles and presses a kiss to my thigh. "You smell like coconut. That's your scent. It drives me wild."

"You smell like lemons." I blush. I don't know why. "Dylan, you're everything, you know that, right?"

His eyes gleam molten gold. Black and gold, I fall into it again.

He kisses my hip bone and reaches around me, running his hands up my thighs. I lift off the wall and quiver as his fingers trace the contours of my ass.

"Dylan, I need to touch you. See you."

He steps back and stands up, reaching for his top. I cover his fingers with mine and pull his shirt over his head. My thoughts scatter as I press close to him, his hot skin brushing my nipples and sending bolts of pleasure into my body. I fling the top away from us and reach down for his pants.

I hesitate on his buckle, but now he covers my fingers with his, flipping open the button and dragging the zip down. I watch our hands with a dry mouth. My heart is thundering in my chest, but my mind is just whispering one thing: Is this real?

His cock sticks out, bouncing against my stomach. It's hard and long and leaking. I reach out, touching him. His skin is so soft and warm, and he jerks when my fingers trail lightly over the slit, dancing through his slick.

"Taste me," Dylan whispers.

Somehow, we're back against the wall. His arm is leaning over my head, keeping him against me but holding his weight off me. I encircle his cock and tug twice; slick spreads down my hand, down his cock.

A groan slips from me as he pants into my face, his eyes locked on me.

I drag my hand up between us and, with my gaze on his, I lick my palm. The sweet caramel taste of him is both surprising and not. My eyes drift closed as I moan.

His breathing turns ragged, and he moves into me, pressing his hips against me.

"I need you," Dylan whispers. "Please, I need you. Don't deny me, Nyx."

"I would never deny you, Dylan. You have me, I'm yours," I whisper against his lips, and then I kiss him. My tongue pushes into his mouth, and he groans. I know he can taste himself on me.

He lifts me up, pressing us against the wall. I wrap my legs around him as he reaches between us and presses himself into me.

I gasp as I sink down onto him. It's slow and controlled, but he's longer than the alphas, and he reaches deeper. As soon as he bottoms out, he stops moving.

For a couple of minutes, we just exist, fused together. Neither of us speaks, nor do we attempt to move. This is more than sex.

I feel like he's touching my soul.

"Dylan, please," I beg, at last, my body betraying me.

He grunts and moves slowly out. I almost whimper at the loss, but then he thrusts back in. I mouth at his shoulders and run my fingers over his short hair.

"Onyx," Dylan growls.

"Yes, do it."

He thrusts up, picking up the pace. I gasp and bounce against the wall. He is relentless, thrusting in over and over. And then he moves us both off the wall and pulls out of me. He kneels down, dragging me to the floor. I lay on my back and open my arms as he nuzzles my neck and face.

He slips back inside me. I'm so wet, and his slick has filled my channel, making his entry effortless.

I can feel his slick pumping into me, seeping out and running down my inner thighs and ass. The squelching sound is deliciously erotic. I clutch at shoulders, dragging him down to me. His pupils are blown, but he keeps them focused on me, not daring to look away.

He dips down, seizing my mouth, and grinds his hips into mine.

"Dylan," I whisper when he pulls away. "Dylan."

"Onyx, I-" He cuts off and drives into me, his hips pistoning faster and harder. "I need you to come. I need to feel you. Please, come for me," He whispers in my ear.

I reach down between us and find my clit, stroking it. I lift one of my thighs, throwing it over his ass.

"I can't hold back. I can't," Dylan grits out.

His teeth bury themself in my shoulder, and he thrusts wildly into me. My hand is trapped, but I can just move my fingers. Just enough. My orgasm screams through me, wrecking havoc. I tighten on him and hear him curse around a mouthful of my flesh. His thrusts turn feral. I hang on, clinging to him, and he sends me straight into another orgasm. The scream tears from my throat.

"Fuck!" He shouts and thrusts up into me, harder than before, and freezes there. He drowns me in his slick and cum. There is so much heating my insides, leaking out. I groan at the feel. It's so deliciously wrong.

"More," Dylan growls.

I laugh softly. But to my surprise, he moves again. He's still hard.

My eyes widen, and I look up at Dylan in shock. He grins down at me savagely.

"Come for me again, Onyx," He purrs.

He slams into me. My eyes roll, and I groan out my reply as I lift my hips to meet his.

I pull my dress back up and turn to find him staring at me. I cup his cheek, gazing into those gold eyes I love so much. This isn't awkward. It might have been, but not between us. Instead, I move closer to him, needing to be near.

"Thank you," My whisper breaks the silence between us.

He inhales on a shudder and nods once. "I have something to show you."

When he holds out his hand, there's no hesitation. I'm reeling. I'm not sure I'm even awake yet. But I follow the omega through several doors into a huge domed greenhouse.

But it's all the birds that take my breath away.

"What is this place?" I ask as I turn in a circle.

All around me are parrots and birds I've never seen in the city parks. The reds and blues are striking, the greens are entrancing. All the patterns and colours, dipping and diving, effortlessly in the air above us.

"When they bought the resort, I said to them I wanted a tropical paradise that doesn't hurt." Dylan says calmly. He stands on the bench and spreads his arms. "It should have been impossible, I said it as a joke. They built this for me. A paradise. A place where the birds here are rescues that have been saved. The water is rainwater, the plants are all especially chosen and relocated from places that were being torn down." He pauses. "Falcon organised this for me, Silas went to all the rescues and handpicked the birds, took them to vets. Grayson designed the garden. This was their courting gift. I found it yesterday. I figured they wouldn't complete it because I left. Silas held me right here while I tried to absorb it all. I wanted to show you."

"That's why you offered Falcon your bond?"

"He didn't want it," Dylan says bitterly. "He didn't want me."

"He wanted you. He just didn't want you to be afraid." I reach out and touch his shoulder. "If you hadn't been afraid, he would have done it in a heartbeat."

Dylan scowls. "Perhaps."

"Trust me, that alpha belongs to you."

He closes his eyes and tilts his head back. A moment later, a bird swoops down and lands on his arms. The thing is huge, with cyan blue feathers and a beak that looks like it could take my face off. This omega is a miracle, how he appeared in my life, how he's stayed, everything since and now, standing like some kind of mythical man with this giant bird on his arms.

It's joined by smaller rainbow birds and a couple of green ones.

I don't dare close my eyes, for fear I might miss something.

He laughs and smiles as he opens his eyes to focus on the birds, talking to them calmly.

I watch him from near the ferns. A bird drops, landing on my head, and I stand still, amazed by how light it is. It explores my hair and then lifts into the air, letting out a shriek and being joined by seven others.

I turn as a red bird flies past me with huge wings, turning so effortlessly it steals my ability to think. When I spin back to Dylan, he's staring at me. Everything inside me goes still. A part of me breaks and is remade, and the knowledge of that is both incredible and devastating.

My heart swells, my mind fills with happiness. Fear fades away. There is only awe and this newness that suddenly makes sense.

He is...my everything.

"I love you," I say to him. It's simple and honest and it's not shouted or loud. I just say it, and I mean it more than I've meant anything.

His eyes widen, and he drops his arms. The birds protest as they launch into the sky, but it doesn't matter. My words have broken us both. And set me free.

I wipe my face and laugh. "This is insane. It's so crazy. But I love you."

He seizes me by the waist, pulling me up against him, and wraps his arms around my back. "My Nyx," Dylan purrs and buries his face in my neck. Then he laughs, and through the laugh, a deep vibration starts in his chest.

I lean into it, pressing my cheek to his chest. We stand there forever and not long enough. Me and the omega in the paradise his alphas courted him with.

Twenty-Three
ONYX

I duck back behind the plant as I see Falcon come out of a room and close his eyes. He looks tired. I almost make myself known, but then another woman comes out of the room. She's young and beautiful, clearly an omega. He shakes his head and throws her hand off his arm.

"Go home, Leisel. This is your last chance," He warns.

She wrings her fingers. "I can't. I have no choice. I didn't mean to. She told me you wanted me. I'm sorry. But I can't leave until she lets me."

He stalks towards me, and I don't have time to move; he slows when he sees me. I can see the rapid calculation in his eyes as he looks back to the woman retreating.

"Was that the woman-"

"From the camera, yes," Falcon snarls and lets out a frustrated sound. "I know you're working right now, but I need you for something else."

"Of course, Alpha."

He winces. "Don't call me that."

I duck my head at his growly tone. "Okay."

He reaches out, barely touching my wrist, before he moves his hand. He chews on his words for a long moment and then sighs.

"Come with me."

I follow obediently as he leads me to the lift. He doesn't press the penthouse, but the button above it. I've often wondered what the button was for, but I don't dare ask Falcon now. I'm not scared of him, per say, but I'm wary, I tell myself. To be honest, most of me wants to take him back to the penthouse, take off his shoes, put a hot mug of chocolate in his hands, and dim the lights. This sick urge to comfort the terrifying alpha is obviously some kind of infatuation that has taken over my normally logical mind.

It is not my place to offer him comfort.

THE BETA'S BARGAIN

The lift stops, and the doors slide open. My eyes widen as we step out into a glass house. I turn in awe, watching the crazy weather attack the sturdy building. It's a viewing deck.

Falcon walks to the bar and leans against it.

Inside the glass house is a bar with twelve chairs that go around three sides of the interior. A door at the opposite end opens onto the roof. And a table and chairs with a candle that's got almost no wax left sits in the middle. I peer up, you'd be able to see the stars from here.

I walk to my boss's side and stand beside him. He stays still and then relaxes bit by bit.

"How do you do that?"

I tilt my head to the side. "Do what?"

"Calm me."

I shrug. "I don't know."

He moves quickly, picking me up and putting me on the bar before stepping in-between my legs.

"How are you going with your end of the bargain?"

My throat gets thick. "Good. He's happier, smiling, and he is more receptive to you."

He leans closer and rests his forehead against my chest. I wonder if he can hear the way my heart is pounding.

I suddenly need to know what's going to happen after? How will it happen? Where will I go? Have they decided where they'll send me? Can I say goodbye to Silver?

I push all those questions aside and throw my arms around this alpha who has far too much responsibility on him. I stroke his back and hold him until my ass goes numb.

When he eventually stands up, he reaches for my chin and touches his lips to mine. "Thank you."

"Uh, Falcon?"

He smiles slightly. "Yes, Onyx?"

"You won't hurt him again, will you?"

His smile dims, but then it gets brighter. "No, I'd rather hurt myself."

I nod and wiggle towards the edge, but he grips my waist and lifts me off the bar. I follow him back to the lift and down to the penthouse. He leaves me in the lounge room and disappears back into his office. There's something so heavy about the set of his shoulders. It breaks my heart.

I purse my lips and then decide to do it, anyway. Opening cabinets and searching drawers, I hunt around in their kitchen and then start cooking. It takes an hour, but I finally bring a steaming hot brownie and a cup of chocolate into his office.

He looks up and frowns, but when the smell hits him, his lips part, and his eyes widen slightly.

"Here. If you aren't going to sit and relax. At least do something nice for yourself." I put the brownie down and the mug beside it and step back, but he grabs me before I can go anywhere.

"You didn't have to do this."

"I know I didn't." Fuck, I can't meet his eyes. I bite my lower lip. "I wanted to."

I pull my arm free and walk back out to the lounge. None of the others are back yet, and I feel aimless. I clean the dishes and put them away and wipe down all the surfaces. There's a slice for each member of the pack.

But I keep finding myself standing in the hallway, watching his door. I take a step towards it, turn around, force myself to do something else, and then end up back there again. In desperation, I go to my room and lie down on the bed.

My mind races, replaying everything that's happened. Every touch, every lingering look. I lie there with my chest heaving and an ache inside me. It's hopeless. So hopeless.

I reach down and inch up my skirt. My cheeks burn, but when I slide two fingers between my folds, I'm soaking. As soon as I brush my fingers over my clit, my entire body tenses as my nerves fire. I spread my legs wider and slide a finger into myself. And then another. I imitate the way they touched me and replay it in my mind.

My door opens, and I freeze. No way!

Falcon stares at my hand between my legs. For three seconds, all he does is stare, and then he comes inside, pushing the door shut.

"Continue." When I don't move, he repeats his demand.

I let out a frustrated groan and keep going, but now my eyes are locked on him. The way his scent is filling the air and the almost inaudible growl he releases sends my hips bucking off the bed.

He moves closer, and his pupils get even bigger. He puts his hands on my knees and spreads my legs even more, and then he leans down and inhales.

I grit my teeth together as I grow even wetter. I need more. This isn't enough. He growls low in his throat and watches as I plunge three fingers into myself.

"Please," I beg.

"What do you need?"

"Something, please. More. You, please, I need you, Alpha." I let out a thin whine and tilt my hips up, shoving my fingers to the knuckle.

"Ah, your pretty little cunt needs more than you can give? Greedy little thing." He whispers and kneels on the bed.

My heart thuds, and I watch him through slitted eyes.

"What were you thinking about to get you so wet?"

My cheeks burn. "Silas and Dylan fucking me. Grayson fucking me. You kissing me like how you did before."

His eyes find mine, and he gently removes my hand and runs his fingers languidly up my pussy. I shudder when the tips of his fingers graze my clit.

"Falcon?" I plead in a broken whisper.

He doesn't answer, and when I open my eyes; I find him staring at me with a blistering gaze that makes my stomach clench.

"You are so lovely."

My bedroom door opens, and Grayson walks in. He pauses on the threshold and then closes the door behind him; it opens immediately, and Silas and Dylan almost crash into him.

"What the fuck, Gray?" Dylan growls. "What are you doing in here?" Dylan stops, inhaling the air, and goes still.

"So this is why you disappeared. I approve," Gray murmurs. "Omega, clothes off."

Dylan bares his teeth, but he does slowly take his clothes off, throwing them across the room. Silas grabs him by the throat the second he's naked and slams him against the wall. Their mouths collide.

My core clenches around Falcon's fingers, and I grow even wetter. He drags his fingers out and plunges them back in. Grayson growls, his head whipping between me and Dylan.

"On your knees for me," Silas purrs.

Dylan drops to his knees. I let out a whimper, but now my view is blocked. Falcon pulls his fingers out, and I move to sit up, but the alpha pins me with a glare. He and Grayson steal my attention, moving in closer to me.

"Put your fingers in that pretty pussy, love," Grayson purrs. "Show us how wet you are. Let me see you."

I whine and try to close my legs, but Falcon slaps the inside of my thigh, and I fling them back open with a yelp, exposing myself to their heated stares. I obediently do as Grayson tells me, holding up two soaked fingers that he sucks into his mouth. My body heats, and I writhe on the bed.

"Gray," Falcon growls and shoves two fingers in, plunging in and out three times until I'm panting and breathless, "get down there and make your mouth useful."

"Yes, sir." Grayson pulls his tie off and then unbuttons his shirt. He kneels on the bed and reaches up, grabbing a pillow.

"Scooch up," Gray murmurs and winks at me.

I scramble up the bed, feeling Falcon's fingers leave my body. I want them back, but when I peek at him, I don't dare say anything.

Gray nudges my hips, and I lift while he shoves a pillow under me. My clothes are ripped off me by the two alphas, and within moments, I'm as naked as they are.

He lies on his stomach between my legs and laughs lightly. "Hold on, love."

"What?" I ask absently, rolling my head from Falcon's scorching stare into Gray's.

His mouth descends in a furious, searing heat. If there's a pattern to his madness, I can't find it. I squirm and arch my back as the pleasure intensifies. He is remorseless, holding my thighs wide apart with his shoulders, lifting my ass so he can get his tongue inside me. I clutch at his hair, moaning as he grabs my clit with his mouth and sucks. I scream and beg, I'm wordless and blind. All that exists is his mouth licking me into my next life.

My hips roll towards him of their own accord, picking up the pace. His teeth graze over my clit, and I gasp, hanging onto the very edge of the cliff.

Silas growls, and the sound of him thrusting into Dylan's mouth makes me groan. I thrash my head from side to side, I'm so close. I reach up with one hand and squeeze my breast, then tug mercilessly at my nipple, the pain sending pleasure tingles straight to my core.

He growls and slurps up, pressing his tongue hard over my clit and sucking it into his mouth. The sultry heat, the tingling pressure, spirals upwards and explodes out.

I scream, pulling his hair, holding him to me as my hips jolt into him. My back arches, my toes curl, and then it eases, and I come down, floating on cloud nine.

"Holy shit, make her do that again," Silas growls. The bed thumps, and I turn my head and find Dylan laying on his stomach, ass in the air, watching me as Silas presses into him from behind.

I whimper. Dylan's mouth opens wide, and his groan sends flickers of heat through my body. Again. Already.

Grayson continues to lick me with slow, languid laps, holding my shuddering body close to him. I go past the painful pleasure and back into that aching, empty need again. My hips roll against his face.

I'm covered in sweat, feeling more alive than I ever have when he gets up and pulls away. He kneels on the bed, and I peer at him stroking his gigantic cock, the thick knot at the base makes my stomach jolt. It's the first time I've seen one appear. I glance at Dylan, his presence must trigger it.

"My turn," Falcon growls. He's wider than Grayson with a knot that looks huge. I'd never be able to take it. But the desire to try teases me, briefly, before I push it away.

Falcon crawls over me. He freezes above me. For a long moment, we stare at each other. I wonder what he sees in me. I see the tired man. I see the kind and caring protector. I see a man who wants me.

"You can't move your arms," Falcon whispers. "Keep them above your head. Can you do that?"

He settles back on his legs and gently guides my hands together over my head. He closes a hand over them and squeezes.

"Stay right there."

I inhale sharply and nod. I glance to the right where I can just make out Silas and Dylan staring with burning gazes. Their fucking has changed to slow love-making. The erotic way Silas pulls and holds Dylan melts me.

Falcon pulls the pillow out and throws it to Grayson, who puts it to his face and inhales. My cheeks flame even as my hips tilt. More, begging silently for more. But then a scrap of material covers my eyes. Nerves flutter to life inside me.

"Trust me," Falcon whispers.

I leave my hands where he told me to and try to forget that I can't see anything.

Falcon lowers himself to me and rubs his huge cock between my folds, soaking himself. I groan at the feel of him. Yes, this is what I need.

"You're going to keep your arms right there, or I'm going to get something to hold them there," He growls.

Falcon thrusts over and over, gently dragging his cock over my clit, dragging my juices all over both of us. Each pass brings me closer and closer to begging, but I keep my hands where he instructed. And then his mouth finds my neck. He sucks hard. I cry out, arching, and he slips inside me. Just the tip.

He lifts himself up off me, and then his hands land on my breasts, massaging a warm liquid into me.

"Gray?" Falcon growls.

I pant, but then I notice my breasts are getting hot, almost a burning heat. Falcon pulls at my nipples, rolling them softly. I cry out, arching up into his hands.

"Feel good? You should see yourself offering your tits for us to feast on," Falcon growls. "Our sexy little beta."

Something cold and wet drips onto my stomach. I hiss, and then it presses against my jaw. It trails down my neck and encircles my breast, spiraling in towards my nipples. I cry out. The heat that's been burning me turns to an icy pain.

Falcon growls and shifts his hips, entering me a bit more. I shift my hips, trying to get him deeper.

"Please?"

"Fuck, you drive me insane, Nyx," Falcon groans. He leans over me, his voice loud in my ear. "Beautiful girl. Do you want me to fuck you now?"

"Yes, Falcon, yes." I scream and shatter around just the tip of him. He grunts and goes rigid, holding himself perfectly still.

I think it startles him as much as me. He reaches out and tears the blindfold off my face. Our eyes meet, and I see his control is ragged, shredded. He lets out an inaudible sound that makes me tighten around him. He surges in, bottoming out in one quick move.

I cry out. This is what I needed. This feeling of fullness. No, I just needed him, Falcon.

I wrap my thighs around him and hold on as he thrusts into me. Each drag of his cock in and out of me sets my nerves jangling in so much pleasure that I forget the others. That I forget everything.

The powerful way he slams into me, drives us up the bed, but I keep my hands where they are. His arms engulf me, giving me no space, no room. All there is is him.

"Fuck!" He roars. He grips my ass and changes the angle, and he hits something inside me. A spot that instantly dials up everything. I pant and let out a low keening sound.

Falcon thrusts harder, slamming into me, hitting that spot over and over. His knot hits me hard, sending delicious bursts of pleasure. I groan and part my legs wider. I seize his neck and suck hard, raking my teeth over his salty skin. He tastes like menthol and Falcon.

I tighten my fingers around each other, desperate to touch, to move, but loving the fact I can't. His hand slams on top of mine, and our fingers lace together like he knew temptation was trying to break me.

He growls into my mouth, and his thrusts grow choppy. Our teeth clash together in a heated kiss. He tears his mouth away and ducks down, sucking my nipple into his hot mouth. I cry out, teeter on the edge, and then free fall into an implosion. I cling to him as my body tightens. A shrill scream escapes me as liquid gushes out of me.

Falcon snarls and slams into me over and over. He gets up on his knees, grabbing my hips, and hammers into me, and then he thrusts once more, a vicious movement that gets him even deeper, and he stills. His cock pulses inside me, and I feel his hot release.

"Oh, god, oh, god, Nyx. Fuck!" He roars, his face scrunched up in ecstasy.

I look up at him, my mind still reeling. His eyes are closed, and his teeth gritted. His knot is inside me. He fucking knotted me. The thought blows my freaking mind. He grits his teeth and looks at me.

"Are you all right?" He takes a moment to get the words out. His tendons are standing rigid in his neck.

I nod my head, and when he twitches, I clench. His hiss is instant, his head goes back, and he moans. Slow curls of heat push the panic away. The harder I try to remain still and be unaffected, the faster I lose the battle. I pant, my hips rising and falling in tiny thrusts that make him growl. His eyes gleam as he studies me.

"Bad girl," Falcon purrs.

I smirk at him.

Dylan, Silas, and Gray are watching intently. I can feel them, but I don't dare look away from the alpha who's knotted me.

Falcon smiles. "One more time, huh?"

My eyes widen.

He reaches between us and brushes his fingertip over my clit. That's all it takes. My body implodes again. I scream. I hear it from a long way away. My body is a conductor of a wave of pleasure so strong that it can't be denied. Distantly, I hear Falcon roar, and then there's darkness.

I wake up in Falcon's arms. We're still locked together, but I'm laying on him now. Cradled in his arms like a lover.

"You're...something else, Onyx Davies." Falcon whispers tenderly. "Are you hurt?"

I smile, shake my head, and kiss his chest. I turn to the left and find Dylan curled up in Grayson's arms beside me. Gray winks, and for once, I don't blush. Silas strokes my back in long, comforting touches. He's lying on his back on my other side, staring at the roof with a half smile.

My happiness fades, and I close my eyes as I realise the huge...critical error I've just made. This feels right. The five of us together like this.

This is my dream. The one I'm not allowed to have. In the darkest moments, when I don't have the strength to remember reality, I dream of this. With that clarity comes a deep fear and then a resolve.

I'm going to enjoy it while I can. For a little while, I can pretend I can be more, have more, and then I'll take the job on the other side of the world and go back to where I belong. I shift in Falcon's arms, getting comfortable.

I reach out and wrap my fingers around Dylan's hands. He smiles in his sleep.

But I don't have to go just yet.

Twenty-Four

ONYX

I need distance.

Those three words go around and around in my head as I scurry through the hotel, finding my way to the dining room. I'm not too proud to admit that I'm running. But this...it's all too much and too big for someone like me.

I exhale and enter the room. The lights are bright and only a half a dozen tables have people sitting at them. Everyone seems subdued and relaxed. I spot Simon and sneak up until I stand right beside him.

He glances from his tablet down at me and raises his eyebrows. "Miss Davies."

"I need to clean something. An oven or a pool. Perhaps some windows. Got a carpet that needs to be beat?"

Simon frowns slightly. "Alpha Treyfield, Hastings, and Waters would be irate if I made you clean-"

"I'm asking. Like, as a favour. One normal working person to another. Give me some manual labour. I've searched the hotel high and low, and everything is disgustingly clean."

He presses his lips together, and I get the distinct impression he's laughing at me. But he's far too professional to let me see.

"Follow me."

I let out the breath I've been holding. "Thank you."

He shakes his head and mutters something we both pretend not to hear.

"How long have you worked for Falcon?"

"I've worked for Alpha Treyfield for five years. But I worked for the Hastings Hotels from the time I was seventeen."

"Wow. So you know it all, then?"

"I have a good understanding of how the hotel works."

"They are...stunning. When I worked at the Lillith and the Evelyn hotels, I really saw how impressive the Hasting Hotels really are. But Ingrid was legendary, she's my favourite of the hotels, with those painted walls and such classy charm."

"I noted in your file that you worked for us. How did you find it?"

"It was good money. Long hours. We didn't get breaks, but we were temps."

Simon grunts. "I'll have a word with them. Temps are supposed to get breaks."

I shrug. "Work is work."

Simon's mouth parts, and I think it's his surprised face. He pushes a door open, and I find myself in a dark storage room. It's huge, but when he flips the light, it's got white floors, it's clean, and there are dozens of metal shelves full of boxes and different equipment. It's the nicest storage room I've ever been in.

"Right, I need you to find all these crates. Confirm what's in the boxes and mark next to the tablet."

The crates are right near the door. There are easily a dozen or more of them. They range in sizes, but most of them are big enough that I'd struggle to pick them up.

"Sounds easy," I say with a shoulder shrug. Now, this is my element. This is where I feel good.

"It is. You just need to ensure that you get the numbers correct."

I open one box and look inside to find bottles of wine. Familiar, menial tasks that I've performed before.

"When you've marked the box off, put them on the racks." Simon jerks his chin in that direction.

"This seems too bright for a wine cellar."

"It's our temporary one." Simon says. "The other broke down yesterday."

"Ah, I see." I don't see, but I'm too busy looking around curiously.

He narrows his eyes. "If they ask where you are, I'm going to tell them."

"I'd expect nothing less, sir." I smile at him and lean into the crate.

"You can't hide from them forever, Miss Davies. Alphas are...well, they won't let you run for long."

I wince and don't say anything, but as he leaves, my estimation of him goes up a bit. I think underneath all that pomp and circumstance, Simon might be an interesting man.

Loyal, too.

I check the stock and put it away until midday. Only then does the door open up and slam into the wall, causing me to jump. I turn my head and find Grayson and Dylan scowling at me.

"What are you doing?"

"Stock take," I mutter and keep working.

Gray growls and struts into the room. He takes the tablet out of my hand, despite my protest, and tips my chin up.

"Beautiful girl. What are you doing?" He asks the question, but this time, layers it with meaning I can't hide from.

I sigh and try to look away, but he ducks his head, following me.

"Have we done something?"

I jerk my head, almost head-butting him. "No, of course not."

Dylan moves in my peripheral.

"No one did anything wrong." I snap at them both and yank my chin out of Gray's grip. He drops his arms and stares at me.

"Well, something's clearly wrong."

I bare my teeth at the wine bottles in my hands and put them onto the rack. Gray grabs my hands from behind me and holds me still.

"Talk to us," he whispers.

I close my eyes as his hot breath wafts across my neck. "I...this just..." Why can't I enjoy something? Just for a little while. Doesn't everyone say it's better to have loved and lost than never to have loved at all? I can control this. I can hide how I feel. I've been doing it for my whole life.

I just...want more time.

My hands go lax, my body refusing to resist when Grayson turns me in his arms.

"Hey, hey. What's this?" He sweeps his thumbs across my cheeks, swiping away my tears. "Did we hurt you? Scare you?"

I shake my head and laugh. My hands reach up and cover his. "It's okay, I'm okay. I just needed to have a moment."

"Oh, okay." It's clear that Grayson doesn't understand my need for space, but he smiles. "Have you finished your moment?"

I laugh again. "I need to finish these bottles."

Dylan elbows past Grayson and peers into the boxes. "What are we doing?"

"Checking them off against this list and putting them on the racks."

Dylan starts helping, and then I notice Grayson opening another box. I move to help him and show him quickly what to do. By the time he's settled, Dylan has finished with his box.

"So, this is...what is this?" Grayson asks when we get halfway through his box.

"Hard labour," Dylan says with a smirk.

"It's just a task to do mindlessly to let my brain think," I explain.

"Oh." Gray scowls. It's cute and almost petulant. "What did you need to think about? Us?"

"Kind of, yeah," I say bluntly.

Grayson is obviously not expecting that answer. His fingers fumble, and he almost drops one of the bottles.

And now I have to elaborate. "I was thinking that you four are perfect together. Seamless. I don't understand why you're all fighting it. To have a pack, a family...there are so many people who don't get those options. They don't get happy endings. You should fight for your happiness."

They are both frozen, staring at me. I'm lecturing them, berating them. Argh, what is wrong with me?

Gray glances at Dylan. He clears his throat and edges closer to me.

"We're not taking this second chance for granted," Dylan says softly.

My cheeks burn, and I turn away from him and start on the next box. "I'm glad. It will be good for you four to be together."

Dylan grips my shoulders and stops my movements. "Would you-"

I tense, terrified of what he goes to ask.

"Dylan!"

We both turn around to find Silas in the doorway. He glances around and then clears his throat. "Come with me."

"Silas, we're kinda busy," Dylan growls in frustration.

Silas meets my eyes and sees the plea there, and because the man has more empathy than is decent, he inclines his head minutely and turns to Dylan with a smile. "I really need your help. It won't take long."

Dylan hesitates and then removes his hands and walks to the door.

"I'm going to stay and learn this stock-take nonsense," Gray says cheerily. He waves to Silas. Gray is okay for thirty seconds, and then he holds up the tablet. "I did something."

I sigh heavily and take the tablet from him.

He bites his lower lip and winks at me.

"How can you create such amazing gardens and not understand the workings of your tablet?"

Grayson snorts. "I draw on paper or the desktop. I really don't like phones or tablets."

"Really?"

"People call me and want stuff, so tedious."

"What about your sister?"

"Oh, when she wants me, she calls Falcon or Silas. I have a phone. I'm not completely out of the loop, I just...don't use it."

"Huh." That's all I can say because he seems the type to be glued to it.

"Oh! That's how it is, is it? You pegged me and put me in a box of your own stereotypes, didn't you?"

My cheeks flame. "No! I- no."

"You totally did," Grayson crows. He grabs me by the hips and pulls me into him. "But that's okay. I'll forgive you. If!"

"If?"

"If you kiss me."

I smile slowly, with genuine happiness, and stand up on my tiptoes to kiss him.

"Ah, that's better. I feel like I can really get down and toil now."

"Oh, no, I'd hate to see you break a nail," I tease.

"It would totally ruin my frock's aesthetic."

I roll my eyes.

"So, tonight is the comedy night, and we were thinking, since the weather's cleared, that we'd like to take you on a date."

I tilt my head to the side. "You mean Dylan."

"Do I look like I'm asking Dylan? No. I mean you." Gray waggles his eyebrows at me and runs a hand down his white shirt, flicking open the top button on the way back up. My eyes are drawn to the extra piece of skin he's just exposed.

His words completely stump me. My jaw unhinges, and I just stare at him, completely wordless.

"So?"

"So...you want to take me on a date?" I clarify.

"No." Grayson growls and grips the back of my neck, pulling me close and pressing his lips to my forehead. "*We* want to take you on a date."

I stumble over that again. "Okay," Slips out of me before I can stop it.

His arms wrap around me, and we just stand like that. It's bizarre, and yet, I feel that if he lets me go, I might very well fall over sideways.

Silas comes back in with Simon. The pair of them have identically blank expressions of polite interest.

I snicker.

Grayson sighs and lets go of me. "Tag. Silas is it."

The other alpha scowls and perches on the edge of a box while Grayson walks backwards out of the room. He blows me a kiss, grabs Simon, and slams the door closed.

I turn to Silas and see his dark eyes studying me intently.

"So, uh...a date, huh?"

"Is that okay?" Silas asks with a frown. "You looked panicked before."

"Yes. It's confusing, but it will be good to help you guys romance Dylan. I think you're really winning."

Silas scowls and prowls towards me. "Come with me."

He grabs my wrist, ignoring my protests, and drags me through a door at the back of the room and up a narrow flight of stairs into a simple white room. It got the lightest dove grey carpet and huge vaulted ceilings with exposed wood beams. He doesn't stop until he drags me to a huge glass window.

"What do you see?" Silas whispers in my ear.

"I see a stunning landscape, your hotel gardens. It's lovely."

"I see a beautiful woman in my arms, a woman who fits with my pack the way we've cultivated our hotel to complement the landscape."

His words take a moment to sink in.

"What are you saying, Silas?" The words strangle me.

"I'm saying that we're enjoying being with you and maybe this date is about you, not Dylan."

"Does he know?"

Silas chokes on a laugh and grips my hip, leaning in to whisper in my ear. "Oh, he insists."

I exhale roughly.

His fingers ghost over my ribs, grazing the side of my breast. My skin breaks out in goosebumps. His hips press against my ass, and I feel the evidence of his arousal. People walk past the window, and I fight to control my facial expressions.

"We could make your entire world flip over and over."

I pant. "I'm pretty sure you already have."

Silas growls and drags his teeth over my ear. I shudder.

"You are a beautiful woman," Silas says. "My omega can't stop looking at you. It took me a while to see what he sees in you, but now that I can see it, I can't look away. You glow with an inner fire."

He steps back while his words echo in my head.

I whirl as he clasps his hands behind his back, the suit jacket pulling tight across his chest. His hair is swept back, not a lock out of place. He's immaculate and so very hot. His lips quirk up, and his smile punches me in the gut.

"Let us spoil you for one night, Miss Davies. Allow us to show you our gratitude and express our interest."

His words can be taken in two directions. The first sends my overactive heart into overdrive. The second is more like duty.

"Can I ask you something first?"

"Sure."

"Why did you take all the birds to the vets? They'd already seen vets, they're at rescues. Why didn't you send someone else to do it?"

"Because Dylan deserves the best. I wanted to give those birds their best chance."

"So best doesn't necessarily mean healthiest to you?"

Silas cocks his head to the side. "There is a bird in that enclosure that can't fly. He can only hop and climb. He is perfect in his own way and a favourite among the staff. What others might see as broken doesn't actually mean they are broken, it just makes them different. I wasn't trying to get Dylan healthy birds, I wasn't choosing the best, prettiest, most aesthetically pleasing birds. I was taking the ones that no one wanted, that no one was looking at, that no one thought had value. Then I took care of what he loved, protected them, and then, Onyx, I gave them forever."

I stare at him in wonder. "You see him, don't you, Silas? He could hide in any shadows in any room, and you could find him."

I reach out, lifting my hand to press my fingers to his jaw.

"You understand him. Why haven't you told him yet?" I ask.

Silas covers my hand with his. "Because I see you, too. You think you have nothing to offer, that people forget you, that you can fade away and no one will miss you, but the truth is that you change lives just by being you. You're a broken bird, too, Nyx. I would give you forever as well."

His words knock the air from my lungs and leave me feeling like I'm standing on the edge of a cliff. One stiff breeze and I might fall, but where would it lead me?

"Okay, Alpha Hastings, you can express your gratitude and take me on a date."

He smiles wider, and it almost ends me. He leads me to the dining room and speaks to the waiter.

"What are we doing?"

"Lunch," Silas says with a grin and pulls out a chair. He sits next to me. I realise we're in the corner of the room, away from the prying eyes of the guests. It's intimate and confusing. He's staring at me like I'm something special.

But I'm not. I am exactly what he said, just another broken bird.

Twenty-Five

DYLAN

Watching her has become an obsession. Wherever she is, I'm not far behind, and my alphas have figured it out. My weakness is on display, and they are using it against me. To draw me in to trap me. It took me a while to figure it out, but now that I can see it. I'm disgusted with myself. Their trap was too sweet for me to resist.

And I've trapped her.

Grayson runs his hand down my arm, but I draw away from him. Silas just watches me with those sad, deep eyes of his. Falcon doesn't even bother. He keeps his eyes on the beta. On my beta.

I lift my lips in a snarl, fully directed at the alpha in question. He turns with a half smile and raises a glass to me.

They brought her on a date. We talked about it; they asked me; I okayed it, but then I saw the bigger picture.

She panicked and backed away from us. And with those few backwards steps, the veil lifted. They want me, but do they really want her or is this just a game?

The glass house on the roof is lit up with candle light. The red roses are fresh from Gray's garden, the food is exquisite and looks like art arranged on delicate black plates. There is soft, melodic music playing in the background. Each of my alphas are wearing dark suits. Silas has a pinstripe, Falcon is wearing solid black, while Gray has lost his jacket and has his shirt undone to the third button, revealing that tiny bit of collarbone I love. But Nyx is in a sleek, crimson slip that is vibrant and full of life and so her, and she doesn't even realise it. When I look at her, I feel so much of everything that I want to shout, scream, cry, fall to my knees, it's overwhelming. It's the perfect place for romance. Including the night sky full of more stars than you can ever count.

So, why is my skin crawling? Why am I feeling so unhappy in myself? I can't take my eyes off her. The soft smiles, the glances she darts towards us. There is a beast in my chest trying to rip his way out. I don't trust them with her. I don't trust them not to hurt me.

I close my eyes as the realisation crashes down on me. I'm waiting for the other shoe to drop.

The longer they talk, the more they touch, the hotter my anger burns. If they are toying with her, I won't forgive them. If this is just a game to get me back, I will never, ever forgive them.

I narrow in on her wrist. So thin, so breakable. Silas's fingers graze the inside, and her breath hitches.

No. No. NO.

A moment later, I'm dragging her into the lift. I press the button for the penthouse and step off, watching the doors close with her inside. She's safely out of their reach for the moment. And I turn, my chest heaving, as I try to control the panic inside me.

My back is tight. All my muscles are rigid with tension. I can feel them staring at me.

"What are you doing?" I snarl once the lift is gone. I turn with a feral growl. "What are you doing with that woman?"

Falcon glides to the stool and sits facing me like he has nothing better to do, and maybe he hasn't.

"We aren't giving up on you." Silas says.

"Leave her alone," I say the words, but I know it's gone far too far.

"We can't do that," Gray murmurs and gives me a sad smile.

"WHY?" I shout at them. "Why can't you leave her alone? She is pure and the kind of person you don't find anywhere. Why are you doing this? I won't let you ruin her."

Falcon gets to his feet and stops in front of me, his eyes are dark, but his expression is deadly serious. The graveness almost makes me afraid. He feels things so deeply, my alpha, but he never lets anyone see. Well, he's letting me now. "We want you back. We've shown you our intentions."

"And if I come back, will you leave her alone?" I plead. I'm scared for her.

"That ship has sailed," Falcon explains softly. "You wouldn't have us without her. Now, in order to have you, we're going to take her."

I blink at him as the crushing realisation that these alphas, that I, will destroy her life. "I…"

"Come on, Dylan, we know you're in love with her. We know about how she saved you on the streets and your midnight activities. You love her, and if she means that much to you…we'll give her to you," Gray says easily, his face serene, his eyes like ice chips of green, without regret. He's serious, he will give her to me. He means it.

"She's not a thing!" I gasp out, appalled. "She's a person with dreams. With a life."

"And we can give her a family, power, wealth. All her dreams will be attainable." Silas explains soothingly. He reaches out to me, but I duck away from his hand. How can they be so, so, manipulative? This is wrong, isn't it? Silas makes an irritated noise and leans on the bar, his face is set in marble. He's decided as well. How did I miss this? She will hate us. Won't she? My head is reeling. I don't even know what I'm arguing anymore.

"She deserves more-"

"What? Like love? Like devotion?" Gray snarls and pushes past Falcon so he's walking me backwards. "She will have those, too. It's easy to fall in love with the woman our omega loves. You took our choice away from us. You ran. You chose her."

"You're still mad at me?" I spit out and shove him. "You're the ones having secret meetings with Vienne Hastings about female omegas and heirs to the future empires. You're the ones who had a female omega in your suite, able to kiss you."

Gray's ire is replaced by a look of complete exhaustion. "We were stalling for time with Vienne. Getting her off your back so you could have a chance."

"You insulted everything I am. Does your mother even know who I am?" I snap at Silas.

Silas hesitates and shakes his head. "No one but we know your identity. But we love you."

"How can love exist without trust? Without honesty and respect?" I throw at them. "How manipulative are you three that you think you can force me back by stealing the woman I love?"

"That's not what-"

"I don't want to hear it!" I roar.

Falcon growls. "We will court the beta, and we will court you. We will have you both. It no longer matters what the plan is. She is…ours now."

I curl my upper lip. "Yeah, you probably will, me because I had no choice due to my biology, and she because she couldn't withstand your wealth." My voice is bitter. "But I'm not going to let her walk into it blind."

Silas puts his hand over his eyes and whispers a curse. Grayson throws himself onto the couch and glowers at his hands, but Falcon just stares, a challenging lift to his eyebrow, all but daring me to make do with my promise.

"Tell her then. Tell her we want her and we don't intend to lose."

I whirl and slam my hand on the button, but then Falcon is slamming me against the wall, pinning me in place. His scent wraps around me, the feel of him holding me down has my cock hardening painfully in my pants. The whining growl that comes out is almost embarrassing.

He leaves a scorching, open-mouthed kiss on my neck and then eases back. Somehow, his hands manage to get under my shirt. My head falls back. His nails graze over my nipples, then pinch and pull them. My hips rock. I'm panting, desperate, all around me, all I can smell is caramel.

The doors open and tear the cloud of seduction away from me. I throw myself free, hitting the wall of the lift and staring back at him.

He spreads his hands and shrugs. "I'll do anything. Whatever it takes. I'll have you both now, omega."

I understand what he's saying. It's terrifying.

"You're never letting me go, are you?"

Falcon smiles. "Not in this lifetime or the next, my omega."

I shiver at the promise in each of their eyes at his words. "I'm not ready."

Falcon's smile fades. "We can wait for you."

The relief those words give me soothes the sharp edges of fear. The doors close, and I fight myself. I want to get back off, go to them, get their bites, have them claim me. Make me forget the pain of their betrayal.

But she's waiting for me, and that gives me strength. She's my shield, she might not ever know it, but I don't trust my instincts anymore, but I trust hers.

The lift opens the doors on the penthouse, and I find her sitting on the couch. Her arms are wrapped around her chest. But she's changed out of the dress and is now wearing one of my jumpers and leggings. I can't help the flare of heat, seeing her like this. I think there's a shine on her cheeks, but she wipes it away. The smell in the room is full of pain, and the lights are off but for the blue light of the TV that isn't showing anything.

"Onyx?"

She lifts her head and stares at me. "What are you doing here? I thought..." She cuts herself off and looks away.

I walk around the couches and crouch by her feet. "Come with me."

"Where?"

"Trust me and come with me."

She puts her hand in mine and follows as I lead her to the lift. I don't say a word as I lead her out of the hotel and deep into Grayson's gardens.

We get to the end of the path, and I stop. My shoulders are tight.

"I'm sorry."

"Why?"

I can't look at her. "I brought them down onto you. I...should have known better."

"I'm confused. Who did you bring down on me?"

"I fell in love with you months ago," I say in a husky voice. "I am in love with you."

She's silent, and suddenly, I need to see her face. I need to know what she's thinking. I whip around and find her staring at me. She doesn't look disgusted or appalled. That's a start, but I can't identify her expression. Perhaps shock?

"Did you hear me, Onyx? I love you."

She shakes her head. "You have scent matches," She whisper-shouts. "Do you know how rare that is? You have a pack."

"And because of my feelings for you...they want you in our pack, too." I spit out a laugh, trying to dispel the raging chaos inside me. I don't know what I want, but everything's driving me towards her, towards this confrontation.

She blinks and staggers, catching herself on a wall of shrubs. "That's ridiculous. They can't want me...I'm just a b-"

"Don't finish that sentence," I growl, furious.

She presses her lips together, and I think I see agony in her eyes before she shakes her head. "Well, we'll just have to show them how wrong they are."

I bite my tongue at the urge to shake her and shout. I get this sinking feeling that this impulse is going to backfire in my face like I'm standing on the side of a road watching two trains collide.

She's ignoring my confession. At least she heard it. That's progress.

"You're upset, Dylan. I don't know what's going on, but it will all be okay."

"I'm angry," I snap.

"At me?" She blinks up at me.

"I just told you I love you."

She blushes and looks at the end of the path. The pavers spread out and gradually sink into the ground like they were never there. And she ignores me again. The agony of it is...a whole new level of hell.

"We're like this garden, Dylan." She waves her hand at the wall of shrubs.

"How so?" I snap.

"We're an illusion. A beautiful illusion, but one that isn't real."

"Bullshit. I'm real. How I feel about you is real. How you feel about me is real. I know you care..." Am I so desperately fishing for confirmation? Have I sunk so low?

She flinches. "You are an omega with a pack. Who loves you and wants you. You should be in their arms."

"You want me to go to them? Leave you here alone and get bond marks to take me away from you forever?" I know I'm being cruel, but I don't care at the moment.

She flinches and turns away from me. "My wants have nothing to do with it. It's what should be. Omegas need packs." She says it like she's said the same thing a million times before. I curse her bitch of a sister.

I gnash my teeth and growl. "Whether I have those bonds or not, you will still be ours. I didn't tell you to make you afraid. I told you so you'd know what's going to happen. Not one of us will give up on you. We won't accept you walking away from this. I needed you to know there will be no choice for you now. They won't allow you to escape."

She sucks in air but doesn't turn. I stare at her back in frustration. "You know what it's like having nothing. You know what it's like to be cold. Take their hand, Dylan. Take the fairy tale. Don't look back, not even for me."

I growl at her, but she turns with a smile. She's not hearing me. I can't tell if she's deliberately not understanding or if she really believes she's not wanted.

"I'm just glad I could watch and experience it a bit."

Is she completely insane? Is that all she thinks she's worth? Scraps? My entire world is rocked by the realisation that this woman can't see her worth. She's so blinded that she can't even acknowledge someone like me expressing my devotion. What even is that? Panic scrapes at my insides, and a desperate whine sounds in the air. She looks towards me but clenches her hands, refusing to step closer. I turn in a tight circle, trying to rein in my emotions, stamp down the omega I've been suppressing all these months.

I need to rethink this. I need to talk to...them.

We fall silent, and I follow her as she leads me back to the hotel, and when she veers off down the employees only section; I don't follow her. I return to the penthouse, my steps measured, and stand before my alphas.

Grayson lays with his head in Silas' lap, who gently strokes his hair. I feel an overwhelming desire to crawl over to them and squeeze myself in. Fighting their pull has become almost inescapable. I'm not sure how much longer I can resist.

Why am I resisting?

Maybe I should accept their bonds. But would it change their desire regarding her if I gave in? I can't take that chance. I have to hold out as long as I can. Onyx and I are a package deal, even if she doesn't know it yet.

"Dylan, what's wrong?" Falcon asks as he pads into the room. He puts his hands on my shoulders and ducks down to stare into my eyes.

"I need your help."

"Whatever you need is yours," Falcon says without hesitation.

Twenty-Six
ONYX

The cloying scent of alphas and omegas is stronger tonight than I've experienced before. This combination makes my stomach curdle.

"How the hell do they live like this?" I mutter and briefly feel sorry for anyone with a nose stronger than a betas.

I catch sight of a pack that I'd thought would be a good fit for Silver. Pack Vore spot me and hesitate. Ian inclines his head slightly and turns away. The two second exchange has me slowing my steps and glancing around nervously.

"Hey, long time no see? How are you loving this job?" Moira whispers in my ear and skips to keep up with me. She's got an armful of linens and a wicked smile. I try to be happy, but I can't muster it.

I push open the dining room door and hold it for her while she goes inside. "It's great." I follow her and scan the room, searching for *them* even though I know they aren't here. There are a lot of people milling in between meals, but the tables are emptying, and it's just the staff rushing to change the room from breakfast to luncheon.

"It's the best, and the eye candy, too. Primo seats." Moira's shoulder checks me, and then she reaches out and grabs my wrist. "Come and help me."

I don't have anything better to do. I'm not avoiding them, exactly, okay, yes, I'm totally running, but to be fair, I'm almost angry that they are being so ridiculous. Have me in their pack? I'm not falling for that. There's no way they are serious, and if they are, then they should seek professional help and wake up.

"See that lady there in the gold sitting with your sister?"

I pick her out straight away. I don't recognise her, but the way she surveys the room makes my stomach tight. She seems cold.

"Who is she?"

"That's Vienne Hastings, the omega of Pack Hastings."

Oh...that's Silas' mother.

My brain accelerates, snatching all the gossip I can recall about her. Omega, seven mates. Runs the pack rather than bowing to an alpha. Rules the empire. Richer than almost everyone. Rude to the point of cruel. Can make, break, or destroy with a single glance.

And my sister is sitting next to her.

"Don't you worry about Silver. Those two are two peas in a pod."

I glance sharply at Moira. "What?"

Moira flushes. "Oh, um, nothing."

"Has Silver been..."

Moira hisses. "I shouldn't have said anything. I'm sorry."

"Onyx, how lovely to see the pack let you out to breathe."

Warmth spreads through me, and I grin even as I turn. I find myself enveloped by Hazel. She inhales near my neck and pulls away with a frown that disappears instantly.

"Hi, Hazel. How are you enjoying the resort?"

Hazel winces. "You can tell my nagging brother I had a fabulous time and didn't find a match."

I reach out and take her hand. "I'm not going to say anything to him, Hazel."

She looks up, and the bitterness falls from her face. "Nyx, you are one of a kind. No wonder my brother's obsessed."

"Yes, well, we know what questionable tastes the Waters have."

Hazel stiffens. "Hastings."

The omega might be old, but she's powerful. Her aura allows nothing near her. Her hair is gunmetal grey, her lips pinched in an unhappy line, but it's those eyes, Silas's eyes, narrowed in disgust that makes me hold my tongue.

"Your brother's influence has ruined my family's chances for a future," Vienna snarls.

"Get over yourself, you old bitch," Hazel barks out.

The room goes still around us. Tension turning the air thick and tempestuous.

"Just like your father, abandoning his responsibilities and family to take that...that beta as his bride."

Hazel rolls her eyes. "With no regrets."

"Hazel!"

Falcon crosses the room and stops beside us. He edges me away from him. "Moira, Davies, get back to work."

Moira nods her head sharply and drags me away. But his words slice deep inside me. Hazel glares up at him.

"You idiot," I hear her whisper before she turns on her heel and stalks in the opposite direction.

I follow Moira and work hard long into the night. Falcon and the pack avoid me. I don't see Dylan, but that awful woman and Silver disappear early.

I chew my lip, worrying it as I consider what I should do. At the end of the night, I pause by the gold lift and study the button. Am I supposed to go back or not? I check the clock hanging on the wall. It's after two in the morning. I turn on my heel and make my way out to the pool, where I sit on one of the chairs and gaze at the water.

Steam rises off it in clouds that evaporate. Tonight, I feel as real as those clouds. I kick off my shoes and roll up my cuffs and slip my aching feet into the water.

I lay back and throw an arm across my eyes. I'm so tired. Everything seems so futile and exhausting.

I hear a splash and move my arm with a groan. Our eyes collide, and I freeze. Silas is crouched over me, his naked chest on display, wet from the pool. His hair is slicked back and dripping. He looks like an underwear model. I have no words, I can't make myself think let alone speak. He cocks his head to the side and studies me.

I shift my weight but don't look away from him.

"I..."

"Did my mother upset you?"

I blink up at him. "No. She was talking with Hazel. She didn't even acknowledge me."

He looks relieved. "Ah, good. You were supposed to sneak away and come upstairs, not work in the kitchen and dining room."

"I did as my employer told me to do," I snap out with a touch of bitterness.

Silas frowns. "Is that all we are? Your employers?"

My breath catches. "Dylan has feelings for you. Deep feelings, and he's trusting you. Our deal is almost finished."

Silas peers at me. I can't tell what's going on in those dark depths. But I get the sense he isn't happy with something.

He leans down until the tip of his nose brushes mine. "I'm going to tell you a secret."

I stay completely still, trying desperately not to clench my thighs or shift my weight and alert him to the ache that has started.

"I'm afraid of my mother. The bravest thing I did was choose Grayson and Falcon and fly away from the cage she kept me in."

"You fear her? Why?" Instantly, my protective side comes to the front.

"She never hurt me, but she never needed to. She has so many people she can pay to do it. To teach me a lesson. To make me earn my place. But she knows all my weaknesses and used them against me mercilessly."

"Silas," I murmur and reach out, cupping his cheek. "You don't need to earn anything from her."

"I know that now," Silas says and brushes his lips against mine. "I'm just making a point that anything she says should be considered poison and ignored."

When his teeth tug at my bottom lip, I let out a helpless groan and wrap my arms around his neck.

"Dylan is upset," Silas murmurs. "Really upset."

"Don't worry, I made him see that he needs to choose you," I soothe.

Silas growls. He pulls back and studies my face. "I thought I was right, but I can't tell."

"Can't tell?"

"We'll just need to push a little harder."

"Silas, what are you talking about?"

He smiles, and it's blinding and confronting and completely and utterly devastating. My stomach flips, and I feel weak. I lay back, staring up at him while explosions inside my mind go off.

Silas stands up, then bends and lifts me to a standing position. "Come on, let's go home."

I don't think I slept more than an hour last night, I spent the entire night pacing, washing linens, cleaning, setting up supplies. Silas and Dylan's words keep going around and around in my head. I keep telling myself that I have to leave. And one word keeps growing, getting louder and louder in my mind.

Why?

My legs almost give out, dumping me on the couch where I close my eyes in exhaustion. I just need a couple of hours, and I can face the sun. Just a little bit of sleep, a rest or something. When I hear them, I almost jump out of my skin, but then Gray walks in, the huge expanse of his muscled chest bare. My eyes run over every curve, noting with horror the butterflies in my stomach, the way my pulse jumps. I can't look away from him.

Breathing in through my nose, my gaze focuses on my hands. I think I'm shaking. I've really gone too far this time, way too far.

Footsteps slowly approach, and my body tenses.

Falcon and Dylan come out at the same time and with each, I'm nearly bowled over by the physical and emotional reaction I have to them.

Dylan spots me and freezes. Our eyes lock. Shame curls through me like those damn smoke clouds on the pool's surface.

"Nyx." He growls, and then he's beside me, pulling me into a hug, and I'm weak. I'm so weak. My horrible thoughts drag me into the depths of misery that I don't understand. I curl my arms around him and hold on for dear life. I cling to the feelings that I suddenly recognise.

Dylan is someone I trust. He is someone I can respect. I won't ruin his fairy tale. Nor will I steal his happiness. But maybe…

Silas comes out of his room and stops beside Falcon, resting his forehead on Falcon's broad chest and his light grey shirt. I watch in stunned silence as Silas tilts his head back and the two kiss. It's soft and intimate. There is no space between them. My throat is parched, and I can't think at all.

"They look beautiful together."

I don't even realise I've said it out loud until Dylan growls in my ear. "They do."

He breaks away from me, and I find Gray in front of me. He beams and puts a muffin in my hands. "Eat, Onyx. Falcon told me to feed you."

I nibble at the muffin while I catalogue just how incredibly screwed I am. My feelings are real and intense. I'd been ignoring everything, so focused on the novel experience and doing my job that I'd neglected the one rule I had to remember.

The rule I imposed on myself when I came into this world. Don't get swept away. This is not my life.

I think...I think I might have fallen for them. It's like loving the sun, it's not possible, I'd burn up.

Suddenly, I'm seeing their penthouse with the blinders ripped away. The lavishness, the expense. I choke, my throat tight with panic as I scramble up. They live on a different planet from me. I slept on a couch that was owned by no less than five owners. My clothes came from thrift shops. I didn't have a choice of food to eat. No one brought me artfully arranged plates to choose from. I mean, the cushions on the couch probably cost a month of my wages.

I wheeze. Panic rips up my throat, and it's everywhere I look.

Gray follows me, his head cocked to the side. He can sense my struggle, and he's trying to figure out how to fix it. I choke, unable get a single sound out. He looks me up and down and then nods to himself, but his eyes are kind.

"Me and Nyxie got something to do. Don't wait up." He blows the others a kiss, drops an impossibly heavy arm over my shoulders, and leads me to the lift.

He doesn't speak, for which I'm grateful for. He doesn't ask a single question, not even with his eyes. We get off on floor ten. He drags me through into the gym and pops me down on the floor with a heavy hand on my shoulder.

I peer up at him. "What am I doing here?"

"You're going to watch me workout."

I fold my arms over my chest and shrug. But inside, I'm melting because he's pulling those grey pants down and revealing a tiny pair of black shorts. I snap my mouth closed and try but fail to not look at him. All those muscles, all that smooth skin. And is he flexing?

I lick my dry lips as he starts to run.

Music comes on the speakers, causing me to jump, and I swear he gets even bouncier. It's revolting. I'm so down for it. At some point, Dylan and Silas join us. Silas sits beside me while Dylan gets on a treadmill and starts running. And now I'm divided between the two of them.

Is it hot in here? I reach out and grab Silas' hand. He laughs and pulls me up from my spot on the floor. "Shall we go and see what's on the roster for today?"

"Sure."

Silas pauses. "Oh, we need to meet the jet quickly."

I frown but follow him as he leads me down to the foyer. A car is waiting for us. I slide into the back and sit quietly while Silas pulls out his phone and barks a set of instructions.

We drive for thirty minutes and then stop. I climb out and feel something shift inside me. A huge jet with Treyfield written on the side is sitting fat and silent on the tarmac. Silas walks towards it. I follow him up and step on the jet. If I thought the penthouse was luxurious, then I was mistaken.

This jet is a whole new level. Silas walks towards a man in a suit.

"Mr Anders."

"I have the paperwork for you, sir."

Silas nods and signs four times. "Fantastic. Take these back and call me if there are any issues."

Silas does a double take when a small child peers around the seat. Mr Anders flushes red.

"I'm sorry, sir, I couldn't find a sitter."

Silas clears his throat. "No, it's fine." He crouches down and smiles at the little girl, holding out his hand. "Welcome to my resort, Miss?"

"Miss Jazzy."

"Miss Jazzy, that is a beautiful name," Silas coos. "Have you enjoyed the flight? Do I need to give the staff a lolly for good behaviour?"

She claps her hands and laughs. "Me, too!"

"Of course, you, too," Silas says and reaches into the side of an armchair, pulling out three lollipops. The girl throws herself into his arms and giggles.

"Right, well, I think your dad's going to get you home now. But when you get home, Dad's going to take a few paid days off and do something fun with you as a special treat. On me."

"Really? Anything?"

"Well, how about the zoo?" Silas asks. "I got some connections with Mr Hippo, and he says he's doing a tour tomorrow. Would you like to go see him?"

"Sir, there's no need, you don't have to-"

"I know I don't have to, Anders, I want to. Take the next couple of days off and enjoy yourself while she's young. Pass me the papers, I'll sign the other set now so you can get back." Silas pulls out his phone and sends a message.

He had a jet fly him his papers to sign? My knees feel wobbly and weak as I watch him turn back towards me. He takes my elbow and smiles, but there's something strange on his face.

"Whilst I'd love to kidnap you, the others would be furious, but I'm making a note to take you away another day," Silas murmurs in my ear.

"Silas? What's wrong?"

He looks away as he leads me back to the car. "I'm okay."

"You looked spooked when you saw the little girl, don't you like children?" I don't know why I'm prodding at this, but it feels important.

He lets out an explosive breath. "I love children. I just resigned myself to not having them."

"But you want them?" I ask slowly.

"More than I want all the money I'm going to inherit," he says ruefully. "We've talked about children a few times. Falcon and Grey wanted to wait for an omega or for us to be more settled as a pack."

I can't help but smile.

"I have seven fathers, but I'm the only child. All I wanted growing up was a big family of siblings. When I got older, I realised I wanted my own children. When we saw Dylan, I realised that it wouldn't be in the traditional sense. We might need to adopt or foster. But then I didn't think we'd ever get him back. I'd almost given up hope. I hadn't realised it was even an option again." He frowns. "Not until right now."

"Does adoption bother you?"

He shakes his head vehemently. "Not at all. I just…" He purses his lips and looks up at the sky. "I feel like it's what I'm meant to do. Children are gifts, and I have the money and the means. I have the desire to do this. I want a family, Nyx. Love and laughter are the dream. I want snotty noses and missing socks. School runs and teenage angst. I can't explain it. I just want it."

"You make it sound like a dream."

"It would be for me," Silas says back.

I lean into his warmth for a moment before I slip into the passenger seat of the car. His desire is heartfelt, I can tell. I don't think I've really, seriously considered having children, but being so poor and seeing the world how it is hasn't been constructive towards dreams. I love that he feels like this. It's like seeing a whole new side of him. But there's an uneasy feeling stirring inside. We're worlds apart. My feelings and that jet are two considerations that I bury to dissect later.

For now, I just let Silas pull me into the car, his arms holding me close, his heartbeat and mine throbbing in sync.

It's a perfect moment, one I commit to memory. It's just too bad that panic deep inside me is reminding me that good things don't happen to me, and as soon as I open my eyes, I'll find this is all a dream and the fire is burning down my house.

Twenty-Seven

ONYX

Some days you wake up and the day is just the freaking day of all days that you wish you could kick to the curb. Today, the day has decided to send all the signs and portents into the universe that I do not belong with this pack. Starting with a dream where my father sat down and mocked me endlessly, telling me they'd see my true value and dump me soon enough. I can still hear his vicious words ringing in my head.

After the jet, Silas took me to the office, where he casually agreed to build a tennis court during a video conference with Simon. He didn't ask the cost. He just said to use whatever funds it took to do it properly. I'd sat, feeling like a child, out of my element, as he went through several more emails and then smiled at me like it was all nothing. I was still reeling.

That was followed by Falcon ordering a steak, taking a single bite, and then getting a phone call and walking away from his food and not returning. I'd watched as his plate was removed and the food dumped into a bin. It made me feel sick and dizzy. I'm from a different world where food is not to be wasted.

Everywhere I look, their wealth is a slap in the face that just reminds me of where I came from. I never had a bed like the one they've given me. I've never eaten so well in my life. Suddenly, I feel like a guest who overstayed their welcome. Even the clothes are so far out of my realm of reality that I would never even try them on.

It's hard to look them in the eyes. It's hard to face the truth.

I spot Silver and wince as she struts towards the table. If anything, she looks even better now. Her hair is silkier, her clothes are more expensive. I wince at the bill she's racking up, then remember that the pack is taking care of it.

Somehow, that's worse.

Silver flounces to the table and sits between Silas and me, turning her back to me. I stare at her for a long moment. I get a flash of an image in my head of gripping her hair and ripping her off the chair, but in the end, I just lower my chin and turn back to the table.

"Silas, you're looking so hot this evening," Silver croons.

My eyebrows raise. I shoot her back a glare and pick up another mouthful of my pasta.

"So, I've been thinking. I'd love that private tour Falcon was going to take me on. Perhaps you could show me?"

"It wasn't private. He was organising a group." Silas says and sets his cutlery down.

I look up, drawn without my understanding, to see Dylan crossing the dining room floor. His glare lands on me and then Silver, and a flicker of rage passes over his features before he goes blank.

His gait smoothes out, his long legs eating up the distance between us. He rounds the table, dragging his fingers over the chairs, and then grabs Silas' chair and jerks both the alpha and the chair away from the table.

Silver snarls, but Dylan snarls back louder. He straddles Silas' lap and leans in to kiss him so deeply that I feel myself get wet just watching.

My sister lets out a sound of deep rage and stands up. She barely looks at me as she whirls away, stalking over to Pack Leeway. The alphas barely acknowledge her, but when they do look at her, their expressions are hostile. Silver doesn't notice, but I do.

I make a mental note to ask Moira for any gossip. What the hell has Silver done to make not one but two packs that angry at her?

Dylan grabs me and leans towards me. I grab his wrist, squeezing hard enough to make him stop.

"Not here," I say tightly.

He studies me, his eyes flicking between mine. There's a guarded look that makes my stomach drop out. "Are you ashamed?"

"Not of you," I whisper back.

His lips press into a line. "Are you ashamed of him?"

I glance at Silas and shake my head.

"So, you think you're not good enough to be kissed?"

I hiss.

He pulls me towards him. "Tell me to stop, then. If you really don't want me, tell me you don't want me."

I let out a low growl but melt towards him as his lips collide with mine. I get so heated, so lost in the kiss, that I forget where I am.

He lets me go, and I sit back with my head spinning. Fuck, he can kiss. I remember Silver and look around to see her staring absolute murder at me. Sucking in a breath, my head ducks away so I don't have to look at her accusing face anymore.

I'm going to face that fall out. I betrayed her. She's going to think I stole them. But they aren't hers; they aren't even mine.

Silas sighs heavily and stands up. He holds up his hand for me. I stare at it and then put my hand in his. It feels almost like I'm putting myself in his hands. He pulls me up and lets Dylan lead us out of the dining room.

We get in the lift, and the moment the doors close, Dylan slams the emergency stop button. His breathing is fast and raspy. I take a step away, but he reaches out and pulls me away from Silas.

"I want you. No, that's not right. I fucking need you. Nothing makes sense without you," Dylan growls out. His nose runs over my skin, drawing goosebumps. He inhales and then sucks on my pulse point. "I know you're confused right now, scared, but you have to hold on to this, it's real. What we have is real."

"Dylan," I moan. "What are you doing?"

"I need you," he moans and thrusts against me. "Don't make me beg. I hate begging, but I will for you. Please, Nyx."

He turns his face, his mouth right beside mine. I taste his breath. The warmth of it bathes my face. I hesitate, trying to recall why this is a terrible idea. But I love this man, and I want him, even if it's just once in a gold lift with his pack mate watching.

Dylan's hands trail down my upper arms and then up my back before he abruptly loses control and pulls me up against him. I gasp at the feel of his hard cock pressed against my stomach.

Silas clears his throat. I glance up to find him pressing the emergency stop button. The lift rises again, but Dylan is beyond it. He presses me against the lift rail and lifts me, holding me in place with the sheer strength of his body.

I forget Silas and the lift in seconds. All that exists is kissing Dylan back. He's a drug, I decide. My favourite. I'm never going to have an experience that will match this. He's ruined me. They all have.

I lock my legs around his waist as the doors open. He spins us and stalks into the penthouse. When Silas gets too close, he lets out a deep warning sound that just makes this all the hotter.

He takes me down to the room with the glass and sets me on the bed. His eyes rake over me as he peels my clothes off with a single-minded intensity. He seems frenzied. I wish I knew what was going through his mind. I reach up, stilling his hand, and stand up on the bed.

It takes me a half a second to gather my courage, and then I unzip my skirt, letting it pool on the floor. I reach for my shirt, undoing the last two buttons, and shrug it off my shoulders.

Dylan is frozen, staring at me, but the moment I'm in my underwear, a purple bra and thong set, he rips his clothes off.

I swallow hard when I see the omega naked. He's breathtaking. He reaches down, stroking himself, and I follow the motions with my eyes.

I lick my lips and then step out of the thong and release my bra. If I thought his look was burning before, it's got nothing on what he's wearing now.

"Lay down." I think I surprise both of us with my command.

He frowns but goes to the bed and lays down. I walk to the window and flick the switch, making it transparent. I need them to be there, I need them to be part of this.

I like knowing they're watching. It makes me feel like they are part of this, too.

Dylan groans as I lean over, kissing his ankle. I draw my mouth up his body. He doesn't have much hair on him, leaving just acres of smooth skin over bulging muscles. I work my way up to his thighs and find slick from his cock all over him.

Slick. I want to taste it. The compulsion pulls at me, so I let my instincts take over.

I lean down and lick his inner thigh. I close my eyes and moan. So damn sweet like caramel, with an earthy tone that is him. I'll never get enough of this taste. I lick my way up his abs and reach his nipples. My lips and teeth suck and toy with them until he's a whimpering mess. His fingers burrow in my hair, holding me still.

I smile and then lunge up and kiss him, biting at his bottom lip before I slide back down and take him in my mouth. He lets out a sound like a hiss and thrusts up into my mouth. I slide my tongue around his crown and suck. With every move I make, I learn a little more about how to undo my omega. When I swallow him down, my nose brushing against his groin, he lets out a sound that makes my insides flutter.

For a moment, I wonder if I could come without being touched. I feel so close to it. I don't think I've ever been this aroused.

And in the back of my mind, I know there are three alphas sitting in another room watching as I make their omega mine.

I hollow my cheeks out, sucking hard, and then let him go before bobbing my head down again. He lets out a wordless scream and thrusts up into me. Over and over, crying out hoarsely, flooding my mouth with his release. It dribbles out of my mouth, there's so much of it, but I swallow what I can.

I don't know if omegas have magic cum, but I want more of him. He thrusts up once more, his body spasming, and then falls still. I pull back, licking at him, lapping up his fluids. I run my tongue over his balls and his thighs. And when he's erect again, I crawl up his body.

I straddle him and look down.

We don't need words. But he gives them to me, anyway.

"Please, Beta, fuck me, please." The words make me feel beautiful, desirable, wanted. Needed.

I grind myself over him, watching as his head falls back. Over and over, I roll my hips, slipping on him. Our fluids combine, our pants synchronised in the huge room. Our hands map out each other's body. This feels different, more intimate than anything we've done before, but I push it aside to think on it later.

"Nyx," he croaks out, "please."

I smirk, lift, and reach between us, stroking him twice before I slowly line him up, letting his crown press against my entrance. Only when he looks up at me, desire and heat turning gold to black, do I sink down onto him.

I bite back a curse as he slips inside me, stretching me out. Dylan sits up, mauling my breast and sucking hard enough to tear a cry from my throat. I arch and move faster than I mean to, impaling myself on his cock.

I toss my head back, let out a keening noise, and focus on the feeling of being full. This is heaven. Dylan lifts his head, dragging me down, and swallows the sound.

After a moment, I move. I experiment with speeds and rolling my hips until I find something that makes him curse. He thrusts up into me, meeting me halfway. Our movements are unhurried as we run our hands over each other. We talk with our eyes. I think I can almost understand what he's saying. Almost.

I slam down harder and turn our sensual love-making to a fiery blaze of lust. I grip him to me as we both move in a frantic rhythm that has our bodies slapping together. He growls and bites my neck. It hurts, but it feels so good. I hold his head to the spot as my body tightens. I clamp around him, screaming as I shatter.

He thrusts up and roars as his cock drives into me. He shudders, and slowly, his body eases until he's relaxed and mouthing my shoulder, then transitioning to pressing heartbreaking kisses to my throat.

"That was-"

"Incredible," he whispers. "Perfect."

He's not wrong. I feel like I should say something else, but I can't find it in me. I'm happy. I'm content. It was perfect.

I'm ruined. I know it. But I'm glad I got this one moment.

"Coming in," Grayson shouts out and throws my door open. I tense, but Dylan holds me tight, glaring over my shoulder. Grayson ignores the nasty look and kicks off his clothes then crawls across the bed towards us. I eye the tawny-skinned man as he comfortably stretches out. He's far too lion-like.

"You need a knot, baby?" Grayson purrs.

Holy shit, Dylan's cock flexes inside me. He looks torn, though, and I do appreciate that.

I decide for him and climb off him, wincing as hot fluids run down my inner thighs, but a moment later, Silas pushes me forward. My elbows hit the bed, and my ass hovers in the air. A hand between my shoulders pins me to the bed, and then a hot tongue laps at my pussy from front to back.

I let out a deep groan. My fingers curl in the bed, clamping onto the mattress. I arch my hips, giving him more access, and shift my thighs apart when he nudges at them. My eyes bulge when he licks up to my ass, probing gently before dipping down again.

"Si!" I cry out.

His muffled laugh comes a moment before he smacks my ass. I yelp and try to glance back as he rubs and kisses the burning spot better.

Grayson grunts, and I hear flesh hitting flesh, and then the rhythmic sound of sex begins in earnest.

"Getting wetter," Silas teases and buries his face in my folds.

My orgasm flows through me like a hot wave, pleasure blooming and rushing through my limbs before easing, leaving me a pliable mess of contentment. Silas crawls up my body, kissing up my spine.

"My new favourite flavour," he murmurs.

I shudder and realise it won't take much to get me close to the edge again.

He sits up and pulls me with him, sitting me in his lap, his hard erection pressing against me. But he doesn't attempt anything, he just turns me to face the dark.

Falcon is standing in the shadows with a long strip of black material.

"Give me everything," Falcon demands.

If I say no, he will let me leave. I know it. But this offer might not come again. It's a once in a lifetime, and I really want to see what memory this will leave me with. Last time was incredible. Can I give them my trust?

Wait. He wants everything. He wants me.

"It's your call, Onyx," Falcon purrs. "Give me your sight, give me your taste, give me your hearing, give me your touch. Give in to me, and give me it all."

Grayson and Dylan have paused, both twisted around to watch me. Silas licks the shell of my ear.

"You'll love it," He purrs. He shifts me up and impales me on his cock.

My head falls back, and I groan as he bounces me, up and down.

"Yes." I'm saying yes to more than just this, and we both know it. I'm saying yes to anything and everything they want for as long as they want it. I'm choosing to trust them. I push my family's voices from my mind, and I focus only on this.

Falcon reaches out and gently takes my wrist and secures it with satin bindings. I'm nervous as I'm pulled taut on the bed. He pulls out another one and hesitates. I give him a nod. That one goes across my eyes.

Music fills the room, startling me. It's loud enough that it blocks a lot of sound from the bed.

"Relax," Falcon soothes. Cold liquid pours onto my chest, and I let out a startled sound, but immediately, hands roll through it, rubbing and massaging. My skin feels alive without the ability to see. My nipples respond to the slightest touch. I'm panting and writhing against the bonds, frustrated, but the hands are relentless.

"This one isn't heated," Silas says with a chuckle and mouths my ear.

My chest, stomach, and legs are massaged, and then another set joins in, rubbing more lotion into my arms. The difference between them is startling. One set of hands is sensual, confident, the others tease and play.

I'm panting heavily, so aroused that I can't lay still when my legs are pulled open and someone kneels in between them. A tongue forces its way into my mouth, and I kiss Silas back. Fig and sea salt. That's what he tastes like.

"You're wet for us," he says. "Needy beta, almost as wet as our omega. But I want to hear you scream tonight. I want to hear you howl. And no one's stopping until I get that scream. You remember how to do it?"

"Yes," I whimper.

Silas growls something and shifts away from my ear.

I almost scream the next moment. A mystery mouth sucks hard on my clit, while two more close on my breasts, and Silas presses his tongue back into my mouth. When he draws back, I'm so overwhelmed by need that I miss his words, it takes my brain a moment to catch up.

"Not yet, beautiful beta." He turns my head to the side and nibbles on my neck, but then Falcon growls, and Silas backs off.

"What do you smell?" Falcon whispers in my ear.

"Methol," I whisper back.

"That's my scent. That's what Dylan craves," Falcon whispers. "You'll crave it, too." He licks up my chin and kisses me with so much passion that I melt. "And can you taste it?"

"Yes," I whisper and turn my head to where I think he is. I can't see anything though, the black is complete.

His huge hands skate up the sides of my body and grip my breasts hard. He squeezes and molds them and then lets them go. Each path his hands take, he makes his. I can hear Dylan cry out, the sound of slurping and flesh hitting flesh. I squirm, tightening my legs together.

"Hear my voice, the sound of my breathing, the sounds of Silas fucking Dylan's mouth while Gray owns his ass. Those are the sounds of this pack."

I whimper.

"Hear yourself, whining so prettily for my cock," Falcon murmurs. "I'd like to suspend you from my ceiling."

My core clenches at the visual. His hand, pressed on my stomach, pauses and then dips down in between my folds and slips into my drenched body.

He chuckles and presses his body down on mine, and I discover he's naked. No clothes to be felt. My heart races.

"You like that idea," Falcon teases and lifts my thigh to wrap around him. "Next time," he promises and surges into me.

This whole experience is out of this world. I can hear the sounds of the pack fucking. Falcon has dominated all my senses. My pleasure is in his hands. His cock impales me over and over, filling me, hitting spots I didn't know could feel the way he's making me feel. I'm helpless, crying out, sobbing for breath. His hands roam freely over my body, his words hiss into my ear, promising, coaxing, and commanding.

He reaches down between us and strums his fingers over my clit. "Come for me."

The next time his finger touches me, I shatter. My back bows off the bed. I thrust my hips into his. The world flashes white and black behind the mask. He slams into me over and over, and then, with a roar, he thrusts up even harder, gripping my hips and emptying himself inside me.

"Damn," Falcon hisses.

"What?" I ask, alarmed.

"You. You're perfect," he says softly. "We're going to need to do that a lot more."

I giggle softly. But then he moves out of the way, and fingers press into me. I wince.

"Sore?" Silas asks.

I hesitate. But Silas laughs and crawls up my body, undoing the restraints and removing the blindfold.

Then he turns me onto my side and wraps himself around me from behind. He positions himself and slips inside. I gasp at the feeling of fullness and the need that starts building again.

"It's okay. I get to hold you like this," Silas whispers and hums against me.

"And that's okay?" I ask hesitantly.

"For now, until you're ready, and then I'll finish what we're starting." His fingers pluck at my nipples, and when Gray comes close, Silas throws my thigh over his hip, opens me up wider for him to lazily move in and out of me.

He groans and presses his lips to my ear. "Beautiful beta, so tight around my cock. But so wet, you want this, don't you?"

"Yes!" I groan. Gray is lying face to face with me, and now he leans across, kissing me deeply. Mangos. Silas moves faster but still doesn't let me move. He and Gray handle my body like I'm nothing, touching, driving me hotter and wilder.

Silas pauses, and then I feel his fingers between us, circling the tight ring of flesh of my ass. I gasp out, my eyes wide. Gray chuckles as I get used to Silas feeling around. A moment later, he presses into me. I let out a whimper.

"That's it, that's it," Silas purrs. "Can you take another?"

I jerk my head in a nod. He adds a second, and not long after, a third.

I'm a leaky, needy, wanton woman now.

"Can you take me?" Silas asks in a purr.

I want it. I nod my head.

"Words, beta," Falcon chides.

"Yes, I can take you, Silas."

He groans and gets up on his hands and knees, rolling me on top of Grayson. I spread my legs wide so I'm straddling him. The heat of his cock presses against my core. I whimper, but then Silas is there, pressing into me from behind.

It stings for a moment, but he goes slow, panting as he works into me. Then he's in. It's so different from when he's fucking my pussy. It's exciting and new and feels amazing in a different way. He fucks me in slow, measured thrusts, like he's clawing to hold on to his control. It's like nothing I've ever felt before, but I'm here for it.

"She's soaking me, bro," Gray grits out, thrusting up.

I pause, staring at him, considering. I have seen it done before.

"Do it," Dylan goads me, his eyes gleaming as he gets closer so that he can get a better view.

I glance over at him and Falcon and find them watching us intently. Hmm, I glance over my shoulder at Silas. His eyes widen, and he pulls out a bit. I reach down between Gray and myself, grip his hard cock in my hands, and then lower myself onto him. I'm barely given time to adjust before Silas slams back into me.

It's so tight, I'm so full, and I can feel them both. Everything is stretched and there is feeling everywhere. I pant as the stimulation becomes overwhelming. They thrust in and out of me. The look on Gray's face of absolute pleasure sends a bolt of power straight into my brain. Silas growls and increases his pace, which affects Gray.

I don't even care, I tilt my head back and wail as my orgasm hits me with the force of a tidal wave. Gray arches up, his face turning red, and roars, his hot cum hitting my insides. Silas curses and slams into me, his cock twitches and seems to grow bigger.

"I'm going to knot you one day, but not today," Silas growls in my ear. He wraps his fingers around my hair and pulls my head back and drags himself up into me. He stiffens, gasping, and growls as he comes in my ass.

We lay there in a tangle for a moment, and then Silas rolls off me and walks to the bathroom. He returns with a couple of washcloths, throws one at Gray, and then gently cleans me up. It's a strangely vulnerable moment.

I snort a laugh.

"What's so funny?"

"You're really sweet and kinda perfect, Silas," I whisper.

"Shh, don't you dare let anyone know that." He kisses my shoulder and tugs the blanket that Falcon puts over us up to my neck.

Dylan lies facing me and smiles sleepily. Gray flops on his back, smiling at the roof.

Falcon walks towards the door. I sit up, making a sound of protest. He turns back and, with a shake of his head, flicks the light off and returns to the bed.

"This is not going to be a thing," Falcon warns. "It's only ten in the morning. We have things to do."

"Meh, we'll do them tomorrow," Gray says with a happy grin.

I cuddle deeper into Dylan's arms and kiss his chest. "We could have a nap."

"And then do it again," Silas purrs.

I notice even Falcon doesn't argue with that.

Dylan's teeth gleam as he wiggles closer to me. I think maybe this might have been the most perfect day of my life.

The start of my new life.

Twenty-Eight
ONYX

Silas leans in and kisses me with so much intensity that I forget where I am. When he pulls back, I have to rest my hands on his hard chest just to balance myself.

"Have a good morning," he croons and nibbles my neck.

I swear my ovaries just about explode.

He steps back into the lift, and I watch as the doors close and the lift disappears. It still takes another thirty seconds for my brain to stop replaying those incredible panty-melting memories of last night.

I turn and stop dead, a wash of icy fear killing any lingering arousal faster than anything ever could. Three alphas from Pack Drest scowl at me. There's a feeling when you are the focus of an alpha pack and not in a good way, you feel like prey; you feel scared. Despite myself, I feel that now. One snorts out something that makes the three of them crack up. But it's seeing the burning in Silver's eyes when she sees me that shakes me out of my frozen state.

I know she thinks I've done her wrong, but I haven't. This is my life, and I haven't done anything I'm ashamed of. Still, my apprehension grows as more and more people stare at me as they walk past. My skin itches, and I feel exposed.

In the dining room, the whispers of my relationship status sweeps ahead of even me. I catch snippets of whore, prostitute, slut, greedy bitch. The words don't mean much, but it's the fact that the people I've worked with are saying it. My face burns. I keep it down, watching the floor as I cross to grab a trolley.

Out of the corner of my eye, I see Moira walk in. She casts concerned glances under her lashes while the rest of the staff talk in hushed groups of two and three.

"You'd think they'd have better things to talk about than you and Pack Treyfield," Moira growls. "So jealous. Petty," she hisses, and a blonde, thin woman with a fierce scowl turns away abruptly.

I half smile at her. "You don't see anything wrong with it?"

"No, but then I know you. They don't. They're just hearing what she's been saying," Moira spits. "That bitch needs her tongue cut out."

"She?" I cut in sharply.

Moira curses and tilts her face to the ceiling. Her frustration is clear, but when I growl, she looks at me and blows out her cheeks.

"Fine, okay, but don't shoot the messenger. Look, you just need to remember that not everyone believes her."

I raise a brow and glance around the quiet dining room. I have a sinking feeling I know what she's going to say, and it's going to ruin my day. "Tell me why everyone is talking about me."

"Because of her," Moira spits out and turns her head to Pack Drest and Silver.

"Her?" My eyes are on Silver, and she's staring back. Glaring back. *Silver, what the fuck did you do?*

"Silver. Who else?" Moira snarls. She straightens the table cloth and puts out the silverware. "She's been saying you do this wherever you work. She says you whore yourself out for the money. For advancement. That you don't care about them, that you'll break the pack and hurt them."

The words sting, and the accusations burn. The fact that it's my sister, my twin, saying it is agonising. It's embarrassing. Shame makes my shoulders curl.

"Silver," I say her name like I've never said it before. Like she's alien, something new and hostile.

"Yes. The bitch queen herself." Moira glares across the room. Silver stands up, graceful as ever, puts her nose in the air, and swans out of the dining room.

I nod slowly. "I'll deal with her."

She looks at me sharply, but we finish setting the dining room, and when I'm done, I find Dylan waiting for me.

"Hey." I sweep into his arms, hugging him tight. I just want to wash the day away from me, get rid of it. Dylan's scent is a balm I didn't know I needed.

"You don't need to do this, you know," he says.

"I like it. There's something about the routine of it that makes me feel like I'm still on this planet and not in some distant dream."

He laughs and guides me out just as people filter in.

"I need to speak to Simon for a moment. Come with me?" I ask him playfully.

He grins and laces our fingers together before he follows where I lead. We exit the dining room and I stop dead. He crashes into me.

"Hey, what's going on-" his words cut short.

Silver is pressed against Silas, her lips against his. All at once, I'm aware of my rage, his fury and despair. It's a painful vortex. The air grows dangerous around us.

Silas pushes her off, his face ice cold, and I realise how she got so close. She's wearing a replica of my clothes. Her hair is styled the way I style mine. From a distance, he might not have known. How did she get changed this quick? She must have been in the dining room to see exactly how I looked this morning.

I feel sick. What has she done?

Silas snarls with rage, and that breaks the spell we've been captured in. Dylan lets out an anguished sound, but he doesn't run away. No, this time, he sweeps towards his alpha and presses between him and the threat. The noise that comes out of him makes even me pause, but not Silas. His alpha puts his arm around his omega's waist and drags him back against his chest.

She's not moving. In fact, I can see her working up to one of her tantrums. Oh, god, they might actually kill her. I'd regret her death, but even more, I regret Silas or Dylan ending up in prison. I need to get her away from them.

Silver puts her hand on her hip, but I cross the space, snag her arm, and tug her away from them. She doesn't even realise the danger she's in.

"Don't say a fucking word, Silver, if you want to survive, shut the fuck up," I hiss.

She glances at me in surprise, but when Hazel joins us and grabs her other arm, helping me drag her away, she comes quietly, stunned.

"No, this is wrong!" Silver shouts. She struggles against us, but Moira joins us, and the three of us tear her away from my pack, step by step. I'm panting and let out a screech when she grips my neck, her nails ripping my skin.

"Onyx!" Hazel says sharply.

"Fuck this," Moira says and elbows Silver in the face. The fight goes out of her, and we move her quickly to the other side of the foyer, near the glass doors. I need to get her out of here.

I glance back and find Grayson glaring at me, from just in front of the lifts. I shiver at the ice in his eyes. Falcon doesn't even look at me as security swarms in. Simon and Yvette bark orders into microphones. Silas and Dylan are locked in an embrace that I don't think anyone could tear them from.

Call me back, I think in my head. *Call for me.*

But no one calls for me. The only person who even looks at me is Gray, and the expression is one of icy rage.

And just like that, I realise I've achieved the bargain I made and damaged myself beyond repair. I delivered their omega into their arms and fell in love. But I'm not one of them, I never will be. And it looks like they just found their reason. Fate is a real bitch.

Hazel urges us outside and deep into the estate. She leads us to a section with lots of trees and walking paths, but few people bother coming. I throw myself into frantic pacing to stop from screaming.

Silver sobs and makes excuses, but none of us listen. I have no words. Guilt for my sister's actions and pain at their dismissal. I see-saw between the two extremes. But at the heart of it all is the resignation that I should have known better.

"They'll want to speak with you," Hazel says to me after a few minutes. I think she's trying to reassure me.

"Yeah, I know," I admit. Things have changed, and things need to be said. I get it. They will need to officially let me know I'm no longer welcome here.

Silver sobs. "I made a mistake. Nyxie, fix it. Please. I'm sorry." She reaches for me, but I snatch my hand away.

"We just need to wait, see what the fallout is going to be," Moira says. "They'll forgive you, Onyx."

I shake my head, already knowing they won't. "It doesn't matter. I need to take Silver home. She is my responsibility."

The sound of shoes on the path makes my stomach jolt. For a moment, I perk up, hoping, praying, it's them. But as soon as they get closer, I realise the shoes sound wrong. It's not them.

Simon and Yvette walk side by side. The expressions on their faces make my stomach tighten and my eyes burn. They are bearing grim tidings. I know what they're going to say. I know it. They approach us and stand shoulder to shoulder. This is what is called, in employment terms, an execution. They aren't going to speak to me. They've sent in the attack dogs.

I am devastated. My head reels, and all I can do is watch them and blink. My throat is tight, but no tears come.

"Pack Treyfield would like to rescind your invitation to stay here, Silver Davies." Simon says with a sharp look at me. I think he's expecting me to protest, but I'm not going to. Of course Silver needs to go. There's no way she can stay.

"What? No! They can't do that!" Silver stands up, and between the crying and screaming, I ignore her. My heart is hammering as I wait for the rest of it.

Hazel snaps her fingers. "Where the fuck are you, Grayson?" She paces away. "You fucking idiot," she snarls into the phone. "You absolute moron. You don't deserve her, and neither do the others. I don't care. I'm going home. Yeah, you can shove your orders where the sun don't shine, big brother. Yeah, I don't care at all. Try locking me up, just try it. I'll call Angel and tell him you've imprisoned me. Oh, I know he's not mine and will never be mine, but he won't let anyone, even you, hurt me, either. You might be the impressive Grayson Waters, but Angel's a cop. I'd love to see how you do behind bars. So, just try me," Hazel snarls. She whirls back, her eyes aglow and her hair a mess.

Moira whistles. "Wow, you are some kind of cool."

Hazel shakes her head. "I'm sorry, Onyx, I tried."

I shrug my shoulders, hiding the hurt. "It's okay. I knew they wouldn't come."

Simon and Yvette exchange dark looks. My anxiety returns full force.

"They want me to leave as well?" My voice trembles.

Yvette's expression goes perfectly blank. "Falcon said the decision is up to you. You can stay for the last four days or leave. He doesn't care, but your sister is to be escorted from the property before nightfall."

I wheeze at the agony those words give me. They don't even care enough to send me away. Did they care at all?

Hazel catches my elbow just as the world tilts.

"My brother is an idiot. I need to make a call," Hazel says and steps away. Moira takes her place, holding me up.

"Hey, girl, no, everything's not all right, we need to talk." Hazel moves out of earshot, and I refocus on Yvette.

I look at her. My eyes are so wide they feel weird, but I can't seem to control my body right now. "I didn't do that...I didn't know. Do they think I had something to do with that, that I would do that to them? After everything?" My voice is a tiny squeak of hurt sound. I feel like I'm facing my father again after the fire. Bracing for the verbal blows that will destroy me. I can't get a deep breath, I feel weird. It's so cold.

Moira presses her lips into a firm line. "Simon?"

He appears beside me with a flask. "Take a sip, Nyx. It will settle your nerves."

The burning liquid runs down my throat, and I almost choke on it.

"For what it's worth, I think when they calm down, they will realise they've made a mistake." Yvette says softly. "You aren't your sister, and deep down, they know that."

Simon clears his throat. "Here's the key to your new room. Falcon asked me to assign it. He said to thank you for your service. Your wages have been paid. Your employment with Treyfield Pack is terminated and, due to the circumstances, they feel they must rescind the offer of permanent placement, especially since no contract was signed."

My skin turns to ice. Moira clutches me closer, almost holding me up by this point. They are wiping their hands of me. Oh, god, how can words hurt so much?

"They think I conspired with her, don't they? Damn paranoid idiots," I mutter. I shake my head and reach for the key because I can't leave.

I'm going to stay for the last four days. I'm going to make sure they believe me. That they know I would never do that to them.

"Nyxie?" Silver says in a tiny voice. "What am I going to do?"

"You're going to go to a cheap motel and stay there for four days. When I'm done, I'll decide what we're doing," I snap at her.

"But, Onyx-"

"Don't!" I cut in. "Just don't. This time, I'm choosing me, Silver. This time, I'm doing something for my life. So sit in the hotel room and stay there until I'm done. I need to do this."

Silver sobs, large, heavy, heartbroken sobs that we all ignore.

"I'll book a hotel at the Smiths Inn. It's an hour away on the road back to Silver Falls. I'll organise a car and her bags and put it on the company's dollar. No, don't protest, if they have an issue with it, I'll pay for it myself. I warned them about this one." Simon casts a flinty glare at Silver. "Good luck with everything, Beta Davies. I hope you succeed."

Moira and I watch them go. The four of us wait until Hazel gets a message from Simon saying that everything is prepared, and then we escort Silver to the car. She crawls in the back, looking small and scared. I have to harden my heart as I watch the car pull away.

Hazel wraps her arm around mine and drags me back into the hotel. I stay with her, ignoring everyone else long into the night, staring at the door, but my pack never appears.

Twenty-Nine

SILAS

I can still taste that bitch on my lips. I can feel her clutching fingers on my arms. With a shudder, I scrub my arm across my mouth, desperately trying to remove it. Through a gap between people, I watch as Silver smirks at me. It's a knowing, evil smirk, and I wonder what her real motivation for doing this was. My mind is in panic, working up to a soundless scream deep inside me as I realise that history is repeating.

Dylan's grip on my arm is tight, almost painful. He's gone past rational thought and is deep in his instincts. I need to pull my shit together for him, but the smell of burnt caramel is driving my own alpha instincts to the front. The urge to destroy the omega who touched me, who hurt my omega, pulses stronger and stronger in my veins.

I strain to see past the people that have appeared, needing to see that omega so I can hunt her down, but when the man in front of me shifts his weight, I catch sight of Onyx. How did I forget about her, even for a moment? The rage stills and subsides. She looks back at us as if she's in pain. The expression makes my stomach jolt. Why is she leaving? Where is she going?

Everything is so messy and confused. There are people everywhere. But Dylan doesn't leave me. In fact, to my surprise, he growls possessively at anyone who comes close to me. I recognise people. Falcon, Grayson, Simon, Yvette, Elaine. Other employees. The Vore Pack holds back any of the crowd that tries to press through. I don't know why they do us this boon, but I will remember it.

"Dylan," I say at last as we're alone inside the gold lift. Falcon and Gray will be right behind us. They just did what they needed to do and got us out. I get it, but I need them right now.

My omega turns, and his eyes are so dark and filled with pain that I flinch. He prowls angrily around.

"She chose someone else," Dylan spits and slams his fist into the walls of the lift. I wince and reach out, pulling him into my arms.

What is he talking about? Onyx? Is he talking about Onyx?

"No, she-"

"She didn't choose me," Dylan growls again, and the sound of his pain tears me apart. "She was supposed to choose me. But she chose that woman. She betrayed me."

Okay, there's something else going on here. I think about her, the only her that could reduce my omega to tears, going off with Silver and try to see it from Dylan's point of view.

Bitter lemons fill the lift, vibrant and intense. The doors open, and Dylan goes to the couch and drops onto it, staring blindly into space. Time passes slowly as I fight to figure out what's going on.

"Where is Onyx?" I ask Falcon when they stalk into the suite.

He looks at me and then at Dylan and shakes his head. I stand up and pace over to him. He tries to pull his tablet away from me, but I snatch it from his hands.

"Show me," I growl.

"Fine, just go down there and watch," Falcon hisses. He goes and sits on the couch, pulling Dylan into a hug.

Apprehensively, I go down the hallway and press play on the security feed.

In the camera, Onyx leans in and talks to my mother. I feel ill just watching it. I feel homicidal.

"Don't worry, I have them eating out of my hands. As soon as I get the right moment, I'll sneak Silver in. She'll be in her heat, so it will be perfect. She'll be bitten, bonded, and packed without anyone ever seeing through the hormones."

"Are you sure about this? What if anything goes wrong?" My mother asks with far too much glee.

"Nothing will go wrong. They are completely blinded. You'll have an omega daughter for your son's pack. You just make sure you wire me the money. Once I've been paid, I'll be out of your lives forever."

I narrow my eyes, watching my mother's evil expressions. They seem to be sincere, but I never can tell with her. I can't believe what I just heard. There must be some mistake. This can't be Onyx.

THE BETA'S BARGAIN

Grayson walks up to me and shows me the feed for the garden. I look at the time stamps and find what appears to be Silver walking around in the garden at the time Onyx was speaking to my mother. Grayson switches the feed to dining room an hour and a half earlier and shows Onyx and Silver in the dining room. Onyx is in her uniform, while Silver, who is sitting with Pack Drest, is wearing the same dress the girl in the garden's is wearing. The same dress she was wearing when she kissed me forty-five minutes later. It was Onyx talking to my mother.

The betrayal is intense and bitter.

"Son of a bitch!" I spit. "She played us."

"Show me!"

Dylan's demand leaves us no choice, and by the time he's finished watching it, we have an omega in crisis. He deflates, and something lively just fades away. I think that I'm watching a heart breaking.

I leave him with Grayson, who is more angry and bitter than I've seen him about anything ever, and walk out to Falcon.

"I've given Simon instructions. She won't get close to him," Falcon says calmly.

"Don't you think we should hear her out?" I protest.

"Do you think there's anything she could say right now that will get you to believe anything else? You saw it with your own eyes."

I press my lips into a thin line. "I'll be back. I need to take care of something."

My mother smiles when I walk into the yellow room where I've asked Simon to direct her. The smile fades away as she gets a good look at my face.

The rage of decades of manipulation and bullshit has built and built, and now I can't contain it. Dylan is distraught and broken. We've waited and worked so long to get him to trust us and…and her, Onyx. Her betrayal hurts me in places no one has ever hurt me. I feel sick and insanely angry, and I can't let myself think about it, so I'm directing it all where it deserves to be directed.

"Silas, don't pout. It was in your best interests."

I slam my hands down on the table. "How dare you conspire with people to manipulate my pack? Have you no shame?"

"If you weren't sneaking around with that, that omega, then we wouldn't be having this-"

"He is my scent match," I growl out. I clench the table edge so hard I leave marks in the wood. "He is perfect for our pack. He is mine. This is the second time that your interference has almost cost me my future."

My mother gapes at me. "Now, Silas-"

"If I don't have him, I won't have another. I will kill anyone you try and put in my bed."

"Fine. But if you want him, you can't have the beta."

"MY PACK IS NOT UP FOR DISCUSSION!" I roar at her.

She recoils and stares at me with bulging eyes. "Si-"

"This is my last warning, Mother. If you interfere one more time in my life, I will go to the head of our companies and have you cut off. I will move in and take over every aspect of Hastings' Empire. I will take the mansion. It's mine in name already, but I will take it all from you. Every cent. I will leave you with nothing," I snarl. "Now, I'm happy with Dylan. I'm in love with my alphas and my omega. I don't want any of the whores you've brought in. And the next one that hurts my pack will end up burning in the fires of my rage."

"Silas!"

"Stay out of my life," I snarl one last time.

I turn and stalk from the room. Silver's waiting at the lift and I see red. I stalk over to her and furiously grab her shoulder, whirling her around. Her protest dies on her lips, but so does my anger. It transforms into rage.

It's not her. The woman looks nothing like the twins. However, she is the woman who destroyed us eight months ago.

"Get out of my hotel," I growl so malevolently that several people around us freeze.

"Silas, I'm sorry-"

"Alpha Hastings, and get out. How dare you come here? How dare you come anywhere near my pack?"

I look over my shoulder at Simon. "Get security. Escort her out of my hotel."

"But Falcon-"

"Simon, Falcon doesn't run my hotels. Get her out, or you'll never work in another one of my hotels again," I bark.

Simon inclines his head. "At once, sir."

Sarah? Cattia? I can't even remember this whore's name, but her lilac scent is burned into my memory, reminiscent of the most painful time of my life. Lilac is misery, betrayal, and loss. It's treason.

"Get out, and never, ever come near my pack again."

Simon takes her arm and pulls her away from me. I watch until I can't see them anymore before unclenching my fists.

I mutter an apology to the crowd and stalk to the gold lift. Only when it closes do I let myself sag. I close my eyes, seeing the look of pain in Onyx's eyes as she dragged her sister away.

I wonder if that will be the last time I see her. Falcon decided. But is he right?

It doesn't matter. We have Dylan. I've warned my mother away. We can be happy again. It will just take time to heal. Now, I need to put all my time and energy into protecting my omega like we should have the first time around.

Thirty

ONYX

I sleep in late and wake up panicking about where I am. When I remember all the events of yesterday, my heart sinks, and I scramble for the shower and clean clothes. I spent most of the night awake. Every painful moment had to be relived and dissected to figure out where I went wrong. Going over and over what I would say, playing out their reactions, going from angry with them for just abandoning me to devastated that I brought my sister here and she hurt them.

But the truth is simple: without them, I am destroyed. I'd assumed it would be hard to walk away, but not like this. I'd made my choice, I was starting my new life. To have it snatched away. No, that's not right.

It was almost daylight when I fell asleep. I'd cried so much my eyes were almost swollen shut. But today, I rush through my shower with renewed determination to see them, to face them. I need to explain.

It takes a lot more courage than I'm ready to admit to leave the safety of my ground floor room. I approach the dining room and peer inside.

I'm wearing the only pair of jeans I own and a long-sleeved black t-shirt. I don't have the fancy uniform or the fancy clothes to shield me. This is me. My hair is loose around my shoulders. There's not a bit of make-up on my face. My shoes are scuffed but still have wear left in them. Onyx stripped back to her true, honest self without the bells and whistles. Will they still want me?

All I have in the way of jewelry is my bracelet. I wrap my free hand over it, hiding the numbers. I've grown fond of the stupid thing. The number, I think, might be lucky for me, but perhaps that, too, is wrong. I need to give it back before I leave.

They aren't in the dining room, which leaves me with both a sense of relief and disappointment. I leave and go out to the first event, which should be Grayson's big reveal of the Alice and Wonderland Garden Experience. My access to the tablets has been withdrawn, so I don't have the itinerary, but luckily, I memorised it.

I find Grayson standing in front of a group of guests. He looks incredible. The sun hits his golden hair, lighting it up. His words get laughs and chuckles, and even though I can't hear what he's saying, I can tell he's captivated everyone. I wish I could tell him how proud I am of him and that it will be exceptional.

He looks around, smiling, but it falters when he sees me. I edge closer to the crowd, staying at the back. A few people see me and move away, leaving a space around me, but I don't care. I only have eyes for Gray.

My alpha abruptly turns and speaks to Simon beside him. Simon's eyes find mine and hold. He shakes his head minutely. A moment later, with a hint of resignation in his normally blank expression, Simon nods.

I would put money on the fact that Gray just gave instructions to Simon to get rid of me.

The wind is cold, and I wrap my arms around myself, wishing I had a jacket. I've felt alone before, but the way people are avoiding me, the way their eyes find me and linger, is a whole new level of alone. My loneliness is complete, so I stay where I am while the guests follow Grayson on their tour. I just wait for Simon, my heart shattering inside me. I turn away after Gray disappears into the hedges, biting my lower lip and looking up at the perfectly miserable skies. My sarcastic, sad laugh is the only sound around me.

A hand lands lightly on my back. "Hey, sweetheart, it's going to be okay." Hazel whispers.

"It won't." I shake my head. "I'm all right, Hazel, I'll see you for dinner, yeah? See the gardens. They are incredible, and he'll need your opinion on them."

"He needs a whack upside the head."

Simon approaches us and clears his throat. For the first time, he looks embarrassed. His cheeks are red, and he struggles to meet my eyes.

"Hazel."

"Simon, I'm going in. No need to report on me."

Simon flinches. "Sorry, Omega Waters, but they pay me."

"I know, I know. I understand it. I just hate it. Be kind to my friend." Hazel narrows her eyes and then turns. The white shirt looks adorable with her jean shorts and the wide black belt. I wonder what she would do for love.

"I've been instructed to ask you to please refrain from joining the events." Simon says reluctantly when we're alone. "They are for paying guests only."

I flinch. "Yeah, guess I deserved that." I peer up at Simon. Really getting a solid idea of the roadblock that's in my way. "They aren't going to let me speak to them, are they?"

He huffs and hesitates before shaking his head. "It would appear not."

My heart aches. "I'll wait, then."

"For how long?"

"Four days. It's all the time they will give me, isn't it?" My chest aches so badly, I wonder if I will ever feel normal again. "I didn't do this, Simon. I don't know what happened, but I didn't do any of this. I just wanted to make sure Silas and Dylan didn't end up in prison. I wanted to protect them. Silver's not worth it. I just…I don't know what happened," I say on a whisper.

"For what it's worth, I'm really sorry, Nyx." He seems genuine.

I swallow hard. "Thanks, Simon." I turn and walk back into the resort. There are still three more inside I might be able to corner. I just need a tiny bit of luck.

My aimless travels take me all over the resort. The staff keep far away from me, and the guests pretend I'm not here. Hazel is kept so busy that she barely has time to get a word to me about our rescheduling plans.

So, it's a surprise to me that during my midnight wanderings, I press the button for a lift and find Silas inside. Instinct tells me to back away. He's angry. I can feel that much. I don't need to be an omega to know that. But my heart begs me to be brave. I hesitate and then step inside, sending a prayer to whoever is watching.

My impulses grab me before I can think it through, and I slam my hand on the button of the lift. The emergency stop button. The lift jerks and stills.

There is only one sound over the rushing of my heartbeat in my ears.

Silas' growls.

I turn to him and raise my eyebrows. Fake it, just fake it. You've done this at a hundred parties and functions. Force that smile, own that confidence, just talk. "It's customary when you break up with someone to do it to their face." WHAT THE FUCK? Why would I say that? Why would that even come out of my mouth? I clap my hand to my mouth, but it's too late. The words are out there.

He lets out another sound, but I can't interpret what it is.

"Fine. It's over. We're done." His words are ice cold, stark, emotionless.

His words cut straight through me, slicing through bone, muscle, and stabbing my heart. It takes me a moment to control my facial expressions. For some reason, at that moment, I think of my father.

"Just like that?" I choke out.

"Just like that," Silas sneers.

I peer at him. "Who even are you? I thought I knew."

"Oh, that's rich, coming from you," Silas snaps. He reaches for the buttons, but I jerk in front of him, and he withdraws. He could manhandle me out of the way, push me with one arm, but he simply retreats. "Get out of my fucking way, Beta!"

My mouth parts at the venom coming from his mouth. "Silas, I don't know what's going on here-"

"Nothing. It's over. We had a deal, and it's done. Dylan has returned to us. There is nothing left between us. You aren't from our world, and you're..." he hesitates before he swallows hard, "you're just a beta."

I flinch away from him. Swallowing a couple of times. Those words take the fight out of me. I depress the emergency stop button, allowing our journey to continue.

To my dismay, he gets off on the same floor that I'm getting off on. The deep burgundy carpets are lit with dim lights, and directly opposite the lift is a painting of a woman sitting with an orange cat on her lap. She looks heartbroken, and I feel a flash of understanding before I look away. Her eyes stare at whoever gets off the lift.

I stumble out and freeze at the combined scents that are so painfully familiar. The entire pack is here. Falcon is dressed in a black jacket and a deep grey shirt. He looks perfectly rumpled. Dylan is wearing a singlet and jeans low on his hips. While Gray and Silas are both wearing light slacks with darker shirts. I've never seen them like this before, so casual. I drink them in, unable to stop staring at them.

Gray hits me with a glare that could strip flesh, and that's what pulls me out of my hypnotised state. Falcon doesn't even react to my presence, but it's Dylan rushing towards me, slamming me into the side of the wall that hurts the most.

My heart thunders in my ears as he glares down at me. I'm not hurt, but I am rattled.

"What are you doing?" I ask him in horror. For the first time since I've met him, I'm afraid.

"You lied to me," He spits out in a bitter growl.

The hair on my neck stands up, and I struggle to find words, but all that comes to mind is, "You lied to me, too."

He snarls.

"We made a bargain," I whisper to him as his fingers tighten around my throat. "I have not once broken that agreement. But you have."

He stares down at me. "Liar," he hisses.

"Says the guy with his fingers around my throat," I point out in a hoarse whisper.

He lets out a moan. His eyes widen, and he throws himself away from me, stumbling back, staring at me with a pale face. "No, I don't, I didn't mean-" Whatever stricken feelings he feels, he pushes deep inside himself because his face turns cold and hard.

I rub my throat and then flinch when Falcon invades my space.

"This, whatever this was between us, is over. It's done," he clarifies with perfect coolness. "I will no longer tolerate you hurting members of my pack with your sinister games."

I think I might be breaking apart, piece by piece, crumbling to dust from the inside out.

"Falcon," I protest. "I didn't do anything wrong." I reach out and grab his arm, but he deftly shakes me off.

He pulls out a tablet while the others stalk away. Silas and Gray don't even look back at me. I focus on the screen and watch my sister talk to Vienne about how she's going to steal the pack from Dylan. Do they really think this is me? Do they believe I'm capable of such deceit?

My shock holds me silent while I watch the video.

I almost protest when she steps out of from behind the ferns. On the security footage, you can't see the difference between us. I watch impassively as she promises that her sister Silver will end up with the pack, one way or another.

"Do you see now?" Falcon asks. "I've allowed you to stay until the end of the week to make a point, Onyx. Your kind will not be tolerated here. This brand of attention-seeking, pack-hunting, greedy, selfish cruelty will not be welcomed here."

I glance down at the tablet. It's on the tip of my tongue to protest, but a little voice inside my head asks me why? They should believe me. They should know me. If they felt anything for me at all, they would believe it. How could they think that I could do this to them, to Dylan? It's insane.

For a moment, I almost throw it all away and beg and plead for him to listen, but then I grab hold of that tiny part of hurt and pride I have left and wrap the shattered rags around me.

I turn and step back on to the lift.

"Nothing to say?" Falcon growls with the first display of emotion I've seen since it all happened.

"No, Alpha Treyfield," I say in a monotone. "You don't have faith in me. Now, I don't have trust in you."

His eyes flicker, but it's too late, the lift doors close and take me away.

Thirty-One
ONYX

They are happy. For three days, I watch from a distance, unnoticed as the pack lives their lives. They touch each other, love each other, be themselves. Grayson kissed Silas in public yesterday. It was so sweet. It made me ache. But they are hurting. They are closed down. I see the hypervigilance in the way they watch everyone approach. They keep Dylan close, safe. But this behaviour it's not right, it's not them.

I'm not sure why I'm still here. I have my stuff packed, but every time I try to leave, I find myself sitting on the edge of the uncomfortable bed and having this argument with myself. One half of me wants to leave and be done with them forever, the other half wants to give them a chance to come to their senses. One more chance.

My mother always said that people deserved second chances. She always said that we, the world, was too quick to make snap judgements and hold onto anger when a simple explanation could be found.

My mother was wise. I've thought about her a lot in the last few days. I wonder if she would be proud of me.

Today is going to be the biggest day for the pack yet. It's the end of the Omega Meet. From the whispers and gossip I've heard, it looks like several of the packs found omegas. The event has actually turned out to be a success, despite Silver. Despite everything, it somehow worked.

I turn away from those thoughts as I sneak into the dining room. There's a short speech ceremony and announcements before the fun starts. I stand near the back wall in the shadows and watch as Silas, Grayson, and Falcon give speeches. At the end, six packs stand up and announce their omegas to the room. There are gifts and more speeches, but I ignore all that.

My pack stands up again, taking the stage, demanding and commanding the attention of the room.

"We'd also like to thank everyone here for being patient and allowing us time while we courted our omega and convinced him to join us." Gray beams. "Allow me to introduce Pack Treyfields Omega. Dylan Wryven."

The applause is deafening.

I lean back against the wall, taking in the way they all lean into each other. The soft touches. They're in love.

I should be happy. I am happy.

No one notices me sneak out of the room. I hide for most of the day, but I need to see them one last time. It's taken me all day to come to that realisation, and I hate myself for it. I'm a masochist.

My bags are downstairs. A car will be waiting to take me home. All I need to do is flag down Simon. I've said a long painful goodbye with Moira and Hazel over lunch, and we've promised to keep in touch.

It's been a long time since I had friends, and if I walk away from here with just that, I'm luckier than I can hope to be.

But I also have a plan. One that's taken me a while to come to terms with, that I couldn't have done with Silver beside me. A plan to take back a part of myself that I lost a long time ago. These four days have been a chance for me to really reflect on how I used to live my life and how I will do so going forward.

I put on the dress that Hazel, in her generosity, gave me. It's jet black with a mother-of-pearl translucent layer of tulle over the top, giving the impression it shimmers as I move. The fabric hugs my bodice and hips tight and flows out in a-line. It's an illusion of dark dreams and fantasies. I look like a princess.

We combed my hair until it shines and hangs down to my mid-back. My make-up is subtle but sultry. If I'm going to go out, at least I'll look like a queen doing it, right? I tighten my clammy hands and then force myself to relax as I step into the dining room.

It's been transformed. All around, the round tables have been swapped out with rectangle ones. Little floating lanterns hold hundreds of flickering flames. And a woman in a glittering red dress sings about love on the stage. There are rose petals on the floor and each table has a red and white or red and black theme.

It takes my breath away, and I ache in that moment to be so alone.

As people see me, they go silent. I move through the room steadily, keeping my eyes on where I need to go. My courage is broken, but I keep my chin up and focus on moving one foot at a time. I wonder if these judgemental packs know about what happened? Does anyone know the full story? Then I decide I don't really care who knows what.

There are only four opinions that matter.

Grayson is the first to spot me. His eyes widening before his face closes down, but then Dylan and Silas follow his gaze and lock on me. Their reactions are identical to Grays, and my heart sinks a little bit more. I almost falter.

I pull out an empty chair at their table and drop into it. Falcon puts down his knife and fork and stares at me with exasperation.

"What do you want now?" He snaps.

I lift my arm, holding my wrist up to him. "Please, remove this."

His face freezes. "I forgot. I apologise." He stands up and rounds the table before he kneels beside me. I stare at him as he takes my wrist and presses in the security key code to remove it. Does he linger a moment too long? Is that touch accidental or intentional? My skin tingles where he touches me. I stare down at him and will him to say what I need to hear them say.

Understand me. Forgive me. Trust me.

As soon as it's free, I wish it was back on there because I know nothing has changed. He stands up and slides it into his pocket.

"I also," I clear my throat, "I also wanted to offer you congratulations."

Silas scowls and picks up his drink and downs it. "Because we won?"

The words sting. "I'm not sure you did win," I say sharply. "I wanted to offer congratulations for finding each other. I hope you are happy."

Dylan isn't even looking at me. I stare at him, willing him to look up. Silently begging because we can't be done, how could we be done?

"I looked for you in the shadows every night," I whisper, my voice breaking.

His eyes jerk up to mine.

"I always knew you were there," I admit and swallow hard. "You were more real to me then."

His mouth opens, but Grayson growls and puts his hand on Dylan's arm, effectively ending whatever moment I was having.

"You're wrong, you know," I say and reach for the jug of water. I fill a glass and take a sip. "You're so wrong about all of it." It doesn't even matter what they think of me. Nothing can hurt more than I'm hurting right now.

"What are you talking about?" Silas growls.

"I don't care what she's talking about. I want her gone!" Gray snarls so viciously my heart starts to race.

I close my eyes. I could tell them, but they wouldn't believe me. And if they did, I'm just a beta. They made that clear.

"It doesn't matter. Congratulations on your happy ending." I stand up. "I truly wish you the best. Be happy, Dylan. Don't come back into my world anymore, you don't belong there."

I leave before I start to cry. People watch me, I can feel them staring holes into my back, but I don't even care. They will whisper and talk about me, but at the end of the day, when the next scandal happens, no one will remember my name.

Falcon catches me just outside, swinging me around and staring into my face. "What were we wrong about?"

I peer up at him, exhausted and sick of seeing the accusation in his eyes. "All of it, Falcon. You were wrong about everything, and you won't even hear it." I shake my head.

He growls, "Tell me."

"And you'll believe me? You'll convince the others?" I peer up at him and see the truth in his eyes. I bark out a laugh. "No, you won't risk them, not a third time." I exhale heavily and look at the buttons on his shirt.

"It's my duty to protect my pack." Falcon says succinctly, "Tell me, Beta, or don't. I'm simply curious."

I shake my head. "What's the point? We all deserve better than this."

My answer annoys him, and before I can move, his fingers thread through my hair, messing it up, holding me in place. His lips hit mine, hard and demanding. His tongue invades my mouth. The kiss is punishing. It's cruel. It's what my happiness is made of.

Then he's stepping back, his brows furrowed. He searches my face as if looking for the answers to a problem he can't solve, and I do something I'm not proud of. I run away.

It's late. People are leaving. I'm still here, I'm not sure why, but I'm sitting in the shadows outside the hotel watching as Treyfield Pack sees off their guests.

"They work well together, don't they?" Only one person has a voice that mercurial.

I look up and find Vienne Hastings walking towards me. She plunks her ass beside me on the bench I've claimed. She leans both her hands on her walking stick. Her eyes narrow as she watches the pack with a satisfied grin.

"I wasn't happy about the boy, but he's a better choice than most. There is something alluring about him. I will happily change my mind over him with you gone. Though it will need some finagling in the future. He has class," Vienne says with curiosity.

"Better than my sister?" I snarl, but my heart's not in it. I truly just want this horrible bitch gone.

"Oh, your sister was never a serious choice. She was just a means to an end. I would have had her killed before allowing her to bond with my son's pack." Vienne clucks her tongue and pulls out a cigarette. She lights it and inhales deeply before smoothly blowing it out. I briefly think about seizing her walking stick and beating her to death with it.

I lift my head and angle my body slightly so I can study her better without her knowing.

"What was the purpose of driving him away?"

"A male omega can't reproduce the way I'd like, but there are surrogates and artificial insemination. We can organise other options. Originally, I was against the idea of having some no-one, no-name bitch birth the scions of our family. But no beta will carry the bloodline of three empires. I won't allow my grandchildren to be bred in such an inferior womb. A no-name male omega would be better than a beta any day of the week. I'll buy them a womb. Everyone has a price. Hell, for the right amount, I could drop a whelp in the Waters bitches' womb herself."

My disgust at this woman grows to a level that has me barely able to speak. I grind my teeth and force my hands into my lap and clench them so I don't do anything stupid. I'll kill her before she touches Hazel.

"That's ridiculous," I hiss with loathing. "Who the hell cares about all that in this day and age?"

"I care!" Vienne Hastings snaps. "I care. When the entire world will look to us for our advice, for where we walk, how we talk, what we do, what stocks we buy or sell, every choice scrutinised, and we pin all our hopes and prayers for the future on not just a beta, but a beta with no breeding, no money, no class, you don't even have a home."

I wince.

"You have no idea of the life I saved your from." Vienne shakes her head. "People from the ultra rich to the poor will look at you, judging you every day on what you wear, the bags under your eyes, the style of your hair. They will judge what you say, where you came from, what you believe in. They will slander you in magazines and come out with the most outrageous stories that will destroy your relationship with them."

"That shouldn't have been your decision to make," I say numbly.

"A mother knows best. A mother who was born and raised in this world knows best. You won't survive in this world, Onyx Davies. You're too nice."

I make a sound of pain. She laughs.

"Not to mention the question of who started that fire that killed your parents."

I stiffen.

"Silver says you left the stove on."

I shake my head, the same note of denial that I've had for five years. I didn't cook anything that night. I'm sure of it. Mama was in bed. I got home and went to sleep and then woke up to the smoke alarms going off and the fire engulfing the house. Silver and Dad were dragged out ahead of me, but I went back for mama. It didn't help. That's the source of my guilt. I couldn't get her out. I failed her.

Maybe she's right. Maybe I'm totally wrong for them. My presence would probably screw them over completely.

"So, you know everything?" I ask softly.

"Well, even if your sister wasn't so forthcoming, and she was, she sang like a little bird. My background checks are incredibly thorough."

"Well, congratulations, Omega Hastings, you've won."

She snorts and stubs out the butt of her cigarette.

"Yes. I do that. I'm surprised to see you still here, though. Have you no pride? Why did you insist on staying?"

"I needed some time to think things through," I say truthfully.

"Oh?"

"It occurs to me that if I can be thrown aside so easily, then the feelings weren't genuine. Manipulation or otherwise, I needed to know that they really believed all this."

"And?"

I laugh bitterly. "Oh, they've swallowed your bait, hook, line and sinker."

We watch them in silence for a few minutes before I clear my throat. This is the last time, I promise myself. This is our ending. This is our goodbye.

"Can I ask what you promised my sister?" I don't look away from the pack.

Vienne doesn't even look at me. "Nothing. She did it because she thought she could. I just encouraged her. But it was her plan. She really wanted to be the next Omega Treyfield. I just didn't tell her that it was never a possibility."

Swallowing that information takes a long moment. "Okay," I say roughly. "Okay. I'm going."

"For what it's worth, you seem like an okay person, for a beta. Hard working. Loyal. Someone I might have hired had circumstances been different."

"Yes, thank you for destroying my career, too," I say dryly.

Vienne shrugs and stands up. She looks perfectly put together in her charcoal suit. A woman of power and money. "All's fair in love and war."

"They'll find out what you do one day, Vienne, and when they do, you'll lose something even more precious."

"It doesn't matter. I'll have protected our future."

I can't even be near her anymore. She's toxic, and I'm exhausted. I walk out, signaling Simon. He and Yvette walk to the drive where the cars are pulling up, ignoring the pack. They wait for me. A sleek black car pulls up and stops right in front of me.

Simon hugs me tight when I reach him, ignoring the growls from his bosses. "Call me if you need anything. I'll give my brother, Adrian, a ring and see if he's got a position for you."

"Thanks, Simon. I'll miss you," I say softly and realise that it's true. In the last four days, especially, I'm not sure I would have survived without him.

He sniffs loudly and lets me go. Yvette hugs me, too, but tighter, almost punching the air out of me.

"Be careful. Call me. I'm calling my friend Kandi and letting her know she needs to keep an eye on you."

"I'll be fine." I protest.

"Wait!!"

I turn and almost crash into the car as Moira and then Hazel slam into me. Moira sobs and buries her face into my shoulder.

"You call me. Anytime. Come stay when I get back," Moira sobs. "No more sleeping on the streets, promise me."

I laugh and disengage from her. "I will, of course, I will. We're friends. No more sleeping on the streets," I promise.

Hazel glowers at her brother and turns to me. "You keep an eye out, I'm sending you a present."

"Hazel you don't have-"

"Yes! I do. Just accept it and be grateful." She kisses my cheek and steps back. I peer up at the semi-circle of friends I've made and want to scream and rage at the injustice of it all.

"I'll miss you guys."

Over Hazel's shoulder, Dylan is staring at me, stricken. I wait, letting the moment stretch out, giving him one last chance, but he keeps his mouth closed.

So, I force a smile and climb into the car, leaving my heart on the Silver Rocks Resort Driveway with the pack that I'm in love with.

Thirty-Two
ONYX

Silver whines at me for the entire three-hour drive back to the city. Sam, our chauffeur, drives us to where I've specified. As soon as we park in the carpark, my nerves rise. I wrap my arms around myself and force steady breaths in and out. Outside the car, the world is dreary and grey; the rain has just started to fall in fat, heavy drops. I thought it would be easier with distance, but no, I'm lost without them.

"Onyx?" Silver pleads. She reaches for my arm and tugs at me. "Why are we here? Where are we?"

"Silver. I'm sorry that it had to come to this." My voice sounds cold. I need to be cold to do this, she's all I have left, and the temptation to keep familiar around me is strong. But I have to do the right thing for both of us.

My self-centered sister looks around and spots the Silver Falls Omega Refuge. My twin who ruined my life finally realises how far we've fallen. "No! No! Onyx, no!"

"Silver," I say loudly, cutting off her shouts. "You have ensured that I won't get a job where I can work enough for both of us. You sabotaged not just my chances but your own with this greed, this feeling that you deserve more than what you're offered, but the fact is, you are a spoiled brat." I don't have any emotions left in me. I'm numb.

I look out the window. The rain has begun to pour. Great, a fitting homecoming. I left here thinking I could change my life. It seemed so long ago.

"You really fucked things up this time, Silver," I murmur.

"No, I didn't. I just need to go back and explain," Silver shouts. "Just let me go back. I can explain. I can fix it. I promise. I can get your job back."

"They chose him. He's their scent match," I say absently. "They think I was going to hurt him," I snap and finally turn to face her. "I loved him, Silver, and never, ever would have taken them from Dylan."

She scoffs. "He's male."

"He's their scent match. You don't know them, you don't like them, you just wanted to be rich and powerful. Well, you failed. So, here are your options. This car is going to let you out here, and you can walk into that center, and they can find you a pack. They have options where you can stay there, work for them in exchange for their help. Or you can get out here and go find a job and take your chances."

"But I can't. I'm an omega."

"I'm aware. But there's nothing I can do. I can't afford your suppressants. I can't afford rent. I've just lost all my references. This is it, Silver. The end of the road."

She stares at me and looks back at the white building. "What if you go back and fix things with them?"

I laugh bitterly. "Oh, no, your plan with Vienne destroyed those options."

She makes a choked sound. She tugs the expensive red coat closer around her. They let her keep everything. Simon refused my money. I am grateful for that. "You know about that?"

"Yes, Silver, I know. Thank you for making sure they hate me. Yes, thank you for that, too."

Silver flinches, her eyes well with tears. "I wasn't trying to hurt you."

"I know. You were just trying to get what you deserved. Except, maybe *this* is what you deserve. Maybe I should have brought you here years ago instead of starving and working myself into the ground. Go inside, Silver, and good luck."

"No, I can't. We're sisters, twins." Silver grabs at me, but I fend her off and finally push her away roughly. She peers at me with huge, hurt eyes.

I stare at her. "Go inside and find what you deserve, Silver, because if you come with me, it will be starvation and rape. I can't protect you from alphas anymore than I can protect myself."

Silver sobs for a few minutes, but I sit in silence, staring out the window. I feel cold inside. She needs to choose her own path. I can't influence her and make her choices anymore.

"Will you come back and visit me sometime?" Silver asks in a tiny voice.

I turn my head and look at her. "Yes." I soften my voice. "I'll come back and check on you."

"Thank you, Nyx." She pauses. "Dad was wrong about the fire. It was an accident. The fire inspector said so. I read the report. It wasn't your fault or mamas." She pauses again, longer this time. "I didn't realise you cared about them."

"Would it have made a difference?"

Silver deflates. "No," She whispers.

I absorb that blow with a curious lack of care.

"For what it's worth, I'm sorry, Onyx. Really sorry."

She climbs out of the car, slams the door, and runs towards the building. I watch until she's inside. I keep the car there for another twenty minutes. A woman comes out in a long coat, she gets into the backseat and studies me. She's got a hard face, like a woman who won't be pushed around.

"Onyx?"

"Yes. You're Jenny Lathem? You run the omega refuge?"

"I am. Silver has agreed and signed up to stay with us in the omega center. She'll work for us and with us. We can keep her here for three years or until she finds a pack. Her bills are all paid with the money you have wired us. There is some left over. Would you like it back?"

I shake my head. "Just keep it in a deposit in case she needs something."

Jenny brushes her grey hair behind her ear. "We'll find her a good home. You don't need to worry."

"Thank you."

She gets out of the car and runs back to the door and passes through.

"Hey, Sam?"

The driver looks back. He doesn't remark on the tears on my cheeks or the tight sounds of my voice. "Can you take me home now?"

"Sure, Miss Davies, I can do that." He clears his throat. "I just want to say that what you're doing, giving your sister this chance, paying for her to stay, it's really beautiful. After everything she did, I'm not sure she deserves it, but I think you're a really decent human being, Miss Davies."

I feel so alone, but his words reach out and warm the broken pieces of my heart. A hug with words.

I smile through my pain. "Thanks, Sam."

What is home? Home is the alley at the side of a convenience store. It's a bit of brick wall that I lean against now. Sam's long gone, and I'm soaked through, but I can't make myself move from the spot. It's the happy and the hope and the memory of innocent love before it all went wrong.

Shivers run up and down my body. I've never been this alone before. I've never been this broken before. Even when I've had men try to force themselves on me and seen some of the brutal things I've seen in hotel rooms, in alleys, in parks. Even when I've had to barricade the door to keep us safe, I've never been this scared of what my future will look like.

Because I don't want a future without them in it. I feel like I've lost everything. A naïvety I didn't realise I had is gone. My sister is gone. This love that I grew inside me is now gone. All that's left of me is a broken shell. No home, no job, no future. Just memories of when life was better.

I let my feet slide out and lean up against the wall. I sob brokenly to the symphony of the stormy night and remember when I met a dying man and saved him.

My shadow, my stalker, the man I fell in love with, he never comes.

Thirty-Three
GRAYSON

Two weeks since she left, and I still can't believe she's gone. I can't believe she'd do that. I didn't think I could hurt like this. Dylan murmurs something in his sleep, and I curl around him, stroking a hand down his chest. My attempts to soothe us both fail miserably.

"Nyx," Dylan whispers in his sleep. "Nyx."

I close my eyes to the pain. When I open them, I find Silas staring at me from the other side.

"He's not moving on," Silas says.

"Neither am I."

I close my eyes and then abruptly roll off the bed and pad out of the room. We're back at my mansion in Silver Falls, having made the trip just after our guests left. I jump on the treadmill and start running.

He's withdrawn and quiet. His dreams always end with him searching for her. When I ask him in the morning what he dreamed about, he always tells me he's in the dark trying to find her, but she's gone.

I run faster on the treadmill.

Falcon walks into the gym and closes the door behind him. He folds his arms over his chest and that stiff white shirt just pisses me off. Why does he have to look so perfect all the time?

"Spit it out or fuck off," I snarl.

"She's got a job now."

"Great."

"But she's still staying in the shelter."

I grunt and keep running.

"She's not seeing anyone," Falcon says and tilts his head to the side. "Sam has not talked, after he quit, he went to work for Darion, and no amount of money will get me an account of what happened."

"I don't care, Falcon. What the fuck?" I howl at him and jump off the treadmill. I pace back and forth, unable to contain the energy.

"Why are you so upset about this?" Falcon snaps coldly.

"I'm upset because she betrayed us."

Falcons eyebrows raise. "So, Grayson. We're not a hundred percent sure of that anymore, are we? Vienne made that slip of the tongue and let out that she and Silver had become friends. What if we're wrong?" Falcon prods.

"If she was innocent, she would have said something," I snarl and grab my towel, wiping the sweat off my face.

Falcon's brows lower. "We didn't let her say anything. We never gave her a chance."

"She could have-" I stop and then sweep my drink bottle across the room. "I trusted her, and she betrayed me, she hurt me, she took everything-"

"Does this have something to do with your past?" Falcon interrupts.

I stiffen, but the words are a bucket of ice water down my spine. "Don't be fucking absurd."

"Your nanny kidnapped you and your sister for two weeks and tortured you both. It was a huge betrayal. She was a beta, too, wasn't she?" Falcon asks.

I snarl. "She's not like that woman."

Falcon paces closer. "I know she's not. Do you?"

I open my mouth but don't answer because the door opens, and Silas walks in.

"What are we talking about?"

"Falcon's got an idea that, in my mind, I've been associating my kidnapper with Onyx."

Silas tilts his head to the side. "Are we finally having this conversation? Thank god. Well, Gray, it makes sense. And your level of anger is way over the top. Like, way."

I shove at him, but he slings an arm around my waist and pulls himself back to me.

"Calm, Gray. It's not a criticism. You suffered horribly when you were a child. You trusted that woman, and she betrayed you. Onyx is the first woman you've trusted since then, isn't she?"

I stare at Silas in shock. That can't be true, can it? I think about it and finally breathe the answer. "Yes."

"My mother is a terrible person when she wants something. I'm more inclined to believe that she had more to do with this than what we think." Silas lets me go and paces the space between Falcon and I.

I exhale and close my eyes. Are they right? I pull myself free and get back on the treadmill. My thoughts run around and around in my mind. Reliving everything in a matter of seconds.

"We need to find out what happened," I say out loud.

Silas and Falcon stop talking and look back at me.

"How?" Silas asks. "My mother isn't talking."

"Find Silver," I say.

Falcon, the smug prick, just grins and walks out of the gym.

Silver crosses her arms under her breasts, and for the first time since I've met her, she doesn't try to impress us. No, she's closed off and defensive. She is angry at us.

"We need to know what happened with you and my mother," Silas says.

She shrugs. "We became friends."

Falcon growls. "Talk and talk fast, Silver, or I'll make sure things go awfully for you."

Her lip curls, and she narrows her eyes. "You don't deserve her. You just assumed she was bad. Fuck you."

I lean over the table and slam my hands on it. "Was that you in the security footage?"

She leans back and snorts. A huge smile spreading across her face. "What footage? Be specific."

I growl, but it doesn't deter her at all. "Do you pretend to be your sister?" I hiss in rage.

She smiles. "That was the right question. Bingo, we've got a winner. Yes. I do pretend to be Onyx, a lot, actually. She has far more freedom than I have."

I hate this woman. My temper is so close to snapping.

"Falcon," I hiss. I have to go, I'm going to hurt her. Crush her.

"It's all right, go," Falcon says calmly.

I close my eyes and rush from the room, ignoring the woman at the reception desk. I go outside and put my hands on my waist and stare up at the sky. It's taken two weeks more to find this bitch, and now she's playing games.

Fuck this.

She pretends to be Onyx. We got the answer we needed. And the heartbreaking mistakes we've made become crystal clear. There was a third woman at the hotel. The omega who broke us the first time. The one who looks like Nyx and Silver from the back. Vienne, Silver, and the omega working together.

What the fuck have we done?

I send an SOS to the only other person in the world that I trust. She sends me back an address and a time. I sit back, closing my eyes. I don't know how to fix anything, but tonight, I'm going to start.

Thirty-Four
ONYX

The first few days were a blur. I remember thinking that I won't survive the pain. I remember thinking a thousand times an hour that perhaps today will be the day they come. It will happen right now, any moment. All day, I'd peer at the front door of my new workplace. I'd sit up all night in the shelter bed clutching the stiff, itchy blanket, but they never came. The constant weight of expectation crushed me. But with each passing day, their smells faded in my mind, replaced by coffee and the real world, and time brought resignation and reality. I discovered that though I might feel like I had torn my heart out of my chest, my body was going to keep on keeping on. I wasn't going to die simply from missing them. Heartbreak would not be my demise.

With my references from jobs I'd worked not related to Treyfield, I found a job at a café. It wasn't a great job, and my boss was a raging dick, but it was work. The few hours a week I worked allowed me to save almost seventy percent of my wages in the hopes of being able to move out of the shelter and into a place of my own. That's my entire dream now. Just somewhere safe to pass the hours.

The doors to the cafe open, and I almost cry when a woman walks in. When will I stop willing them to appear? The omega comes in with her fruity scent. Her clothes are new, expensive, and stylish. She looks badass compared to the omegas at the Omega Meet in her skinny jeans and leather jacket and with this confidence I've never seen on an omega before. She lowers her sunglasses, searching the cafe until her eyes land on me.

She smiles, white teeth flashing, and a pang hits my chest. Dylan.

The way she moves is sinful. Her ginger hair falls to her mid-back and her green eyes sparkle.

"I've been looking for you everywhere," She says and leans on the counter. She inspects the menu and then peers at me. "This place is a dump."

"I'd like to disagree, but I wouldn't eat anything here, and the coffee is mediocre at best," I say with a polite smile.

She's obviously mixed me up with someone else. My mind immediately goes to Silver, wondering if she's tried to steal this omega's alphas, too.

"I'm not sure why you've been looking for me. I don't know you," I say hesitantly.

"Onyx Davies, you are a hard girl to find, but found you, I have." The omega says with a wink. "And, yes, I'm looking for you, not Silver. And," she stresses, "you don't know me yet, but you will."

She smiles and glances at the door as it opens with a cute little chime that I'd happily destroy. An incredibly handsome dark-haired guy pushes in, scouring the cafe like he's searching for people to kill. My money's on he belongs with her.

"No, you don't. Not yet. But you will." She laughs as a couple scurry out of the cafe, giving the man a wide berth. "I'm Missy."

"Missy?" I say absently, still warily watching the alpha prowl towards us.

"Raptore, formally Clark." She hooks a thumb over her shoulder. "I belong to him. That's Darion. The idiot lying on the bonnet of his car is Lukas, and the viking is Seb."

I study the three men intently. "I see." I don't see, but neither do I care. "What do you want?" I almost wince at my bluntness.

"We run a security company."

"Okay." I'm still not following, and this conversation is getting boring and painful. I grab a cloth and wipe down the counter. It doesn't need it, but I need to do something, anything, else but focus on how the wrong omega walked into my work looking for me.

I glance at the white-blond guy who has sat up off the car and is now doing a handstand on the footpath. I seriously question whether he can run anything, but I'm not going to put my thoughts into words. But judging by Missy's sigh, she's picked up on my hesitations and isn't sure how to combat it, especially with the three-ring circus happening out the front.

Missy covers her eyes with her hand and mutters something about strength. "Look, I'm looking for a seriously organised individual, and you come highly recommended."

"I work with food," I point out stupidly. "Hard not to be organised around food."

"Ha, you're funny. No one mentioned you were sarcastic and bitter. You'll get along great with Darion. Yes, but food, security. It's all interchangeable."

I narrow my eyes. "Um, no, it's not."

"Fine, I'll train you." Missy rolls her eyes.

"So, this is a job offer?" I clarify and laugh at her.

"Yup. I'll give you...um, I have an envelope." She pats down her chest and then her jeans until she finds a bit of paper, pulls it out, and passes it to me.

This has got to be a joke. An absolute joke. I take the envelope. "If this is a revenge or something else, I'm not playing. You may as well go find someone else to screw."

I unfold it quickly, my brows rising as I read it over. It's a lot of money. Its lodgings. It's everything I need to get back on my feet and get out of sleeping in the abandoned buildings on Fifth and Noble or the shelters. I read it three times.

"What's the catch?" I snarl quietly.

Missy smirks. "No catch, love. I need good, trustworthy people."

"Who said I was trustworthy?" I snap back instantly.

"Scarlet Waring."

The name takes the wind out of my sails. "Oh." I half expected her to say Falcon. It almost hurts that it's not him. Wait, Scarlet Waring? The female alpha of Pack Knight? The woman in crimson?

"Scarlet doesn't know me," I say cautiously. "We met in passing once," I amend. "Why would she help me?"

"Your name is running in bigger circles now, sweetheart. Scarlet has heard of you, and she told me to snap you up. I listen to her because Scarlet is a good friend of mine. She said you're a good person. So, here I am, recruiting people of excellence to our security team. Also, Adrian Shultz called me, his brother is a guy named Simon? Oh, and there was a call to Kandi, who works for me, from a woman named Yvette. And, finally, Sam joined our team and begged me to help you."

I stare at her. There's an excitement and hope that I haven't had in a while running through my body. I can get out of the shelter. Enough money to do anything I wanted. I could travel. I could run. Far away. And maybe it will stop hurting.

But all those people, helping me? I'm speechless.

"Will you take the job? You come highly recommended."

I glance around the empty cafe; I see the empty future that awaits for me, and I reject it. I want more.

"Yes. I'll take the job." I know I should be happy. I should be enthused, but I'm dead inside. If there was any justice in the world, people would be able to see the wound I'm walking around with. "There's nothing left for me to do, anyway."

Missy sits on my desk and swings her legs while I type up the report. She was right. Between Darion, Seb, Lukas, Missy, a beta named Kandi, and an older woman with a radiant smile named Ava, I found this job easy. It was similar to the work I'd done for Silas, a lot of compiling reports and information and presenting it in a logical way. It keeps me busy, and that makes the hours pass faster.

"I don't know. I mean, I could get him what he asks for, but where's the surprise for a present if I get him what he asks for?"

I give the omega an exasperated look. "Missy, I'm working."

"I know. But hear me out…"

Instead of listening, I send a 'help me' message to Kandi through our computer message system. The omega's bodyguard and best friend laughs and comes over to stand beside her.

"Missy. Just get both."

The omega's eyes widen and then get a glimmer of excitement that gives me butterflies in the worst way. Missy's ideas get us on the wrong end of Pack Raptore's fury, and while they might forgive Missy, I still can't get used to their disapproval or the fear of losing this job.

"I've got an idea," Missy says with excitement.

"Nope!" I snap. "I'm not getting involved."

"Oh, come on. Help me," Missy winks at Kandi and then lets out a little squeal when she spots her sisters walking inside.

Elise and Muse are cute, but what I really find different is the way the betas here are part of everything. More than half the staff are betas, but Missy treats them like family. And when I overheard Elise telling Lukas about a boy she liked, but didn't want to say anything to him because she was just a beta, he calmly but firmly told her that no one is just a beta, that she was important and integral to their family, and anyone, alpha, omega, or beta, would be lucky to have her.

I'd stood in the hallway blinking back tears, wishing someone had said that to me.

Being here has given me time to let the voices of my father and Silver fade away. I'm starting to see that the rhetoric I've lived my life with is wrong. Designations are important until they aren't. We each have a place in this world, and we are all useful to each other.

I press my hand to my mouth to hide my smile and watch the omega with her sisters. It's sweet. This whole place is nice. It's just…I miss the pack.

I miss Falcon's calm and the way he would push his glasses up the bridge of his nose absently. Those glasses that I'd been so surprised to see because it was just another sign my alpha was actually human. And I miss the way Silas would silently pause at the doorways and watch us. Grayson had a bigger than life personality, but he always made me smile. He'd be teasing a smile out of me right now. And Dylan. I miss him more than all of them. I miss looking into the shadows and finding him there; I miss his eyes on me.

I feel broken without them, like I've lost a part of myself that I won't ever get back. But most of all, I miss their casual touches, the reassurances, the feeling of connectedness, I'm a boat adrift without an anchor.

Blinking the tears away rapidly, my attention shifts back to the computer screen. Missy's family is large and encompasses more than just her pack, but it isn't mine. I rub my temple, trying to dispel the near constant ache that exists there.

This was the right choice, I tell myself again. Silver is no longer a problem for them. Vienne won't hurt them.

Dylan must have gone into his heat because the pack official withdrew for ten days four days ago. I abused Missy's trust and reached into their secure networks to read the email Treyfield sent to Darion. It was a polite notification because Treyfield does use Raptore Security occasionally. I'm sure they know, but no one has said anything. The official bonding announcement will come out soon, and that will be that. I'll be out of their lives.

One thing Vienne said was true. The tabloids were ruthless with reporting the 'mysterious male omega dating Pack Treyfield'. Between that, the missing Donahue heir is all they seem to talk about.

I tried really hard not to feel destroyed over that. I am happy for them, but I'm devastated for me. They are a pack. No one can separate them now.

"Good. That was my plan all along," I whisper. If I keep telling myself that, I'll believe it one day.

The last hour of the day drags, but finally, it's over. I head back to the apartment Darion had secured for me. It's way too posh for me and far too big, but it's nicer than anything I've ever lived in before, except, of course, the Treyfield Suite penthouse. I'm not sure anything could top that. But this at least looks loved and lived in. I push open the rusty gate and pause. There's a woman standing on my painted porch with two men on either side.

She turns, and I suck in a startled breath.

"Alpha Waring," I say respectfully because no one can forget her once they meet her. Scarlet Waring is beautiful, but more than that, she's a rare female alpha who owned multi-million dollar companies and tamed the elusive Knight Pack. She's also the woman who rescued me all those long nights ago when it all changed.

She smiles and turns even more, and I notice how incredibly pregnant she is. I jump forward, ignoring the growls of the alpha and omega, and unlock my door.

"Come in, sit down," I say and usher her through.

She sits down on the lounge, right in the middle, and lets out a relieved sigh. "Thanks, Onyx. I have to admit, it's getting awkward to, well, do anything."

I hesitate with my back to her. She remembers me? Why is she even here? I turn around and take in the other alpha. He's got auburn hair and a smile that I'm sure broke many hearts before he settled down.

"That's Jet." The omega says with a playful grin. "I'm Barren."

"You're Pack Knight," I say reverently. There is a tremendous hit to my heart when I look at Barren. He's nothing like Dylan. Barren is happier, friendly, and more open. But he's a male omega, and apparently, that's enough to make my ridiculous heart ache.

"Yep."

There's a tense silence where my frustration grows until I finally snap. "Why are you here?" I groan and turn away. "I didn't mean that the way it came out. I'm sorry."

Scarlet tilts her head to the side, watching me. I meet her eyes, and this time, I don't look down or away.

"You've grown, little beta."

I shrug. "Do you want a drink, something to eat?"

"No," Scarlet says with a laugh but takes the hint anyway.

I tense and sit on the armchair. "Okay, let's get straight into it then. Did Falcon send you? Or did Darion?" It's the first time I've spoken Falcon's name in weeks, and it hurts.

Scarlet's smile falls away. "So much pain when you say his name. You love him."

I flinch but straighten my shoulders, anyway. "That's not relevant."

Scarlet and Barren exchange a look that I don't understand.

"Actually, it wasn't anyone from Pack Raptore or Pack Treyfield. It was a very good friend of mine. Someone who saved me in this very room when I needed it."

I blink at her. "This was your house?"

Scarlet smiles, but it's soft now, sympathetic. "Onyx, this is my house. You didn't think we'd let you fall, did you? You are destined for so much more than a shitty job in a café. Any one of our packs will gladly find you a place. And that includes Falcon. He has said to Taylor that you are to be given anything you desire. Money is no object. He still cares."

I bite my lower lip to hold back the tears, but I can't stop the arrow of pain into my chest. It rips open the wound and makes it hard to breathe. If he cares so much, where is he?

"The person who sent me to you was Hazel Waters." Scarlet says at last when I don't answer her.

I blink rapidly. "What?" Hazel. Grayson. The links and reminders are everywhere. I can smell him like he's standing beside me. Mangoes. My throat squeezes closed.

Scarlet shakes her head. "That girl, she's got to fix everything that's broken. I can understand why, though, her story is tragic and with no happy ending. She can't stand to see us all like this. She has a message for you."

I tense. "I didn't think she cared. I haven't heard from her since the day I left."

"Of course, I care, but sneaking away from my brother, the new dictator of Waters, is getting harder and harder. He's impossible, I swear. But I'm here because you made them love you. And you loved them. You protected them." Hazel says suddenly from the front door. I stare at her, confused. What are they doing here? "That kind of loyalty is rare. We are destined to be sisters."

I shake my head, denial, confusion; I don't even know anymore. "What's the message, Hazel? Why are you here?"

Silas would look at her and know. He would stand beside me, his arm touching mine. A silent show of support. I miss him.

"She said to tell you she knows what you did to save them, and she knows that living without you will never give her family the happy ending they deserve. So-" Barren glances at Hazel and obediently falls silent.

I look between them. "What are you two talking about?" I thunder.

"I challenge you to come home." Hazel lifts her chin, glaring at me with all the superiority of her damn family line. "To see them, to stand before them and tell them how you feel. To show them what you've done and let them decide once and for all. The truth, Onyx, tell them the truth. You let the lies fall between you, and you didn't fight for them," Hazel shouts at me. "They won't listen to anyone else. I've tried. You can't let them believe a lie. If you won't fight for yourself, fight for them, fight for their happiness."

I stare at her, stunned. Is she for real? All I can think of is her words hitting into me over and over. Is she right? Did I give up on them? Did I give up on myself?

Missy sneaks through the gap between Hazel and the door. She grins at me and then ushers Moira through.

"Hey, hun." Moira waves at me. I let out a cry and explode towards her. We embrace, and I hug her to hide my tears. The last time I saw her was the night I left. All the memories come back.

"I'm so glad to see you," I say and brush a tear away.

"I've missed you, too. It's the first weekend I could get off."

I approach Hazel, who is glaring at me.

"Pause so I can say hello, then you can yell at me some more?"

Hazel's frown vanishes, and she throws her arms around me.

Missy and Scarlet exchange a look and roll their eyes. "Haze, we could have handled one brief message," Scarlet says.

"It needs to be done right," Missy and Hazel say at the same time.

I look between the two of them. Missy pokes her tongue out at Hazel.

"She's a control freak," Missy stage whispers.

"You don't know what it's like living without the ones you know are yours. I know, my pack, my scent matches are out there, they turned away from me," Hazel says in a rough voice.

I make a sound of protest even though there's nothing I can do. How could anyone turn away from Hazel? Moira reaches out and grabs Hazel's hand, squeezing her fingers.

"I don't want that for my brother. So, I'm being selfish here, Nyx. I'm being greedy. I'm going to fight whatever I have to fight to get you to go back to him."

"It's not them," I say, my throat tight. "I'm a beta."

"So?" Scarlet snaps icily. I wince and backtrack.

"So, they are rich, and-"

"Lonely, scared boys who turned into cold men surrounded by people who didn't or couldn't show love," Hazel interjects. "Men who found an omega they could love and almost lost him because they didn't know how to be a safe place for him. But you taught them with words, with gestures, with actions how to be that, but they need you."

I shake my head in mute protest.

Hazel closes her eyes. When she speaks again, her voice is bitter. "I never pegged you for a coward, Onyx Davies."

I flinch.

"In two weeks, there's going to be a party held at my mansion. This is your invitation. Come and see them. Prove that you can live in a world without them by facing them. If you can walk away from them again, I won't pursue you. We will all let you go."

"You can't do this. They hate me," I breathe those last words into the air with so much pain that everyone in the room flinches.

"I'm a Waters. No one can stop me," Hazel says with a lift of her chin. "And they don't understand what happened, but when you tell them the truth, they will forgive you. They don't hate you, Onyx. If they hated you, they wouldn't be so damn miserable."

"Oh, the arrogance." I whip around and find Missy in the kitchen. She's found a stash of my chocolate and is shoving pieces into her mouth.

Kandi is leaning over the island, watching with undisguised glee.

"How did you get in here?" I ask, blinking rapidly. Kandi wasn't in here before, I was sure of it.

"Kandi either has mad skills and climbed the gutters, or she used the key I gave her," Missy says. "Hazel, enough with the dramatics. We're here to celebrate."

"Celebrate?" I protest.

"It's your birthday, Onyx," Scarlet says. "I didn't know what to get you, but I spent too many birthdays on my own, so this is my present to you. A birthday with many people who care, even if you don't know us well yet."

I pause, confused, and then suddenly realise it is my birthday. I've never celebrated it before. Not once. I stumble backwards and drop heavily into the armchair.

"Get dressed, sexy beta. We're going to drop Scarlet home before Taylor and Gold can go crazy, and then you, Haze, Moira, Kandi, and I are heading out to have some fun."

I raise an eyebrow.

"Oh, all right," Missy grumbles. "Sven, Lukas, and Darion are coming, too, but I promise they'll be invisible."

"You don't have to do this."

Missy walks towards me and crouches beside the armchair. "We've known each other for a month, yeah?" She flicks a glance at Scarlet. "We're the kind of friends that are going to be annoying staff in a nursing home. Friends, Onyx. Haven't you realised? You, me, Kandi, Hazel, Moira, and Scarlet all old and wrinkled, shouting at our packs while they fight each other off with walkers. Defending our honour. It's going to be epic."

"I can just see Darion with adult diapers, glaring at the nurses who come to change him," Scarlet says with a laugh.

"He and Gold will have to be taken out the back and hosed down from a safe distance." Missy claps back.

Kandi roars with laughter, Scarlet snorts. Hazel shakes her head in disgust, but Moira looks delighted.

I swallow hard, blinking moisture out of my eyes. I have friends. I think of my mother at that moment, and I know she'd be happy for me. She'd tell me to take a chance. To be brave. She would say betas can do and have anything.

She would have told me to fight for them. She would have loved them, I know she would have, even Falcon.

I look at Hazel, and the world narrows down to just her and I. "I'll come to your party. I'll explain everything I did. I'll give them the words they deserved to hear from me. But they won't take me back, and I won't chase them again. It's all-or-nothing, Hazel."

Hazel lets out a breath and then squeals and throws herself at me. Missy ends up sandwiched between us as the omegas hug me tight.

I don't know how I got here, but I guess I'm glad for the detour. There's a tiny burning flame of hope inside me again. I'm going to see them one last time.

Thirty-Five

FALCON

I hate this place. I don't know why Grayson needed to be here tonight. He'd insisted. The thumping of the music is too loud, and there is too much stimulation. I've never felt more like an old man watching my pack dance with my omega than I do right now, longing for home. Or rather, for her and the quiet of my study.

Dylan looks up at me and waves.

I will admit, watching the sultry way he moves and grinds with Gray and Silas is bringing out two conflicting urges. The first, to shove him to his knees and claim him as mine in front of everyone here, and the other, to grab him and run.

I turn my head, scanning the rest of the club. It's packed tonight. A dissatisfaction rolls through me, and I shift as I try to push it aside. Ever since she left us, the feeling has popped up mercilessly. This discontent, this anger that I can't extinguish, this ache in my chest.

Forcing her image from my mind takes more effort than I'm willing to admit. But then, when I open my eyes, she's there, on the other side of the club, with other alphas and omegas.

Blind rage has me up on my feet, staring in her direction. A moment later, I feel the reaction of my pack. Dylan is the one that forces me to pull my own emotions back in. His pain is excruciating. I can smell it from up here. Silas aches in a way that is dull and resigned. Grayson is less angry, but it's all a front to hide the longing inside him.

She looks different. She's laughing and dancing with the Raptore omega. Has she replaced us so soon? Is this who she is? A human leach sponging off the wealthy. I immediately feel ashamed of my thoughts. I know that's not who she is, but when the omega puts her hands on Nyx's hips and moves in close, swaying and laughing, I see red.

No one touches what is mine.

And whether I want her right now or not, that beta is still mine.

A low, menacing growl erupts from my throat, and I watch as Nyx lifts her head, looking around like prey who suddenly has a sixth sense they are being stalked.

I have my eyes on you.

Is she thinner? Are those shadows under her eyes from exhaustion? She's not smiling her normal sunny smile. I curse myself five times a fool and force myself to look away.

My eyes meet Dylan's distraught ones, and the feeling of wrongness intensifies and explodes into panic.

He melts back into the crowd faster than Grayson and Silas can realise. I try to follow him with my eyes, and as soon as I see the path he's taking, I rush down the stairs, pushing bodies aside, but knowing that I'm going to be too late.

The crowd clears, and I see her on her own. He's not there, but he should be. Her head whips around, confusion changing to fury on her face. The expression does something to me, but then the gap closes, nearly obscuring my view. I push harder, forcing my way through. My direction changed.

The gap clears, and Dylan, my omega, is shoved hard against a wall by an alpha. I can see the shock and anger on his face, but also a touch of fear. But just when a fist flies, there she is.

Her own fist comes up, hitting the alpha's chin. It's followed by a second arm sweeping across his face. She hits him again and again, forcing him back by sheer will and fury. She is a blur of movement, and Dylan is against the wall, in shock, watching her.

I'm stunned into inaction. I hear a grunt and catch Silas' scent of figs and sea salt and then Grayson's mango. Their scents strengthen. Hunger. Longing. Possession.

She's ours.

Dylan pushes up off the wall and reaches for her. She doesn't see it, but we do. But then he withdraws his hand. Hesitates. No, damnit, no. Take her, I want to shout at him.

She barely turns, and Dylan is already backing away. He's already got his mask back in place. He's retreating.

Gray makes a wordless protest, but she's already turned. She sees his back as he disappears into the crowd, and I wonder if Silas and Gray see the agony on her face a moment before she looks up and spots the three of us.

Silas is the first to move, breaking away from my side and stalking after Dylan. I force myself to move, step by step, until I'm barely a foot from her.

She tries to meet my eyes, but she drops them, staring at the third button on my shirt. It pleases and enrages me that she's unable to meet my eyes.

I catch that faint whiff of coconut, so weak, like how I wake up sometimes, chasing that scent out of sleep only to realise it was just a dream.

"Thank you for your assistance, Beta." I pull out a handful of notes from my wallet and force them into her stiff hand. "For your trouble."

The coconut gets fainter and fainter. I study the red in her cheeks, the way her hair hides her face.

"Falcon, no!" Grayson groans as if in pain.

"Falcon!" Hazel snaps, giving me a look of deep warning.

I look at the interfering omega and scowl. "Just making sure she's compensated for the effort she's expended." The words come out all wrong. I just want to make sure she sees a doctor, but all the words just come out hostile and wrong. The world feels as if it is shifting and shaking and tilting. I want to bite her and end this now. I want to pick her up, throw her over my shoulders, and fuck her until my scent bleeds from the inside out. My thoughts are a jumbled mess as I try to contain the need to have her.

A low growl slips through my teeth, and I watch as her skin pebbles, her nipples tighten, her damn coconut scent turns sweeter. Reacting to me. Mine.

Hazel bares her teeth, but it's Onyx who captures my attention, lifting her chin.

"He's right. It's all about the money, don't you know, Hazel? I hope you'll excuse me, but I'm not feeling like being out after all. I'm going to head home." Though her voice shakes, she doesn't hesitate, and as she spins, the money falls to the floor.

She leaves, just like that. So easily. Walking away from us all over again. I rush after her before I can even stop, throwing off Lukas' hands and shoving Sven out of the way. I catch her arm and spin her around.

Her furious eyes meet mine, look over my shoulder, and then land back on me.

"Don't come any closer."

For a moment, I think she's talking to me, but her gaze jerks to a spot over my shoulder again and gets cold and hard.

I can't get the words out. I can't even think past the need to have her. She doesn't understand, but Sven sees me and whispers something to Lukas.

My fingers tighten around her arm, drawing her attention back to me. For a moment, it's just us, and I read into everything I can, using every sense that I have.

THE BETA'S BARGAIN

I yank her closer and press our lips together. Her arms wrap around my neck, holding me tight. Our tongues duel. Coconut is every-fucking-where, just like it should be.

I pull back from her; the insanity sated for a minute. "Happy birthday, Nyx."

Her eyes widen and then narrow. She wrenches her arm free and whirls, her hair fanning out behind her, and then the crowd has swallowed her, and she's gone as if she was never there.

I close my fist to preserve the feeling of her skin on mine. My anger has taken a bitter, sour taste in my mouth.

I stand there in that crowded nightclub and realise that I'm barely in control anymore. I need her. I'm hurt and all I want is her back, and if I don't do something about it soon, I might just take her.

She is mine.

In the same way that Dylan is mine.

Her walking away from me, walking out of my life, is only tolerated because he needs me. I soothe my inner self and promise that, soon, I will take her. Soon, I will chase her down. And it's a promise I intend to keep.

But I push the unsettled feeling aside and focus on the pain in the pack bonds. I have priorities and responsibilities, and the beta made her choice. For tonight.

Tomorrow, all bets are off.

Thirty-Six

SILAS

Only Hazel would organise a masquerade. I lean over the rails, watching the crowd of people hidden behind their glittering costumes and their masks. The drinks are flowing, the live band is a hit, the food is being delivered on white and red platters by men wearing card costumes.

I put the fingers of my left hand against my eyes.

"Is this a thing with you, Waters?" I ask. "This Alice gimmick?"

"It's kinda cool, actually," Grayson says and leans on the rail beside me. "Hazel has set herself up as Alice." He points, and I see her. The sexy blue dress that does somehow also convey innocence also somehow implies Alice. The long blonde wig is the finishing touch. Despite looking somewhat daring, she still manages to do it with class.

"I would have pegged her for the queen of hearts," I say and twist around, taking a champagne from a passing Ace of Spades.

Grey snorts, and when I turn, I find a cat-like mask on his face, he smirks and turns, flashing me his tail.

I roll my eyes and put the tall hat on my head.

He'd bullied us all into dressing up. He's the Cheshire cat. I'm the Mad hatter. Falcon is the caterpillar.

And Dylan is wearing a waistcoat with a pocket watch and two very long white ears. He looks adorable and really unhappy.

I spot princesses and queens, monsters and myths. Characters from stories. It's actually a really fantastic turnout.

The doors open, and someone walks in that makes my heart pound. I stand up and stare down, unable to believe my eyes. I'd recognise her in a million masks, in a million different rooms, in the dark, in the light.

She's in a suit of black with red pinstripes. She's not wearing a shirt, and the jacket shows a huge amount of skin as it dips down to just above her navel. The flare of her hips, the long black hair braided with red roses, the black mesh masque with its gold roses, and her crimson lips.

It can't hide her.

She's here.

I push off the balustrades and walk down the stairs. My pack is with me. I can feel it.

She looks up and sees us coming. For a second, I think she might run, but instead, she straightens her shoulders, snags a drink, and turns on those ridiculously tall shoes.

Where the fuck is she going? Who cares? I'll follow her anywhere.

"That's our queen," Grayson says beside me.

Falcon growls and pushes through the crowd as we follow her through the massive house.

She leads us to the back doors and steps outside. The gardens are beautiful. Grayson designed them, but Hazel has them glowing with little balls of light and crystals. It looks like a sea of flowers.

She walks to the edge of the terrace and stops, her hands on the rail. Even her nails are long and crimson.

Onyx, my Onyx, glances back, and she's nervous. I see it now in the tightness of her shoulders, in the line of her jaw.

"Onyx," Dylan murmurs.

She turns then, and when he steps forward, she holds up her hand to stop him.

"I'm here to tell you the truth."

Falcon tenses.

"Why now?" Grayson growls.

She gives Grayson an amused smile, though it seems forced. "Your sister is a powerful, persuasive presence."

She reaches back, gripping the railing, making the jacket pull tight, giving us a view of the curve of her breast.

Fuck.

"Okay, so, um. God, this is harder than I thought it would be." She bites her lower lip.

I surge into her space, gripping her hips and dragging her to me. She gasps and grips my jacket, holding herself steady.

"Silas?"

"I don't care anymore," I say into her mouth.

"I didn't do it," she whispers.

"My mother-"

"Vienne," she says at the same time as me.

We stop, and I find myself lost in her eyes. I need to remove the mask. I reach up, but she steps sideways and stops when she finds her way blocked by Grayson.

He looks hungry. His mask is hanging forgotten in his fingers. Nyx responds with a blush that deepens the pale colour of her chest.

She turns and finds Falcon. Her eyes hit him, drop to his lips, and then rise back up.

Once more, she turns and, in the darkest shadows, she finds Dylan. I almost can't see his face, but whatever moment they share is strong enough that she shudders.

"Listen to me, Onyx. We're prepared to hear you out. Tell us everything. All of it, but you need to know that we already made a decision."

She tenses. "So nothing will change your mind?"

"No," I say to her. "Nothing you say is going to make us change our mind."

She scowls and stalks past us. "So arrogant. Entitled. Bastards."

"Tell us how you really feel," Gray purrs, and he and Dylan start stalking her.

Falcon and I separate and walk around her in opposite directions, cutting off her exits.

"I will tell you how I really feel!" she shouts. "I didn't do it. It wasn't me. Your mother is an evil, evil, horrible human!" She points at me, but when Falcon gets too close, she whirls to him.

"And you, you just shut me out with a message from your lackeys. How dare you!"

Falcon dips his head but stops moving, focusing intently on her. "It was a horrible decision, and the only excuse I have is that I was trying my best to do what was right by the pack."

She makes a feral sound and tosses her head back, that intricate braid swinging.

"You don't deserve me," Onyx growls.

"We know," I say with more remorse that I think I've ever felt. "We don't deserve Dylan or you."

She whirls, and her head whips towards Dylan.

"I trusted you," she says in a plaintive mewl.

It destroys me.

Dylan inhales on a shudder. The pain is excruciating. I can smell it, I can feel it, I can see it.

"I didn't betray you, nor did I dump you. I didn't conspire against you. Honestly, can't you see how much I trusted you? How far I went to help you?"

Dylan reaches for her, but she slaps his hand away.

"I kept thinking about this moment, that you'd come for me, that you'd be different, be better, be more, and now we're here, and I'm so, I'm so, I'm so angry!" She shouts.

"We're sorry," Falcon says. "We realise that now."

She huffs. "Hazel said to give you another chance. She said you love me, but I don't believe that now."

"Onyx-"

"I'm not finished talking," Onyx snaps, cutting Gray off. "All right, so here's how it's going to go. You have five hours. If you can find me in the only place that feels like home to me, if you can bring me the food I love, if you know me well enough to be able to tell me the words I need to hear, and if you can give me an offer I can accept, I will give you this one chance." She hesitates, then nods to herself. "But if you fail...I will walk away and rebuild my life without you."

"I fell in love with you, Dylan, in the shadows. I told you I loved you. I tried to give you your pack back, and I succeeded. But," she looks at Falcon, Grayson, and then me, "I love you, too."

"Nyx-"

She holds up a hand. "I can't hear your words because you'll say something, and I'll give in, and then I won't ever know. So don't. Just prove to me you know me."

The rainbow lights of the fields of flowers dance on her skin. Her chest is heaving, and she looks like she's in pain, but she's determined.

"A challenge, to prove ourselves?" Gray says with a high voice. "To prove we know you, that we love you?"

"Fine. And when we find you. When we bring you what you need, you will know that we're not letting you go," Falcon growls.

"Ever," Grayson says with heat.

She takes a step, but I reach out and grab her hand and hold her back.

"When we find you, you will know that we're more sorry than words can say, Onyx."

"When we find you, Onyx, you'll accept everything we offer, bonds and forever. I'm not losing you again," Dylan growls. "That's the deal."

Her eyes are wide behind the mask.

"That's the decision?" She asks

"Yes," I say in silky seduction. "That is our decision, and it's not going to change."

Dylan grabs the back of her neck and kisses her. When he lets her go, she sways back, stumbling.

"Ten minute head start," Dylan growls. "I'll be seeing you soon, Onyx."

She reaches the doors and looks back. The Queen of Hearts and the queen of our hearts challenging us to chase her, to find her, to hunt her. To prove our love, and earn her forgiveness.

Thirty-Seven
ONYX

My braid is long gone. But I've left the mask on. The man inside the convenience store gave me a look like he thought I was insane, but I don't care.

I pace the depths of the alley, back and forth, and check the time again. I've been here for two hours, but I'm getting nervous. They have one and a half left. Will they appear?

Is this the right choice? All I need to do is go somewhere else. Go home. They won't find me, and I can live an extraordinarily boring life without them. The idea turns my stomach, though.

Perhaps that was a fleeting option in my mind at the start, but their words have caught something inside me and set it blazing. Perhaps it was just even seeing them. Instead of living with their ghosts, I got to see the real versions, and they are my weakness.

What of bonds? I've heard rumours that betas can be bonded. It's not the same as an alpha to alpha bond, or an omega bond, but there is some extra feeling. But having that ring of silver scars on my skin, proclaiming my belonging to them? Do I really want that? I can't bond them back, but I can take them. I can be theirs forever.

Now, my brain is running with what ifs. What if I could have a forever with them? What if they are serious and are offering bonds? What if they aren't? What if I accept them? What if? What if? What if?

Do I want them?

Yes.

I want them in my life in any capacity.

Do I love them?

There was never a question. My heart beats for the Treyfield pack.

Well, I laid down the challenge. Whether they appear is still undecided.

I still can't believe the audacity of myself. But I can't deny I want them to prove themselves to me, I want them to fight for me. Just this once. Prove that I'm important, that I mean more to them than just an employee, just a secret bargain, just the beta they are fucking.

If they want me, they need to show me that I'm more.

A sound has me spinning. I have to step quickly to catch myself on these towering heels, but then I see the huge shape of a man in the alley's mouth.

My heart races, and I chuckle. I can't believe it. They found me. I laugh again, louder, pull off the mask, and swipe at my eyes.

"You found me."

Dylan snarls at Silas. "It took us a while to find wings with the right assortment of sauces." But when he looks at me, there's hope and fear in his eyes. "We found them, and we're here." His voice softens to an intimate murmur that makes my eyes water.

My heart beats double time as Falcon appears. He looks around curiously.

"This is where you saved Dylans' life," Falcon says with satisfaction, like I've done something exactly the way he wanted me to do it. Like he expected this of me.

I look around. Dylan. I came here for Dylan.

"How do you know that?" I ask to buy time. I swallow hard as he tosses his mask in the dumpster and moves closer.

"Trade secrets," Grayson shouts. He pauses on the edge of the alley mouth, whoops loudly, then jogs towards me. He picks me up and spins me around. "You're ours now."

I can't help but smile down at Gray. He's lost his mask, too, I note. Good, I want to see their faces. I need to. Everything depends on their answers.

"Almost," Silas says. "Gray, put her down." The command sinks into my skin and leaves me painfully aware of my alphas. *Yes, Silas is right, we need to finish this.*

The alpha sets me down and steps back. My attention slides to Silas as he stalks towards me. His expression is predatory, and when he smiles, he smirks.

"We found you," Silas says and circles around me. "We brought you wings, and," he glances at Falcon, who pulls out a sandwich and a drink, "It's the same drink and sandwich you gave Dylan on the last day before you came to work for us."

I stare at them and feel tears burning.

"We also bought the convenience store, just in case," Falcon shrugs. "I'm taking no chances. So, help yourself."

I splutter a laugh.

Silas reaches out with one finger, stealing my attention back. "You want words? We're sorry. More than sorry, we will regret it for our dying days. We are in love with you. We can't live our lives without you. There is a hole inside our pack that only you can fill. So know that our words are heartfelt, honest, and true, and we will prove them with actions every day."

"And the offer?" This is the one I'm most concerned about. I don't want their money, I don't want their things. I'm betting on them knowing me enough to know that.

Grayson clears his throat. "I'm offering you life."

I raise my eyebrows. "Pretty sure I have that one already, Gray," I tease.

He snorts a laugh and circles behind me, hugging me and pointing his hand out to the street. "I'll give you a life of fun, of experiences, good and bad, because I'm Gray, after all. A life that's lived not survived."

I don't know why his words reach deep down into me and twist. But they make it really hard to see. He hugs me tight and kisses my neck before he moves away.

"My offer is for safety," Falcon says. "I will keep you safe in this world by protecting your body, providing you a safe place to sleep. I'll keep your nightmares from you, and I'll be the ear to listen. In this world, when you are afraid, know that I will always be at your side, fighting for you, from this day on."

A tear slips down my cheek, and he thumbs it aside and presses his lips to mine in a chaste kiss.

"Good offer," I whisper.

"I thought so," Falcon murmurs back. He reluctantly lets me go and steps away.

"I'm offering you my trust," Dylan says. "I haven't told you the truth, not about everything, and it's the reason why I got so scared and withdrew when things went wrong."

I peer at him anxiously.

"You see, I, uh," Dylan scratches the back of his head. "Fuck! My name is Griffin Dylan Wryven Donahue. I'm the lost heir to the Donahue fortune. I took off when all that happened. I wanted nothing to do with that world, with money. With anyone."

I stare at him, stunned into silence.

"You saved me when I had nothing. I was probably going to die. But you had kindness, mercy, for a no one. You didn't see money when you looked at me, you didn't see power. That's why I loved you, because you saw me when I thought no one else could."

"I never cared about your money," I say to all of them.

"We know," Falcon says in amusement. "We know what you did for your sister. With all the wages you'd earned."

Dylan clears his throat. "So, my truth is that I was scared. You were my hero, you saved me. My happy ending isn't going to be complete without you."

"So, you're, like, really, really, uh, well off, then?"

Dylan laughs. "Just a bit."

I swallow, but my stomach's jumping, full of nerves. I close my eyes and have to squash the familiar feelings of inferiority.

"Money means nothing," Silas purrs in my ear.

I snap my eyes open to watch him circle around me.

"What do you offer?" My voice is sultry, Silas always brings out the sexual side of me with ease.

"I'm going to give you wings, my little broken bird."

My heart clenches and then lifts in my chest. I reach out, and he steps into my embrace.

"I accept."

Silas laughs and kisses me. When he comes up for air, I'm passed into someone else's arms.

"Okay, now can we get out of this alley?" Falcon asks. "I really feel a need to shower."

Dylan leads the way, the red waistcoat shimmering when it catches the light. There's a bounce in his step, and when he looks back, a huge smile on his face.

We've come so far from those desperate days when we were dying for a bite to eat.

I'm content with what they've given me tonight. Everything else is a negotiation. All I wanted was for them to know me and know me well enough to find me, to know what I'd want and what I wouldn't. To prove they knew what my heart was.

They know my heart.

I've found the pack of my dreams.

Thirty-Eight
ONYX

I thought that night would be the end of it, but the pack has been determined to right their wrongs.

Life's been like a fairy tale. I've moved in with them, and getting used to needing a map to remember when I am in my own home is slowly losing its shock factor. The quality of clothing is impressive, but the price tags make me a bit ill.

Of course, I'd had to resign from Raptore Security, but now we had a huge mansion and a pack that was trying to get on my good side. Which meant weekly catch ups with my friends, hosted by yours truly.

The trick to conquering the media world was to let Hazel and Grayson do their thing. The siblings twist the media around their little fingers and introduce Dylan and me in one elaborate party. Dylan's identity revelation basically made me a non-subject, which I was eternally grateful for. Between the two of them, they have protected me from the world's scrutiny and taken to sneaking me to the most incredible places. There's a hotel with a forest room that blew my mind.

I'd pulled Gray aside and tried to tell him he didn't need to, but he'd kissed me softly and smiled. *"Of course, I need to. I love you, and I want you to have everything."* But I think we both know that a little bit of guilt is still driving his behaviour.

Dylan took me out one night to another one of the hotels with painted walls. He spent the entire night telling me about his life. His parents, his family, what happened to him on the streets, why he didn't feel safe trusting people who knew he was a Donahue. He struggled with it, but he did it.

Falcon was a whole new level of promise. He immediately set up the paperwork for me and Dylan to be listed as owning part of each of their companies. It sets both of us with financial independence forever. When I argued this, Falcon said that since he and the others were prone to fits of stupidity, this was his safeguard. Then he gave me the keys to a separate property with the reason 'just in case'. Oh, and the car. And announced my authority over the staff. My head is still spinning. Our argument lasted two days, and I only caved because he got on his knees and pleaded with me to allow him to do this to protect me from them.

How could I refuse?

Silas, though, he's building me a beautiful world to live in, like I am one of those pretty, broken birds. He's pulling in contacts and friends, strengthening ties with Pack Raptore, Pack Knight, and the friends I'd made. In true Hastings fashion, he's planning an enormous charity event for the Omega Refuge, and he's bought the buildings I used to live in with intentions of making them hospitable and make them cheap housing. He also organised Yvette and Simon's promotions and gave Moira a position in management of the Silver Rocks Resort.

I can see what he's doing. And I love him for it. I love them for it.

The weeks have been exhausting in a way I never even realised. The hours of getting ready, dress fittings, the interviews and introductions. Dylan's parents came at the end of the second week. The reunion was beautiful. His parents adore him, and despite their concern, once they met the guys, they were totally on board.

After they'd left, I sat down on the stairs, tears running from my eyes. Grayson had sat with me, his hand holding on to me.

"They like me," I'd whispered, feeling brittle.

"Yeah, people do that."

"But they're okay with me. She called me daughter."

Grayson had enfolded me in his arms then. Holding me while I erased more of my father's vitriol. It's hard letting go of all these beliefs I held about myself, but I want a life with the pack, so I'm working hard to erase my lifetime's worth.

I wake up, my heart pounding, feeling strangely on edge, like the house has grown teeth. The scent of lemons soaks the air, and the pack is MIA when I go hunting through the silent house. Even the staff are gone.

It takes me well over an hour to track Dylan down, but I found him in a room at the back of the mansion.

I take a step inside and freeze. The hairs on my neck rise, and I wondered why we hadn't gone over this in our pack meetings. Dylan turns slowly towards me, but he's not really seeing me. His head tracks my movements. I hold my hands up and back out of the room, my heart pounding. The sexy way he growls has my whole body tingling, but he doesn't ask me to stay, and it doesn't feel right to push.

Grayson bursts out of a room and seizes me around my waist and swings me into a library, softly closing the door and leaning against me. He trembles, and I reach up, holding him to me, wondering what the hell is wrong with him.

"Gray?"

"He's in heat." He then says the words with both awe and horror. "Won't be long now, and it will be..." He trails off and swallows hard.

I look at him carefully. "You look like you're about to be sick."

"What if we mess it up?" he says in a stricken voice. "It needs to be perfect."

I can't believe what I'm hearing. "What happened to the cocky alpha I know and love?"

"He's in heat," Gray stresses.

"Yes, but I'll be here this time. Well, in order to make it perfect, we need to get organised? Do Falcon and Silas know?"

"Yes, they're canceling everything."

My words aren't making a difference to the distracted alpha.

"Good. So, let's go get towels, stock the bathroom and the fridge. Prepare for days in the nest." I try for a calm, soothing tone while I think about what he might need.

Gray's mouth pops open, and he sweeps his hand through his hair. "Of course. Shit, yes. All right, let's go."

Together, we get everything ready, and the realisation grows and crystallizes in my mind.

"This is the second heat?" I ask cautiously. "Isn't it?"

Gray looks up and nods once. "First."

I stop dead, my arms hanging uselessly at my side. "But didn't you, with the bites and..." I trail off at Gray's blank expression.

"What are you talking about?" he asks with a bite of anger.

"But you've been together for two months. Surely, you've had a heat and…" I stop and realise I haven't seen bite marks on Dylan. I don't know why it didn't occur to me to ask. I reel, stunned, as I change information around in my brain.

Grayson frowns and stalks towards me. "Dylan wouldn't stop taking his suppressants after you left. He didn't feel safe enough to go into a heat. And he wouldn't take our bonds, he wasn't ready."

My mouth opens and closes. I know I should say something, but I can't get anything out. "He waited." A tear streaks down my cheek.

"For you. Yes." Gray swipes it away and sighs. "You two are going to kill me."

"But we couldn't have known it was going to work out." I protest. How did he know? How could he have known? Maybe it was just hope.

"I think he would have found a way to figure it out, Nyx. He's been in love with you for a very long time. You are the woman who rescued him, who protected him when he had nothing. We might be his scent matches, but you're his love match."

I squeeze my eyes closed on those words, feeling something shift inside me. Grayson pulls me against his chest, hugging me tight.

"This is a dream."

Grayson laughs, but we break apart when we hear footsteps. Dylan walks into the room like something else. His pupils are huge, and when he inhales and catches our scents, they get even bigger. His hair is mussed like he's just gotten out of bed. He doesn't have a top on, just a pair of black sweatpants hanging low on his hips, giving a tantalizing look at the V that leads down below the waistband. And he's hard.

My heart slams against my ribs, and I find myself moving across the room towards him. He keeps his eyes on Gray and then switches to me so suddenly I freeze.

"Dylan?" I murmur his name, a mere whisper of sound.

He moves so quickly I almost tip backwards, but his hands grip me, pulling me close enough that we touch almost everywhere. He leans down, inhaling, and the scent of sweet lemons fills my nose. I don't know what it is, but I suddenly find myself wet and squirming in his embrace.

"Dylan." I try again, but he cuts me off with a tongue shoved into my mouth.

Oh, the taste of lemons is better than the smell. I cling to him, kissing him back. I feel high, like he drugged me just with a kiss. Time ceases to have meaning, and then we're moving, and the world is rolling, and I'm lying on soft cushions. An alpha purr brings me back, and I find Gray kneeling behind Dylan, kissing him.

It's so hot. I reach out, running my hands down his smooth flesh, and then following the same path with my tongue.

He whimpers a high, needy sound I've never heard before, and its answer is Gray's growl.

"Please, Alpha, I need you," he whimpers.

Gray growls. "It's going to be hard and fast the first time. I'll be gentle next time."

Dylan turns to me and pushes up my skirt. His fingers dive into me, and I groan, helplessly spreading my legs further apart.

"Omega," I whisper. "Fuck me. Please."

Dylan tenses, and then he struggles free of Gray's arms and pushes me back onto the cushions. His mouth closes over mine, and he then slides into me. I gasp into his mouth, but he doesn't stop kissing.

"So perfect. Both of you. Can't imagine one without the other," Gray says in a deep growl.

I feel the moment Gray slides into Dylan. His movements are hard, fast, the pace brutal. He fucks Dylan into me, and with each slam, I gasp, reaching out and gripping on to them, holding them to me. I need them closer.

Dylan tears his mouth away and stiffens. My eyes widen as I feel the release flood into me. I whimper as he thrusts again. Scarlet and I had a discussion about male omegas and what to expect in the heat, but I'm still surprised.

"More," Dylan demands.

I sense the arrival of Falcon and Silas, but they just close the nest door and come closer, so I refocus my attention on Dylan. Gray slams into him again, harder and harder. Dylan pants and thrusts hard into me, hitting a spot that sends my body careening into a rushed orgasm. I scream at the intensity of it, and then cry out as Gray and Dylan slam into me half a dozen times, and then Grayson thrusts once more even harder, and Dylan goes insane.

His eyes open wide, and he shouts as he thrusts into me, climaxing again and again. His movements are erratic, and the moans are down right dirty. Grayson is growling, his teeth sunk deep in Dylan's shoulder.

Bonded and knotted.

Holy hell, I stroke Dylan's trembling form as he rides out the non-stop pleasure the knot sends him into. Liquid seeps from where he's still inside me, running down my thighs and ass to soak the sheets.

If I wasn't so concerned about my omega, I'd be turned on right now I'd be joining them, but I just want to watch him come through this and out the other side.

I don't know how long it goes for, but Dylan is a weeping, boneless mess when Gray withdraws from him. I expect him to sleep, but Dylan nuzzles me and whines, thrusting his hard cock inside me still. I expect to feel sated, but instead, flames of need start to ignite in me. I'm shocked by how easily I respond to my needy omega.

I groan and hold onto Dylan as he fucks us both into another bone-melting orgasm. I'm panting, covered in sweat, and my brain has short-circuited. *Wow. Just wow.*

Dylan whines. I send a frantic, searching look to my alphas. What's wrong with him? They need to fix it!

Silas reaches for him and pulls him away, distracting him with that magic mouth of his. I glance at Falcon and crawl to him. He strokes my hair and kisses my forehead.

"Are you okay?"

I smile and nod. "Course, I am."

The room is a rich, warm umber. A huge mattress covers the entire length of the floor on one side. On the exposed floor is a shag carpet made of black and red fibers. It's a strange and eclectic nest. There aren't many pillows, but there is a crap tonne of blankets and a lot of knitted materials. I make a note to get more of them later.

There's an enormous bathroom attached to the room. I can see through the slightly open door it looks modern and barely used.

I know that there's a fridge in the room next door with anything we could want. We discovered that someone, probably Falcon, had discovered the nest's location and had a fridge installed weeks ago.

I jerk to attention as Dylan crawls over to Falcon.

"You're beautiful, Omega," Falcon purrs. He grips Dylan's jaw and presses a controlled kiss to the omega's mouth. "So pretty."

Dylan whines, and I realise that he loves it. He'll probably deny it when he comes out of the heat, but right now, he needs to hear that we think he's attractive and wanted.

Silas nips at his ass and licks a long stripe up his spine. "So tasty, too."

"Gray?" I ask in confusion as the alpha picks me up and moves me away from the other two. "What are you doing?"

"Hmm?" He doesn't really pay attention to me as he lays me on the bed and lays between my legs.

I whimper as he buries his face in my pussy, eating with abandon. My toes curl, and my gasps join Dylans. I reach down, gripping his hair, forcing myself to uncurl my fingers every few minutes, but in a short amount of time, my hips are rising, and I'm fucking his face, unable to stop.

My orgasm sends me blind, and when I come back down to Earth, I sit up on my elbows and find Gray pinned to the mattress on his back. Falcon holds him by the throat and is licking my release off the other alpha's face.

"Fuck me!" I breathe out in shock.

My core clenches painfully, and I let out a whimper that draws both their eyes. Falcon smiles and licks into Gray's mouth, he grinds himself against Gray, and the other alpha growls. But then Gray lifts his chin, submitting to Falcon.

Holy...

I sit there and watch Falcon as he fucks Gray, and Silas rails our omega. It's erotic, it's magical. It's so hot I think I might have died and gone to pack heaven. I move closer for a better look and get snagged by Silas. He pulls me up and kisses me deeply.

"Beta," He growls. "Get in here."

I whimper, but he pulls out of Dylan, flips him over and pushes me to straddle him. I look down at his lust-locked eyes and stroke his cheeks.

"Okay, baby, let me take care of you." I reach between us and slide down on his soaking cock. I groan at the feel of him and then pause as Silas pushes me down.

"Wanna try something?"

I glance over my shoulder and smile. "Always." I love all of Silas' challenges, and I've learned to love the dark paths he leads me down.

He beams and pushes his finger inside me alongside Dylan's cock. The sensation makes me gasp. Dylan whimpers and thrashes his head from side to side. I keep moving slowly, riding Dylan with painful slowness, while Silas continues to finger fuck me at the same time. When he adds a second finger, I swear my eyes roll.

He grunts and then pulls them out. I flick a look over my shoulder, and he narrows his eyes.

"Don't give me that coy look, baby girl."

He grips his cock and walks on his knees until he's right behind me. I don't know what I'm expecting, but when he pushes himself inside me, with Dylan, I almost faint. There's a frisson of fear, but a whole heap of excitement. Dylan reaches up, drags me down, and bites my neck.

The pain and his thrusts send pleasure skating over all my nerves. Our combined fluids seep out of me, slicking up Silas' cock. He manages to push in even more and finally bottom out with a pant. I'm in a vortex of feeling.

"Oh, yeah, good darlings," he purrs and mouths my shoulder. "Is this the spot, Dylan?"

"Yes. There. Do it."

"Do it? DO what?" I ask.

"Bond. We want to bond you."

My eyes widen. At that moment, I melt. If there was anything holding me back from wanting them, it disappears. "Yes."

Silas rocks back and forward, grunting with the effort. He worries the spot with his teeth. I get even wetter. Dylan stares at my face, straining and thrusting up.

"Mine," he growls almost incoherently.

Silas pushes me down so Dylan can mouth my neck from the other side.

"I love you," Dylan says with clarity.

"I love you. I love you all," I say, almost near tears because my body is so over stimulated.

"We love you both. Now, Omega, claim your prize," Silas growls and then bites. The bite goes straight into me. On the other side, Dylan's bond flares up. I scream as they break through my flesh, just a flash of pain followed by such intense pleasure I'm hurtled into a climax that makes both of them follow me. The force of my orgasm has me throwing my head back in a silent scream. Only then do the bonds really hit my insides, tying me to the pack with chains of love and ropes of trust.

The next thing I'm aware of is lying beside Silas. He's licking at my bite mark and purring deeply. Dylan is asleep beside me, with Falcon lying beside him.

"Go to sleep, Nyx," Gray murmurs. "You did perfectly."

Silas' arm slides over my hip, bringing a sense of safety, along with that deep well of emotion through the bond.

I sleep.

THE BETA'S BARGAIN

Grayson has taken my ass, claimed it for his own. He's currently balls deep into me, while Dylan fucks my face. His cock slams into the back of my throat, making me gag, but it just seems to spur him on. If I wasn't so turned on, I might want to laugh.

They seem determined to push my limits. Except, I don't really have them right now. This is too much fun, and I'm loving every minute we're spending in this nest.

His fingers thread through my hair, holding me still while he roars and sends his cum shooting down my throat. He falls backwards and lies there panting. His entire chest is heaving, and for a moment, I feel sorry for him. His body can't get enough, and he can't stop. I think it's the third day, but I can't be sure.

Grayson growls in my ear. He grabs me by the throat and pulls me up so my back is pressed to his chest. I whimper at the new position and how it changes the feel of him inside me.

"I'm going to bond you now," Gray growls.

My eyes widen. I want it, boy, do I want it. "Do it, Alpha," I whine.

He fucks me harder. I don't know where he gets the stamina, but he can't seem to stop anymore than Dylan can.

"Bond me, Alpha," I plead.

Dylan is wearing three bond marks on his body. One on his neck, one on his shoulder, and Falcon bit his inner thigh. They did get closer with the bonds, I don't think they could tell, but I could.

I have waited, impatiently, and now I get my third one.

Falcon smirks at me and looks down at Dylan, who is sucking his cock. I watch the omega tug at the alpha's balls and turn his head to wink at me. Dylan is insatiable, and I love it.

Grayson takes that opportunity to grab my breasts and squeeze them before letting them go and rolling my nipples gently. I moan and rock back against him.

He reaches between my legs with one hand and rubs my clit.

"Tell me when you're going to come."

It doesn't take much. All eyes are on us. The sounds of Dylan sucking Falcon should be obscene, but it's so damn erotic. Silas reclines on the bed beside Falcon, stroking his dick and smirking.

"I'm coming!" I grate out.

Grayson fucks me hard for thirty seconds and then growls and latches onto my shoulder with his teeth. I let out a wail as the orgasm that was already moving, intensifies by a hundred. He supports us, holding me up while I convulse in his arms. I pant and whine and claw at his arm, but it keeps going, and then it eases and fades back, allowing me to feel Gray inside me.

My eyes burn as I feel what he feels. His bond flares up and shines with warmth and love. He pulls out of me, but before he can go anywhere, I turn and slam us together, sobbing against his lips and holding on to him.

"Thank you, thank you."

He smiles. "I should be thanking you."

Gray and Silas pull me into their arms, stroking and cuddling me tight, allowing me a moment to be emotional and feel the bonds.

And all I feel is love for them and from them. I lay on Gray's chest while Silas strokes my back and just feel.

This is what it means to be loved.

Thirty-Nine

ONYX

The heat continued on for another five days. By the time it finished, we all needed about two more days to sleep, and then another week to recover. I still blush and simultaneously get aroused when I think about what we did in that nest.

But there's one thing that's bothering me.

Falcon never bonded me. He hasn't mentioned it, and I've been too scared to ask.

I find my way to his office and walk inside. He's standing at the huge window with a phone to his ear. When he sees me, he points to one of the seats and holds up a finger.

I shift uncomfortably on the chair and resolve to do this. Then lose my courage and then find it again.

Dylan, Gray, and Silas have been putting bets on when I would actually get the courage to confront him. If I go through with it today, Gray and Silas owe Dylan one huge favour.

I need to know the answer so that I can stop wondering if I've done something wrong.

Falcon hangs up the phone and comes around to lean against the desk in front of me.

"What's up, Nyx?"

"How do you know something's up?" I ask.

"You have the thinking face on."

I hesitate, feeling stupid.

"I won't think it's stupid, whatever it is," he says, and it feels like he's reading my mind. Perhaps the bond isn't necessary. No, I need to do this.

"Why haven't you bonded with me?"

He straightens and frowns. I watch his face carefully until he crouches in front of me and takes my hands.

"Did you think I didn't want to?"

I look away from those cerulean eyes. Why is he so pretty?

"Maybe, no. Sometimes."

Falcon blows out a breath. "That was not my intention. I was just giving you time."

"For what?" I almost shout.

"I feel things more intensely than the others. I was giving you time to get used to the bonds."

"I don't want to wait anymore. I just want you." I bite my lip and look away, but he touches my jaw and turns my face back towards him.

"You have me," Falcon whispers. "You have all of me, all of us. We belong to you and you to us." He sighs and bites his knuckle, hiding a smile. "My gorgeous beta, you are so mistaken, but let me put your worries to rest."

He stands up, drawing me with him. He takes my hand and leads me out of the room.

"Where are we going?"

"To rectify this situation," Falcon says. "You have to understand, Nyx, the moment I decided I had to have you with Dylan, I would have bonded you in that moment. Prepare yourself, Beta, because this is your future. I am possessive and territorial, occasionally jealous, bossy, anal, I have likened myself to a dictator and to a tyrant. I expect perfection and honesty."

"I want it all," I snap. "I know you are, Falcon. I want you."

He opens his bedroom door and brings me into the room. I expect him to lead me to the bed, but he doesn't. He brings me to a chair that faces the window. Then he turns and looks at me.

"You are beautiful, miraculous. Accept this bond and join pack Treyfield. Be mine, Nyx. I need you, I want you. You're my everything."

I nod and kiss him. The menthol taste of him floods my senses, making me feel alive. He strips me out of my dress, letting it pool on the floor. A moment later, my bra is thrown across the room, and then my panties drop off, too. I shove at his shirt and reach down to undo his belt. It takes me a moment, but I manage to get him undressed. He steps around me and sits on the chair. Then he reaches out and pulls me down to sit on his lap, facing the window.

His fingers ghost up my thighs, causing me to shiver. I lean back into him and duck my chin when he presses light kisses to my shoulders. He reaches out and touches my chin, and I turn, kissing him.

Our kiss turns heated. He adjusts my legs so that they're parted by his and dips his fingers into me, curling them.

I whimper as he strokes in and out of me. His thumb grazes my clit. I sob out a cry, and then he lifts me up and impales me on his monster cock.

"Falcon?" I whine.

"Shh, soon."

His hands are everywhere, leaving a heated path as he thrusts up into me. I grind down on him, squirming.

The curtains open suddenly on their own. I freeze, but Falcon chuckles and reaches out to cup my breasts, pulling my nipples until I'm moaning. If the whole world were standing outside, I still couldn't stop.

The sun is setting, and it's turned the entire sky orange. The estate ranges in front of us, anyone could see us. I whine.

"Our lives are about to start. Are you ready?" Falcon growls.

"I'm ready," I pant.

He thrusts up harder and harder and then reaches and takes hold of my wrist, bringing it to his mouth. I cry out as his teeth sink into me. My core locks down on him, but he thrusts up, forcing his knot into me again. He growls and makes a strangled sound into my flesh as he chases and rises his own orgasm.

I sob as our bodies meld together. Joined. Locked. His knot inside me. I shouldn't be able to take one, but I can take theirs. A sign that I belong to them? The ecstasy eases, and I find myself floating, and then when it clears, I feel the river of feeling that is inside Falcon.

I can't believe I thought this man was cold. He's the opposite. The orange is fading, but I don't even care. He wraps his arms around me, and I hold onto him.

Then I think about what I feel about him. He grunts, and I smile as his arms tighten around me. He shudders and rests his forehead on my shoulder.

"In the nightclub that night-" He breaks off and swears. I feel his shame through the bond. "I was going into a rut."

His words stop my movements.

"What does that mean?"

"It means my feelings had surpassed everything, and I was ready to kidnap you. My nature was driving me towards just making you mine. I was abrupt and inexcusably rude, not because of not wanting you, but because I did. So badly."

"I made you lose control?" I ask.

"Don't be so pleased, you little vixen. Nyx, you make me lose control all the time. I plan everything, but since you came along, I go with the flow. You make me afraid and make me brave, and I find that I love it."

"Hmm, well, I like the sound of that, Alpha Treyfield. Looks like tonight is the beginning of forever."

I hear the sounds of the pack creeping into the room. I don't need to check because I can feel them through the bond. My bonds. My pack.

"Now, about that suspended from the ceiling comment. Can you elaborate a bit more?" I tease.

Forty

EPILOGUE- ONYX

Silas finishes writing and turns to me. I slide off his desk and into his lap.

"What's wrong, my love?"

I purse my lips and shrug. "Nothing. Okay, something. I'm worried about Hazel."

Silas heaves a sigh. "There's nothing we can do."

"I know. I just think we should convince her to come with us."

Silas raises an eyebrow, and I scowl and cross my arms defensively.

"Fine, I just don't want her to be alone. We're going to her gallery next week and then flying to the other side of the world. It just seems cruel."

"She won't be. Missy is here. Scarlet is in June Haven, not too far away. She'll have Simon, Sven, Yvette, and Kandi. Hell, even Moira will be keeping tabs on her."

I shift my shoulders, adjust myself so I'm closer, and lean my head on his shoulder.

"Your mother called again. She sent gifts and wants to know if we got the flowers," I whine.

Silas laughs, a deep, evil sound that reaches inside me and turns me molten.

"What happened to the flowers, Si?" I reach out and run my fingers down his throat, then flick open the top button of his shirt.

"I threw them out," Silas murmurs.

"I told Simon and Yvette I'm going into the office to work on Monday."

Silas grumbles, "No. I'm not done with you yet."

"It's been months. We need to return to the world, besides, I have some ideas for the hotel-"

Silas slams his lips across mine and effectively makes me forget my next thought.

I break the kiss, snort a laugh at his grumpy face, and continue to slowly flick open the buttons of his shirt, working my hand inside. "Silver is doing well, too. I went and saw her. She actually apologised and didn't look like the words would strike her dead."

"I'm glad."

"She refused my help. Is it bad that I'm glad she refused?"

"No. I don't think so. Silver betrayed your trust, and now she's learning to atone and become her own person. It's good she's not leaning on you."

"I know. Just years of my father's voice in my ear. It's okay. I'm ignoring it."

"Uh-huh."

I peer up at Silas and then look back at his chest. "You seem a bit distracted, Si."

"You want to tell me what you're doing in here, my cute little beta bunny?"

"I'm not a bunny!" I snap in outrage, but I shift my hips, moving myself higher on his lap.

He slips his hands under my shirt and cups my breasts. I moan and curl my hand around his shoulder.

"You're so my bunny." He stares at me with a dark light in his eyes and, with a smirk, leans closer, his hot breath on my ear. "I'm going to fill that belly of yours, too. Until we have a pack full of little bunnies. Yes, I think now. I'll fuck a baby into you, starting right now," Silas growls in my ear and scrapes his teeth over my neck. There's so much intention, so much possessiveness, in that tone that I know that he means it.

My cheeks scorch, they burn. But my traitorous body lets out this wanton moan. There's still this strange mix of arousal and horror when he starts talking like this. I'm leaning towards letting him put a baby in me. I mean, one couldn't hurt, right? Ruby is super cute. No! No! What am I thinking?

"You're not saying no!" Silas teases, his thumb flicks my nipple hard enough to draw a squeak.

My eyes shoot wide open, and I throw myself off his lap. "Uh," I peer at him and lose my train of thought. His eyes have gone sultry and dark, and he's giving me that look that makes my brain melt.

"Still not a no," Silas says, his voice rolling with pleasure.

I swear, sweat breaks out on the back of my neck, but I still can't form the word. The door opens, and Dylan slips in, looking between us suspiciously.

"You were supposed to delay and then bring him to us, Nyx."

I open and close my mouth and then suck in a lung full of air. "Yes. That. Sorry."

Silas stands up, looking pleased. "Still not a no."

I skitter out of his way and hide behind Dylan, who gets even more suspicious. "What's going on?"

"Nyxie, bunny, my love, are you going to let me do naughty things to you? Are you going to let me get you fat with my child?"

Just the words, the words are disgustingly, creepily arousing. What is wrong with me? I don't want children, do I? But I see them in my mind, little girls with Falcon's serious aura, boys with Dylan's golden gaze, children with Gray's laugh and Silas' smile. My heart thumps heavily in my chest. Yeah, I kinda do.

Dylan gapes at Silas. "Cheating, Si, cheating. We were going to ease her into it."

Silas just winks, and my knees get weak. I'm soaked, and without my underwear, which is currently in Grayson's pocket, that moisture is spreading to my thighs.

Fuck.

"Wait!" I interrupt with sudden recall of my vocal faculties.

"Yes?" Silas asks and crosses his arms over his chest like he has all the time in the world.

"You need to come this way first," I mutter and dart for the door.

Dylan mutters something, but I ignore him until he captures my wrist and tugs me to him.

"Pause. Stop. Serious talk now. Onyx... Do you want a child?" Dylan asks.

I stare up at him. My omega. I reach up with my free hand, touching the spot that holds his bite. His claim. He shudders.

For me, bringing a child into our pack would mean the ultimate level of trust. Do I trust them enough to try this, to want this? They have groveled in the most extravagant of ways, giving me everything I could ever think of wanting. Is there any doubt in my heart?

"We are a family?" I ask hesitantly, aware of Grayson and Falcon in my peripheral view and Silas behind me.

"Yes, we're a pack and family. Forever. No take backs or exchanges," He growls. "Do you doubt us?"

"No." And those two letters, that one word, clear any concern from my mind. I smile. "Do you trust us?" I ask Dylan because we both got hurt in this. We both need to be okay with this choice.

"Yes."

There's no hesitation. No fear in his eyes. He does trust us. There are no doubts in our hearts, no wounds, no shadows. We are a pack. For me, his answer is enough to cement my answer. My giddy heart flips inside my chest.

"I want everything with you," I say simply. "I want a family, a pack, an adventure. I want love and hope and honesty. I want trust and respect. I want children. I want old age. I want forever."

The pack moves in closer. Falcon's eyes are wide, uncertain for the first time I've ever seen them.

"You're sure?" Falcon asks.

"It's a bit late to change my mind, Fal," I say tartly. "But I wouldn't even if I could. You four are it for me. Let's give Nana Hastings some heirs. I want to record her reaction so I can play it over and over when I'm sad."

Silas' arms come around me from behind, and his purr causes me to inhale sharply and lean back into him. There is so much love and gratitude soaking through the bond that I can't tell who it's coming from.

Falcon turns away, swallowing hard. I know how lonely his childhood was. I know he thought having children was something he would never have. He and Silas have that in common. I wait until he turns back and smiles before I really relax.

Grayson hugs Dylan from behind and laughs. When he opens his eyes, they are wet and filled with joy. He lets go of Dylan and cups my face. "All the experiences, then?"

I grin up at him. "All of them," I swear.

"And a new chapter in the story," Dylan says with a soft smile. It's the one he gave me all along. A secret language between the two of us that I never understood, but now I hear it. I love you, that smile says. You're my world.

"And we'll write it however we want." My smile is a bit wobbly, but his kiss is anything but. His kiss is a promise we make to the future. It's another silent bargain we make with each other.

ACKNOWLEDGEMENTS

So, there's a few people I need to thank, so just hang with me.

Melissa from Homestead Book Services. You are amazing!! Silas is yours.

I want to thank my family and friends. Of course. But especially to my mum. *Time heals all things. I love you.*

Emilie who listens to my book summaries and is *so very* scandalized, but who understands the struggle.

Mr H and Miss E who forced me to take breaks. Frequently. Even when I just had one more line! One more chapter! One more...

Mick. Who listens with glazed eyes of pure boredom, and has taught me so much about the person I am, who I want to be, and how to get there.

Ron, Valerie and Jeff. For believing in me, no matter what. I could pack bags in a supermarket and you'd still think I'm amazing. For being so proud of who I am, even when I struggled to be. For knowing I could do this, without me saying a word.

But most of all, I want to thank the readers. Those people who picked up The Omega's Contract in the first few days of publishing, who found Scarlet, or are just discovering Onyx.

Thank you for reading. For loving them. They aren't perfect, but I'm not trying to give you a perfect story, because I don't believe any story can be. I love these stories, I love these characters and I am so glad I can share my not so perfect worlds with you.

I am truly humbled by how much you have loved these characters, stories and worlds.

You said keep em coming...and so I will

ALSO BY TEA RAVINE

The Omega Accords
The Omega's Contract
The Alpha's Arrangement
The Beta's Bargain

About the Author

My name is Tea I live in Australia on the coast. I grew up devouring books, all kinds of books! If it was written, I wanted, no needed to read it(And back in those days it was a daily expeditions to the local library and a sore back or sadly, reading the backs of discarded bus ticket). Peopling- not so much, though age has improved my skills vastly, I can hold a full conversation now without showing how incredibly introverted I am.

As an adult, writing books became a impulse that was impossible to resist. So I write, feverishly pouring out pain and love and all the crazy I dream up. I am occasionally seized by my artist muse to paint. Birds. I paint birds and dogs. It makes me happy. And I obediently obey the whims of my bossy blue dragon dog. He's the tyrant in this house, traipsing all over my orderly plans but he is my heart.

I like long walks with my dog that may or may not include long conversations with my dog. Creating stories for the people I pass on the street, cause I'm a nosy fucker. And delicious things that aren't good for me or my thighs. Also books, birds and anything phone box blue.

Reading and writing is my lifeblood but educating myself is my religion.

So if you like my tasty people pretzels, in their paranormal worlds and this 'why choose' book. If you hunger for more magic and twisted tales, more love and alternate worlds, more heartbreak and hearts made whole, and you need, no must have that fix. If you want more steam, more heat, and more happily ever afters. Well you can have more. I can be found on Facebook, Instagram, Goodreads and Amazon.

Email- Tear@TeaRavine.com

Made in United States
Troutdale, OR
05/29/2024

20198427R00176